# The Bratva King's Twins

## Age Gap Pregnancy Romance

### Levov Bratva Book 8

## Deva Blake

Copyright © 2024 Deva Blake

All rights reserved. This copy is intended for the original purchaser of the book only. No part of this book may be reproduced, scanned, or distributed in any printed or electronic form, including recording, without prior written permission from the publisher, except for brief quotations in a book review.

This book is a work of fiction. Names, characters, places, and incidents either are products of the author's imagination or are used fictitiously. Any resemblance to actual persons, living or dead, events, or locales is entirely coincidental.

# Contents

| | |
|---|---|
| Chapter 1 - Ari | 5 |
| Chapter 2 - Vivian | 11 |
| Chapter 3 - Ari | 19 |
| Chapter 4 - Vivian | 24 |
| Chapter 5 - Ari | 30 |
| Chapter 6 - Vivian | 36 |
| Chapter 7 - Ari | 42 |
| Chapter 8 - Vivian | 48 |
| Chapter 9 - Ari | 56 |
| Chapter 10 - Vivian | 60 |
| Chapter 11 - Ari | 65 |
| Chapter 12 - Vivian | 70 |
| Chapter 13 - Ari | 77 |
| Chapter 14 - Vivian | 82 |
| Chapter 15 - Ari | 88 |
| Chapter 16 - Vivian | 93 |
| Chapter 17 - Ari | 99 |
| Chapter 18 - Vivian | 104 |
| Chapter 19 - Ari | 109 |
| Chapter 20 - Vivian | 115 |
| Chapter 21 - Ari | 123 |
| Chapter 22 - Vivian | 129 |
| Chapter 23 - Ari | 136 |
| Chapter 24 - Vivian | 142 |
| Chapter 25 - Ari | 147 |

| | |
|---|---|
| Chapter 26 - Vivian | 153 |
| Chapter 27 - Ari | 160 |
| Chapter 28 - Vivian | 165 |
| Chapter 29 - Ari | 169 |
| Chapter 30 - Vivian | 176 |
| About Deva Blake | 184 |
| Books by Deva Blake | 185 |

# Chapter 1 - Ari

The thick smell of smoke and freshly sparked gunpowder traveled through the air, greeting me as I shoved out of my office and moved down the hall with urgency.

Shouting came from the distance, along with the volleying gunfire, both inside and outside the building. I listened closely as I loaded my pistol and cocked it, mouth fixed in a scowl. Unfortunately, it was nothing new.

It was another raid, no doubt. The second one in less than a year.

There was something about being a Levov that seemed to draw the other families, both major and insignificant, like flies to shit. Apparently, the warehouse had a big red target on it, begging for the others to try and bring us down.

But try as they may, it always ended the same way.

The guys were already on it, calling out commands according to rank and gunning down any men trying to enter the building. They shot on sight, working hard to not let any of them get away.

So long as they wanted inside our house so badly, they could die there, too, right on the cold concrete for all I cared.

They were nothing but cannon fodder, and regardless of who their families were or who they worked for, it didn't affect me. If they were stupid enough to work for someone willing to send their men into a Levov den, then in a sense, they already had it coming.

More shooting rang out inside, and I spotted flashes of light on my left side from where I stood on the second floor. Positioning myself over the railing, I fired down below, knocking down one of the assailants as they tried to sneak in.

The other beside him fell after, pulling my attention to the metal platform across from me.

There stood Benedikt, having the same idea. He winked, I scoffed, and we both descended our respective staircases.

He was a good shot, at least.

More shouting came from the south side of the building as our men flooded out, and we followed in tow, picking off whoever we could find.

It seemed we had missed the initial showdown, given how the moment we reached outside, the surviving assailants peeled away in their vehicles, leaving behind anyone who was either dead or dying still. Their tires squealed, trying to get away without being caught in the middle of the chaos.

"Send a unit after them!" I shouted, gesturing to a group of our guys, who all nodded once and ran for the nearest SUV.

"That's too bad," Benedikt said, sucking his teeth in slight disappointment. "I was hoping to get more practice in."

"There's always the firing range."

He shrugged. "It's not quite the same as real, moving targets."

"We're lucky we have the forces we do," I muttered in return, tone laced with a slight warning. "The faster they're taken care of, the less damage they do, and the less money we have to shovel into fixing this place."

"Andrei wouldn't whine about a few hundred grand going into renovations. He's used to it."

"And I am not Andrei, unless you've forgotten," I began, giving him a side-eye. "His resources here are a lot more abundant than what we had in Russia. Forgive me if I got used to counting every dollar."

Benedikt sighed, clicked the safety on, and absently scratched the back of his neck with his pistol. "Don't remind me. You were on my back about every little thing."

"Speaking of, get me the details on who did this, will you?"

Toeing the line between brother and subordinate, Ben gave me a disinterested look. "That's what Lukyan is for."

Narrowing my eyes at him, I let that authority come through, even if it was undercut with slight amusement. "I don't care who reports back—

just make it quick. I'd like to know what bastards decided to halt our productivity today."

"Alright," he said with a sigh, pulling out his cell as he walked away. "Lukyan it is."

As the others collected intel and did the usual running around to get things organized again, I made my way over to the attackers' point of entry. Assessing the damages, I found myself scowling all over again.

A handful of our men were down just outside of the north wall, right where someone had cut through the steel wall and forced their way through. From there, it seemed their guys had piled in with their weapons drawn. Fortunately, they only made it so far.

I couldn't understand what would've given them the idea that they could successfully infiltrate our operation and take whatever they wanted.

Regardless, it made my blood boil.

My branch of the family may have been new to the city, and new to America for that matter, but we weren't small fish. We were Levovs, sharing the same blood as the most notorious family in New York.

Andrei certainly left his mark, but it seemed I still had to make mine.

Before long, Kir and Benedikt strolled into my office, the former holding a tablet. My youngest brother moved with more urgency, as he was still new to how everything worked and didn't want to slip up along the way.

His green eyes were still bright with the desire to work hard and earn his place. Benedikt, on the other hand, was quite the opposite. His face was stern and usually tired looking from everything he'd seen over the years. He didn't tolerate any bullshit well, which was why he was my second in command. He knew what needed to be done, even if he did it with reluctance most times.

"I have the surveillance footage," Kir said, placing the tablet in front of me. Wearing a black tank top tucked into his dark cargo pants, the aggressive-looking scar on his shoulder from the conflict with the Caprises was on full display.

He had initially been frustrated with the mark left after his wound healed, but after being reminded he had earned his first true scar from working the family business, he came around and showed it off more proudly.

Kir wasn't a kid anymore, after all. Even if we teased him for being the youngest brother, he was still one of us, and he worked damn hard.

Pressing play on the footage, I watched as the scene unfolded as I had predicted. Our men were taken out, the access point was created, and they snuck their guys in. But from what I could see, their group split apart, some running forward and acting as a distraction while the others snuck into our inventory.

My brows came together as I looked closer, watching as they grabbed bundles of product and filed it out through the access point, seemingly directing it to their awaiting vehicles. More went out than I had anticipated, and my skin started to burn with fury.

Once the video ended with them fleeing and our forces pushing them out, I looked between my brothers with my expression hardened.

"How much did they take?"

Kir glanced at Benedikt nervously, whose eyes gave away the devastation. "According to my numbers, at least two hundred thousand's worth."

Blinking back at him, I processed that sum in my head, unable to say anything at first.

While it wasn't the biggest number in the grand scheme of things, especially given our wealth, it was the principle of it. The very fact that someone else in the city decided to steal from us. They felt entitled to a piece of what we had and simply took it.

That success would be more than enough incentive for them to try again. Hell, once word inevitably spread to the families of New York, we'd have everyone and their distant cousins on our doorstep.

I had to put an end to that idea.

Scrubbing a hand down my face, I shook my head. "This can't fly. We need to know who did this, and what else they might be planning. And where the hell is Lukyan?"

"He should be on his way," Kir murmured, glancing down at his phone.

"Right here," Luk said as he entered the room, immediately brought up short by the tense atmosphere in the room, largely charged by my anger. He glanced around before handing me a fresh folio. "I have that intel you wanted. Some guys are still working on it, but this should stave you off for now. Does the name De Luca ring any bells?"

There were many dominant families in New York, some more prevalent and vocal than others, but still active regardless. Many names floated around, all with varying reputations. Some popped up from time to time to form alliances and reinforce their turf, while others came onto the scene aggressively, throwing everything at the wall hoping something might stick.

De Luca, however, had been the quiet type. The kingpin, Edoardo, had reached out to Andrei before for an alliance, but when he didn't have enough to bring to the table, the offer was rejected. It seemed he must've harbored some bad blood since then. It made me wonder if Andrei would even recognize that name if it came up again.

Likely not.

"It certainly does," I murmured, leaning back in my chair as I considered what that meant, leafing through the printed pages.

"I figured as much. The name was highlighted in the database," Luk added, dropping himself onto one of the leather chairs in my office.

"There's a brief history with him and Andrei," I returned as I looked down at a black and white copy of Edoardo's picture. "It didn't end in his favor, so I can only assume he was ready for some retribution."

"But why attack us? Andrei doesn't work too closely with us," Kir questioned.

Letting go of a breath, I closed the folio and placed it on the desk. Ben was quick to look through the contents for himself. "Because De Luca thinks we don't have the same teeth as Andrei and his ranks. Since we aren't as established, he probably assumes we don't have the numbers or forces to fend for ourselves."

"I'd say we proved otherwise back there," Ben murmured as he flipped through the pages.

"I doubt he'll try again after that. He may have gotten away with some inventory, but it was a slaughter on his side," Luk chipped in, not seeming all too bothered by any threat posed.

"He may not try again on his own, but there's no telling if he'll come back with reinforcements. He could use the profits from what he stole to leverage an alliance with another family on our bad side. Or perhaps he just wants to smear our name throughout the city—let everyone know he pulled a fast one on us. Either way, Edoardo cannot get away with this," I said, using my voice of authority.

My brothers looked between themselves, surely wondering what was to come next.

I was pissed that the old man assumed he could push us around and poke at our defenses without us biting back. Assuming I was little league and wouldn't properly defend what was mine and my family's.

It seemed my time to prove otherwise had landed right in my lap. The chance to flex what made me a Levov.

"Get me more information on the De Luca family," I murmured, stroking my chin absently as I thought.

Kir lifted his brows with curiosity. "What are you going to do?"

"Something drastic. Something that'll show Edoardo and his family that while I'm not Andrei, I'm a completely different beast he'll have to contend with now," I said, brainstorming on the spot. "Soon enough, he'll wish he never rocked the boat."

While they still didn't completely know what that entailed, they exchanged glances, anticipating something that would truly show what we were capable of.

My brothers and I may be another vein of the Levov name, but we were just as willing and determined to secure our legacy as Andrei and the others had. We had our own battles to conquer and reputations to create.

And De Luca was about to find out the hard way.

# Chapter 2 - Vivian

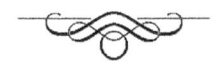

There was nothing worse than a family dinner.

Sitting down and having a meal wouldn't be all that painful if I had a different family—one that functioned normally. One that didn't make me feel like shrinking into myself every time I was stuck in a room with all of them.

Lounging in the living room while I scrolled through my phone was supposed to be a moment of reprieve, a chance to collect myself before having to sit around the table and pretend like we all got along swimmingly.

It was always Dad's idea. After spending all week ignoring his kids, he'd announce that we needed to have more 'family time.' As if having a sit-down dinner once a week would solve all our problems and traumas.

If it wasn't clear enough, it never worked. It did virtually nothing and caused more stress than necessary.

But still, if it was Dad's idea, then it happened regardless.

Letting go of a deep breath, I continued scrolling, looking through pictures posted by the equestrian center I went to during the week. It was the one thing I had that my family couldn't ruin, and I cherished every moment I had there.

I had a few prized horses, but I had trained my best one from the ground up and spent as much time with him as possible. Being around the horses was my favorite thing, and even in the worst times, it gave me comfort and stability in a life where I had very little of both.

While I certainly had opportunities that many others didn't since money was never an issue growing up, it all came at a price. Those privileges were monetary Band-Aids—Dad's solution for everything.

If he knew he'd been gone for a while, he'd sign me up for prestigious lessons somewhere. When he missed school events, graduations, or birthdays, he'd get us something expensive. After Mom died and I caught him getting too close with a woman much younger than him far too soon, his would-be new wife, he decided an all-expenses-paid trip to Greece was in order.

It didn't matter what happened or how he messed up; Dad would find a way to use his money to fix it for him.

I didn't always mind the lessons or trips, since I never had much to do outside of those things, but Dad's absence seemed to hurt my brothers the most. Two eager boys wanting nothing more than to have their father's approval were caused an endless storm of anguish and anger when he didn't give them the time of day.

Dad may have ignored me at the best of times, leaving me to do whatever I pleased within reason, but he was something else entirely to them. He was a ghost of the man they looked up to—the man they expected to show them the ropes and include them in his work.

His disappointment in them was palpable. Whether it was because of their behavior that stemmed from his absence, or if there was just something he didn't like about them, it was evident enough.

And of course, being the youngest and only girl in the family, I was the sole target of said bad behavior.

Since he wasn't there to nurture and guide them, it certainly meant he was never there to stop either of them from picking on me and choosing me as their outlet to let out those tumultuous emotions.

It had been silent while I scrolled through the photos, biding my time until this evening was over, but the moment Dante dropped himself into the armchair across from me, it felt like all the oxygen had been sucked out of the room.

I felt his eyes burning into me immediately, and I risked a glance up to find him staring.

Letting go of a breath, I returned my attention to my screen, hoping he'd just forget it for Dad's sake.

"What are you doing?"

"Nothing," I mumbled, already aware of what was to come.

"That looks like more than nothing."

"So?"

"You're always distracting yourself with useless things." he sneered, wearing a smug smirk on his face.

I didn't say anything, knowing he always just wanted to get a rise out of me. Instead, I kept scrolling, feeling like the world was caving in around me.

But that was an obvious mistake.

With a rush of movement, Dante was up faster than I could register, and he snatched the phone right out of my hand.

"Give it back!" I said, gritting my teeth to hold back from shouting too loud.

"I don't think I will," he said, wearing a triumphant grin as I stood and tried to take it from him, but he was much taller than I and able to hold it above both our heads.

"Dante, stop it," I muttered, trying to reach for it despite how useless it was.

He flipped the phone around and noticed what was on my screen, only to pull a mocking look of innocence when he met my gaze again. "Aw, you're looking at pictures of your precious Seabiscuit again?"

"His name's Arion."

"Same thing," he mumbled, looking disinterested. "I think Sunday Roast is more like it. What a useless beast."

The thought made me recoil, disgusted. "You're cruel."

"You're still a horse girl. You could do anything with your time, and you choose horses? You're embarrassing," he chided, still holding my phone out of range while he pressed the screen. "I wonder what else you have on here…"

"I said give it back!" I snapped, tired of always dealing with the same thing from him, reminding me of when we were kids. Not much had changed since then. "You're a spoiled, rotten man-child! Harassing me won't get you Dad's attention no matter how desperately you want it."

"Ouch," Elio, our eldest brother, said as he entered the room, hardly looking up from his phone. "Watch yourself."

Immediately, Dante's eyes darkened, and he forgot all about my phone as he tossed it aside to snatch my wrists.

Pain erupted across my skin as he pinched both together, using his strength against me. He pinned me there, eyes searing into me. "Want to say that again?"

"Stop, you're hurting me," I managed, sucking in a scared breath. "Dante, let go!"

"Kids," Dad mumbled from the other room, voice distant. "Whatever you're doing…quit it…"

Another half-assed attempt to restore order in his own house. He was probably too preoccupied with his wife to care.

Of course, Dante knew he wouldn't do anything, just like always. He tightened his grip on me.

"I think you've forgotten who you're talking to," he muttered, nearly making my wrist pop from the pressure. "How would you feel if I made my way over to that precious equestrian center and put that beast down, huh? An apparent man-child with a gun can do a lot of damage."

"Elio, help me!"

Elio only snickered and got up again as he made his way toward the dining room. "You started this, so you can fight your own battles."

"But I didn't!"

"And I don't care," he muttered, already leaving the room.

Panic rushed through me as Dante brought a hand up, pointing a finger in my face. "Disrespect me like that again and you'll learn to regret it real fast. Remember that."

"Everyone get in here, dinner's ready!" Dad shouted, voice reverberating through the big, cold house.

With a final glare, Dante shoved me down, dropping me onto the couch as he scoffed and turned away from me.

I took a moment to regain my bearings the moment I was left alone, aware of how fast my heart was racing. Tears welled in my eyes, bringing me right back to my childhood, reminding me of how badly I wanted out of there.

Even in my early twenties, I was just as much of a target as when we were young.

I should've been out on my own, going to school and starting a life for myself, but Dad wouldn't allow it. He said I was his little girl still, and I couldn't leave until he 'made arrangements.'

While my brothers were useless to him, I apparently wasn't. He was only waiting for the best offer to make it all worth it.

Sucking in a shaken breath, I reached for my phone, only to find the screen completely shattered.

The broken screen didn't matter. Of course not. There were always new ones, and Dad would tell me to put it on his card and pretend like he'd do something about Dante.

But he wouldn't. He wouldn't stand up for me or put my brother back in his place. Instead, he'd ignore him and pretend like Dante wasn't his flesh and blood.

And I would be just as alone. Just as susceptible to his bullying, his number one target.

"Vivian!" Dad yelled, snapping me out of it.

Letting go of another breath, I wiped my tears and reassured myself that Dante wouldn't really follow through with his threat. At least, I told myself he wouldn't. I pulled myself together as best I could and joined the rest of my family in the dining room as if nothing happened, despite the bruises already forming on my wrists.

Avoiding Dante's scalding eye, I looked down at my plate while the chef brought out the last of the meal, and Dad said grace before we dug in.

Having retreated within myself once again, I didn't say anything, afraid of earning more ridicule from my brothers.

Dante was always the worst of them, but with Elio's passive disposition, he seemed just as bad at times. He could help me, but he usually didn't. On the worst days, he would even join in.

Dad talked about everything and nothing at the same time, not allowing much room for anyone else to join in except for his wife, Shannon. She was a tanned, blonde-haired, and blue-eyed young woman who was far too beautiful to be with my dad, but it didn't take much to realize exactly why she put up with him.

She certainly wasn't the brightest, but she had her priorities straight, and even if I didn't agree with them, she knew what she wanted.

Shannon loved expensive things, and if it took flocking to a rich man to get her said things, then flock she would. She scarcely paid any attention to us. Even if I had been angry with Dad for the fact that he was already moving on when Mom was hardly buried in the ground, I still tried to get to know her. Yet she didn't care to give me the time of day.

While none of us particularly liked her, Elio especially wasn't fond of the situation. Shannon was nearly his age, and she was Dad's biggest distraction. Despite trying to get his attention, hoping to be brought into the fold of the family business, it never seemed to work because of her.

Dante was right behind him in vying for his mentorship, but it was always fruitless.

I would've felt bad for them if they didn't treat me like their personal punching bag.

Barely picking at the herb-crusted chicken and sautéed vegetables in front of me, I couldn't help but focus on how badly I always wanted us to be normal. How much I wanted to not feel like a prisoner in our family home.

"We were thinking of taking another romp to the Caribbean," Dad began, throwing back some of his red wine.

Elio's face tensed as he met his gaze. "Again? What about business?"

"What about it? It'll be here when we get back."

"I was hoping you might show me your recent dealings," my brother tried, reaching out once again. His hints were far too obvious, and yet, Dad still dodged them.

Dad waved the sentiment off. "No need to worry about that."

Looking down at his plate, Elio's jaw clenched, but he dropped it. Dante looked just as frustrated.

"The water was so blue the last time we went, wasn't it, dear?"

Shannon nodded enthusiastically with a pressed smile. "Yes, so blue."

Letting go of a discreet breath, I tried to ignore her half-assed attempts at seeming like one of the family, and Dad's desperation to make her exactly that.

"In fact, I was hoping—"

A loud pop traveled through the house, making us all freeze. We glanced at one another before we all looked at Dad. More loud sounds followed.

He seemed just as confused, looking toward one of the guards waiting in the hall. "What's going on?"

The guard turned to speak to him, pulling his phone away from his ear, only for a shot to sound closer, and his mouth to hung open with surprise. Red seeped into the front of his white button-up, tainting the fabric as he dropped to the floor.

My eyes widened, and my skin froze over.

Dad stood up just as a handful of men dressed in all black rushed inside, making for us immediately. Their rifles were pointed at us, shouting at us to stay where we were.

"You," one of them said, stepping into the room with a pistol aimed at Dad. He loomed over everyone with his great height, built as intimidatingly as possible. Like a wall of muscle, he commanded everyone's attention with ease. "Sit. Everyone else, get up."

Shannon was a blubbering mess as she stood, and my brothers were just as afraid, their eyes wide. When they didn't stand fast enough, the other men swooped in and roughly brought them to their feet, forcing the barrels of their guns against their necks.

Dante's hands were shaking, and something about it struck me.

They were terrified. For once, they were at the receiving end, forced into a state of complete fear and submission.

It was surprisingly satisfying to see, despite the circumstances.

But it was nice to watch them cower instead of me.

As soon as one of the men grabbed my arm and murmured a 'get up' to me, that satisfaction came crashing down, and I snapped back to the present.

Fear coursed through me then at the reality that there was a swarm of heavily armed men in our dining room, and we were all at their mercy.

I trembled in the man's grasp, but my gaze was fixed on the man who seemed to be orchestrating the whole ordeal.

His black tee hugged every hard muscle on his body, impossible to ignore regardless of how scared I was. Even if he was wearing clothes appropriate for combat, paired with black gloves and heavy boots, he looked clean-cut, his loose black curls maintained and the sides tapered.

The moment he glanced over at me, all the oxygen in the room seemed to vanish, and I was stunned.

Those icy blue eyes found mine, hard with his fear-inducing intentions, yet a slight glimmer in them made my heart race.

He was ridiculously beautiful with his tan skin and a few tattoos peeking from beneath the short sleeves of his tee, so much so that I couldn't look away no matter how much I wanted to.

I couldn't understand why I was so attracted to him, especially while his gun was aimed at my dad and he ambushed our family dinner.

That eye contact felt like it lasted a lifetime until his lips barely pulled upward in a slight smirk before he faced Dad again, focusing on the task at hand.

That expression didn't reach his eyes, making them seem even darker than before.

With villain-like satisfaction, he murmured, "It's about time we officially met, Edoardo."

# Chapter 3 - Ari

The dining room was mostly silent aside from the occasional whimper of fear from the blonde woman restrained by one of our guys. She could hardly stand it, but she had no choice.

With everyone pinned and exactly where I wanted them, I had the chance to check them all off. They were all accounted for, and the plan was going smoothly.

The alarm and confusion from the family made the room tense while they awaited my next move.

I couldn't help but chuckle at how afraid they looked.

But as Edoardo looked at me and tried to hide just how scared he was by the whole ordeal, his fear turned into irritation.

"What the hell is going on? What do you want?" he demanded, at least using his voice instead of a weapon. He was unarmed and completely at my mercy.

That sheen of sweat on his face told me he was preparing himself for the inevitable. He was bracing himself for death, but it wasn't going to be that easy. I wasn't there to murder anyone.

"You don't know who I am?" I questioned, feigning surprise. "That's funny. Normally, you'd know your opponent before targeting them."

Through his confusion, recognition came over him, and his eyes widened. "Levov…"

The name rolled off his tongue like something from folklore—a beast to be feared and revered.

That was exactly how I wanted him to see me. By the end of the evening, he would be a fool to not cower and flinch at the very sound of my name.

"Aristarkh Levov, to be precise," I hummed, relaxing my gun arm to put it down at my side. "Fortunately, I was able to find out your name. I made sure I knew all about you and your family before I decided to come here."

Fear lingered in his eyes as Edoardo looked back at me, seemingly trying to keep his wits about him. "How did you locate my home?"

"You'd be sick knowing just how far my reach goes in this city. Between the databases, surveillance, and the vast number of men we have on patrol at all times, you could never hide from me. If you got even a glance at how much information I have on each and every one of you, your dinner would make a reappearance."

Edoardo grimaced at me, surely bearing the weight of that reality. Even if he kept his business low-profile, I knew all about it. He wasn't an exception to our sheer power.

Gritting his teeth, he murmured, "This is about the recent hit, isn't it?"

"Correct," I affirmed, leaning closer to him smugly. "I have to hand it to you, De Luca, it was brave of you to go up against any Levov. Surely, you know about all the other families who have tried before, only to fail as miserably as the others. People call us dogs for a reason."

"Just don't hurt my family…please…"

Sighing at how soon he pulled out the family card, I pulled back and chuckled. "Don't worry, Edoardo. Nobody's going to die today so long as everyone cooperates. But you will learn how relentless we can be. It's my hope that by the end of this, you'll learn every reason you shouldn't cross a Levov. You'll walk away from this put back in your place, and you'll know exactly what I'm capable of."

"I know I haven't been the most honest man or the most devoted father, but don't take your anger out on my family," Edoardo began, voice shaking. "They had nothing to do with this. Nobody else here knows anything about the business. Not even my sons."

Rolling my eyes, I didn't want to hear it. I wasn't in the mood to be appealed to. "Please, old man, spare me. In fact, you should be delighted,

Edoardo. We're not here to mourn anyone but to celebrate a wonderful day. There's to be a wedding right here."

As my grin lingered, Edoardo's expression slowly fell as more of that confusion plagued him. "A wedding?"

Nodding, I gestured toward the hallway, and before long, an officiant walked in carrying their book. Despite the overwhelming scene of guns and terrified family members, he kept a straight face and did as instructed, stepping forward.

"What's the meaning of this?" he demanded, looking between me and the officiant as if realizing I wasn't bluffing.

With a cold laugh, I lifted my arms from down at my sides and addressed the room. "In exchange for targeting my warehouse, stealing from me, and assuming you'd get away with it, I'm here to take the one thing you can offer me as payment. Although, that exchange is much cheaper than I'm sure you had been dreaming up in your mind, and I won't be taking no for an answer. To let you know just how seriously I take my job, and how you will never win against me, I'm going to marry her."

Pointing at the frightened young woman to my right with her light-brown hair pulled back into a low bun, and her green eyes set on me, I singled out the last bargaining chip he had.

Her eyes only widened like a deer in headlights, completely frozen in place.

While it was a drastic and life-altering decision, I felt pleased she was just as pretty in person as the photos I had been studying for weeks. If not, it would've been difficult to follow through.

"You can't be serious!" Edoardo barked back, suddenly angry as he pushed himself up to his feet. "She is my only daughter."

But the moment I cocked my pistol and aimed it right at him, the old man fell back in his chair, alarmed by the silent threat.

"Exactly," I snarled at him, hoping it would cause him as much anguish as possible to know he was losing out on a crucial business deal. "I don't know if you've realized this yet, but I'm not here to be nice. We're not negotiating or making terms. I'm going to marry your daughter right in front of you, taking away your chance at picking the highest bidder for her, and there's nothing you can do about it. You picked the wrong man to mess with, and I want you to know that."

He looked furious as he stared at me, but as I said, there was nothing he could do to stop me.

Looking over at Vivian De Luca, the one I had my sights set on, I gestured for her to approach. "Come here."

She was frozen in place, taking in nervous breaths as she glanced over at her dad as if silently hoping he'd step in and beg for forgiveness. She wanted someone to save her.

But of course, he didn't move a muscle.

When she finally approached, Vivian kept her eyes averted, unable to look at me as the officiant stepped forward and asked if we were ready. Her cheeks were flaming.

Keeping my chin up, aware that everything was going according to plan, I nodded, and the impromptu ceremony began.

Right in the dining room where De Luca was forced to watch every second of it, the officiant went over the usual lines, to which we repeated them back, even if Vivian needed some encouragement.

Wearing a smug smirk, aware of how torn up and defeated Edoardo seemed, I knew it had been an easy win. But a win nonetheless.

Word was going to spread through the city before long, and he'd have to bear the shame of being one-upped by a Levov, tormented and forced to watch the union of his precious daughter to one of his enemies in his own home.

While it wouldn't get our money or product back, knowing he had no choice but to submit to me made it all worth it. The sweetness of victory was more than enough to have me grinning.

Foregoing the kiss and skipping right to signing our names, it was a done deal, and I officially had my bride.

"Be glad, Edoardo," I said once it was all said and done. "Your previous attempt at forming an alliance may have failed, but at least now you have a child blessed with the Levov name. It's a shame you won't see a single benefit from it, though."

De Luca was practically shaking with fury in his seat, but it was already too late.

Satisfied by the job well done, I reached for Vivian's wrist to sweep her out of the house. "Come along, wife—"

But the moment I grabbed her, she winced with a nearly silent whimper and snatched her hand back.

My brows furrowed immediately at the reaction. She hurried to pull her sleeves down, but not before I caught sight of what looked like bruises tainting her skin.

A surprising anger filled me then, as I couldn't help but wonder what it was from. But given how she shied away as I took notice of it, it was clear she didn't want anyone to point it out.

Deciding it wasn't the time or place, I put a hand against her back instead and led her toward the hall. Glancing back, I gave Edoardo a sarcastic wave.

"It was a pleasure doing business with you, De Luca."

The old man said nothing as he slumped into his chair, running a hand down his face in defeat.

On a victory high, I left my brothers and men to take care of the room while we exited the house, but I couldn't take my mind off those bruises on Vivian's wrists.

Something about it made me wonder if I was inadvertently doing her a favor by getting her out of there.

Regardless, I had made my mark on the De Luca family as I planned, and I intended to enjoy that win for quite some time.

# Chapter 4 - Vivian

I had no words to describe the compounding shock and disbelief I was feeling.

My body was completely numb as the realization sank into my skin, and the scene continued to repeat in my mind over and over again. Haunting me, I couldn't escape the memory of that ceremony.

More so, I couldn't forget that smug smirk and just how brutal his ruthlessness had been in that moment.

I was so out of it that I wanted to believe it never happened at all, and that I had just imagined it. But a panicked voice seemed to be screaming in the back of my head like a cold reminder of what it all meant.

I had been married. I was married.

My last name was no longer mine, and I was married to a man I didn't know completely against my will.

It didn't make any sense. None of it did.

In the beginning, I'd enjoyed watching as my brothers were brought down a peg and forced to listen to someone of higher authority for once, but they weren't the ones forced into a ceremony against their will.

Even if they were embarrassed by the ambush after the fact, they didn't face the same consequence I did, despite not doing anything to deserve it.

I had been begging for a way out of my dad's house, for the chance to start a life of my own, but that wasn't what I had in mind. I was essentially changing hands, going from one prison to another.

A part of me had found his directness and domineering attitude alluring, especially how easily he could command an entire room, and it didn't hurt that he was easy on the eyes, but I didn't know him.

Given how Dad never shared much of anything about his business with us, I didn't know what a Levov was, or why that name was significant. But apparently, given the papers we both signed, I was legally one of them.

I was Aristarkh's wife, and I didn't know the first thing about him.

Walking stiffly out of the house, I couldn't understand how it happened.

I went from sitting through a painful family dinner to being whisked into a sudden wedding ceremony and swept out of the only house I had ever known. Before I could blink or do anything, it was already said and done. My whole life had been turned upside down, and I couldn't help but feel like a bystander in all of it.

Without another word, my family was behind me, and I couldn't see a way out or any kind of silver lining.

I was on my own and left to fend for myself, unable to do anything against the lumbering giant I was supposed to call my husband.

Chilled to the bone, that thought made my whole body tense.

How could I ever feel even slightly connected to the man who took me from my home unprompted and decided to start calling me his wife? How could I live with knowing I had no choice in the matter, and my input didn't matter?

As attractive as he was, Aristarkh was a terrifying man built of steel. He could overpower me in a second, capable of ridiculous strength, even to the point of striking fear into my entire family.

He had shown unmistakable evil in our house, and I wasn't sure I'd ever be able to look past that.

I couldn't fathom his power and influence, and how easily he could enter our home and immediately make demands without any pushback. Of course, his guns far outnumbered us, and we weren't willing to find out how readily any of them would pull the trigger, but he did it all with such ease.

His men took out the guards Dad had posted around the place, he strode in like it was a simple thing to do, and he didn't give anyone the chance to force them out again.

Aristarkh stunned me with his looks, then paralyzed me with the most ridiculous demand he could make.

Feeling his hand against the small of my back made me shiver, alarmed by the fact that I was so close to someone capable of ending me on a whim.

Unable to even squeak out a word of protest or at the very least a question, the pressure of his hand deepened as the rear door to an SUV opened, and he prompted me to climb inside.

"Get in," Aristarkh said, voice clear and triumphant. "And just cooperate with me for your own sake."

Even if I wanted to fight back, I couldn't. I was still too confused and alarmed by everything that transpired.

Swallowing back the dryness in my throat, I did what I was told and got inside, boosted by his hand. Before I could even sit down, the door closed behind me, and I watched as he went around to the driver's side. He climbed in, and the vehicle locked completely.

Blinking through the haze of it all, I tried to understand how any of it could be real, and why it happened to me.

I couldn't accept the harsh reality of it, and I had no idea what was going to happen to me.

Did he marry me just to drop me off to be abandoned somewhere? Or did he really mean to keep me in his place like a doll to be placed on a shelf somewhere?

There were too many flustered thoughts moving through my head at once, fighting for my attention. But I couldn't dwell on any of them, not while it felt like my life was on the line.

The engine roared to life, and before I knew it, he was pulling out of the driveway.

He put his arm against the back of the passenger seat, letting me see how his muscled biceps flexed while he reversed. His strong hand was gloved, making my mind wander. There was no doubting how well he took care of his physique, and how clearly experienced he was in all aspects.

But embarrassment cloaked me the moment our eyes met, giving me a brief chance to take in his strong features before I couldn't handle looking at him any longer.

I managed to catch that amused grin of his as he chuckled to himself before he popped the SUV into drive and pulled onto the highway.

My face felt like it was on fire, stretching up to the tips of my ears.

The man forced me into marrying him, kidnapped me from my home, and he found it in himself to be amused.

Better yet, I was flustered because of how beautiful he was, even after everything he had just done to me and my family.

He was certainly one of the best-looking men I had ever seen, but he had been nothing but a beast for using me to humiliate my dad. For forcing my hand despite us having no prior connections.

I didn't know who he was until he introduced himself, but somehow he knew me. He mentioned something about having a database and information on us, but I didn't understand how he could possibly get ahold of that kind of thing.

But the more I thought about it, the more tense I became. If he had access to crucial information on me and my family, then that likely meant he had more power than I could ever comprehend.

I had the feeling there was so much more to it all that would only make me fear him more.

As Aristarkh drove us somewhere, I sat in the back of the SUV and fumed over it all.

I didn't know him, but I hated him.

I hated how he could just swoop in and ruin my life even more than my brothers did. How he dared to make a life-altering change on my behalf and demand that I simply go along with it.

Beyond that, I hated the idea of moving from one cage to another even more. Especially when I didn't have a say in it.

All my life, I had only wanted to make my own choices. I took advantage of whatever freedom I had in high school, despite going to a private school. I tried to let myself think I was free despite knowing I wouldn't be going to post-secondary. After that, I was supposed to wait to be married to whoever my dad eventually picked.

But it seemed Aristarkh had taken that decision from both of us, even if it had never really been mine to make in the first place.

Some feral part of me wanted him to suffer. I wanted him to face immediate repercussions or karma of some kind. Whatever he deserved, I wanted it to happen, even if it meant getting hurt in the process. I didn't care at that moment. I wasn't thinking straight, not while my mind was racing with panic and fear.

But regardless of my silent praying, nothing happened.

Instead, he drove without issue, listening to the radio quietly. When he pulled up to a red light, he even drummed his fingers against the steering wheel.

Looking out the window, I had the fleeting thought that someone might be able to see me if I caught their attention. But there was no missing how dark the tint was. Nobody would be able to see me, no matter how hard I tried to flag someone down.

I glanced at Aristarkh in the rear-view mirror from time to time, plagued with combative thoughts of how much I hated him, yet how painfully beautiful he was to look at.

It felt like self-sabotage to admit how appealing he was, deceived by my own mind while in a moment of crisis. That fact alone made me realize how doomed I really was.

Eventually, he flipped on the left signal and pulled into a driveway, sliding into a massive garage. The heavy doors closed once we were inside, and he turned the engine off.

Wordlessly, Aristarkh got out and closed the door behind him. The sound rattled my distressed brain, forcing me to realize what was coming next.

My door popped open, and he threw me an expectant look. But I didn't move.

"We're here, let's go," he said, gesturing for me to get out.

When I didn't, he sighed.

"I told you to cooperate."

"No," I muttered, finally finding my voice as that pure anger coursed through my body.

I had been forced to cooperate all my life, regardless of my own thoughts or desires. I was tired of being pushed around and being exploited for my more passive demeanor. My gentle nature had been taken advantage of since before I could remember, and I was sick of it.

"Vivian," he said with more demand in his voice. "Don't make me do this."

"Leave me alone," I forced through gritted teeth, moving to the other side to put more space between us.

Forcing out a huff, Aristarkh shrugged. "Don't say I didn't warn you."

Furrowing my brows, I didn't know what he was getting at.

Before I could blink, his massive, muscular body was pushing his way inside the back of the SUV as he reached for me. His fingers wrapped around my ankle, and in one heave, he pulled me out.

I would've fallen right out if it weren't for his waiting arms. I sucked in a surprised breath as he used my shock to his advantage and put a hand against my back. With ease, he hoisted me onto his shoulder, leaving me completely disoriented and off-balance.

"Let go of me!" I shouted, letting out every combative nerve I possessed as I tried to hit his back and kick my legs.

But it was no use. He was stronger than me, and my attempt to free myself did virtually nothing.

"Shut up," Aristarkh muttered as he closed the door behind him and carried me toward the interior entrance to the nice house. "The sooner you give up, the better we'll both feel."

Regardless of what he said or how compromised I was in his grasp, I didn't want to give up.

I wanted to fight for myself, and for my freedom, even if my abilities paled in comparison to his monstrous strength.

# Chapter 5 - Ari

I had learned from an early age to appreciate every win, big or small.

In our business, you never knew when the next one would come, so it was best to take it all in while you could.

With everything said and done, I was feeling good about it all.

I humiliated Edoardo in his own home, making him look like a spineless fool in front of his family, and his only daughter was officially my wife.

Everything should've been perfect, because every detail went according to plan. The job went swimmingly, and I had exactly what I wanted.

Except the deer-in-headlights look Vivian previously sported had worn off, and she apparently came to her senses after we reached the house. I didn't want to lock her in the guest bedroom, but I had no choice. Not after she found her courage and started fighting me.

Sitting in the living room with a glass of whiskey in my hand, I tried to soak in my victory and savor the look of defeat on Edoardo's face after everything was complete.

But her incessant screaming and shouting was ruining my immersion.

Regardless of how big the house was and the fact nobody would be able to hear her outside of these walls, she did it anyway, yelling at me to let her go, along with all the creative obscenities she could think of.

Even if I grew tired enough of listening to that noise to let her go, I couldn't do that. It was done, and there was no backtracking now.

Legally, she was my wife, and even if it was mostly a rash decision, we both had to deal with it.

Sitting in the living room by myself while she shouted herself into exhaustion wasn't the wedding night I had in mind for myself. In all honesty, I never really pictured myself tying the knot, regardless of wanting it deep down.

Something had always appealed to me about finding the right person and settling down with them, making as many heirs as we could. But with my line of work and how brutal it forced me to be, I wasn't so sure it would be possible.

I couldn't envision any sane woman wanting to marry me, so I never went out of my way to try to make it happen before.

But with De Luca causing trouble, it was the one way I could really get a one-up on him and get into his head to the point of making him throw in the towel.

It wasn't by any means an ideal union, but I couldn't complain.

Having a more agreeable wife would likely be a better circumstance, but that wasn't an option anymore.

After my first glance at her, I assumed Vivian would remain as passive as she seemed in the house, too afraid to fully look at me. I thought she would fawn like all the other innocent women swept into the mafia world for the sake of convenient marriages and making babies.

But it seemed she was hell-bent on proving otherwise.

Letting some of the whiskey burn its way down my throat, I sighed and wondered how I managed to get myself in this position, anyway. Or how I convinced myself that getting married would solve my De Luca problem, when in reality, it seemed to create a whole new one.

As annoying as her tantrum was, I had been taken with her. Ever since I started digging into Edoardo and his family, I couldn't deny how the young woman had caught my attention. I learned as much about her as I could, and while I didn't have much to work with, it was enough to let me build an entire identity for her in my mind.

From what I knew, she had been a private school brat like most of them were. Beyond her good grades, she didn't accomplish much academically. She certainly could've had her dad grease some palms to get her into whatever prestigious school she wanted, but that obviously never happened.

As far as I could tell, she had been a stay-at-home daughter, with no further education under her belt and no career as a result. But, of course, that made sense.

Edoardo would've never wasted that kind of money on getting her a higher education when she would inevitably be sold to the highest bidder.

Something about that thought irritated me, knowing he had other plans for her when I was curious about her.

At first, I was simply intrigued by her photo and wondered what she was all about. But the more I dug into the family, the more attracted I became.

It may have seemed like I married Vivian only because of wanting to humiliate her father, but truthfully, I had my eye on her long enough to want her for myself. There was something so interesting about the mafia princess, and I needed to get to the bottom of it myself.

All of that determination landed me exactly here: sitting in the living room alone, sipping whiskey, and forced to listen to her never-ending protests.

Really, it had been a flawless plan, except for the fact I didn't consider that part. I never stopped to think about what would happen once I got her home and had to face what I had done.

It was hard to say if the trade-off was worth it just yet.

As irrational as the move had been, all things considered, I didn't want it all to be for nothing. I really did want to have a genuine connection with her, even if it took time to get there.

We were certainly very far from making that happen, but I wanted to be optimistic. I wanted to believe I didn't make an excruciating mistake all for the sake of revenge.

As the whiskey pooled in my gut and made my system feel more sluggish than it had before, something in the back of my mind manifested like an annoying sound that I couldn't shake. It pulsed, growing louder and louder until it seemed to fall into step with Vivian's shouting from upstairs.

That little voice in my head was nagging me, letting me know I'd gotten myself into a bigger mess than anticipated.

The lengths I would have to go through just to prove to Vivian I wasn't only a cruel man who stole her away from her family suddenly felt too monumental to ignore. It was a more daunting task than I planned for, and it made my stomach churn to think about.

Staring into the electric fireplace in front of me as my mood dropped more with every passing minute—and every curse and scream Vivian could hurl at me—the tantrum started to grate against my head to the point of making my blood boil.

My cell ringing shattered my clouded thoughts, making me jolt from my seat.

Glancing down, I caught Ben's name as it lit up my screen. Easily enough, I grabbed it and answered the call.

"How are things over there?" I asked, noting how defeated I sounded despite my victory.

"According to plan. We left De Luca to regret ever striking the warehouse, that's for sure. We're on the way back now," Benedikt replied, sounding chipper about getting to go home. "More importantly, how's your creature doing?"

I scoffed. "She went from fawn to bobcat."

"Really? I wouldn't expect someone like her to put up much of a fight."

Holding the phone away from my ear, I let it pick up her distant screaming. Putting it back again, I murmured, "You'd be surprised."

Ben chuckled from the other end. "Good luck with that one. Once we get back to the warehouse, we're going to head out for the night. Let us know if you need anything else."

"Will do," I said with a sigh as I pinched the bridge of my nose. "Tell Luk to keep an eye out for any kind of retaliation. Edoardo is likely beaten down for now, but we won't know how he might react after the fact. I don't want him assuming the ball is in his court now."

"You've got it."

After we said our goodbyes and I ended the call, I forced out another breath.

My heart seemed to synchronize with Vivian's heavy steps upstairs, along with her never-ending howling. As I focused on it, my pulse quickened to the point of making my skin crawl.

Unable to take it any longer, I tossed the phone to the side and forced myself out of my chair.

Even if I understood why she was causing such a fuss, I didn't want to listen to it anymore. I wanted to bask in my triumph, but her noise was keeping that from happening.

I refused to sit there while she disturbed my peace.

Put on edge with the booze in my gut, I went upstairs, hoping it wouldn't take much to put her back in her place.

Regardless of how angry I was, I didn't want to be too forceful. She would likely doubt that, but it wasn't fun for me.

I had no issue yelling at my men or brothers when they screwed up, but women were a completely different matter.

Making my way down the hall until I reached the spare bedroom, I pushed the door open to find Vivian standing there with a vase in her hand, looking at me in surprise. Her screaming stopped.

The anger slowly dissolved from her face, turning into slight sheepishness as I took her in, and her cheeks filled with color.

"What the hell do you think you're doing?" I demanded of her, approaching with tense shoulders.

Vivian heaved in a big breath as if scrounging up her courage, and she held my gaze despite my initial impressions of her. "You can't keep me here!"

"I can and I will," I muttered.

She wound her arm back with the vase still in her grasp, flashing a look of defiance at me, to my surprise.

"Don't you dare," I snapped, cutting the space between us. Before she could throw it to the ground, I snatched it from her hand, forcing her to let go. "No matter how loud you are or how many things you break in this room, nobody is going to hear you."

Vivian blinked back at me in astonishment, startled by the proximity. "This isn't fair, and you know it."

If she hadn't been so defiant and arrogant, I would've been interested in how close we were then as I towered over her, noticing just how small she was in comparison. But I was at my wit's end, and I wanted her to be quiet.

"You're wasting your breath," I added, gritting my teeth. "It's already done, and you might as well get comfortable. Like it or not, this is your home now, and it would do you some good to respect your surroundings."

Vivian's brows furrowed at the statement, letting those words sink in. She studied me closely before taking a step back to put more space between our bodies. Shaking her head absently, there was no mistaking the anger and disbelief on her features.

"You're a monster," she muttered, holding back tears and the rage she previously had shown for me. "You're sick, and I hate you."

Not that I would say it to her, but I was ashamed to admit those words had enough bite in them to sting.

I knew I shouldn't care about what she thought or said, especially not so soon after bringing her home, but of all people, I'd never wanted my future wife to think that of me.

I was big and imposing, and I could certainly make any man cower, but that wasn't all there was to me. Of course, she couldn't see that—not yet, anyway.

Still, it didn't numb just how venomously she said it, or how much she meant it.

Forcing myself to keep it in, I straightened my back and looked her square in the face.

"Call me whatever you'd like, but the sooner you accept this new arrangement, the sooner you'll get to roam the house," I told her with a slight edge of warning in my tone. "Get used to it, wife. You'll be here for a while."

As fury gathered in her once again, I chose to ignore it, and I made my way back toward the door.

Closing it again behind me, I paused just outside. At once, she started at it again, screaming and cussing at me to let her go.

With a sigh, I knew it was no use, and I just had to wait until she inevitably tired herself out.

Hopefully, it wouldn't take too many more glasses of whiskey to make my brain cancel out the sound of her tantrum.

As irritating as it was, I didn't want Vivian to think I was a complete brute. But at the same time, I knew I couldn't sway her opinion from nothing.

# Chapter 6 - Vivian

Every hour that passed was more torturous than the last. I felt like I was hallucinating and making up the entire thing.

Part of me wished that was true, but my nightmare was far too real to question.

I couldn't wrap my head around how it happened, or why I was locked away in Aristarkh's house. I didn't know how I ended up being his wife, or why he chose me in the first place.

Nothing about it made any sense, and I was struggling to see how it could get any better.

I felt like a caged bird in my family's home, waiting to be sold off to the highest bidder in exchange for an alliance or something else Dad could use to his advantage, and it had seemed like the worst treatment possible once.

But now, here, I felt just the same, only with my name on a marriage license and stuck with a man I didn't know or care about.

For the first time in my life, I was silently begging for my brothers to come to my aid. They didn't have much of anything to do with the business—through no choice of their own—but that desperation within me was holding out hope that they might take the reins and step up anyway.

But as I sat on the edge of the soft bed, I thought about that idea.

Would Elio or Dante do that for me? Would they pull themselves together again and put their lives on the line to save me?

Throughout my childhood, and even into adulthood, I had only ever been their punching bag. I was their anger outlet no matter what they were going through, regardless of what I had or hadn't done.

Despite my innocence, they chose to bat me around and scar me with their abusive words. They constantly reminded me of why I meant nothing to them, and how I was useless to them and the family.

It didn't bode well for my chances of being saved.

I wanted to think my disappearance would bring them to their senses, and remind them that I was their family, but that deeply rooted disdain they held for me couldn't be cured quite so easily.

The trouble was, they didn't see me as family, and they didn't care about what happened to me.

Just like Dad, they were waiting for me to be shipped off somewhere far away from them. They had no interest in keeping me safe, and surely my being swept away by Aristarkh came as a relief for them.

I couldn't even rely on my brothers, and I knew I shouldn't hold my breath for their help.

It hurt to think about it, but it wasn't out of the ordinary.

We were a dysfunctional family at best, and they weren't going to save me, no matter how long I screamed for them.

My lungs and throat ached as I lay back on the bed, exhausted from yelling and trying to get Aristarkh to let me go. I had stopped screaming about an hour after he came in to shut me up; as much as I didn't want to, I had no choice.

My voice went raw, and it hurt to even swallow at that point. I didn't have anything left, and his words had sunk in, anyway.

Given how long I had been shouting with nobody coming to my aid, I knew he was right.

Nobody could hear me. The house was big and fancy, and surely sound-proofed. It made me squeamish to consider why he would bother adding that feature.

As bold as I had been during my protest, I was still afraid of him. He made me angry, and I hated him, but still, I wasn't prepared to underestimate a man like him.

I didn't know what to expect, and I could only imagine all the ways he meant to mistreat me.

It was surprising that he didn't do anything beyond trying to defuse me, especially after all the noise I had been making, but I wasn't out of the woods yet. There was still time for him to prove otherwise.

If my life with my family had been bad, I couldn't imagine what I'd have to endure with Aristarkh. Like a rock in my stomach, I carried that dread, unable to let go of it.

While I had been given seemingly endless peace and quiet while locked in the bedroom, the downside was how boring it was.

I didn't have anything to occupy my time, and that boredom started to get under my skin to the point where lying down seemed irritating.

With a sigh, I pushed myself up from the bed and wandered across the room.

I had no idea how long he intended on keeping me there, but a part of me didn't want to find out. I didn't want to be the one to discover just how cruel he could really be.

Glancing over at the door, I looked at the handle as an idea popped into my head. Even after I spent hours screaming and trying to open the windows that wouldn't budge, I never tested the door.

Immediately, I hurried over and reached for it. When it turned without much effort, hope sparked within my chest.

That rush of optimism fizzled out the longer I thought about it, watching as the door opened soundlessly.

I had the feeling he either forgot to lock it—unlikely—or he didn't think it was necessary in the first place.

If he wanted to confine me in one room and was worried about me breaking out, he would've been sure to lock it.

That only told me one thing: the house had so much security that he had no reason to be concerned.

Given how nice the place was, and how wealthy he claimed to be, I had no doubt the house was monitored better than a high-security prison.

Even if I tried to run, I probably wouldn't get anywhere, anyway.

Letting go of a breath, I felt just as stuck, even knowing the door opened.

As two choices laid out in front of me, I didn't know which one I preferred.

I could either leave the bedroom and explore the house, or shut myself in again and refuse to be anywhere near Aristarkh.

The more I thought about him, the less I wanted to see him. It was a shame, too, given how attractive he was. Even if I felt like I was going crazy in that room, he had caused me more than enough pain and distress for me to be willing to stay put.

The more distance between us, the better.

Regardless of how tempting that first option seemed, I accepted defeat and closed the door softly.

Stewing over what happened and how awful things were for me, I flopped back onto the bed and tried to soothe that burning ache inside my gut, where dread and deep sadness mingled.

Helpless and completely lost concerning how I was going to move forward, I tucked several pillows beneath my head and closed my eyes just as my nose tingled with emotion.

My tears burned down my cheeks, reminding me that only pain was ahead of me, and there was nothing I could do about it.

---

The contrast of night and day streaming through the windows was my only indicator of the passage of time, but beyond that, I had no idea how long I had been there once the days started blurring together.

As much as I wanted to believe Aristarkh was a monster for locking me away, nothing was stopping me from leaving the room. The door was unlocked, a constant reminder coursing through my head. He brought me food throughout the day, sighing whenever he found the previous meal untouched, only to take the old one away and leave the new bag.

He attempted a few words to me, but every time he entered the room, my lips seemed to seal shut. I couldn't bring myself to speak to him, especially not when he had forced my hand and left me with no choice. I could tell he was growing tired of it, but the motivation and will I previously had was sucked out of me.

I tried resisting the food he brought me for as long as I could, but when the growling in my stomach turned into stabbing pain, I took what

I wanted and left the rest. The same applied to the new clothes he brought me, all with the tags still on, and all name-brand.

Aristarkh's attempts at smoothing things over by buying me new things started to feel reminiscent of my dad's tactics, as if he had taken a page straight from his book. Like offering an olive branch to me, he wanted the food, the clothes, and the free access to the house to make him seem charitable.

He wanted to convince me he wasn't so bad, but I could only assume he didn't realize just how similar it was to my old life. How it turned my stomach to think about how closely he was following Dad's playbook.

Despite all of his attempted niceties, it wasn't enough.

I felt like I was going crazy. Staring at the same four walls, looking outside the windows I couldn't escape from, and being forced to stew about my current situation only made those dark thoughts even worse. I needed a break from that isolation, even if it meant running into my supposed husband in the meantime.

Heaving out a sigh as I pulled on a cream-colored knit sweater, I reached for the doorknob for the first time in days and opened it without thinking twice.

I hated him, but I hated being stuck in that bedroom even more.

Glancing both ways down the hall, I couldn't hear or see anyone walking around, and I relaxed somewhat. Aware of which end led to the staircase, I chose to start in the other direction.

Walking down the hall, I took in everything as if I were in a museum for the first time, noting everything with a critical eye.

From what I could tell, Aristarkh didn't have very many sentimental items decorating his house. Instead, he had fairly basic yet obviously expensive decor, almost like he went with the furniture and pictures used for staging.

It was minimal yet chic, and despite the lack of any personal touch, the house was warm enough.

Turning a corner, I peered into a nearby room, catching sight of several rows of bookshelves.

My interest piqued, and without hesitating, I made my way inside. The sleek shelves were lined with books—stuffed to the brim as if that was the only thing he collected in his life.

Despite the situation, I was in awe. From old textbooks and non-fiction books to leather-bound, limited-edition copies of mystery, horror, and fantasy novels, he had it all.

I knew I wouldn't be able to fathom how much everything must've cost him, so instead of dwelling on that, I inspected the small library from top to bottom.

It made me wonder if he had inherited them from a bookworm in his family since I couldn't fathom someone like Aristarkh willingly reading anything.

Regardless, I was so engrossed with the ample variety of books that I completely forgot about the bedroom or any kind of protest I had been participating in. Instead, I sifted through the collection, letting my fingers glide against the spines while I waited for one of them to catch my eye.

Pulling out a leather-bound book, I cracked it open and found a deep armchair to sit in. Next to a window, the seat offered me a different view of the property, which was surprisingly refreshing.

As I allowed myself to fall into the book without any other care in the world, it was the most relaxed I had felt in days.

It wasn't a cure to the situation he forced me into, but it was a distraction at the very least.

# Chapter 7 - Ari

Even with a body other than my own in the house, that week was the loneliest one I had ever experienced.

Just because we were married, it didn't mean I was entitled to her time or attention. I knew that. But as I went about my usual routine with the addition of making sure she was eating and somewhat taking care of herself, it was easy to forget about the union altogether. It had felt more like a figment of my imagination.

The worst part about it was how much it bothered me.

While she didn't know me and I didn't know her, something in me wanted us to find a common ground, or, at the very least, speak to one another.

Wanting to get to know Vivian and to at least be in her presence seemed like such an innocent thing, but the longer it went on, the crazier it made me feel.

For a moment, it made me wonder if we were experiencing the same kind of cabin fever, even if I left for work every day.

After a week of being married, I had never felt more alone, and I was sick of Vivian shutting me out.

Regardless of how she would feel about it, something had to change, and I was determined to make it happen.

Even if she hated me, or if it would push her away even more, I had to try.

Being so affected by her iciness easily took away the shine of outdoing her father, which was the one thing I had clung to ever since following through with the hasty decision to get married to a woman I didn't know two things about.

Pushing through the front door, I let go of a deep breath and tried to push away the thoughts that lingered from the workday. If I wanted to appeal to her in some way, I couldn't let that irritation follow me.

After dropping my keys on the kitchen island, I made my way up the stairs with that slight concern pulsing in my chest.

That feeling would hit me every time I went to check on her, afraid I might not like what I saw when I opened the door. I assumed Vivian was too stubborn to do anything she might regret, but given how she had been left with no other choice but to accept her new situation, I couldn't write off that possibility.

I hoped that she would come around eventually and that I wouldn't have to worry about her in that way.

Swallowing back that hesitation, I approached the bedroom door, only to find it cracked open. I peered inside, but the bed was empty, along with the ensuite.

Immediately, my heart skipped.

Did she get out of the house somehow? Did she slip through the security system?

Those questions bounced around in my head as I pushed away from the room and continued down the hall, surprised she finally left the spare bedroom.

I immediately let out a discreet sigh, relieved to find her in my library.

She sat in the armchair with her legs tucked underneath her, book in hand, while she quietly read by herself. It was one of my favorites, too, and I couldn't help but think she must've had good taste.

Even if the scene in front of me was a simple one, I was glad to see it. She looked at peace and comfortable, and it was nice to find that faint smile on her lips as she was completely immersed in the book.

Something in me hoped it gave her a sense of normalcy through everything going on, no matter how small.

Regardless of how things came to be, I didn't want her to suffer. She would likely say otherwise, but I didn't take any pride in knowing she had been uncomfortable and reduced to moping around in the spare bedroom.

With some regret, I watched as Vivian realized I was there and jolted in place, face blank as if she had seen a ghost. She immediately closed the book like she had been caught committing some sort of crime, and she regarded me with caution.

Seeing how she hesitated around me as if I might bite at any given moment stung, but I told myself to push it away. She looked prepared for me to shout at her, but that wasn't what I had in mind, and I didn't want to fuel her preconceived notions of me.

When she still didn't say anything, I murmured, "We're having dinner with my family tonight. I'm making arrangements now, and you'll have the chance to meet them all."

There was no missing the fear as it flashed in her eyes, truly alarmed at last. The color drained from her face.

Instinctively, she shook her head. "I don't want to."

"You might not want to, but it's happening anyway," I returned, bracing myself for another tantrum. "You have a few hours to get ready, then everyone will be here to meet you."

As much as I didn't want to push her too much or cause any more problems between us, I needed her to acclimate herself to our new life together. It was strange and uncomfortable, but it had to be done for the marriage to work.

The sooner she accepted it, the sooner we could develop some sort of genuine connection, rather than just what was printed on paper.

Despite her fear, there was no denying how beautiful Vivian looked in that moment as the early evening light streamed in through the window and brought out the natural blonde highlights in her hair. While her eyes were wide and bordering panic, the green in them seemed to sparkle.

There was nothing extraordinarily done-up about her appearance, wearing a simple outfit consisting of an oversized knit sweater and yoga pants with her locks splayed over her shoulders. It was simple, yet put her natural beauty on full display for me to appreciate.

It made me wish there hadn't been any kind of discomfort or rockiness between us. If we had met organically and had the chance to get to know one another, everything would be so much easier.

But I didn't exactly enter her life in a way that could've built a solid foundation for us to work with.

Again, I could only blame myself for that, but it didn't change how I wanted her to see me beyond the brute she assumed I was.

Even if she hated me, just looking at Vivian was enough to evoke such a strong yearning to be near her, and to understand how she affected me without even trying. She caught my eye the moment I started doing research into her family, and while I assumed it would fizzle away with time, that desire to know her never did.

My moment of adoration for her features and how perfect she looked shattered the moment she stood with a look of complete refusal on her face, and that startling reality brought me back down to earth.

With resolve, Vivian fixed her lips in a straight line as she tucked the book underneath her arm and went straight for the hallway. "I'm not doing it. You can't introduce me like some happy bride who wants any of this."

Sighing, I followed her out of the room, able to take longer strides than her, despite her hastened steps as she headed for the bedroom again. "Give me a break, Vivian."

"I don't think you deserve one," she snapped, attempting to slam the door in my face.

But I caught it with a hand before it could hit me, and I pushed it open again as she hurried over to the bed and hid. We were back to square one again.

My blood was boiling once again, but I bit my tongue. There were so many things I could've said to her at that moment, but they would do more harm than good.

If I wanted any kind of peace between us, I had to lead by example. Fighting her fire with even more would burn the whole house down, and I wasn't willing to go through anything worse than our current condition.

"Listen," I began, even as she faced away from me and pulled the covers over her head. "You can either get ready in the time I'm giving you, or you can be prepared to head down in your current state. Either way, it doesn't matter to me. You're going to eat downstairs for once and meet my family regardless."

There was a moment of silence before her muffled voice came through the duvet. "You could force me into marrying you, but you can't make me do anything else."

Tempering my irritation, I straightened my shoulders and drew from my well of authority. "Fighting me won't make this any better. The sooner you realize this won't just go away, the happier you'll be."

"Happy," she muttered, voice bitter. "I don't know what that is anymore, thanks to you."

Scoffing, I scrubbed a hand over my mouth. "Apparently, you didn't know it back home, either."

As that silence settled between us again, I immediately regretted the words, but I couldn't take them back.

Forcing out another breath, I didn't know what to say to make it better. I had the feeling it was just more salt in her wounds, and trying to fix it would make everything worse.

"I don't want to hear any more arguments or whatever else you might have to say about it. Get ready, or don't. Your choice. But either way, you will be at that dinner table by seven."

Not caring to hear more of her grumblings, I left the room and headed straight for the master bedroom with my phone in my hand as I made catering arrangements. I had to cool off before I said anything worse.

Feeling the need to wash away the anger and any residual frustration from our lackluster conversation, I stripped down and hopped in the shower.

As the hot water streamed down my body, cloaking me in some semblance of comfort, I couldn't keep my mind straight. There were too many thoughts and concerns moving around in there, forcing me into a constant state of questioning.

I wanted to believe everything would work out fine, and that marrying Vivian wasn't for nothing, but that ever-growing doubt in the back of my mind seemed relentless.

Given how back and forth she had been with me, favoring her outbursts, I had no idea how she would behave in front of my family. They were the people I did everything for, and if she were to disrespect them, or make a mockery of me, I didn't know what I'd do.

They would certainly understand her resistance, but something in me didn't want that risk. I didn't want to deal with any headaches in that department.

I could only silently pray over and over again for everything to go well.

However, I had the hunch that regret would be the one thing she'd like me to feel. That would be her only possible exit from her current situation.

As I scrubbed myself down and tried to clear my head, I just hoped for the best.

# Chapter 8 - Vivian

My heart was in my throat as I looked at myself in the mirror and decided there was nothing else I could do to prepare myself.

Since Aristarkh didn't exactly give me makeup or anything to style my hair with, I could only make it look more presentable, and I changed into something a bit more formal. I swapped the yoga pants for tan trousers and put on a fitted black off-the-shoulder top.

I didn't know just how dressed up I was supposed to be, but I figured it was good enough.

No part of me wanted to be involved in the dinner, but it seemed no matter what, he was determined to have me there. I didn't know what angle he was playing at, especially since his family had apparently been at the impromptu wedding. Even if I didn't know them, they were still present at the time anyway, and already knew of me.

Every fiber of my being was begging for it to be over.

Regardless, I told myself to calm down. They were just people, even if they were related to someone like him.

Knowing how much of a beast he could be, I couldn't imagine what his family was like, and that thought didn't make me feel any better.

I didn't know much about the Levovs. More precisely, I didn't know anything about them.

Given the context clues from the night he forced my hand, they had a notorious reputation in the city for being brutal and taking what they wanted, and that thought alone made my hands shake.

I didn't know what to expect, but the mental image I had provided no comfort.

With full reluctance, I was ready and standing around in the bedroom by the time a knock came from the other side, and he popped his head inside.

As much as I hated admitting it, Aristarkh looked incredible. With his hair freshly washed and full of volume, I couldn't get enough of his loose curls, and how well-manicured his undercut made him seem.

He was in a navy button-down that hugged his muscled arms, reminding me of his sheer power and strength. His leather gloves were nowhere to be seen, and instead, he wore a Rolex that caught the light as he rolled up his sleeves.

"You ready?"

The part of me that was still angry with him for what he said earlier, and how he refused to take my feelings into account in any respect so far, wanted me to lash out and refuse. It wanted me to throw myself back into bed and forget all about the dinner.

But I could hear his siblings talking downstairs. They were already waiting, and something about embarrassing myself by being disagreeable made me want to crawl out of my skin.

As much as I hated the idea of being introduced to his family, I realized it was no different from what was required of me back home.

I just had to sit there, be quiet, and bear it until the dinner was over. If they asked me anything, I'd answer them right to the point and leave it at that. I didn't want to give my family credit, but they prepared me for exactly that moment without even realizing it.

Swallowing back my reluctance, I nodded.

Relief moved through his eyes to briefly mask his look of surprise. "Alright. The food's here, and so is everyone else."

"My dad would never believe I was about to be introduced as Aristarkh's wife," I mumbled, reaching for anything that might break the awkward tension between us.

"Ari," he returned lightly.

"What?"

"My family calls me Ari, so you might as well do the same," he said, sounding surprisingly vulnerable from such a minor detail. "It's just easier, I suppose."

It was such an oddly personal disclosure, yet it seemed endearing. In a way, the nickname was disarming and almost humanizing. Ari sounded much gentler than his full name.

"Ari," I said, as if testing out how it sounded.

Something new moved through his gaze, so quickly I nearly missed it. In the time I spent trying to understand what made him soften for a beat, it was already gone, and Ari nodded once before gesturing toward the door.

"After you."

My curiosity faded as the reality set in, and I silently reminded myself to breathe, to keep it together and face his family regardless of how anxious I was.

Together, we left the bedroom and headed down the stairs. As we approached, the chatter from his siblings grew in volume, but the moment we stepped into the large dining room, it was like they all went mute at once.

Looking around the room in one initial sweep, I was startled by how much they resembled Ari. They were like carbon copies of him but with varying hair and eyes. There was certainly no denying those Levov genes.

That silence lingered for another moment before Ari cleared his throat. "Everyone, this is Vivian."

In near-perfect unison, his four siblings greeted me at once. Bracing myself through the initial awkwardness, I pressed a smile for them and returned the sentiment.

"It's only fair I tell you their names too, I suppose," Ari murmured, gesturing to the brother nearest us.

He was introduced as Benedikt, followed by Lukyan, then Kir. Lastly, the only sister's name was Lara.

While they all had the same faces and similar noses, Ari and Benedikt were the only ones with black hair, which the latter had slicked back instead of maintained like the former's. Lukyan, Kir, and Lara all had dark brown hair and varying shades of blue eyes.

It was interesting to see how identical they looked at first glance, only to notice their differences upon further inspection.

Once everyone's names were in my head, Ari sat at the head of the table while I sat to his left side across from Benedikt and beside Lara.

Various dishes were spread around the table, along with appetizers, wine, and whiskey with a Levov label on the bottles.

There was a tangible discomfort in the air, yet I couldn't tell if it was just me. Although, given the circumstances, I could understand why they might seem somewhat off-put, or at the very least wondering how they were supposed to approach the situation.

I was still learning that myself.

Regardless, they looked mostly happy to have another person joining them.

With Ari's go-ahead, everyone started digging into what looked like a feast in front of us, and soon enough, Lara's voice broke the remaining awkwardness.

"Can I just say how happy I am to have another woman around?" she said, sounding exasperated as she put a gentle hand against my forearm and gave me a look that screamed I was somehow saving her. "They wouldn't think so, but dealing with so much testosterone in one room is exhausting."

"What?" Lukyan questioned sarcastically as the others immediately stirred, laughing at her dismay. "Too much testosterone in this family—what could you possibly mean?"

Lara rolled her eyes and reached for one of the dishes in front of her. "I mean, you only ever go on and on about guns, and heists, and whatever the hell else you get up to during the day. You bore me to death."

The others oohed at Lara's comeback, getting themselves worked up. Based on Ari's amused grin, I could tell it was a recurring thing.

"But you love us all the same," Kir said with a teasing hand on her shoulder.

"Unfortunately," she uttered, lightly shoving him off with a smile. "You Neanderthals."

Everyone chuckled at their banter as we finished filling our plates before we dug in. Initially, my stomach had been in knots, but as I tasted some of the buttered lobster on my plate, I realized just how hungry I was.

"All I'm saying is, thank you, Vivian, for giving me a break from them. I'm glad you're here," she added with a warm smile.

"I know you love yourself to pieces, Lara, but I think you'll have to share the spotlight tonight," Lukyan said with a smug look as he gestured to me. "There's someone here we actually want to hear about."

Lara scoffed at her brother and grabbed a roll off the plate, throwing it at Lukyan, who cracked himself up. "See? You're proving my point!"

"Alright, rein it in. Let's not scare Vivian tonight," Ari interrupted, raising an authoritative brow that pulled them all back in line.

Lukyan held up his hands in defense as Lara scowled at him and straightened herself out.

A small smile settled on my lips then, surprisingly amused by how warm they seemed with one another, even with the teasing.

That kind of thing never happened in my family's house, not even between my brothers, and it was refreshing to witness it for once.

"Anyways," Kir interjected as he cut into his steak. "Vivian, how have you been liking the house?"

Listening to the question, I thought about my previous resolve to be prim and proper, but at the moment, it didn't seem necessary.

Although there certainly were some aspects of being in Ari's house I didn't want to dwell on, and I chose to step around it instead.

"It's nice, and…peaceful, compared to what I'm used to," I managed, regretting how empty of a response it sounded. "I especially like the library."

Recognition filled Lukyan's eyes as he sat back in his seat. "Ah, Ari's prized collection."

Something about those words settled within my skin, and I immediately felt embarrassed for helping myself to those books without knowing it was something he apparently cared about. I assumed they were just books to him, but as Ari nodded in agreement, I knew that wasn't true.

"I'm surprised he let you get near them," Benedikt murmured with a gleam of amusement in his otherwise cold eyes. "He used to threaten to take our hands if we ever touched them."

"That's because growing up, you lot were exactly what Lara said—Neanderthals. I didn't dare let you read them with your grubby hands, let alone look at them," Ari retorted, waving off the accusation. "Vivian, on the other hand, is welcome to them. It's good for them to be read, anyway."

Heat filled my cheeks at Ari's consent, even if I had gotten it after the fact. It moved something in my heart, too, knowing he didn't mind if I occupied myself with his collection.

"Do you read often?" Lara asked, steering the conversation away from her riled-up brothers as they chuckled.

Nodding, I immediately thought back to how many books I had stashed in my room—even the ones I'd read front to back numerous times, either out of boredom or because I needed to hide away from my brothers. It left a bittersweet taste in my mouth, but I pushed through it.

"My dad couldn't keep up with how fast I was going through the ones he bought me."

She smiled at that, making me feel welcome every time she looked at me with her kind eyes. "You should feel right at home with Ari's books, then. I'll have to keep that in mind for future occasions."

The dinner went on with more teasing and laughing as we cleared our plates, and by the end of it, I was surprisingly relaxed compared to how I started.

I hated admitting it, but I felt strangely at ease with them. They all had good senses of humor, and while their jokes could've gotten out of hand, they seemed to consider one another's feelings before crossing any lines.

It was easy to see how close they all were, and how they respected Ari without question. That fact alone made me curious, and I couldn't help but wonder how they got there, or how that respect seemed to come so easily.

Above all, there wasn't any genuine bickering, and nobody was fighting for Ari's attention. Everyone had their place and seemed just as supportive as one another.

It was nice to see a family that didn't operate like the one I was used to. In a way, it made me hopeful.

By the time dinner was done and everyone needed to head home, it was approaching late at night. They said their goodbyes, with Lara taking her time to welcome me to the family again.

Trying to wrap my head around the fact that Ari and I were married and being welcomed into the family was a necessary step was still incredibly difficult, but with her poise and kindness, it felt a little easier to bear.

Once everyone left and Ari and I were the only ones in the house, he made his way to the kitchen to put the open bottles away, and I followed, not knowing what else to do.

Since I hadn't spent much time downstairs, I took the chance to look around and familiarize myself with the place.

"That went well," Ari murmured as he closed the fridge door behind him.

At first, I wanted to agree. But I was riding on that mild high of knowing it was behind me, and how everything didn't implode in the middle of dinner. But with the others gone, I was forced to see the situation for what it really was again.

We may have been legally married, and his family welcomed me easily enough, but nothing about the situation was ideal.

I didn't ask for any of it.

Regardless of how well it went, at the end of the day, I was a kind of prisoner in that house. I didn't have my autonomy, and I couldn't choose to go home—or go anywhere else, for that matter.

Despite my previously good mood, it all crumbled as I looked at him and felt deceived by his relief, as if it were a kind of victory to him.

"Well?" I questioned as that familiar anger swelled inside me. "You think any of this is going well?"

Ari looked startled by my response, like he'd surely expected me to feel the same. "Vivian—"

"You were parading me around as if I consented to any of this. Like you didn't force me to marry you just to humiliate my dad," I snapped, cutting him off.

Overwhelmed by the fact that I was trapped in that house, forced to play the role of his happy little wife despite how much it made my stomach turn, I let go of the reasonable mask I had been wearing for him.

Recognition moved through his eyes then as Ari raised a calming hand toward me, along with at least a sliver of guilt. "That was the idea initially, but it's more than just that."

"How?" I questioned, feeling the last of my patience slipping away. "You forced all of this on me, and despite hauling me here like I was nothing, you want me to act like things are normal for your family? You want me to pretend like I'm not losing my mind being here? You can't really be that delusional."

I watched as he fluctuated between emotions as I spoke, landing on irritation at last. He put his hands against the island counter and leaned closer, narrowing his eyes at me. "Was it such a bad thing that I took you away from that place? I saw those bruises on your wrists that night, but I didn't pry because it's none of my business. I don't imagine marks like that come from a happy home."

Bristling at the reminder, aware that he was right to think so, I turned away from him and averted my eyes. It seemed he was good at striking that nerve in me.

"You have no right to bring that up to excuse what you did," I muttered, feeling the surge of emotion in my face. "Going from one cage to another isn't mercy."

Ari was taken aback by the statement, and he scoffed. "You think this is a cage? You weren't even locked in that bedroom, for Christ's sake! I've left you alone to do whatever you want in this house, but you spent your time moping around and longing for a place you were clearly mistreated in."

"Stop," I mumbled, hating how he used my upbringing as a weapon against me, as a way for him to earn points in some kind of good book.

"You have no idea the kind of fate you'd have if your dad was successful in selling you off like he planned to. You would've been married to someone two to three times your age, to a brutal man who didn't care about what you wanted or needed. You'd be forced to carry his children, no matter how much he demands from you, and you'd be left to rot like any other breeding mare in the world of organized crime," Ari said, voice raising as he went on. "I offered you an escape, whether you want to see it or not! I gave you a warm bed, clothes, food that you hardly wanted, and all the space you could ever need to come around to the idea of being my wife. Is that such an impossible role to have?"

"You say it like you aren't a brutal man," I retorted, meeting his gaze again. "You did this to me. I never asked for any of it! I'm so sorry a nice bed, food, and complete isolation from the outside world couldn't make up for being forced to marry a man I don't even know!"

Ari gritted his teeth, and I had the feeling we weren't done yet.

# Chapter 9 - Ari

The two of us went back and forth like that for some time, going in an endless circle.

By the time we both stood there, catching our breath in the kitchen with anger flaring in our eyes, we were too worn out to keep going.

At last, the volume came down again, and the room was nearly silent as neither of us could think of what to do next, or how to approach the tumultuous ground between us.

I knew we were at a complete impasse.

No matter how I tried to make the transition easier for her, it didn't seem to be working. She still thought I was the worst person in the world, and I had no idea if I could ever change her mind about that.

That cynical thought left a bitter taste in my mouth as I turned away from her and leaned against the counter with my arms crossed.

Tired of fighting and at a loss of how to make things better, I took a breath and shook my head absently.

Vivian was right. She didn't know me. I didn't make much of an effort to level with her or to help her understand me better, and surely that had only made matters worse.

But that needed to change.

Bringing my voice down to a soft volume, I began, "I've been taking care of my siblings since I was a kid myself. The first time I changed Kir's diaper when my mom was too sick during her pregnancy with Lara to take proper care of him was when I realized how fragile small children really are."

My words seemed to catch Vivian by surprise as she glanced over at me, looking confused yet vaguely interested in what I had to say.

When she didn't speak up, I continued, "We grew up in Russia alongside our cousins. We were a normal family, and all of his children were the apple of Dad's eye. He doted on Mom, and everything was great until after she gave birth to Kir. I guess the delivery was hard, and she didn't heal long enough before getting pregnant with Lara. She passed during the delivery, and while we gained a sister, we lost our mom. Since Dad was so focused on the family business, he left me to parent them all before I was even old enough to drive or go to high school."

I watched as Vivian's head tipped slightly, and her shoulders slumped empathetically.

"I'm sorry for your loss," she murmured, letting me hear the slight remorse in her voice.

"It was tough in the beginning, especially with having two under two. But I had no choice. I gave up my childhood to take care of them, and while I didn't go to school, I made sure the rest did. I stayed back while Benedikt experienced the high school career I should've had, and once they were old enough, I dedicated my time to continuing the family business," I explained, feeling the weight of those memories all over again.

A short moment of silence lingered between us before Vivian mumbled, "What about your dad? Why didn't he take over so you could have a normal childhood?"

I exhaled. It was a whole other beast to open up that trauma involving Dad. "He had been focused on his work alongside my uncles, but after Mom died, he became a shell of himself. He didn't dote on anyone anymore, and he drowned himself in work, becoming more reckless with everything he did. Eventually, he found more comfort in substances than his own children, and we lost him, too. My uncle, cousin Yaro's dad, made sure we had what we needed to keep us all together and avoid any kind of children's aid, but he had his litter to deal with."

"It sounds like your family has always been close," she commented, offering me the slightest show of interest.

"We were as kids, since our fathers were busy running Russia together. You would've thought our cousins were all siblings, but as we got older and as our branches left the country, my unit stayed behind the longest," I continued, feeling strangely comforted by the idea of sharing my story. "When my other cousin Andrei and the others left Russia, I made sure to stay back to maintain the family legacy. I never stopped leading, and I never stopped looking out for my family. Even if they're all grown up and managing lives of their own, that instinct to protect them never left. I'd do anything for them. I was prepared to bring the entire city down when my cousin Anastasia was taken by one of our enemies, and Kir suffered an injury because of it. Luckily, everyone's safe and doing better now."

Vivian's expression softened as she leaned against the countertop opposite me, seemingly understanding more of where I was coming from. "That sounds like a lot of pressure. How did you manage all of that as a teenager?"

I shrugged. "I had no choice. I wasn't willing to see my siblings suffer, and I certainly wasn't going to let any government body take them away. I did what I had to just for them to succeed, and even if I had to sacrifice so much of myself and my time, I wouldn't change that for anything. Dad let us down, but I wasn't prepared to do the same thing to them."

As we talked, I found myself glad neither of us were yelling anymore, and the conversation felt genuine.

It seemed I just needed to be vulnerable to get her to open up more.

I could tell she was curious, and I didn't mind answering her questions. At the very least, we were talking, and it still felt like progress.

"Obviously, you did a decent job at raising them," Vivian murmured, surprising me with the compliment. "Everyone got along so well. It was…nice to see, for once."

Taking that as a hint of how her childhood had been with her family, it warmed me to know my siblings left an impression on her.

"They didn't used to be as polite as children, but at least they're better behaved now," I said with a chuckle. "I was afraid they might be too much, but I'm glad you were able to put up with them."

A small smile settled on her lips then. "They weren't so bad. I always wanted to be able to banter with my siblings like that, but it just didn't happen."

As curious as I was about her family and her upbringing, I didn't want to ask anything she wasn't willing to say. I had done enough in that department, and it always seemed like a sensitive subject to her. I didn't need to make that obvious pain even worse.

"It's a good thing I have more than enough family to share. They liked you, and believe it or not, that's important to me," I added, surprised by even my own words. "While their opinions aren't the end all, be all for me, I still care about what they think."

I didn't miss the slight color that moved through Vivian's cheeks then, and she smiled faintly with a nod. "I liked them, too."

Warmth coursed through me at her admission, and as I glanced over at her, it was hard to fight my attraction. Even if she looked just as tired as I felt, there was something so simple about her beauty that pulled me in.

Something in me wanted to reach out and caress her face. I wanted to feel her skin beneath mine and to know what it would be like to receive her affection. But it was too soon still.

I didn't want to pressure her into anything, especially not when we finally seemed to find common ground.

Instead, I pushed up from my place against the counter and glanced at her. "If it counts for anything, I'm sorry about how all this started. It was never my plan to ruin your life."

Vivian blinked back at me, at a loss of words as she stood in place, unable to speak.

Interestingly, she seemed to lower her defenses somewhat as we spoke, and the slight lust in her eyes didn't fly under my radar.

Before she could say anything, I turned and said over my shoulder, "Goodnight, Vivian."

She was still stunned, frozen, but as I left the kitchen and headed to my bedroom, I couldn't fight my curiosity about that look in her eyes.

# Chapter 10 - Vivian

Even if Ari had shown me a surprisingly soft side to him, a part of me was still on the lookout for anything off-putting about him.

But after the dinner with his family, and how he continued his routine as normal, it was getting harder for me to find reasons to hate him.

He was still giving me as much space as I needed, but as I worked up the courage to explore the house more and spent less time in the spare bedroom, it was easier for us to talk casually whenever he came home.

"Enjoy another book today?" Ari asked from his side of the table, cutting through the seared steak on his plate. He always seemed to be starving after being at work all day. It made me wonder if he tended to put his own needs after his responsibilities, forgetting to eat or doing so scarcely throughout the day.

I nodded as I chewed my food, swallowing before replying, "I did. Well, I started one anyway. You know how long *King's* books are."

Ari snickered with an understanding nod. "I certainly do. They're so lengthy and always disturbing in some ways…but I guess that's what makes them so intriguing."

"What drew you to his books, along with some of the other horror ones?"

He shrugged as the thought, letting light contemplation fill his eyes. "The gore is visceral, even if there's a long build-up before he reaches the final pay-off. It always pulled me in."

I cocked a brow in interest, surprised to hear it. "Don't you get enough gore through your work?"

Ari chuckled. "I suppose I do, but there's a different aspect to that gore in his writing. There's something intriguing about the paranormal aspects. Knowing that violence and destruction is typically caused by something paranormal puts real gore into perspective for me. In a way, real-life violence doesn't seem so bad in comparison."

I really took in his words, understanding where he was coming from. "I suppose I know what you mean. Like when you watch or read something and realize your problems aren't as big and scary as what the characters are facing?"

He nodded, smiling faintly. "Exactly. I'm glad you understand."

My heart warmed at his acceptance, feeling as our mutual connection seemed to be coming from a more genuine place. "I never really had anyone else to talk books with, so I'm interested in what you think."

Ari looked pleased at that, and he nodded. "I must admit, too, it's refreshing to not always talk about work…especially when I'm not there and meant to be unwinding. Speaking of watching things, how about a movie?"

I nodded with a light smile as we wrapped up our meal. "That sounds great."

"Should we test fate and pick something random, or go with something safe?"

Following his lead to the living room, I soaked in that light-hearted air around us. "Surprise me."

Ari let a teasing smile take over his face as he reached for the remote. "Leaving it up to me, huh? I'm warning you now, it will either be the greatest or the worst movie you've ever seen."

"Maybe it'll fall somewhere in the middle?"

He chuckled as we took up our respective places, the curl of his lips hinting at his mild amusement. "Maybe so."

Like most mornings, he was gone early, and I woke up to an empty house, aside from the housekeeper who greeted me in passing as I went to the kitchen.

I felt strange familiarizing myself with the place when Ari was home, but once he was gone, I'd look around and take in everything the house had to offer.

The kitchen was beautiful and open. There were at least two separate living rooms with different uses, a home gym, a theatre room, as much food and snacks as anyone could ask for, and plenty of fully furnished bedrooms to go around. The personal library was a close second, but the grounds were the best part.

The pool was always well maintained and sparkling, the lawn was perfectly manicured with countless places to lounge and sit out in the sun, and he even had courts for tennis, basketball, and whatever else you could think of.

I found myself lingering there, dipping my toes in with a quiet hiss at the intrusive chill compared to the warmth around me.

Surprisingly, Ari became a point of interest for me ever since we fought in the kitchen. When he finally opened up to me, and we started to actually get along, I couldn't ignore how beautiful I thought he was. But it was all so confusing for me to deal with.

I was angry with him for everything, and yet, I got a glimpse of someone kinder and softer beneath that hard exterior when we talked.

Seeing that side of him made me curious, and I knew that was a dangerous thing.

A part of me still wanted to know more about him, even if he'd already given me quite a bit to work with.

I was surprised to learn he sacrificed his childhood to raise his siblings, and while it was admirable, it also made me sad. He gave up so much for them, and while they were surely grateful for everything he did, Ari would never get that time back.

But it made sense why they all respected him so much. He gave them everything they had, and while that didn't completely make up for how brutal he had been, it certainly showed him in a different light to me.

I didn't like the idea of being attracted to Ari, but as we stood in the kitchen together after the fighting died down, and he even managed to crack a few smiles, something in me wanted to see just how much he had been holding back.

Even if I knew I was better off without his attention, I had been prepared to give in.

And in some strange personal betrayal, I was somewhat disappointed when he didn't make any kind of move on me.

It was presumptuous of me to assume that was something he would do, but at that moment, my curiosity had gotten the better of me.

Was it really a crime to be attracted to the man I was legally married to?

Not really, but I didn't know how to deal with those conflicting thoughts and feelings. I knew I shouldn't be attracted to him, given what happened, but it was getting harder and harder to fight.

Most days passed with me struggling to understand why my hate for him was crumbling into an easy comfort, and while it took up a lot of space in my mind, above everything else, I was bored.

As nice as it was to not have much to worry about while Ari went off to take care of the family business, I needed something else to do with my time. I couldn't just sit around all day and wonder what my apparent husband was getting up to.

My family may have been dysfunctional at best, but at least I always had something to occupy my time with. Whether it was lessons, going to the stables, or going somewhere on vacation, there was always something going on.

Resting my chin on my arm against the side of the pool, I looked up at the blue sky above me and soaked in its warmth. I could only hear the usual neighborhood sounds, along with the occasional passing car and birds as they chirped in the trees around me. Otherwise, it was incredibly quiet.

At least something in me knew I should've been grateful in some capacity.

It was peaceful not having to deal with my brothers since I wasn't their target anymore. I didn't have to worry about them being disappointed by Dad, or taking out their anger on me just because they didn't get what they wanted.

The house was beautiful, things were mostly fine whenever me and Ari were in the same room, and I didn't have to be on edge. I didn't have to prepare myself for daily yelling, for things being thrown, or dealing with a mostly absent father.

Things were looking better, and that was only stoking the flames of my conflicting opinions of him and our situation.

But despite all of those good things, I knew I needed to confront him about my doing something—anything—with my time. I had to that night when he came home, or else I knew I'd go stir-crazy eventually.

Following my typical routine, I glanced at the clock while I sat in the living room with a book in my lap, only to find it was three in the afternoon. Sighing, I knew he usually got back at five.

While I tried to focus on the book, I could only think about what I planned to say to Ari about the situation. I ran words through my head again and again, trying to find the right ones that wouldn't cause any kind of fight.

By the time I had another hour left to wait, I stood up with a huff and waited by the kitchen island on one of the stools.

I couldn't wait any longer, surprised by the nerves that stitched themselves in my stomach.

Even if I was dead set on addressing how I needed more, I was afraid of what he might say. I didn't want him to think I was ungrateful, but at the same time, I didn't want to waste away in the house.

Time slowly ticked by as I waited, only to jump in my seat as the door finally opened, forcing my heart into my throat.

# Chapter 11 - Ari

I never imagined a fight followed by a conversation would have the power to shift the dynamic between us, but it came as a pleasant surprise.

Of course, it wouldn't patch everything completely, but it was a start. It gave me the hope to keep going, to stay level-headed around her.

Through the last little while, we had been more cordial with each other, and it was surprisingly nice to see Vivian leaving the spare room more often. I was glad she felt safe enough to do so.

It was a hopeful sign she'd begun to trust and think differently of me, but I also knew my actions would determine whether or not she'd accept me completely. It was daunting to constantly feel like I was walking on eggshells around her, wondering if my words might set her off again, but at least things seemed to be going well overall.

I went to work as usual, thinking of ways to bring us closer if it was at all possible. Her defenses seemed to be dropping thanks to the unspoken truce we reached, and that made me feel better about testing the waters.

But that hope seemed to hang in the air as I stepped inside the house to find Vivian waiting for me. Standing next to the counter with her hands behind her back, her slight anxiousness was palpable from where I was, immediately making me curious.

Before I could say anything, she swallowed deeply and blurted, "What am I supposed to do with my time when you're gone?"

Blinking back at her, I'd scarcely entered the room as I regained my bearings. I was still processing everything that happened at work, and I wasn't prepared to be asked anything yet.

Kicking my boots off, I moved through the kitchen and dropped my keys on the island. "Hello to you, too."

Vivian dropped her shoulders and she stiffly sat on one of the stools. "Hi, I guess. Anyway, what do you want me to do here?"

"I don't want you to do anything," I murmured as I went to the fridge and pulled out a beer. I lifted it in question toward her, but she only grimaced and shook her head. With a shrug, I closed the door and leaned against the counter. "You aren't hired staff. You don't need to worry about any of it."

"But that's the problem."

Cracking the beer open, I swallowed a mouthful. "I'm failing to see how that's a problem."

"I need something to do," she complained, resting her chin on her palm. "I don't like being bored."

"Well, what did you use to do?" I asked, curious about how she used to spend her time. As far as I knew, she wasn't enrolled in any kind of post-secondary program, and her family had some staff, too. Even though I told her my life story, I still didn't know much about Vivian or her upbringing.

"I played tennis, and polo, and usually went to afternoon Pilates. I had violin and piano lessons since I was a kid, even if I'm not that gifted with music, and we'd go to the lake house most weekends so I could see my old friends. But I loved horseback riding the most," she explained, listing everything with at least some nostalgia in her gaze. "I still do love it. I haven't seen my horses in a while."

Everything sounded pretty typical for a rich kid, and since she didn't usually act the part, it was easy to forget how privileged that aspect of her life had been, regardless of her strained family dynamic.

However, most of those activities involved leaving the property. That wasn't something I could swing so easily.

"That's great, but I can't let you leave here without me," I said, trying to keep my voice from rising. "I need you to stay put while I'm not here."

It clearly wasn't what she wanted to hear. Her shoulders dropped and her brows furrowed. "Why?"

"Because I'm involved with people willing to do worse things than kidnapping their brides, and if anyone feels like crossing me, they'd go for you first," I explained, watching as her anger only deepened. "You're an easy target for anyone hoping to blackmail me, which is why you can only leave when I'm with you for now."

Unimpressed by my answer, Vivian sat up straighter and crossed her arms. "So what? I'm supposed to just exist in this house forever until you permit me to leave once a month?"

Knowing she wasn't prepared to back down, I sighed and ran a hand down my face.

As much as I wanted to snap at her and stop any kind of fight before it could happen, I knew I had to tread carefully.

"Look," I started, placing my beer on the counter. "You can do whatever you want on the property, so long as you stay here. We even have a tennis court, and so many other things to occupy your time. I don't care what you do, you just can't leave without me."

I felt like I was being as fair as possible, and despite being passive about the topic before, it seemed to set her off even more.

"I've already exhausted all of those things!" Vivian fired back, letting that anger consume her again. "There's only so much tennis I can play, or how many books I can read before it stops being fulfilling at all. I don't have anything to work towards, and really, I never have. Which is why I'm sick of just sitting by and being useless!"

"I want to help you, but my hands are tied," I returned, pushing away from the counter. "You have to stay here, and that's final."

Hoping to defuse the situation, I decided leaving the room would be the best for both of us. But as I went, her next words stopped me in my tracks.

"I refuse to be some kind of trophy sitting at home waiting for you to get back! That's not the kind of life I want, regardless of what you've decided for me. I need something to put my time and energy into. You have your business, but what do I have? Nothing!"

Pulling in another deep breath, I couldn't let that be the precedent in my house. I couldn't stand the thought of Vivian fighting me on every little thing for the rest of our marriage, and I had to snuff that spark before it could get out of hand.

Turning to face her, I cut the space between us and gripped the counter on either side of her, caging Vivian against the kitchen island.

Stunned, she could only look up at me with those green eyes as a sharp breath escaped her.

With my face in hers, I murmured, "Nothing? You have nothing?"

Vivian swallowed deeply as she looked into my eyes, seemingly measuring her next steps carefully, although that defiant streak moved through her again, and she sat up straighter despite the proximity.

"Providing me with necessities is the bare minimum for storming into my family's home, marrying me then and there, and hauling me here without my consent. Don't act like you've done me a great service," she spat, holding her own against me. "You can't expect me to sit here by myself all day and pretend it's enriching."

While a part of me knew she was right, I was annoyed that she was making demands, that she was pushing against me and asking for more when we were already living more extravagantly than we needed to.

But at the same time, something was intriguing about her stubbornness. Her intensity and fiery will came out of nowhere, but in some strange way, it turned me on.

Vivian knew what she wanted, and something that set attraction stirring within me.

I wanted her, and that was no secret to me. But I had been holding back ever since I brought her back to the house for her sake, and I could feel that resolve started to weaken.

When I didn't say anything in return as I took in her beautiful features, tight with anger, she continued her rant, but I could only focus on how much I wanted to feel her. To hold my wife like any good husband should.

"I'm not asking for much, just something—"

Cutting her off, I connected my lips to hers, unable to resist that temptation anymore.

Vivian froze at the contact, surprised by the interruption. But as the kiss lingered and I hooked a finger under her chin, she seemed to melt into my touch. She let go of a breathless sound that sent shivers down my spine.

It was the relief and encouragement I needed to keep going as I finally gave in to the deepest desires I kept locked away inside me.

# Chapter 12 - Vivian

Whatever was left of my anger dissolved as Ari held my jaw in his hands and deepened the kiss, moving like he couldn't believe how it felt either.

The words he interrupted completely left my mind, along with whatever else I planned on saying. At that moment, none of it seemed to matter, and I could only focus on the flickers of pleasure that moved through me as his lips caressed mine.

Finally, that curiosity of mine had been answered, and I wasn't disappointed by what I found out.

It felt incredible to kiss him, somewhat to my dismay.

That sensation alone made it nearly impossible for me to hate him, even if something in me wanted to try and hold on to that sentiment.

His skin against mine made me long for more of that contact, and to never find myself without it again.

I didn't know what had come over me, but I knew it was too addictive to give up.

Ari let out a content breath as he leaned even closer, forcing my back against the countertop as he kissed me so roughly I nearly fell off the stool. He caught me, chuckling as he slipped his arms underneath my legs, hoisted me up, and propped me up on the island.

My stomach flipped at the swift movement, amazed by the sheer strength that seemed so casual to him.

But the thought faded as he slipped between my legs and held my waist, too eager to give either of us a break from those fiery kisses. Not that I wanted him to, anyway.

My heart raced at the feeling of his hands against me, soaking in his warmth and how strangely comforting it was to know his touch after cohabitating with him for weeks.

Testing the waters as that curiosity claimed me, I put a hand against his chest and dragged my fingertips down the front of him, in awe of the sheer wall of muscle he possessed. I felt every ridge and bump, noting just how strong his abdomen felt.

Ari hummed into my mouth as he pulled my bottom lip between his teeth, biting down just enough to make me squirm.

My skin felt like it was on fire all the while he teased me, exploring my body with his hands without really doing much about it, much to my frustration.

But the moment he pulled back and dipped down to kiss my neck, I couldn't stop my eyes from closing as I took it all in. Those touches felt even more erotic as he occasionally dragged his teeth against my skin in between each one, making me shiver beneath him.

I wasn't good at hiding how greatly he affected me, or how badly I needed him, and while it was vaguely embarrassing, I could tell Ari didn't mind for even a second. Every time I let go of a breathy moan or squirmed from how intense his touch was, he'd chuckle or hum his amusement against my skin, only stoking that desire growing within me.

"I know we didn't start off on the right foot," Ari murmured against my collarbone as he pressed a final kiss there before stepping back enough to get a better look at me. He towered over me as he reached for the zipper on my hoodie and slowly pulled it down, revealing the black bralette I wore underneath it. His eyes darkened. "But if you'll let me, I can try and make it up to you."

His words sucked all the moisture from my mouth, forcing me to swallow back the lump in my throat. Color moved into my cheeks and every fiber of my being wanted to know what he had in mind.

His fingers reached for the slouchy sweatpants that hung from my hips, letting them tease the skin beneath the waistband. "Would you like that?"

My ears burned as he looked down at me with that suggestive haze in his eyes, matching the lust festering within me, too. I nodded sheepishly, too embarrassed to say anything else.

"Come on now," Ari murmured, freeing one of his hands to tilt my chin up, forcing me to lock eyes with him. "Use your words, sweetheart."

Swallowing again, it took all the courage I had within me to say anything, recalling how I had no trouble fighting him earlier. Those words had come from a place of anger and passion, but as I sat there perched on the countertop, needy for whatever he had to offer to the point of almost feeling ashamed about it, it felt impossible to form them.

"Yes, please," I managed, unable to escape the blazing heat from moving through my skin.

Ari chuckled and lowered his lips until they were inches from mine. "So polite."

Excitement sparked within my stomach as he pressed a light kiss against my mouth, barely giving me any relief from how pent-up I felt.

"I'll see what I can do," he said, returning both hands to my waistband as he secured his fingers around it. "Lift."

Doing as I was told while my heart flipped with anticipation, I hoisted myself up as he easily pulled the sweatpants down in a single motion, tossing them aside carelessly. As I lowered myself against the countertop, I hissed quietly at how cold the surface was through my panties.

"Don't worry, you'll need that to cool off soon enough," Ari teased with a knowing grin as he lifted my thighs and forced me onto my back.

Too desperate to care what position he wanted me in, I tried my best to ignore the chill of it, and I was too preoccupied with how he lowered himself closer to my core with his hands holding my thighs up.

The moment I felt his breath fanning against my heat, I couldn't contain that neediness inside me.

That frustration lingered as he left a few sloppy kisses against my inner thighs first, making sure to draw out how much I needed him, riling me up for his amusement.

My breath hitched the second I felt his tongue through the remaining fabric separating us, using the slightest pressure to tease me even more. My legs tensed as he continued, slowly exploring and making me whine for more.

Ari hummed against me and slowly hooked a finger in the material, just barely pushing it to the side. "Looks like you need this as much as I do, princess."

While the new nickname was tempting to rebuke, the desire to resist him disappeared the moment his tongue returned, this time with minimal restraints.

A moan choked out of me as that slippery warmth embraced me, not leaving a single inch untouched. Pleasure shot through me and tingled across my skin, spurring more of that arousal to flood my system.

His grip on my thighs tightened as I squirmed from his expert tongue, forced to pin me down to keep me from moving. He chuckled at my reaction before busying himself once again, not letting up despite how overwhelming it felt.

My mouth fell open as he quickened his movements, flicking his tongue against my clit and greedily devouring me like that was his only chance. As much as I didn't want to fuel his ego, I couldn't stop myself from moaning.

His ministrations were addictive, but I knew it wasn't enough. With every touch and teasing movement he made, I only needed more of him.

"Ari…" I murmured breathlessly, so overcome by how incredible it felt that I was at war with myself, both not wanting it to end, and feeling greedy for the main event.

"I know, sweetheart," he said gruffly between my legs, leaving a final kiss there before he took the panties in his hands and tore them, to my surprise.

Before I could say anything, he tossed them away and hooked his arms underneath my thighs to pull me closer to the edge. His lips were on mine in a second, feeding that never-ending lust inside me.

But the sound of his cargo pants being shuffled off and the break in the exchange as pulled his tee over his head made anticipation pulse between my legs.

Seeing him in only his black briefs made something come alive within me, and I couldn't stop myself from staring at how perfectly sculpted his body was. He looked like an art piece, and I couldn't get enough.

Ari chuckled as he closed the space between us again and reached for the waistband of his briefs. "As much as I don't mind you admiring me, we have something to get to."

Another blush burned my cheeks at being caught, but given how hot my face was anyway, it didn't seem to matter.

Instead, the last of his clothes was thrown away, and his hands caressed my thighs as he secured my lips with his, urging me to lean back on my elbows.

I did as he wanted, too worked up to refuse him, or to delay for another moment.

A chill moved through me as the pressure of his cock weighed against my core as he teased me again, letting his length glide through my arousal.

We both tried to swallow back our moans at the sensation, to no avail. It was pointless to hold back when we both wanted it more than anything.

He slowly moved his hips back and forth as he kissed me, only pausing long enough to line himself up.

That initial connection as he pushed inside nearly made me break. That rush of intensity overcame me, forcing me to gasp at the sensation. Ari hummed his approval as he held me there and slowly filled me.

I could hardly believe how big he was, and just how perfect every inch of him felt. Thankfully, he was careful with every movement as he held me close.

By the time I couldn't take any more of him, Ari dropped his forehead to rest against mine as he pulled in a breath, seemingly fighting back against how good it felt. Steadying himself, he slowly drew his hips back and entered me again with less resistance.

We both moaned at the rush of pleasure that rained over us, making everything we had been through already feel worth it. Instinctively, I reached for him, desperate for something to hold on to.

Ari cursed under his breath while he developed a smooth rhythm, not afraid to squeeze my thigh with one hand while the other kept my opposite side pinned down. Even if our bodies couldn't be perfectly flush in that position, he still did everything he could to keep us close.

Even if he wore a hard exterior and was the leader of his family, I had the feeling he needed that intimacy as much as I did. To know the feeling of each other's touch, regardless of the unfortunate start to our marriage.

With every thrust, I could hardly take how overwhelming it was to be fed that unmistakable bliss again and again. How he had so much power behind him, and it all pushed me closer to the edge.

There was no point in holding back my moans then, especially not while Ari couldn't accomplish the same. Even if his sounds were reserved for muttered groans and breathy exhales, he was just as affected by it all.

As he rutted into me, I could tell Ari was desperate for more, and he confirmed the thought the moment he yanked me closer and I ended up flat on my back again.

The moment I settled into place, the angle of that position completely changed, making my jaw slack from the shock of it. With his relentless pace, he hit the same sinful place again and again, grunting as he gave me his all.

Stars were already burning into my vision as I took it, disbelieving how he was capable of making my eyes go bleary, how one man could make me feel never-ending pleasure.

The more that addictive sensation cloaked me, the harder my body clenched in anticipation as the coil tightened within me, threatening to snap at any moment.

Ari reached up and pulled my bralette down, letting my breasts spill out as I arched my back, far too overwhelmed to stay still.

He hummed his approval once again, reaffirming that he enjoyed my reactions and exactly how I was crumbling for him.

Once Ari seemed to zero in despite how his thrusts became sloppier, my throat felt raw from moaning for him, and it almost seemed to seal shut as he hit that spot enough times to make me clench around him.

Even as that haze consumed me, I didn't miss his guttural sound as he continued to thrust despite my approaching orgasm. Instead, I could hardly breathe as everything came to a head, and that ecstasy flitted through my system.

I gripped his biceps hard as I came undone, crying out for him.

Ari clenched his jaw through a few final thrusts before he grunted and reached his release, his hips quivering. He braced himself against the countertop as he let it wash over him, soaking in that bliss.

A warm fog filled me as I rode out that high, not caring about what led to that moment, only how incredible it felt.

As Ari caught his breath, he pulled me closer and put his forehead against the crook of my neck, letting me feel it against my collarbone.

Too dazed and content to do otherwise, I let it happen and allowed myself to appreciate the afterglow. Absently, I traced shapes against his bicep and wondered what was next for us.

We had just crossed a line in our relationship, and we'd never be able to walk it back.

# Chapter 13 - Ari

There was something about a woman's touch that made a man want to be softer. Made him want to be smoother around the edges and consider all the ways her presence alone could improve his life.

There was no mistaking how Vivian had the same effect on me.

As gentle beams of morning light started filtering into the room, I considered getting up at my usual time and getting ready for work, but as I took in her sleeping form, something told me to stay.

I wouldn't always get the chance to admire her in that way, and I had to take advantage of this new revelation. We were sharing the same bed for the first time since I brought her home, and it was surprisingly nice to watch her sleep peacefully. It was certainly a contrast to her resistance and willingness to fight me on most things.

Admittedly, I was still somewhat annoyed by her demands the day before. Mostly because I gave her more than enough to be comfortable, with no expectation of anything else in return, and because I wasn't used to anyone in my life confronting me in that way.

I couldn't believe how that confidence and resolve in her eyes was enough to break me down and stir those desires of mine. Yet I couldn't complain.

As much as I didn't want her to get comfortable about demanding whatever she wanted, I knew I couldn't expect her to give me respect while bossing her around and dismissing her concerns.

In all fairness, she had been mostly docile and passive ever since she started leaving the spare bedroom, and we had been spending more time together, even if it was platonic before. When I stepped back and really considered it, she wasn't asking for much.

Regardless of the small strides we were making towards resembling a real couple, there had to be give and take. To get her to open up to me, I needed to be vulnerable. I needed to show her the real side of me I hardly ever showed the outside world.

Ever since I was a kid, I had to be reserved about my feelings and emotions to not burden my siblings. I couldn't show a second of weakness out of fear I might not be enough for them, which made it second nature to be closed off from everyone else.

My ruthlessness and ambition could easily be misconstrued as me being a complete monster only out for blood. But I didn't want Vivian to think that of me.

I wanted her to know I was capable of being the person she needed to lean on. That I could be gentle and nurturing.

As her lashes lay heavily against the tops of her cheeks and her chest moved rhythmically with every gentle breath, I couldn't help but reflect on the night before.

Everything seemed to move so quickly, and that shift in our dynamic made it that much more intense. The sex had been mind-blowing and was exactly what I needed after bottling up that frustration inside myself. Luckily, it didn't stop in the kitchen.

While I had given up my control and couldn't resist how much I wanted her, throwing all caution to the wind felt worth it. We both reached a moment of bliss, releasing everything that was pent up between us. It even offered me a glimmer of hope for what might be ahead of us.

Even if Vivian had a way of weakening my resolve and making me hungry for more, I didn't care anymore. I just wanted us to be honest about our mutual attraction, and to not fight those feelings.

As I studied every inch of her features, along with her perfect body that was half-exposed beneath the sheets, I brought a hand up and ghosted my fingertips up and down her arm.

I watched as I caressed her skin, intrigued by how even in sleep, she was one of the most beautiful women I had ever seen.

Despite everything, it was hard to believe she was my wife. I had the pleasure of seeing her every day, all with the potential to become so much more.

Stirring, Vivian broke my trance as her eyes slowly opened, blinking back at me with the slightest bit of confusion in her gaze. But as she regained her bearings, she wore a faint smile as she stretched in her place.

"Morning," she hummed, surprisingly soft as she lay there.

"Good morning," I returned, noting how groggy my voice still sounded.

Even if she was being quiet and elegant like a feline, just looking into those eyes reminded me of her fire, and how determined she had been to prove her point the night before.

I never expected her to be quite so outspoken given how passive and doe-like she had been before, but something was refreshing about it. Knowing she could push back against me excited something within me.

"I have to ask," I began, keeping my tone as gentle and receptive as possible. "Why is being busy such a big deal for you when you already have everything you could ever need?"

A part of me immediately regretted asking the question when she seemed to pull back and retreat within herself again. Wanting to claw it back and apologize, I could only watch as she pulled the sheets higher and moved into a sitting position. She averted her eyes, and while I assumed she was about to leave the bed and bring us back to square one all over again, she sighed instead.

Interested in whatever she had to say, I followed her lead and leaned against the headboard.

"I don't intend to be mean. I'm just curious," I managed, hoping to encourage her to open up.

"I know, it's fine," she murmured, seemingly wrangling with something internally before she gave in again. "I may have grown up with two brothers, but we were never the family I wanted us to be. Elio and Dante…they treated me like I was no better than a verbal punching bag. Dante was the worst one. Dad was too busy with his work, and he didn't let them in on the family business, which bothered them, so they took their anger out on me. To make up for keeping me from pursuing anything of my own, he made sure I wasn't idle for too long with lessons and anything else I wanted. I always wanted more for myself, and the chance to do it on my own, but I couldn't while living there. I felt trapped, and with my brothers treating me like garbage, I only had those things to distract me. I don't want to feel trapped here, too."

As empathetic as I was to hear her reasoning, I couldn't completely temper my anger at how she had been treated, and at the hands of her own siblings.

Given how absent Edoardo had been, it seemed I did pull her out of a bad situation.

"Your brothers should be ashamed of themselves for treating their only sister like that," I murmured, reaching out for her hand. "I'm sorry you didn't experience better."

With a grim expression, Vivian tried to pull a tight-lipped smile. "I wish they thought the same."

Knowing I had been right about assuming things weren't good at home, easily recalling those bruises on her wrists, it made me soften. In that moment, I made the mental note to be gentler around her, and to keep that in mind moving forward.

She deserved better than what her family gave her, and something in me wanted to give her that. No matter what it took, I wanted to be the one to show her she could have so much more.

It all made sense to me then.

"After seeing how your family acted around each other, I couldn't help but wonder where mine went wrong. I questioned why we couldn't be the same way, and why my brothers saw me as their enemy instead of their sister," Vivian continued with defeat in her voice. When she met my gaze, there was no missing the deep sadness there. "How did you get so lucky with your siblings?"

Considering everything we went through together, it was easy to see why we would be close. Thinking back to those times, I shrugged. "We only ever had each other. And honestly, the women in our family are treated better than anyone else. We so rarely had girls born into our family that they were like royalty in their own right."

"That sounds nice," she sighed, looking off in consideration.

Giving her hand a small squeeze, I wanted Vivian to know I'd treat her with the utmost respect, and that my family would do the same. Even if we got off on the wrong foot, she mattered to me beyond our marriage license.

"About keeping busy," I said, deciding it was worth pursuing after all. "I'll see what I can do about it."

With complete sincerity, Vivian gave me a smile bordering on sad gratitude as she blinked back the beginning of tears. "It would mean a lot to me."

Throughout my childhood, I had been completely prepared to give everything for my siblings, and with my wife, it would be no different.

Decided, I leaned in and pressed an affectionate kiss to her forehead before forcing myself out of bed.

"Come down for breakfast and coffee when you're ready. I'll have it waiting for you," I said, grabbing my phone from the nightstand as I headed for the door.

On my way, I caught the small smile on her lips before she rolled over to face away from me with a small murmur in response.

Thinking it was endearing, I chuckled to myself and left the room.

As the coffee brewed, I leaned against the countertop and scrolled through my phone, browsing through listings with a keen eye before finding something that struck my interest.

It was perfect, and exactly what Vivian needed.

With Benedikt's contact open, I tapped the screen and initiated the call.

He answered after the first ring groggily. "What's going on? Did something happen?"

"Nothing to worry about," I replied with a faint grin on my face. "I just wanted to let you know I have an important purchase to make for my wife, and I need you to sort out the details."

There was a moment of silence before Benedikt sighed. "Alright. What do you need?"

At the end of it, I knew Vivian would be completely over the moon.

# Chapter 14 - Vivian

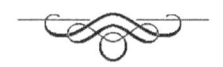

I never considered how much things between me and Ari would improve by simply giving in, by dropping those defensive walls and admitting what we were both thinking.

To my surprise, I was still riding that high of knowing we had sex, and how it changed my perception of almost everything. Not only was he a god physically, but he had changed his tune, too, and everything between us shifted.

As satisfied and relieved as I felt to get that tension behind us, I was still battling the confusion clouding my mind. I couldn't understand why I enjoyed it so much, or how I let it happen in the first place. While he made my heart feel lighter and full of unfamiliar hope, I still didn't know what to think.

My control and willingness to resist him were slipping, and I had no idea how to get it back again.

Worst of all, I didn't know if I even wanted to fight him anymore. It was hard to want to after he had been kinder and more understanding of my feelings.

On top of everything, I had no idea where Ari was taking us as I sat in the passenger seat while he drove. The radio played quietly, and he seemingly knew where he was going without letting me in on that information.

I assumed we were going to see his family until we were somewhere more remote, leaving the city for the countryside. While it wasn't too far, it was a change from what we were used to, and soon enough, long stretches of farmland appeared all around us.

I was somewhat unsettled the farther we went, at a complete loss for where we were until he turned into a long lane.

Ogling out the window, I took in the stretch of pastures, where horses grazed in the gentle winds. Up ahead, there was a huge stable with red siding, along with both an indoor and outdoor riding ring. The property looked immaculate and like any horse lover's dream.

I looked at Ari in complete disbelief as the realization set in.

He took what I said to heart, and surely this was how we were going to spend the day together. That swell of emotions was almost impossible to hold back as he gave me a knowing smile and killed the engine before popping the door open.

"Come on," he said simply, gesturing with his head for me to do the same. "Let's have a look."

As my heart kickstarted again, I undid my seatbelt and followed.

The moment the fresh country air hit me, I felt like I was back at the old stables. Like I was in my favorite comfort place, and I never had to worry about anything while I was there.

"Is this what we're doing?" I asked, falling into step with him as he guided me toward the nearest field. "Going riding?"

Ari could barely hold back his smug grin as he placed a hand against the small of my back and guided me closer to some of the horses. "Sure. Whatever you want."

A bay mare with a white blaze on her face approached us curiously as she chewed on a mouthful of grass, tail swishing the flies away from her.

Holding a hand out, I could've died right there as she blew warm air against my palm before letting me stroke her soft muzzle.

"She's beautiful," I said, in complete awe of her and all the others grazing in the distance. We managed to catch the attention of some in the back, and a few more headed in our direction.

"I'm glad you like her," Ari said, still smirking. "You'll be able to visit as often as you like, so long as you have a driver."

As nice as it sounded, I couldn't help my confusion. "Are you sure? Wouldn't it bother the owners?"

"Not at all," he replied, unable to hold back his smugness as his dimples showed themselves. "We are the owners."

Hardly able to process his words, I blinked back at him in complete shock. "What?"

Chuckling again, Ari nodded. "You heard me. Every horse and building on this property is yours. The farmhands have already been hired to take care of things when you're not here, so you can swing by and ride or just visit with them whenever you want."

As if those words melted what remained of my resistance, a new kind of warmth ran through me. That sheer happiness settled on my shoulders, and every bit of me was singing from how incredibly nice the gesture was.

I didn't take Ari for a thoughtful man before, but he was certainly proving me wrong.

As that joy overtook me, I pressed myself against him and wrapped my arms around his midsection.

"Thank you, Ari," I said, just above a whisper as I fought back the fresh emotions making my nose sting. "This is more than I could've asked for."

"It's my pleasure," he hummed, returning the embrace with more warmth than I expected. When he pulled back, I took in his pleased smile as he kept his arm around my shoulder, surrounding me with that new comfort. "There should be more than enough tack for you in the stable. We can get one of these guys prepped now if you want."

Grinning at him, I nodded. My heart could barely handle the combination of how handsome and at ease he looked doing something so generous for me, and knowing he trusted me enough to let me go without him if I wanted.

Together, we got ready in the stable as I sifted through the brand-new tack like a kid on Christmas morning, then walked the bay mare inside to put everything on her.

Ari watched as I handled it myself since I was used to going through the motions at the stable I used to visit. Once everything was done, I led her to the outdoor riding ring and climbed into the saddle.

The mare had the perfect temperament as I used the reins, giving her commands to test her skills. She did everything I asked of her, and it made me wonder how everything in Ari's impromptu plan managed to work out so well.

I could only imagine that power and influence did a whole lot for him, and it certainly seemed to work in my favor now, too.

Even if my dad had money and tended to flex it whenever he wanted, I knew his wealth paled in comparison to the Levovs. An entire stable with horses, farmhands, and all the fixings likely didn't make a dent.

Overjoyed as I did laps around the riding ring with the mare, getting a taste of that familiar feeling I loved so much, I felt completely at peace. I was comfortable and at home in the saddle, even if the horse was new to me.

Everything about it brought me a sense of security that made everything else feel easier to bear. Like I had been given the tools I needed to feel better about my new life.

Ari watched all the while as he leaned against the wooden fence perimeter, certainly proud of himself for how much of a hit it was. He seemed almost impressed by how quickly I got into the swing of things.

Eventually, I slowed the mare to a stop in front of where he stood. "It feels like it's been ages since I rode last."

"You're a natural," he complimented me, reaching out to give the horse a scratch on the nose. "You look regal up there."

My cheeks warmed as I brushed him off bashfully. "If only you had seen me in my showing uniform."

He cocked a brow at that, clearly interested. "Consider me intrigued."

Smiling, I swung a leg around and slid out of the saddle, noticing that familiar ache in my thighs again. "Want to give it a try?"

As I walked around to face him, Ari shook his head. "That's alright. I don't mind staying on the ground."

I couldn't help but find his sheepishness funny as he obviously wasn't fond of the idea, but at the same time, I wanted to see him out of his element for once.

"Come on, just a lap? She's sound, I promise," I encouraged him, reaching out for his hand.

Ari watched as I twined our fingers together, and I noted how he seemed to relax at the touch. For a moment, he looked like the gentle version of himself again—vulnerable and without that usual cold edge of his.

It was strange seeing him so unlike that man who stormed into my family's home, making his demands and not taking no for an answer.

Instead, nothing other than his size and sheer muscle seemed brutish.

Letting go of a conceding breath, Ari met my gaze again. "Alright, fine. But I'm not wearing that silly helmet."

"Fine," I replied, cracking a smile for him. "Get on and I'll walk her around."

While certainly unsure about the whole thing, Ari let go of my hand to walk around to the mare's side, and he hoisted himself into the saddle.

He sat up there skeptically while he tried to make himself comfortable, flashing me a nervous look. "How do you do this so often? It feels awful."

Snickering, I gently reached for the mare's bridle and started leading her around the ring. "Quit complaining and hold onto the reins. Make sure your feet stay in the stirrups."

Ari grumbled to himself as he did what I told him to, looking completely out of his depth despite moving at a slow pace.

I tried my best to be supportive of him since it was his first time on horseback and very unlike his usual work, but there was something funny about how he looked up there, seeming ready to get down at any moment.

Hiding my laughter as best as I could, I made sure the mare didn't make any sudden turns or movements, and as ridiculous as he looked, it was incredibly endearing.

"See? That wasn't so bad," I said once the mare eventually stopped, and I allowed him to hop down.

The moment he had both feet on the ground again, Ari dusted himself off and narrowed his eyes at me playfully.

"Don't you dare tell anyone about this."

Laughing quietly as I led the horse back to the stable, I found myself feeling grateful for that sense of normalcy. Like the playing field was even for once, and I got to see a less measured and confident side of him.

"Your secret's safe with me."

At least Ari was able to see the humor in it, too, as he chuckled to himself and gently pet the mare's flank. "For such a majestic beast, that is one uncomfortable ride. I'll stick to my cars, thank you."

As we wrapped up our time at the stable, feeling lighthearted and at ease, I couldn't deny that I was seeing Ari in a different light.

He went out of his way to meet my needs in a way I never expected, he didn't complain all the while he let me do as I wanted, and he even gave it a shot for me. As reluctant as he was, at least he tried, and he made me laugh in the process.

Even if he seemed like a brutal, bloodthirsty man before, there was no denying how much he changed, and how willing he was to make things work.

As much as I didn't want to admit it, being his wife didn't seem quite so bad anymore.

# Chapter 15 - Ari

It turned out that horseback riding suited Vivian, and watching her sheer joy suited me even more.

Buying the stable felt like a small price to pay for the chance to see that side of her come to life, able to take in how comfortable and at ease she was. It was a refreshing sight after only knowing her resentment and vague disinterest for weeks.

Giving in to our mutual attraction seemed to be the catalyst we both needed to open up to one another so that we could better understand each other.

I was glad I heard her out.

She had been missing something that brought her so much fulfillment, and I hoped giving that to her again would reassure her that marrying me wasn't the end of her life.

Even while I sat at my desk at work, leafing through some documents that needed my attention, I couldn't pull my focus away from Vivian and how perfect that day at the stable was.

She smiled so much that it was burned into my brain, and her laughter was so sweet that I just wanted to hear more of it. I wanted to be the reason she did both those things more and to prove to her I treasured every moment of it.

It was easy to see then how much I cared about her, and how greatly she was affecting me.

No woman had ever made me feel that way before, and while it made me somewhat nervous, I also felt more prepared than ever to handle it. To accept her time and affection and savor everything I could.

Even if we were still working on our connection, I was already missing my time with her, and she seemed to take up permanent residence in my mind.

For the first time in my life, I felt genuinely drawn to someone, and I wanted her so badly it almost made me feel sick.

But of course, I couldn't just skip out on my work. I had to at least try and pay attention to what was in front of me, even if my mind was actively back at home, wrapped up in the sheets with her.

I knew I was doing a poor job of concentrating the moment I nearly jumped out of my seat once someone knocked at the door.

"Someone looks out of it," Benedikt said as he strode in with Lukyan behind him. He was quick to steal the seat in front of me, dropping himself into it while our younger brother had to stand. He sighed at the realization but didn't argue with him.

"Watch it," I mumbled, placing my pen down as if I had been busy writing anything at all.

His gloved hands went up in defense of himself, and he gestured to Lukyan casually. "We'll be out of your hair soon enough. We thought you might like to hear this."

With my interest piqued, I looked between them. "What did you find?"

"Ever since you told me to keep an eye out for anything suspicious, I've had some guys out there tasked with monitoring the situation. I recently received a report of someone digging into us and our operations," Lukyan began, holding the black tablet in front of himself while he poked around the screen.

"Digging how?"

"They've been staking out nearby and trying to locate our other warehouses. Our guys have been trailing them, and they have no idea we're actively collecting intel. After running some searches and filtering through our databases, we've narrowed it down to some likely suspects," he explained, flipping the tablet around for me to see it.

"And?" I questioned, brow raised as I sifted through a series of photos featuring vehicles I didn't recognize, along with men clearly trying to hide while they watched our properties.

"We believe it's someone from Vivian's family. I'm assuming it's one of her brothers, given the circumstances. It sounds like Edoardo isn't involved, so it must be one of them. They're likely looking for some kind of in to get back at you for what happened."

Stroking my chin absently, I nodded as irritation flared within me again. It was troubling, but it came as no surprise.

"I suspected as much would happen. I just figured it would take longer for them to recuperate. At the very least, I expected Edoardo to retaliate, not one of his sons," I murmured, mostly to myself. "But it doesn't make sense for one of her brothers to be leading the effort. Vivian told me her dad wouldn't let them have anything to do with the business."

Lukyan shrugged. "Maybe you broke Edoardo down enough to cause him to step back, allowing his sons to take the helm? If that's what they wanted all along, I doubt he would take much convincing at that point."

"That would certainly be an interesting development if so," I returned, silently agreeing that the information was well worth my time. As I swiped through the last of the photos, I landed on one that looked vaguely like one of the brothers who had been there the night we stormed them. "There's one of two reasons why they're doing any of this. One, they want revenge for humiliating them and their dad. Or two, they want Vivian back since she was the one valuable asset they had waiting to be used. They're potentially figuring that if they can get her back, end the marriage, and lock her up in the house again, they'll be able to sell her off to someone willing to pay a pretty price."

"And how would you feel about them trying to take your wife?" Benedikt asked, brows lifted curiously.

Leaning back in my chair as I handed the tablet back to Lukyan, I snickered bitterly. "The bastards will know what the concrete outside tastes like before I let that happen. If anyone thinks they're going to pull a fast one on me and take my wife, they'll find out the hard way. I say let them try."

Ben chuckled and nodded. "As I imagined."

"Besides, there's a special place in hell for any man who treats his little sister like a punching bag. I'm more than willing to send them there myself," I muttered, recalling how she had opened up to me about her brothers and the treatment she faced in the family home.

"They sound like a rotten bunch over there," Lukyan commented, sounding empathetic for Vivian.

"You don't know the half of it," I returned, shaking my head in disbelief. "If they are gearing up to try and get her back, it will only be for monetary purposes. They don't care about her, and they likely never will. Which is why I'm going to do everything I can to stop that from happening."

Both my brothers seemed to understand, and Lukyan crossed his arms. "What now, then?"

"I appreciate the work you've done so far. Keep looking into it, and let me know if you or anyone else finds anything of interest. We need confirmation it's really her brothers before we do anything about it."

Luk nodded. "I'm on it."

"And what about Vivian? I take it she's been enjoying the new ranch," Ben added since he finalized the sale of everything for me. "Are you going to stop her from going if her brothers are on the lookout for her?"

Letting go of a tense breath, I shook my head. "I bought the place as a gift, and to show her she's not trapped like she was at her old place. I can't go back on my word now—not after she loved it so much."

Benedikt gave me a look of surprise as he made himself comfortable. "It seems you've grown soft, brother. You better start yelling to save face."

"If you keep pushing, I'll make sure that happens," I muttered, waving him off. "It turns out that not being a hard-ass all the time actually builds trust."

He laughed to himself. "I never would've guessed. You're making strides, Ari."

Scoffing, I pointed at the door. "Show yourself out, you little shit."

Amused, Ben pulled himself up from his chair and moved toward the door. "Gladly, boss. I was planning on finishing my work early so I can go get myself a wife and find out what it's like for myself."

"Good luck finding one in Andrei's clubs," I called after him as he slipped through the door.

Lukyan roared with laughter on his way out, trailing behind Benedikt as he muttered something I couldn't hear under his breath.

Shaking my head at how ridiculous they could be despite the serious nature of our work, the reality of the situation fell on my shoulders once I was left alone again.

The De Lucas were back on my radar just as everything seemed to be going so well with Vivian, and I couldn't help but wonder how it would all play out.

As I looked down at the paperwork in front of me, I still couldn't bring myself to focus on it, especially not with the news fresh in my mind.

While it wouldn't be the worst thing in the world to let Vivian know about the potential situation, I didn't want to alarm her. I also didn't want her sitting at home stewing about it and considering all the bad things that might happen.

Which was why I decided I'd keep it to myself for the time being. At the very least, I wouldn't say anything until I learned more about what was going on.

With us getting closer and Vivian beginning to open up to me, I didn't need anything to put a wrench in it.

Things were good, and I wanted it to stay that way.

# Chapter 16 - Vivian

The sun on my face was a welcome comfort as the wind swept my hair back and reminded me of how much of a joy it was to be out in the pasture, taking in my surroundings with complete appreciation.

I had just finished another perfect ride with the mare and was walking her back into the field with the others. Once I unclipped her lead, they managed to sniff out the treats in my pockets, and I fed the ones crowding around me.

There was no mistaking how much I missed being around horses, and how they had been such a light in my life during hard times. Because of my family, those memories were bittersweet, but with the new stable and the complete escape it was for me, I was able to make new ones.

I was grateful for that and beyond happy that Ari found it within himself to see how much I needed it.

Boarding a horse in another barn would've sufficed, but of course, it couldn't be that straightforward with him. It was still hard to believe the ranch belonged to us, and I could go at my pleasure so long as a driver was available for me.

It wasn't how I'd prefer to go, but it was a decent compromise for us.

Giving the last treat away, I scratched the horse between the ears before leaving the pasture.

I had already been there for several hours, and I knew I'd have to be back home soon enough anyway.

Feeling fulfilled and more than happy with how the day was playing out, I made my way back toward the stable, taking in the sights and peaceful surroundings.

Being in nature and working with horses was something I always enjoyed and pulled a lot of relief from. Over the last few weeks, I was even considering going to Ari about providing lessons for kids or beginners.

It wouldn't be anything too ambitious or overbearing, but something to put my mind to and build some connections. It sounded rewarding, and I liked the idea of it.

But once I reached the stable, I stopped as a wave of nausea hit me out of nowhere. Bracing myself with a hand against the wall, I paused and waited for it to pass, trying to feel out just how bad it was.

Sucking in a deep breath, saliva filled my mouth immediately, and a rush of panic came with it.

I couldn't remember the last time I threw up, but given how sick I suddenly felt, I knew it was coming.

Keeled over behind the barn, I couldn't help as the vomit forced its way out. As ungracefully as possible, I had no choice but to let it run its course, waiting for that urge to pass.

Finally, I wiped my mouth once I felt it was over and tried to regain my bearings. Grossed out by the aftertaste, I tried to ignore it as best as I could and gathered my things before heading toward the SUV waiting down the laneway.

I was somewhat dizzy as I went, wondering why I felt so gross, and what could've caused it.

We didn't eat anything out of the ordinary recently, and regardless of how hard I tried to think about it, I couldn't come up with a reason.

But there was something.

I had been pretty tired recently, and hardly able to finish reading without falling asleep whenever I got home after riding. Yet I had been chalking that up to how busy I had been with the horses. It made the most sense to me.

Ever since Ari and I started connecting, I stopped feeling sluggish and gross due to being stuck in the house. Instead, I was doing a lot better until recently.

As I approached the vehicle while the driver sat with his legs hanging out of the open door, it hit me.

That night when we first had sex. I couldn't remember using any protection.

We had been too riled up and too desperate to even consider it. Plus, I had no idea where I was in my cycle at the time.

There was no missing the worry that swept through me, forcing a wave of adrenaline through me.

Making that connection made everything feel far too real far too fast, and I could hardly stand how it felt to not know.

I could already picture myself going back home and not being able to stop thinking about it, questioning if it was true. I wouldn't be able to sleep, and the thought of approaching Ari about whether I was pregnant or not was too humiliating. I didn't want to say anything until I knew for sure.

I had to get my hands on a test sooner rather than later.

"Are you all right, Mrs. Levov?" the driver asked, poking his head out.

Blinking through my stupor, I shook myself out of it and nodded. "Y-yeah, I'm fine. I was just hoping we could stop at a convenience store nearby. There's a few things I need to grab."

Even through his black sunglasses, I could see his apprehension, as if considering whether or not it was a good idea.

"The boss said I was to make sure you get here and make it right back afterward, but I don't see how another stop would hurt," he murmured, then gave me a final nod. "I'll find the closest one."

Forcing a smile for him, I tried to make it seem like I was okay even though I felt the complete opposite. The panic was looming over me, and I still felt horrible after vomiting, but I had to hold out until I was alone again. I didn't need the driver tipping Ari off about it.

"Thanks, I appreciate it," I said, climbing in.

On the way back to the city, I couldn't think about anything else. My head was a mess as I considered everything, whether I was pregnant or just making myself believe that was the case.

I imagined having to swallow my embarrassment to let him know if I was carrying his child, and the thought alone scared me. Even if he was my husband, and that wasn't the worst thing to happen to a couple, I didn't know what he would think about it.

Would he hate me for strapping him with a child? Would he learn to resent me for how my body would inevitably change? Would he even want to keep it?

The confusion of it all wouldn't let my head work straight, but before I knew it, the driver pulled into a convenience store parking lot and looked at me through the rearview mirror as he parked and killed the engine.

"I'll be waiting right here. Just make sure you come right back out."

I nodded as I climbed out, acknowledging him, though my mind was somewhere completely different.

Walking numbly to the door, I made my way inside and urged myself to find the nerve I needed. I considered grabbing a few things and forgetting about the test since I would inevitably find out eventually.

But as I thought about how much not knowing would bother me, I knew I had to.

Glancing out the window, I caught the driver watching me from his place by the SUV. Of course he'd be keeping his tabs on me.

To not look too suspicious, I browsed through the cold beverages and grabbed one that looked all right before checking out the candy section. I grabbed a few bags, and then made my way over to the small section of feminine products.

I snagged one of the tests and headed over to the counter to pay.

The driver watched, pulling a few drags from a cigarette while he made sure nothing out of the ordinary happened. Although, he didn't seem to suspect anything.

With everything I bought tucked away in a plastic bag, thankful for the card Ari gave me, I thanked the cashier and headed for the bathroom. I could only hope it wasn't too obvious.

Once the door was locked behind me, I let go of a big breath and got to it.

I swallowed back some of the juice I got, glad that I did have to go in the first place, then tore the packaging open and did what had to be done.

As I capped the test and waited for the results, my head was far too full of panicked thoughts for me to string a coherent one together.

Instead, I was too focused on the test coming out one way or another, and questioning what that would mean for me and Ari. If he would accept it, or if a child was the last thing he wanted.

Those few minutes felt agonizing, but once I peered over at the little screen, my heart dropped.

Immediately, my skin felt ice cold, and I could've thrown up all over again.

It was positive.

I was pregnant with Ari's baby.

The floor seemed to move beneath me as I struggled to understand what I was looking at, or what I was supposed to do next. I felt dizzy, reeling from what that meant.

Remembering that I was in a public bathroom, I put a hand over my mouth to stop from making any noise despite how prepared I was to cry from how overwhelming it all was.

Since I knew and would have to get it confirmed at a clinic, that meant I had no choice but to tell Ari. I wouldn't be able to hide it for too long, and I could only imagine how angry he'd be if I kept it to myself.

But the thought of that added so much pressure to my shoulders, I could hardly stomach it.

While I never hated the idea of being a mother, I never thought it would happen so soon, especially not after we had only been married for a handful of months. Sure, I'd have the security and stability I'd need to take care of a child, but if Ari and I weren't okay, there would only be more problems because of it.

Our relationship still felt like a new thing that needed more time and care to make sure it was heading in the right direction, and there was no telling what a newborn might do to it.

Yet, there was no denying how much better things had been, and he was doing his best to prove to me that even if our union was hasty, he had every intention of being a proper husband. He was looking out for both of us and making sure I was as comfortable as possible through the adjustment period.

A strange wave of reassurance surrounded me then, and I wiped my eyes as I tried to calm down.

Whether it was our budding relationship or how paternal Ari seemed given his experience taking care of young children, something in me was almost excited by the idea of seeing him in action.

He told me he had sacrificed everything to take care of his siblings, and I could only imagine how he'd be with his own baby.

Regardless of those conflicting thoughts and emotions moving through me, one thing was abundantly clear: I was dreading telling him.

I didn't know how he would react, and bringing a child into the world wasn't a small thing. I could only hope kids were on the table for him, and that all of my worries were for nothing.

As I threw the packaging out, put the test in my bag, and wiped my tears, I headed back for the SUV, all while mulling over how I would tell him.

# Chapter 17 - Ari

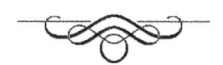

Knowing Vivian was waiting at home or busy at the stable while I went to work every day made the days feel longer in anticipation of getting to see her again. As the week came to an end, I was looking forward to the moment I could be back with her, spending the weekend doing whatever we wanted.

I never thought I'd be the kind of man who couldn't wait to get back home just to be graced by his wife's affection and the comfort I'd learned to appreciate more than anything, but it seemed I did change for the better.

Being married and having someone like Vivian in my life was making me want to reach my full potential, and to never be like most husbands and fathers in the organized crime world. I wanted to prove to her that I would always be there regardless of what happened and that I always kept my word.

As I sat in traffic, I was starting to lose my patience. I was itching to get back to her and to connect with her more. With two free days at my disposal, I intended to take full advantage of them.

The time spent alone at my cold, lonely desk needed to be rectified as soon as possible.

I may have done something nice by buying her the ranch and letting her go out even while I wasn't around to make sure nothing happened, but I knew it wasn't all I could do. I wanted to establish more trust between us, and for her to feel she could depend on me.

I wanted to get to a place where I could have her unwavering loyalty, and she would have mine just the same. To do that, I needed to prove she could trust me first. The foundation had been laid, but with more time and effort, I wanted it to be even stronger.

I pulled Vivian from her old life, whether that was for the greater good or not, and in return, I couldn't let her down by providing a lifeless, loveless marriage. Given how she grew up, she needed to know she was deserving of so much more, I was determined to show her the lengths I was willing to go to prove it to her.

I refused to let her feel like she was nothing more than a release for my anger like her brothers did. I wouldn't make her think she was nothing but a bargaining chip—like something that could be sold off for the highest bidder like her dad did.

I wouldn't let her feel the cold ache of an empty, unforgiving house again. She was at the top of my priority list, and I needed her to know that.

With ample relief, I pulled into the garage and found myself getting antsier with every passing moment keeping me from feeling her and reacquainting with her lips. At the very least, I just wanted to feel her warmth and how easily she could soothe me without even knowing it.

Vivian was the relief I craved, and I couldn't tell if she was aware of how much power she had over me because of it.

Finally, I went inside and found her in the living room, curled up with a book in her lap.

Letting out a deep breath, I could already feel myself reaping the benefits of being near her—of knowing nothing else could stop me from taking full advantage of our time together.

When she noticed me walk in, Vivian smiled. That was enough to put me at ease.

"How was work?" she asked, setting the book aside.

"It was work," I said, always choosing to keep the details to myself. I approached the couch and stood behind her, gently putting my hands on her shoulders. "But I'm glad it's behind me for the weekend."

Carefully massaging her shoulders, I watched as Vivian relaxed into my touch. She hummed her approval. "Shouldn't I be the one doing this for you?"

"I'm sure there's time to arrange that," I returned with a chuckle. Lifting a hand to brush a finger against her cheek, I took great satisfaction in how she leaned into the caress like a cat would. "Two days, to be exact."

I felt her face move with her smile, and I leaned in, leaving a kiss there before I rounded the side of the couch and scooped her up. She laughed, caught off guard by it as I swung us around and sat down, placing her in my lap.

"Speaking of, what would you like to do this weekend?" I asked, taking in how comforting the presence of her arm wrapped around the back of my neck was while she perched there. "I'll be at your disposal the entire time."

Vivian seemed surprised by the proposition, but there was no doubting her pleasure in hearing it as she leaned into me. "You're leaving me with a lot of choices here…and they're all very tempting."

"What's the first thing on your list?"

She thought to herself for a moment as I pressed kisses against her neck, causing her to giggle. "I've been practicing my serves while you're at work, so I wouldn't mind playing some tennis together."

Pausing my ministrations, I tried my best to conceal my grimace at the idea. A part of me cursed whoever installed the net since I was never skilled at the sport. But since it was something Vivian wanted to do, and I'd offered the decision to her, I didn't want to be difficult about it.

Leaning her back so that she was suspended in my arms, I kissed along her jaw until I reached her lips, hovering there as I murmured, "First thing tomorrow morning, we'll head out to the court. You can decide the rest as we go."

Vivian smiled at the idea, accepting the kiss against her lips before having to deal with the many small affections I peppered around her face.

"Ari!" she squealed, giggling as I doted on her.

Unable to hold back my amusement, I laughed and soaked in the addictive sound of her happiness, and I found myself looking forward to what was ahead of us.

Following through with my promise despite how much I was dreading the activity itself, I got myself ready in some athletic shorts and a black compression shirt, at least glad for the chance to get a workout in.

I was already down at the court to make sure everything was in order when Vivian came out wearing a perfect tennis ensemble with her hair in a high ponytail.

The skirt fit her perfectly, accentuating her curves and leaving little to the imagination. I knew the distraction would only work more in her favor.

Cracking a smile for her, I handed her a racket. "Tennis suits you."

She mirrored my expression, and I didn't miss how she seemed to take me in completely, too. "We'll see if it suits you."

Taking it as a challenge, I cocked a brow at her and started stretching. "Don't set your expectations too high, sweetheart."

She laughed at that and joined me.

It didn't take long to see just how skilled Vivian was, and how I could hardly keep up with her.

She had been practicing, given how strong her serving arm was. She maintained an impressive amount of focus as she returned every one of my swings, moving with ease around her side of the court.

I may have been built with a strong frame, but I was hardly coordinated enough to go toe-to-toe with Vivian's evident experience.

I spent more time chasing the ball around than I cared to admit, and as hard as she tried to be supportive, Vivian couldn't help but get a kick out of it.

Once again, I felt completely out of my element, but given how happy it made her, I didn't mind nursing my bruised ego in the meantime.

She was wiping the floor with me, and as much as I wanted to maintain that competitive air, I was more impressed than anything else.

"Mercy, please," I said, bracing myself as I caught my breath.

Vivian smiled as she walked beneath the net over to my side and grabbed two water bottles I had waiting for us. She handed one to me with a grin on her face. "A break wouldn't hurt, I guess."

Letting her be smug, I snickered and took a swig of water. "Can't say I didn't warn you."

"You just need some practice, that's all."

While I appreciated her encouragement and support, I knew it would only be a lost cause, anyway. But so long as she wanted to keep playing, I had to just suck it up.

"Did your brothers ever play tennis with you?" I asked, remembering how I needed to get some insight on her family, given how the current situation with them was growing more concerning with every report I got back.

Sadness moved through her eyes as she recalled whatever memories she had associated with them, and she shook her head. "I only ever played with friends and my trainer. They tended to do things on their own."

"That's a shame. They could've learned a thing or two from you," I murmured, regaining my bearings again. "A part of me wishes I had more practice."

Vivian smiled faintly and capped her water again before asking, "Ready for another round?"

As much as I didn't really want to, happy wife, happy life, right?

# CHAPTER 18 - VIVIAN

I was more than happy for the chance to spend time with Ari and to show off some of my skills, especially since I felt in my element again. His clumsiness was the cherry on top.

Ari was a wall of muscle—brutal in both size and strength. But he couldn't play tennis to save his life, and that was just fine with me. I did as much as I could to conceal how funny it was to watch him fumble around the court, but in truth, it made the experience even better.

After our break, we made our way back to our places, and I was feeling good for the most part, even if I had something plaguing my mind.

From his side, Ari bounced the tennis ball against the ground several times, and he looked contemplative. "Do you think your brothers would ever take over your dad's business?"

As I digested that question, I couldn't help but get the feeling he was trying to make some sort of connection. It seemed like he had been testing the waters with his previous question, which I initially brushed off until I put those pieces together.

I was concerned about why he would be asking about my family, but at the same time, I didn't mind answering. It was good for us to be transparent with each other, even if the topic was a sore spot for me. However, his prying gave me a funny feeling.

"Since Dad never let them in on any crucial information before, I wouldn't think so," I answered, standing in position while I waited for him to serve the ball. "But I can't say anything for sure."

"And you're sure he wouldn't have a change of heart?" he asked, finally sending the ball to my side.

Tracking it, I aimed and swung my racket, sending it right back. "He didn't seem interested in changing his mind before. That's why they were always frustrated with him."

Ari did his best to not trip over his own feet as he went after the ball, managing to return it, much to his delight.

Even if Ari was out of his depth and not the best competitor to play against, I was still having fun. Ever since he came back home the night before and was determined to have a good weekend with just the two of us, I was more than happy about it.

Although, I hadn't forgotten about the positive pregnancy test, and I knew it would have to come up eventually. That night would've been the perfect time, but Ari seemed so relieved to be done with work and excited to focus on just us. I didn't want to sour the mood if a child wasn't something he wanted yet.

We were doing much better than before, and Ari was certainly putting in the work to make something genuine happen between us, but throwing a newborn into the mix would complicate everything. Especially since we were still working out the kinks.

I couldn't hide the news forever, but I was trying to put it in the back of my mind in the meantime.

I wanted to enjoy our time together, even if hiding it from Ari was slowly eating at me.

When the tennis ball eventually hit his side of the court, Ari chased after it in a light jog. "That's interesting. Usually, kingpins train their sons to take over the business…"

As much as I was trying to answer his questions to the best of my abilities, I couldn't ignore the skepticism moving through me. I didn't know what he was getting at, but seeing as he didn't ask about them often, he had to be on to something he wasn't sharing with me.

"I suppose so," I murmured, watching as he bounced the tennis ball several times before catching it again.

As he looked at it in his hand, many thoughts moved through his eyes as if fighting some internal battle. He squeezed it, looked like he was about to serve it, then didn't. His hesitation was worrying me.

Ari let go of a deep breath and looked over at me. "If they were to surround this place right now and ask you to come with them, would you?"

My brows furrowed at that, confused as to what he was talking about, and I relaxed out of my poised position. "What?"

I genuinely wasn't expecting him to ask me anything like that. He didn't seem to work in hypotheticals, and seeing how much it seemed to weigh on him, I knew something was up.

He ran a hand down his face, gazing at me with an expression I couldn't read. "What I mean is, would your loyalty be with me or with them?"

Aware of how much weight that question carried, I knew I had to get to the bottom of his questions. I didn't understand why all of that mattered so suddenly.

"What's going on, Ari?" I asked, approaching the net again.

Ari looked away, not meeting my eyes like he normally did. It seemed out of character for him as he absently fiddled with the tennis racket. "I shouldn't concern you with this…"

But that only made me more concerned. Lifting the net, I walked beneath it so that nothing stood between us. With the game completely out of our minds, I looked at him directly.

"If something is happening with my family, I should know about it," I said, determined not to be left in the dark.

I didn't mind not knowing the gritty details of his work, and I honestly preferred it that way. But knowing how things went down with my family, I felt like I had a right to at least be told if anything was going on.

If we were married and planning on making it mean something, then I didn't want there to be any glaring secrets between us. Even if I wasn't the greatest at following that philosophy myself just yet.

Ari still didn't say as he bounced the ball, only to let it go as it rolled across the court aimlessly. "I know, and you're right. It's just…I don't want you to worry any more than you need to."

"But now I'm going to worry until you tell me," I told him, hoping he could hear my sincerity. "I don't mind answering your questions. I just want to know why you're asking in the first place."

Knowing I was right, he sighed and looked at me as if I had worn him down. "Alright. We've been getting reports lately of your family looking into us. We're still monitoring the situation, and we haven't pinpointed exactly who it is, but it seems like they're trying to gain insight into our operations."

Those words settled into my skin, hitting me at once.

While it wasn't a complete surprise due to the way Ari had stormed into our home and forced everyone into submission, I couldn't imagine any of my family going to that extreme or planning anything against the Levovs.

It would complicate everything.

Not knowing what to say, I could only think about what that would mean, and how that might make our situation worse.

Ari relaxed his shoulders at my visible shock, and he reached for my free hand. While he seemed empathetic, his eyes were serious and almost silently pleading. "Vivian, I need to know. What would you do if they tried to interfere?"

The question hit me even harder after knowing more about it.

In the beginning, I would've gladly gone with them. I had been silently begging for them to come take me back home, even if I'd be returning right back to the poor situation I was already in. A part of me wanted to believe they would do that for me, but as time passed, I assumed they wouldn't.

But if they really were out there, looking for an angle to get me back, I didn't know how to feel about it. It was a bittersweet thought now.

Before, I thought there was nobody worse than Ari. I thought he was a brutal monster who only cared about landing on top. But with time, and after we managed to connect after everything, I realized he was so much more than that.

Beneath that hard, mob-boss exterior, there was a gentle, thoughtful man who was actively doing everything he could to not only earn my trust but also to make me feel the love and affection I had never known before.

There were more layers to him than he let show, especially around others, but with me, he was becoming someone I missed when he wasn't home. His touch made me feel some type of way, and there was certainly no denying the mutual attraction.

He made me see how being his wife wasn't the worst punishment in the world, and with his child actively growing inside me, there were too many elements to consider all at once. I had no idea what my brothers would do if they knew I was pregnant, or what Ari would do, for that matter.

If they were to interfere…I didn't know what I'd do.

My stomach turned at the thought, knowing Ari was still waiting for a response.

But as that nausea cloaked me completely, forcing me to cover my mouth with a hand as my skin went cold, it took everything in my power to hold it down.

Concern stitched Ari's brows together as he inspected me closely, reaching out to steady me on my uncertain feet.

"Vivian?" he questioned, dropping everything else to make sure I was alright.

All the while, I couldn't stomach the idea of having to choose between my blood and the man who was trying his hardest to give me everything I never had.

# Chapter 19 - Ari

Vivian looked paler than a sheet as she stood there on the court, nearly swaying on her feet. If I hadn't been holding her, I was sure she'd be keeled over on the ground.

Concerned why she suddenly looked so sick, I couldn't help but feel guilty. If it was because of my questions, I had overwhelmed her, and that wasn't my intention.

Even if it made me seem doubtful by questioning her loyalty to me, I needed to know. I needed to know our connection meant something to her and that she valued our relationship like I did.

Staying by her side, I pressed the back of my hand against her forehead, only to feel how ice-cold and clammy her skin was.

Not caring about the game or my questions anymore, I brushed some stray hair out of her face and did my best to make sure she was alright.

"What's wrong, Vivian?" I asked, hoping to get to the bottom of it. "What do you need?"

It seemed like she wanted to say something but couldn't since she was stopping herself from vomiting. There was no missing how nauseous she looked, and I didn't want her to have to deal with it while standing right in the sun.

"It's alright," I murmured, wrapping my arm around her waist as I headed for the back door. "We'll get you out of the heat."

Vivian couldn't say a word as she covered her mouth and walked as best as she could, heading inside. She was still so pale, and it worried me.

It was a nice, sunny day and we had been out there for some time, but I didn't think it was hot enough for her to get heatstroke. I could only hope, at least.

As quickly as I could, I took her to the nearest bathroom and helped lower her to the floor where she immediately wrapped her arms around the toilet and couldn't hold it back anymore.

Making sure her hair didn't get in the way, I held her ponytail back and stayed with her while she let it all out.

I had never been great with vomit, even after dealing with my siblings through their illnesses, but I did my best to grit my teeth through it just like I used to. I didn't want to step out—not while she needed someone by her side.

Even if I wasn't fond of it, it had become second nature to me, and I didn't have to think twice about it.

As wave after wave coursed through her, I gently rubbed her back and hoped it was soothing for her. I wanted her to feel at ease even if it was somewhat traumatic for her to go through.

When she hit the handle on the toilet and eventually sat back, leaning against the wall as she pulled herself together again, I put a supportive hand against her shoulder.

"Are you feeling alright?" I asked, keeping my voice calm and quiet.

"I should be fine...I just felt nauseous," she murmured with her head against the wall.

"I guess we haven't eaten anything yet," I added, realizing we skipped food altogether and went straight to playing tennis. "You probably need something in your stomach. I'll go grab something for you."

Vivian nodded absently, and I had the feeling my words went right over her head, but I got right to it anyway.

Slipping out of the bathroom, I made my way to the kitchen and rummaged through the cupboards in search of anything that might be easy on her stomach.

Even if she was playing without any food in her system, I thought it was strange for something like that to cause such a strong reaction. At best, I'd expect her to feel dizzy, not throwing up.

But the more I considered it, the more those recent behaviors of hers came to mind again.

While Vivian seemed to be in better spirits after having the chance to spend time as she wished, she seemed more tired than usual. She looked worn out, as if she had been shouldering some difficult work all day even if she tried to not make it obvious. Plus, getting food into her had been harder lately, and she'd spend some meals pushing her food around instead of eating it.

Since she was more than willing to play tennis, I didn't give much thought to it. I assumed she was still just settling in and getting used to everything.

But those things paired with how immediately sick she was outside, I was afraid something else might be wrong.

Even if that was the case, I didn't want to pester her—not now.

By the time I returned from the kitchen with an armful of supplies, I found Vivian sitting in the living room instead of the bathroom floor with her head in her hands. I put everything down on the coffee table and handed her a water bottle.

"Do you feel better at least?" I asked her, sitting next to her on the couch.

"Somewhat," Vivian mumbled as she lifted her head again, sniffling to herself. She carefully took the water, and her trembling hand wasn't missed by me.

Looking at her splotched cheeks and the tears in her eyes, I couldn't understand what was going on. I was trying my best to help her, but at that point, I was at a complete loss.

"Is there anything else I can do?"

She wiped at her eyes, shaking her head despite another wave of emotion that overcame her. "No, I'm fine…I just…I'm sorry."

Furrowing my brows at her, I was grappling to understand. "What's making you upset?"

Vivian pulled in a deep breath to steady herself as she leaned back into the couch and just barely met my eye with subtle shame. "I haven't been completely honest with you, Ari. I'm afraid you'll be angry with me."

While the statement surely caught my attention, I also didn't want her to think I'd be quick to anger. At that point, I didn't think there was much she could do that would make me mad anymore.

"What is it?" I asked gently, silently hoping to not scare her, or cause her to retreat within herself again. "I promise you can tell me, Vivian."

Meeting my eyes fully then, she nodded and seemed to scrounge up her bravery. "Here goes nothing," she said, just above a whisper. "Ari, I had the driver take me to a convenience store after riding one day, and I took a pregnancy test. It was positive."

Even as those words repeated again and again in my mind, I couldn't fathom what she was telling me. It didn't feel real, even as I felt her next to me, still on the brink of tears.

"I didn't tell you sooner because I was afraid it would complicate things between us right after we started to get closer, and I didn't know how you would react to it," Vivian rambled as her chin wobbled. "I was afraid you wouldn't want it, and I'd be forced to get rid of it, or—"

"So soon?" I questioned, voice so quiet I almost didn't recognize it as my own.

Vivian stopped dead in her tracks then, caught off guard by the innocent question. She nodded slowly.

We both blinked back at each other in stunned disbelief, sitting in that silence until I spoke up.

"That's incredible news, Vivian," I managed to say, struggling with the influx of emotions I felt at the revelation. "We're…we're going to have a baby."

She still looked apprehensive until I leaned in and wrapped my arms around her, pulling her close while being mindful of her nausea.

When she relaxed, Vivian couldn't stop the tears as she hugged me back with her face pressed against my chest.

"It's alright," I cooed to her, holding her as gently as I could manage, overwhelming happiness consuming me. "I'm sorry you were afraid I'd be angry to hear something like that, but just know I'm the opposite. I can't believe it."

"You don't think it'll be too much?" Vivian asked, voice muffled as she pulled back to show me her bleary eyes, sniffling.

"Of course not," I returned, smiling at her. I pushed those loose strands of hair out of her face and gently wiped her tears away. "You're doing an incredibly brave and honorable thing, and I appreciate it immensely. I'd be thankful for any child."

With relieved joy, those emotions hit her again, causing me to feel the same as she hugged me tighter.

"I'm so glad to hear you say that," she murmured, letting everything wash over her.

I could still hardly wrap my head around the idea, but I was grateful regardless.

Even if I had spent years focusing strictly on the family business and my siblings, something in me always wanted children of my own. I wanted the chance to give someone a childhood better than the one I experienced and to prepare them for whatever future they desired.

One would think I wouldn't want them after raising my siblings, but the thought of having a child of my own instilled an incredible pride within me, especially knowing it would happen with Vivian.

"You don't need to worry about anything," I said, pressing a kiss against her head. "I'm going to look after you and the baby. No matter what, you two are my top priority. I'll do whatever it takes."

---

After I managed to calm Vivian down and we both soaked in the great news, I decided breakfast was in order.

Vivian ate as best as she could, not as hesitant now that I knew about the pregnancy and she didn't have to hide it from me. Once she got some food and orange juice in her system, her skin brightened up again, and she looked like she was in much better condition than before.

I was glad to see her up and moving around more comfortably, and not weighed down by that nausea.

"What next?" I asked, taking both of our empty plates over to the sink.

"I think a shower," she mumbled in slight dismay at her current state.

Smiling at her, I returned to where she was and slipped an arm behind her back while the other went under her legs, and I lifted her into my arms. "I can make that happen."

She mirrored that expression and leaned into me, visibly calmer and more relaxed.

With ease, I carried her up the stairs as she giggled to herself, returning to her usual self, to my relief.

In the bathroom, I carefully put her down and started the shower, putting a hand under the water to make sure it was a suitable temperature.

While I did so, Vivian was already stripping out of her tennis uniform, and the moment I glanced over at her, the sight of her perfect body was enough to spark desire in me.

I reached out for her as she met my gaze with those innocent eyes, and once her hand was in mine, I pulled her against my body.

"I still can't believe you're carrying our child," I murmured, letting the warm haze that filled the bathroom take over my mind, too. My hands ghosted up and down her waist, wondering if she'd be up for it. "I can't wait to see your swollen belly."

She gave me a shy smile. "I was afraid you wouldn't like seeing me so big."

The thought alone made my cock stir, aggravated by the light friction of her body pressed up against mine.

"The opposite," I hummed, hooking a finger under her chin to pull her closer. "It's making me hard just thinking about it."

Her smile grew then as a seductive veil covered her gaze, and she murmured against my lips without touching them, "Then get undressed and join me."

Blinking back at her as another wave of desire hit me, Vivian turned away and headed for the shower, making me scramble out of my clothes.

# Chapter 20 - Vivian

Warm water cascaded down my body, immediately soothing me as it rained down all around me. It pulled that uncomfortable sweaty dampness out of my skin and left me feeling surrounded by warmth instead.

It took the edge away from how gross I had felt after being sick and was refreshing, much to my relief.

But it didn't take long to feel his presence behind me, spurring excitement through my entire system.

Ari approached, caging me against the wall as he loomed over me and moved my hair to expose my shoulder. With one hand against the tiles next to my head and the other on my waist, he leaned in and pressed a kiss against my skin before slowly trailing them up my neck.

I sighed at the feeling of his lips against me, pushing me further into a state of anticipation. A shiver ran down my spine as his hand just barely held me, making sure I couldn't get away from him.

Tilting my head to the side, I offered him better access, eager to feel more of those delicate sensations.

He moved with such an agonizingly slow speed that I could feel my patience waning. As much as I wanted to soak in his affections, each kiss made me hungry for more, squirming as his lips continued to crawl upwards.

I let go of a breathless moan as his teeth teased against my skin just below my ear, making me feel just how ready I was for him.

The heat between my legs said it all, aching for his touch and for the relief it would inevitably bring me. The only problem was getting him there.

Even if Ari seemed just as worked up as I felt, he was being deliberate with every action, not diving straight in like I wanted him to. And even if I wanted to let that happen, the raw desperation in me was dying to cut to the chase.

As bravely as I could manage, I turned myself around to face him, finding his lust-ridden eyes staring down at me as a satisfied smile settled on his lips.

Suddenly needing to feel them more than anything, I closed the gap and brushed mine against his, addicted to how full his lower lip was.

Savoring every second of it, I could feel myself getting lost in the exchange. My heart raced as Ari deepened it, sighing against my mouth. Only willing to slow it down just to appreciate how incredible his lips were, I was glad since it gave Ari the chance to muffle his moans into me, and I noted how the roles seemed to reverse.

He gave my hips a loving squeeze as the stream of water hit his shoulder directly and moved that warmth between us as steam filled the bathroom completely.

Keenly aware of the lack of clothes between us, it made everything so much easier as I slipped a hand down and reached for his cock.

Ari shuddered at the sudden contact, breaking the kiss to mumble a curse against my lips before reconnecting them with vigor.

I hummed my approval, gaining more confidence as his body reacted positively to my touch. With a rush of impatience again, I stroked him once before deciding I wasn't willing to wait anymore.

Already in a daze, he looked down at me as I moved, slowly dropping to my knees. "Where do you think you're going—"

The moment my tongue toyed with his aggravated tip, Ari choked back a groan and leaned against the wall.

Watching his honest reaction encouraged me, piquing my interest as his loose curls looked heavy from how wet they were, giving him an endearing look. Water droplets hung from his dark lashes and ran down his sharp jaw as his lips parted.

"Jesus Christ…" he muttered, letting his head tip back as I wrapped my lips around him and let him take in that intense sensation.

There was no denying how gorgeous he was, especially as he tried to compose himself through my ministrations.

But looking at him through my lashes, I couldn't hold back. I needed more of him, even if that meant taking the reins and showing him just how much I adored his body.

Taking as much of him in my mouth as I could, I moved up and down his shaft, watching every twitch and quiver of his thighs while he did his best to hold back. But it was useless as I made a mess of him, and his fingers eventually snaked into my hair, giving my scalp the slightest tender scratches before they flexed at a particularly pleasurable stroke.

I hummed against him, sending those vibrations through his body.

Ari growled back a moan at that and used the wall to keep himself propped up—otherwise, I wasn't so sure he'd still be standing if it wasn't there.

When he glanced down at me through his heavily lidded eyes, his brows were knit together in concentration, but the moment I met his gaze, his head fell back again as he groaned, letting the sound reach me without any restrictions.

Everything from his body's visceral reactions to his tense sounds of pleasure had me feeling like I had complete control over him, like my mouth and hands offered me some sort of divine power.

There was no denying how incredible it felt, especially as his fingers threaded through my hair, and I knew he was doing everything in his power to not reach his release yet.

I continued, letting him savor every stroke of my mouth on him, surrounding him with that velvety warmth until his hands stilled against me.

"Enough," he said gruffly, sneaking a hand beneath my chin to make me look up at him. "As incredible as that feels, I'm not done with you yet."

To my very slight dismay, I gave up the reins as Ari guided me back to my feet and pulled me in for a chaste kiss, pouring every ounce of how much he truly enjoyed the attention into my mouth. But at the same time, I couldn't complain. I did want him to cut to the chase, and it seemed he had exactly that in mind.

"That was very kind of you," Ari hummed, not caring about the stream of water between us as he kissed my lips. "But I should return the favor."

As the words left his lips, his fingers were already waiting, just hovering above my heat. My eyes fluttered shut the moment he pressed his middle finger against my clit and started those agonizing circles.

Jolts of pleasure moved through me, making my legs tense as I stood where he had with my back to the wall. Another breathless moan ebbed out of my lips and into his as he kissed me hard in contrast to the slow movement of his finger.

With his opposite hand pinning me to the wall against my hip, he mumbled against my mouth in between kisses, "I can't wait to see you full and pregnant with my child." Turned on by the thought alone, he growled out the next words like it caused him great strain, "You'll look angelic and perfect, and everyone else will know I did this to you. They'll know you're growing my heir inside you."

His voice was so silky and seductive, and paired with his tracing against my clit that steadily grew more intense, I was already shaking.

"Isn't that right?" Ari questioned with a domineering lift to his tone. He slowly moved his finger down until it slipped inside, letting him feel just how aroused I was. He chuckled. "Who has you this wet, sweetheart?"

I swallowed back the dryness in my throat despite the amount of water I inadvertently consumed, dazed by the sensations evoked by his long, skillful finger as his thumb took its place against my sensitive bud.

"You..." I managed to say, leaning my head against the cold tiles slick with condensation. "You do."

The moment I caught his smug smirk, my stomach did a flip, and my legs weakened. Everything about him was so sensual and obscenely sexy, I could hardly handle it.

"And whose baby are you pregnant with?" he cooed, laying it on thick since he knew just how greatly it was affecting me.

"Yours," I breathed, giving in to his almost condescending tone due to how worked up I was. How ready I was for him.

Another chuckle came from his chest, startling me from my daze. "That's what I like to hear. But I suppose that's enough teasing."

Even if he had managed to get two fingers inside of me already, hardly moving them at an agonizing speed, I needed more of him. The tension was building into frustration to the point where I didn't care about the momentary loss of contact as he pulled out.

I could only think about the incoming fullness I was about to feel as a shiver of excitement moved through me.

"Turn around," Ari instructed, already using his hands to guide me there.

At once, I did as he said, not willing to delay any longer.

I was already panting and squeezing around the absence of his fingers as I propped myself up against the wall, spreading my legs as he nudged them apart.

"Lean forward slightly," he continued, placing a palm against the small of my back to show me what he meant, easing me into that position. He pulled in a deep, satisfied breath. "Just like that. Perfect."

Those words seemed to run across my skin, soaking in and surrounding me with his praise as he settled in behind me, holding a hip as he lined himself up.

Ari hummed his appeasement as his head moved through my slick folds, sucking air in through his teeth. His grip on my hip tightened as he pushed his way inside.

My breath cut off at the sudden intrusion, shocked by the immediate pleasure that position gave me. It moved through me and seemed to spark all over, stretching me in a completely different way than usual.

"Fuck," Ari muttered, holding me with both hands as he sank all the way in, losing himself to the feeling. "You're tight, sweetheart."

My heart fluttered at the complete adoration in his voice as he remained there for a moment, soaking in the feeling. But I couldn't manage any words as I accommodated his sheer size, nearly blindsided by how good it felt.

He cursed again as he held me tight and slowly withdrew his hips, struggling from how tightly I gripped him.

His palm hit the tiles next to mine, needing the leverage to pull out slightly, then shuffled his hand over to intertwine our fingers together once he pushed back in again. Immediately, our groans mingled at the rush of intense pleasure that accompanied his long, yet slow strokes into me, prolonging that blindingly strong sensation.

Ari wasn't shy about his unwavering bliss as he grunted for me and developed a consistent rhythm with his hips. Water pummelled against his back as he thrusted into me, surrounding us with a thick haze that made it even harder to breathe.

But regardless of the sticky heat surrounding us, I was far too immersed in it to care. I just wanted more of him. I needed to hit the euphoric rush that was waiting for me.

With a strangled moan, Ari rocked his hips against me harder, giving in to his own desperation.

Even if he normally maintained decent stamina, I could tell he wasn't as confident in his ability to hold out given the attention I had previously given him, which was why he wasn't holding back. Instead, he set a brutal pace, forcing my lips to part as an endless stream of moans dribbled out of me.

I couldn't help it, not while he hit me with wave after wave of intense bliss, turning my mind completely useless. It took everything in me to stay standing while he rutted into me, allowing me to feel every inch of him at that angle.

My moans were met with his breathless ones, almost like confirmation, as if he knew just how incredible it was and was aware of how close I was as I clenched around him. He wanted me to know he was right behind me, teetering on the edge with me.

The feeling of his fingers coming down to stimulate my clit sent another rush of intense shock through me, causing me to inhale sharply. He was insistent about it as he circled my abused bud, determined to push me across that line before he crossed it himself.

By then, I was incoherent as I took those brutal thrusts along with the extra pleasure of his fingers. I could hardly think beyond understanding I was close as that pleasant fog consumed me, and I didn't care to try and achieve otherwise.

I was beyond content accepting his greedy movements and struggling to stand, all while being unable to fight that impending bliss.

Focusing on getting me there, Ari's pace quickened, shocking me with the power he had left in him. His thrusts were becoming sloppy, and with my ever-increasing slickness, I knew it wouldn't be much longer for him.

But as Ari continued to ravish me, hitting that perfect angle again and again, mingled with the sparks stimulated by his fingers, I couldn't help but clench on him as my throat closed around my splintered moans.

It was all too much to take at once as everything within me came undone, and my legs wobbled as my orgasm tore through me.

I cried out for him, leaning against the wall as he caged me there, pumping me through that blissful high. I continued to squeeze him, resulting in his guttural moans, and that release broke me down completely.

Ari cursed to himself again as he put his arm out to catch me, pinning me to his body as he rutted several times before spilling inside me, chasing right after me.

As his movements slowed to lazy strokes as we rode out that high together, he held me close and made sure I didn't fall due to how shaky my legs were. He leaned over of me, supporting us both with a strong arm against the shower wall while we caught our breath.

I was aching from his intense thrusts, feeling overstimulated until he softened and slipped out of me, still attentive to me even as he did his best to calm down.

In my pleasant haze, I hardly noticed as he turned me around and pressed his forehead against mine while the shower continued to rain down around us. He pulled me to him and wrapped his arms around my back, dipping down to press his soft kisses against my lips.

I savored the taste of him and how perfect his mouth was, feeling delirious after the fact.

But if I knew anything about Ari, it was how seriously he took aftercare.

To my great relief, he wasted no time pressing those kisses to my skin, moving from my cheeks to my forehead, and back to my lips again before he brought his hands up to my hair.

With careful precision, Ari massaged my scalp, making sure my hair was thoroughly wet before he reached for the shampoo and lathered it through my locks.

Eyes closed, I took in the addictive feeling of his soothing fingers and melted almost completely.

Ari's chuckle reverberated to me through his chest as I leaned against him. "Remind me to do this more often."

"Please do," I sighed, aware of how scratchy my voice sounded from crying out for him.

Regardless, he seemed to take great joy in washing my hair, and before long, we were both exchanging soap between our bodies as he took care of us both.

The soft foam made our skin slick as we stood there beneath the water, and unable to resist it, Ari pressed a tender kiss against my lips, causing us to both smile lazily into the embrace.

With his gentle touch and the confirmation that he was completely on board and happy with the pregnancy, my worries dissipated, and I allowed myself to enjoy everything about that moment.

# Chapter 21 - Ari

That paternal instinct was deeply ingrained in me, and with the exciting news, it was all coming back to me again like not a day had passed since the last diaper I changed, or the last bottle I fed.

Even if I knew the pregnancy was very real and it was something we had to prepare for, it almost felt too good to be true. But the test was proven to be correct as we stood in the clinic and that cold gel was spread across her belly.

I stood by Vivian's side and held her hand as the scan was underway, letting her know I'd be there through it all. It was her first visit, and the first time we were getting confirmation since Vivian told me. We had both been excited yet nervous about the appointment, but at that moment, all worry faded immediately.

The technician ran us through everything as she got to it, pressing the transducer against her lower belly and searching for our baby.

As a first-time father, it was a lot to digest, but I did my best to take it in. I was far too excited about it all to miss out on even a second.

It was an impossible thing to fathom.

I had wanted to be a father for years, and to have the pleasure of being called Dad by my little one. I wanted to know what it was like to grow my family and to take pride in knowing I was furthering the Levov name.

For the longest time, it felt like a fantasy. I didn't think I'd be able to find a woman who could look past my hard exterior to get to that place. I assumed my work would be too much, and I'd never have the time to develop that deep of a connection with anyone.

I hadn't been sure I was a man anyone could love, but knowing I was changed everything for me. Even if our marriage didn't start in the best way, and we had more than enough ups and downs in a short amount of time, everything had me feeling optimistic about us lately. We were on the right path, and I did not doubt that.

We made good strides to better understand each other, and we were developing more trust with every passing day. We cared about each other more than I thought possible, and I was beyond grateful for it.

Plus, with the baby on the way offering us another way to connect, I was sure everything would be fine.

"Alright Vivian, so far I can see one embryonic sac," the technician said as she looked closer until her brows went up, and there was a sudden lift to her voice. "Oh. It seems we have a bit of a surprise today."

"What's that?" I asked, pointing at a second lump on the screen ahead of us.

"That's the second sac for your second baby," she said, trying to hold back her lighthearted amusement. "Congrats, you're having twins!"

Immediately, I looked over at Vivian to catch her shared surprise, and neither of us could say anything at first. Facing the screen again, I couldn't believe it.

I swallowed hard as the thought hit me. "You're...you're sure?"

"See right there? That's the second embryo. I'm as sure as can be," the technician confirmed, suppressing her chuckle at our shock. "I'm sure this is a lot to digest right now, but both fetuses are looking great. So far, everything is as it should be."

I almost didn't know how to feel as I considered how much extra responsibility another child was, but at the same time, even more pride swelled within me.

The thought of being a parent to two babies at once was intimidating, but I did take care of Kir and Lara when they were both under two, and I somehow managed it then. I had the feeling I'd be able to slip back into that role just as easily.

At this point in my life, I was much better equipped to handle twins, and even if things became difficult to juggle, there were two of us, and I had the resources to hire a trusted nanny. Plus, I had more than enough family in the area who would be more than willing to do some babysitting on the side.

I only hoped Vivian could trust me with such a big step in our lives and wouldn't feel too overwhelmed by the revelation. I could tell she was nervous when I looked over at her, but when I smiled, accepting the news, she relaxed somewhat. I gave her hand an encouraging squeeze.

"The more the merrier," I said, glancing back at the screen to watch as our growing children wriggled within their warm, temporary home. It brought tears to my eyes knowing we'd get to meet them in a few months, and our lives would be completely different.

---

As the appointment wrapped up and we were on our way out, I made sure to walk with a hand against her hip, letting Vivian know I was content with the appointment and everything going on.

Ever since she shared with me how she had been afraid to tell me about the pregnancy in the first place, I made a concerted effort to be more supportive than angry or demanding. I didn't want Vivian to think I only knew how to respond with those intense and demanding emotions.

I wanted her to trust me with everything, and to know she could come to me about anything. Even with the difficult things.

"That was certainly a surprise," I said as I unlocked the car and opened her door for her.

Vivian pulled a smile for me and climbed in. "I wasn't expecting it at all."

Once I closed the door and climbed in on my side, I added, "This is something we should celebrate. I think we should take the family out for dinner this weekend and share the news with them. They'll be elated."

"That sounds very nice," she agreed, looking down at the scan prints of our growing children.

Before I could pull away, I sent a quick text out to Ben to let him and the others know about the plans and made a mental note to schedule us in somewhere we all liked.

Bringing the car to life, I drove out of the parking lot, smiling faintly as the idea of twins started sounding exciting to me. I was in a good headspace about it, lost in thought of how everything might pan out.

But as we went and the radio played quietly, I noticed Vivian wasn't saying much from the passenger seat.

She was busy looking at the scans, and from my side, I couldn't tell what she was thinking. She seemed to be lost in her head, and I couldn't blame her. It was a big adjustment compared to what we were expecting, and I could only imagine how she was feeling about it.

As subtly as I could, I placed my free hand on her leg and carefully caressed the spot with my thumb.

When she looked over at me, I smiled at her. "I'm glad everything went well and that they're happy and healthy. You're doing wonderfully."

I caught the faintest glimpse of sadness in her eyes until those words settled in, and she gave another faint grin before returning her attention to the picture.

Even if she was feeling unsure about it all, I didn't want her to think I was anything but supportive and happy about the news. Knowing she came from a house that didn't offer her much warmth or attention, I wanted to show her the opposite.

I wanted her to feel every ounce of appreciation I had for her.

When we eventually arrived at the house and Benedikt got back to me about the plans saying everyone was available to attend, I called up my restaurant of choice and made sure the reservations were set.

Since I knew the owner, I could've walked straight in and he would've cleared a table for us if necessary, but I was in a good mood and I didn't want to ruin anyone else's weekend.

Walking into the bedroom to get ready for work, I was surprised to find Vivian sitting on the end of the bed with the scan in her hands still, with tears in her eyes as she sniffled.

Immediately, concern knitted itself within me, and I made an effort to soften my voice as I entered the room.

"Vivian?" I asked, approaching with careful steps.

Aware that I knew she was crying, Vivian didn't bother to hide it. Instead, she put the scan in her lap and rubbed at her eyes. "I'm fine…"

"I can see otherwise," I murmured, kneeling in front of her so that she had no choice but to face me. "What's bothering you, sweetheart?"

At the question, those tears surged even harder, and she pulled in a shaky breath. "I'm scared, Ari…Having one baby was nerve-wracking enough, but two?"

Better understanding where she was coming from, I reached for both of her hands and collected them in mine, silently appreciating how much smaller hers looked in comparison.

"I know this is a lot, and neither of us were expecting to learn we're having twins, but everything will work out," I said, doing my best to soothe her worries. "They'll be a handful, but I'm not going anywhere. If you need anything, I'll drop everything else to help you. We'll get as much help as we need, and I'll do whatever is necessary for you and the babies. I'll be by your side through all of it."

Vivian met my gaze as her eyes softened, and despite her tears, I thought she looked beautiful. "You're not worried about what it might do to us?"

I shook my head with resolve. "Not at all. The twins won't tear us apart, Vivian. They're a significant reason for us to work together and act like the partners we are. I want this family with you, and I know they're going to be perfect."

While she continued to cry, there was a notable shift from fear to relief, and she did her best to rein it in.

"Be as nervous as you need to be, but just know I'm here every step of the way," I reminded her, giving her hands a loving squeeze before I got up and sat beside her instead. "Can you remember that for me?"

"Of course," she murmured, leaning on me for support as she wiped her eyes.

Wrapping my arms around her, I held Vivian close and offered as much support as I possessed. I felt at ease as she returned the embrace, letting me know the words of encouragement helped.

"Sorry for crying so much," she added with a small laugh. "The baby hormones aren't helping."

"There's no need to apologize," I hummed, gently rubbing her back as she calmed down again. "Your body is doing such an impressive thing. You deserve all the slack and grace you need."

"Thanks, Ari," she mumbled, pulling back just enough to look up at me through her lashes, dark from the dampness. "I'm glad this is happening with you. I feel so lucky."

My heart swelled at her words, and I cupped her cheek with my free hand. "I'm the lucky one here."

As she smiled at me, I couldn't help the craving to kiss her. There was something so magnetic and alluring about her that was hard to resist.

Leaning in, I pressed my lips against hers and felt as we both melted at once, soaking in the mutual affection.

I didn't feel any need to worry—not when things between us were better than they ever had been.

# Chapter 22 - Vivian

Initially, I was afraid to have twins. I was scared it would pull us apart and fray that delicate relationship we were still working on. I was still intimidated by the idea for multiple reasons, but Ari was trying his hardest to show me it didn't have to be a source of worry for me.

He had been excited because of the pregnancy before, but after the scan, it was like a switch flipped inside him.

Without needing to be asked at any point, he immediately started coddling me. He was there constantly, checking in on me and making sure I was feeling okay. If I even slightly complained about pain or nausea, he would swoop in without a word and do everything he could to make me feel better.

Ari made sure I always had something to eat first thing before he left for work, and he'd ask me throughout the day if I was comfortable enough.

There was no mistaking just how much he cared about me and the pregnancy, and it helped me to see even more of his sensitive side.

Even if he could be a bit suffocating from doting on me, even with the most minor of issues, it was endearing, and it helped put me at ease every time.

Before, I never imagined being happy with Ari. The thought of being married to him alone was bad enough, but if my future self were to tell me then I'd be having his children sooner rather than later, I never would've believed it.

I thought he was a brutal monster, but I was glad to see the opposite was true.

Ari was as caring as could be, and he made sure my every need was met. He seemed to get better at reading me and understanding what I needed, and that in itself was a great relief.

Given how often I was shut down or ridiculed for anything I said back home, I wasn't always the best at expressing what I wanted or needed. I used to hide away within myself and not let the real me out for fear of receiving another verbal lashing from Dante.

But with Ari, he truly listened, and he made me feel heard. He never made me feel like I was an idiot or a waste of space, but like he was interested in what I had to say. He listened so closely that he often made me feel like I was the only woman in existence.

He could be intense, especially with his work, that world I had nothing to do with. But with me at home, he was a gentle giant. He could be vulnerable with me, and showed me the sides of him he didn't dare show anyone else.

After being cared for so dutifully and seeing the thoughtful parts of him, I was beginning to truly believe that things weren't so bad.

When I was first brought to his place, I thought being his wife was the end of my life. I didn't see how we would ever connect or find a common ground, but with time and effort on both sides, I felt that our future might not be so turbulent.

We were married and spending as much time together as we could, and with the twins on the way, I was looking forward to seeing how he parented.

Given how excited he already was, and how naturally he fell into step with that parental air about him, I could already picture it. I wasn't sure if my heart could handle watching him coo over them, and doing everything in his power to protect them.

As much as my past self would hate me now, I knew I was falling for him.

There was no point in resisting the inevitable anymore—not when I couldn't bear the thought of being without him.

Ari was perfect in every way with his ridiculous good looks, his contrasting abilities to be both domineering and protective, and was the most caring man I had ever met. I had no doubt he would be a good father, and that he'd let the world burn for his family if he needed to.

Whenever he was at work, I wanted him back home more than anything. It was selfish of me to want so much of his time, but I couldn't help it. He made me feel safe and secure, and it was hard to let go of that after he had given me so much.

Being with Ari was like night and day compared to my family, and I knew I'd do anything to stay with him. I used to be ignored if not verbally punched around, and Dante especially had been getting bolder about laying his hands on me. They made me afraid to even exist or express a thought of my own.

But Ari was so different. He proved to me I didn't have to live like that, that I was worth the time and effort.

As I got ready in the mirror, relieved that the nausea had passed for the day, I couldn't help but glance at Ari as he pulled his clothes on in the bedroom.

His pants sat low on his hips as he reached for his button-down, carving out his V-line and chiseled muscle. His fingers made quick work of the buttons, reminding me of all the other ways he was skilled in using them. Even if dinner with his family was supposed to be on my mind, I couldn't help but get lost in those fond memories.

Glancing away with a knowing smile as he turned to face me, I added the finishing touches to my mascara.

Before long, he appeared in the mirror next to me and slipped a hand around my waist, giving me an affectionate squeeze. "Just about ready to go?"

Capping the mascara and putting it away, I smiled at him. "All ready."

"Good," he hummed, leaning in to press a kiss against my cheek. "They're all heading to the restaurant now."

"Do you think this dress looks okay?" I asked, turning to the side to see the faintest bump through the tight material. It was a bit shorter than I'd hoped, but it hugged my curves in a way I liked. "It's not too much?"

"It's perfect," Ari murmured, taking my hand in his and turning me to face him. He pulled me closer and said against my lips, "So perfect I'm considering taking it off you already."

My heart leaped at that, letting the familiar warmth move through me at the idea. Already, I could feel myself longing to feel his lips again and to work out those budding frustrations in me.

"But we can't keep them waiting too long. Later it is," he said finally as he pressed a quick kiss to my lips and swept me out of the ensuite. He flashed me a dimpled smile and chuckled at my look of dismay.

Ari was a tease, and he knew it.

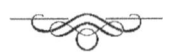

---

Everyone was already at the table by the time we arrived at the swanky restaurant.

I had been to my fair share of fancy restaurants whenever Dad felt bad about leaving us at home for too long, but there was something so romantic about the low light and live string band playing quietly in the background.

A handful of flickering candles sat in the center of the long table we were seated at, along with several wine glasses and fancy bottles sitting on ice. It seemed his siblings had already helped themselves.

We were met with friendly smiles, but realizing we were about to break the news to them made me more anxious than before.

"It's nice to see you again, Vivian," Lara said, handing me a menu. "I keep telling Ari to stop keeping you to himself, but it's no use. He won't listen."

"You can't take what's Ari's, remember?" Kir teased as he looked over the rim of his glass. "He doesn't share well."

Ari released a breath and carefully rolled up his sleeves beside me. "Don't make me regret doing something nice for all of you."

Everyone chuckled at that, and it was nice knowing their banter and jokes were only that. There was never any kind of hidden malice.

"If it's on you, then don't lump me in with these animals. I'm on my best behavior," Lukyan said as he browsed a drink menu. "You wouldn't mind if I got an order of shots with desert, right?"

Ari rolled his eyes and shook his head. "I have something better than shots for all of you."

"That's a tall order," Benedikt snickered.

Ignoring him, he continued. "I arranged this dinner because Vivian and I have some exciting news."

Immediately, I felt their eyes on the both of us, glancing between us with interest.

"Well, don't make us wait. Out with it," Lara encouraged, growing impatient as Ari stalled.

"We're expecting," he said, wearing a proud smile. "Better yet, we're expecting twins."

Immediate shock filled the table as I reached inside my clutch and pulled out the scan photos.

"No way!" Lara exclaimed, softening as she gave us a supportive pout. "You're carrying twins?"

Unable to hold back my own smile, I nodded and handed the photos to her first. "We went to our first scan the other day. It was a surprise for both of us."

His brothers looked just as shocked, as if they couldn't believe those words. But as the photos were passed around, they all wore that same awestruck look, the scan enough to solidify the news for them.

"I'll be damned," Lukyan murmured as he smiled at it. "Two little ones for our big brother."

"I never thought the day would come," Benedikt added with a teasing gleam in his eyes. "Congrats, you two."

We received a complete round of congratulations as they cooed over the photos, seemingly all coming around to the idea of their family growing by two more.

Ari and I were both amused by their reactions, and it made me happy to see his joy. Even if he could be stern and serious with his siblings, he truly cared about their thoughts and opinions, and he wasn't above joking with them.

"Let me see that again," Lara demanded of Kir once he had the scans.

"Wait your turn, I'm connecting with my future nieces or nephews."

Lara scoffed. "You'll actually have to put effort into becoming their favorite uncle, whereas I will be their cherished aunt by default."

Ari chuckled and took a sip from his glass. "It begins already."

"Uncle Lukyan will always be on top," he said triumphantly. "I'll be the fun one."

"Until you let them do something they shouldn't and they go crying back to Ari and Vivian," Benedikt added with a snicker. He looked between the two of us. "For the love of god, don't let him babysit for too long."

Lukyan feigned his offense. "And Uncle Ben will teach them how to curse before they're two."

Unable to deny the accusation, Benedikt only laughed and shrugged.

Everyone joined in as they continued dreaming up what was ahead, wondering what the twins would be like or who they would take after while we ate dinner.

It was easy to feel accepted by his family, especially after sharing such good news with them. They seemed more than ready to welcome little ones into the fold, and as it sounded, they had been waiting for quite some time.

No matter how many times I saw them, it still amazed me how close they all were, and how they treated each other with respect even while they joked and poked fun. It was so different from what I was used to, and I was relieved to see it.

It put me at ease knowing I'd be bringing children into a family that got along and didn't spend their time bringing each other down.

Back home, I was ignored or bullied, and I promised myself I would never have kids in a similar situation. I didn't want my children to know that pain and the heartache of not feeling like they were enough.

I wanted to give my babies the experience I never had, and with the Levovs, I knew that was possible.

In his family, I was treated like an equal, and there were no unspoken expectations of me. They welcomed me with open arms, and for the first time in my life, I felt like I had a family.

It left me warm and comforted, and prepared to reach that next stage in life with Ari.

When dinner was over, we were both embraced by each of his siblings, and Lara especially was completely over the moon about it. We said our goodbyes and the two of us headed back home.

We were both in good moods, but Ari looked completely full of love and excitement.

The moment we parked and he helped me out of the car, he threaded our fingers together and carefully pressed me against the side of the vehicle.

He hovered above me with an almost hazy smile, his lips just inches from mine.

"That went incredibly well," Ari murmured, letting me feel his tempting breath against my lower lip. "Now, what was I saying about that dress ending up on the floor?"

# Chapter 23 - Ari

As he normally did, Benedikt lazed in the chair across from me as he looked through some paperwork, scanning through it at his leisure.

Of course, I never let him act quite so nonchalantly in front of the others, but so long as he was doing his work, I didn't mind. I was willing to make certain exceptions for my siblings if they didn't run too far with them.

"According to my numbers, we would have a better return on our investment by going with warehouse A instead of warehouse C," he murmured, turning the paper around to show me. He pointed at respective pictures. "We'd have to dump more into A initially, but the return would be far more worth the cost than the other."

Nodding, I considered it, stroking my chin absently. "What about B?"

"As far as I know, Andrei put his bid on that one. He's still finalizing the sale."

"Damn him," I mumbled. "He's always on it."

"Maybe, if you ask him nicely, he'll let you utilize some of the space."

"Nah," I said, waving off the idea. "I'd like to keep us as separate as possible. I can't have him thinking we're not capable of running our side of things on our own."

"What, you don't want to owe him any favors?"

"Of course not," I retorted, snickering. "One moment I'm asking him for the space, and the next I'm kissing his ass just to get more. You know how he can be."

Benedikt laughed to himself. "He's Mr. Charity, then conveniently needs our guys for something after."

"Exactly," I agreed, despite being on good terms with Andrei. "We're strapped for manpower as it is. between getting those new jobs ready and keeping tabs on the De Lucas."

"Speaking of, has Vivian asked about her family lately?"

Recalling the last time the topic came up, I could only think about how much of a difficult thing it was for her to talk about. We weren't able to finish our conversation about what side she would choose, but at that point, I didn't need to hear the answer. I already knew she was with me, and that wouldn't change because of her abusive brothers.

"I was the one who brought them up before. I was trying to get some more insight into them, and I didn't plan on telling her the details, but she managed to get them out of me anyway," I explained, walking him through it. "She didn't have much else to share that I didn't already know, but she did seem upset knowing they were interfering."

"Did it come as a surprise to her?"

"It seemed to. I don't think they ever stuck their necks out for her before, so it must be strange to her."

Benedikt cocked a brow. "And if they did come for her, you're certain she'd stick by you?"

Letting go of a breath, I nodded. "By now? Yes. If it happened weeks ago, I'd have my doubts."

He looked at me with scandalized interest. "Things are getting better at home, huh? I had half the mind to assume she wouldn't let you close enough to—"

"Alright, alright," I interjected, waving him off before he could cross any lines. "No more talking about my wife."

Benedikt chuckled and returned to his papers with a shit-eating grin. "All I have to say is, she must be one brave woman to get past that mean mug of yours."

"Shut up, will you?"

Before he could say anything else, shouting came from the first floor of the warehouse, and immediate gunfire volleyed back and forth, echoing all around us.

Looking at Ben in confusion as the sound continued, realization set in, and we were both on our feet in an instant.

"For fuck's sake," I muttered, drawing my pistol as we ran out of my office.

It never seemed to fail. Right when everything was operating smoothly and moving as it should, we still couldn't seem to shake the constant interruptions.

"Who do you think it is this time?" he asked as he followed behind me, focused on the path ahead.

"Doesn't matter until we stop them."

We rushed down the iron steps and hurried through the warehouse, watching as our guys flooded out the bay door. With their guns raised, they fired at the assailants, shouting their usual commands and finding their places.

Given how often it happened, it was protocol to run through the necessary drills to make sure everyone knew where to go and what the main priorities were every time something of this nature happened.

Most of the action was outside, our men aiming for several men on foot as they ran back to their vehicles waiting on the lot.

By the time Ben and I made it to the open bay doors, it seemed the outsiders had been chased off with very little force, immediately making me feel suspicious.

The assailants who managed to get away shouted at their drivers to go once they reached the armored SUVs, and they peeled away. The others were either gunned down or tried to leave on foot, too.

But as one of the cars pulled out and sped away, I recognized the man sitting in the passenger seat firing back at our security, seemingly enjoying the action far too much.

It was Dante. Vivian's brother.

Gritting my teeth, I watched as they rolled out, splitting up the moment they hit the highway.

"Send a group out to trail them!" I shouted as our guys pulled back and assessed the potential damages.

At once, several men did as I said and ran for the nearest vehicle, hopping in before chasing after them.

"What the hell was that about?" Benedikt asked, stepping out as he, too, looked around.

"It has to be Dante leading them," I said, scrubbing a hand down my face. "I saw him."

"Sure, that's likely, but why? What did that possibly accomplish?"

"I have no idea," I mumbled, walking over to where Kir was busy talking to one of our higher-ups with Ben in tow.

"What were they aiming for?" I demanded, angered by the hit itself, even if our forces defended the place easily enough.

"They snuck into one of our flatbeds. They waited until the truck came here, and they blew the back open, but as far as we can tell, they didn't take anything or anyone," Kir said dutifully, getting straight to the point. "Everything's accounted for."

At a loss, I looked around in disbelief. "Either they're trying to distract us, or they're really that dense. How many times are they going to try the same thing and keep underestimating our numbers?"

It wasn't the first time the De Luca family tried to hit our warehouse, and while the first time they managed to get a slight gain on us, they didn't accomplish anything this time. They hardly managed to take any of our men down, and they didn't take anything.

They only succeeded in getting some of their men killed, and Dante threw away any doubt that he was involved.

"Do you think they're trying to test our boundaries? Maybe they're looking for a weak point," Benedikt suggested, watching as our guys took care of the cleanup.

"There's a chance that might be their angle," I murmured, trying to connect the dots. "If they came in on one of our trucks, it's likely they're looking for an in. They got tabs on our operations and now they're trying to find a fool-proof way to ambush us."

"They're trying anything and seeing what sticks," Kir murmured.

I nodded. "That also tells me Edoardo doesn't have a hand in this. He wouldn't waste his resources poking at our defenses. Vivian's brothers don't have any experience in this game and it's showing."

Benedikt crossed his arms over his chest. "If they're inexperienced, then we'll certainly have the upper hand. They shouldn't be difficult to take care of."

"Even if they haven't been much of a threat yet, it's clear they're pulling their punches. That was the first time they attacked directly since I married Vivian, and they're getting bolder," I said, considering all angles. "They could be holding their full strength back on purpose to force our guard down. But we can't let that happen."

My brothers nodded in agreement.

"Tell Lukyan to recover the security footage and send it to me. I need to see what we're working against," I directed to Kir. "If they're using any specific explosives or schemes, we need to know."

"I'm on it," Kir said, pulling out his phone while he walked off and started talking to Luk.

"If they continue at this rate, they won't have any men left," Benedikt murmured.

"Which makes me wonder why they're so willing to dispose of their forces like that. I have the feeling they won't wait much longer to show us their real plan," I returned, aware of how that would complicate things even more.

"I'll wait for any word from the team that went out. If there's anything worth noting, I'll let you know," Benedikt said, making himself useful.

With a single nod, I began back toward the warehouse. "Make sure someone is on them at all times. We can't take our eyes off them."

Understanding what I wanted from him, Ben split off in another direction, and we both went back to work.

My blood was boiling as I went back inside, still able to see Dante's face in the back of my mind. Even though they lost, he looked smug, and I knew that wouldn't bode well for us.

There was something we didn't know about them yet, and I wasn't looking forward to finding out what it was or how it might lead back to Vivian.

The moment I reached my office, my phone went off in my pocket, and it was the surveillance footage from Luk.

Dropping myself into my chair, I hit play and watched the attack all the way through before scanning nearly frame by frame.

I focused as much as I could, trying to discern anything from the video that might give us the upper hand.

From what I could tell, it seemed to be a standard issue explosive, and nothing too technical. They had been inside the C-can, waiting for the chance to blow the doors open and pile out into our lot.

While it didn't tell me much, I did note how strange it was for them to cause so much commotion, just for them to turn around and flee the moment they faced any opposition. It felt more like a drill than anything—a practice run before they tried anything more.

With a sigh, I put my phone down and leaned back in my seat.

It wasn't anything new, and the attack only instilled more questions in me.

I told Vivian about her brothers prying into our business, and while I didn't want to in the first place, she got it out of me anyway. It was enough to let her know they were causing trouble, but I didn't want to mention the explosion.

Knowing she was pregnant and needed to keep a level head on her shoulders for the babies' sake, it was better she didn't know. I wanted her to relax at home and visit the ranch to pass the time—I didn't need her worrying about what her brothers were doing. She didn't deserve to endure that stress just because her brothers somehow got their hands on Edoardo's resources.

But as much as I didn't want to let her in on it, I knew I wouldn't be able to hide it from her forever.

At the very least, I could keep it to myself and handle the situation before she ended up hearing anything else about it.

# CHAPTER 24 - VIVIAN

Even from my place in the master bedroom, I could hear Ari shouting at someone, and as hard as I tried to ignore it, I couldn't.

Given how I could only hear his voice, I assumed he was on the phone giving someone a piece of his mind. Since it likely had to do with his work, I figured it would be over soon enough.

But the longer it went on, the more interested I became. I sat up in bed and tried to focus on what he was saying, but despite his clear volume, the words were too muffled, and I couldn't make the words out properly.

It seemed too early in the morning for him to be laying into someone, and since I couldn't focus on anything else, I decided to pull myself out of bed.

As I moved down the hall and headed down the stairs, listening to how his yelling only got louder, dread filled my chest.

As much as I wanted to believe they were leaving things alone, I had the sinking feeling it was because of my brothers.

Ari hadn't told me anything beyond what he mentioned that one day about them snooping, but that didn't mean everything was perfectly fine on that front. He could've been trying to spare me from something worse, which didn't make me feel any better.

I just hoped they weren't the reason, and nothing else would come of it.

Leaning against the stairwell wall, I tried to listen for any indication if it was about my family, but it was too general for me to understand what was going on. Then, Ari murmured a final demand before he ended the call and let out a heavy breath.

Gingerly walking down the rest of the way, I found him running an irritated hand down his face as he stood by himself in the kitchen.

"What was that about?" I asked, keeping my voice quiet to not alarm him.

As if realizing he hadn't been quiet enough, Ari glanced over at me and sighed. "It was just something work-related. Sorry if I woke you."

Not believing him, I walked further into the kitchen with my brows furrowed. "That sounded pretty serious. What's going on?"

"You don't need to worry about it," he mumbled, ignoring my obvious concern.

"Does it have anything to do with my brothers?"

When the words hit him, Ari looked away, silently confirming my suspicions. That pit in my stomach only grew more.

Leaning his forearms against the countertop, Ari looked like he wanted to keep it from me still, but he was already caught. He surely knew I wasn't prepared to give it up until I heard the truth.

It was a correct assumption.

When he met my gaze, he seemed exhausted. "I didn't want to tell you because I don't need this compromising the pregnancy in any way. You shouldn't have to stress over my work, too."

Understanding his reasoning, I also knew it wasn't enough.

Still, I did my best to be empathetic as I approached him and put a hand on his arm.

"I get that, Ari, but if my family is causing issues, I need to know. You may not want me to stress about it, but I don't want you carrying this on your shoulders alone," I told him, offering him my support. "We're partners in this, remember? You can tell me."

Ari looked conflicted at first, but as he thought about it more, he eventually nodded as he came around. "They've attempted to hit our warehouses multiple times now. One of our higher-ups just informed me they've hit another this morning, and this one caused the most damage. They've been getting bolder over the last few weeks, and I'm worried this might cross over into Andrei's territory. He doesn't need to get pulled into this, and I don't need this getting any worse."

My skin went cold as that reality sank in, and at least a part of me felt numb.

As much as I wanted to believe I could handle hearing the truth, I couldn't deny how it hurt to know my family was causing problems, and there was no telling exactly why it was happening.

"We believe they've been trying to poke holes in our defenses to see where they might find success, but other than that, we don't know what they're after," Ari continued, clenching his jaw as he spoke. "I believe they're trying to throw us off so they can hit us big. Maybe even so they can get you back."

"To get back at you for embarrassing Dad," I murmured, connecting those pieces in my head.

Ari nodded. "I'd assume so. We won't know until I can either get more intel on the situation or until I can confront them face to face."

That struck panic through my system. "You'd do that? Face them directly?"

"If that's what it takes. I'm sorry you had to hear this, but we can't always handle things by proxy. If this keeps up, I can't guarantee they'll come out of this alive."

It was hard to digest that fact, but to my surprise, I wasn't concerned about them.

As far as I could tell, they were messing with something they shouldn't have, and if they were poking the Levovs despite their reputation, they were asking for it.

"I'm not worried about them," I said, realizing I needed him to know that his safety mattered the most to me. "I don't want you or your family to get hurt because of my brothers and their stupid revenge."

Ari softened at that, and he put a hand on top of mine. "I appreciate that, Vivian, but if it comes down to it, there's nothing else I can do but tackle it head-on."

I averted my eyes then as the tears threatened to fall, but I didn't want them to. I was tired of the constant up and down with my emotions because of the pregnancy, and from going through a whirlwind of experiences over a few months.

I didn't want to seem weak. I wanted to seem strong like Ari, even if I could barely handle the thought of anything happening to him.

"Look, I have to level with you," he began, facing me completely with his hands against my waist. "This whole thing has me in a precarious place. I've been wanting to keep you out of this because of the obvious conflict of interest. I can't stand by while your brothers get in the way of our operations, but I don't want to hurt you by engaging with them. It could get ugly, and I need you to know it's nothing more than business. If I had my way, they would stay out of it, and nobody would have to get hurt. I don't want you to think I take any pleasure in this."

Confused for a moment, I couldn't understand why he was trying to emphasize that point so greatly. But then I realized why.

He assumed my heart was still with my family to some capacity. He thought I was worried about them, when in reality it was him I was concerned for.

The more I thought about it, the stranger I felt.

They were my blood, and I should've felt some sort of allegiance to them. I should've been afraid for their lives given who they were up against, but I wasn't.

They were asking for it by getting involved in something they should've left alone, and there was nothing I could do about that.

If anything, they were betraying me by waiting so long to take action, after I had come around to the idea of being with Ari and starting a family together. I couldn't even pretend to be on their side.

They treated me like I never mattered a day in my life, but Ari proved otherwise. He made me see that I was worth something, that I was important to him. No matter what I went through during my upbringing, he was the reminder that better things were possible.

"Ari," I murmured, meeting his gaze with a swell of genuine pride in my chest as I looked at him. "I realize I never answered your question before, but my loyalty is with you and your family. I'm on your side."

He took me in completely then, providing me with his complete and unwavering attention. For once, he seemed to be at a loss for words, unable to return with anything substantial enough. Yet his eyes gave away how much it meant to him.

Working up my courage, I continued, "Whatever you need to do, do it. They never had any love for me before, and I can't ignore the person in front of me offering exactly that. Don't let me or my connection to them get in the way of what has to be done."

Dropping a hand to my stomach, I held the small bump there, aware that regardless of getting my permission to carry out any means necessary to get my brothers off his back, Ari also had to do whatever was necessary for our growing family.

He was doing everything for us, and that was all I could ask for.

# Chapter 25 - Ari

There was no doubt in my mind how Vivian felt about me and our plans to raise our children together, but hearing those words from her seemed to cement it all for me.

Even if the feud was with her brothers, and she was caught in the middle, she didn't hate me for it. Against all odds, she came around to the idea of me so completely that she was willing to put her complete faith in me.

She wasn't upset or opposed to the idea of me stopping her brothers before they could cause any more problems, and it turned out I had been worrying for no reason.

I had her blessing, and that meant the world to me.

I didn't know what to say in return at first, not while I was still wrapping my head around what that meant for us.

She was with me, and she was determined to keep it that way. Even if her family somehow came to retrieve her, she would want to stay.

But with her looking so delicate and committed in front of me, I couldn't help but relax and be vulnerable myself.

"You don't know how much that means to me," I murmured, leaning closer so I could cup her cheek with my hand while I held her. "I'm completely committed to you, Vivian, beyond our marriage license. Beyond those half-assed vows. You saw me at arguably my worst, and you still managed to find something better in me. You've shown me it's okay to be soft, even if I've only ever known had to conceal my emotions. You've brought out the best in me, and I want to be better thanks to you."

Despite her brave face, Vivian's eyes watered as she looked up at me tenderly. "A part of me didn't want to believe you could be caring in the beginning. I kept searching for any reason to despise you and to be vindicated for it, but I stopped being able to see those reasons. I was terrified to be here, and I was even more scared to admit I was falling for you, Ari. I don't know how you did it, but you showed me the things in life I was missing back home, and now I don't want to be without it. I don't want to be without you."

"And you won't have to be," I returned gently, stroking her cheek as I took in every gorgeous feature of her face. "I promise to keep you and the babies safe, regardless of what it takes. I never thought I was capable of being loved, or of letting myself return that affection, but you changed all of that for me. I love you, Vivian."

As more tears gathered in her waterline, I carefully placed a hand against her small belly and mustered up every ounce of sincerity I had. "For us and them, I'll take care of everything."

"I love you too," she managed, despite the slight crack in her voice. Unable to fight back her tearful smile, she beamed up at me as I tried to dry her eyes. "You're going to be an incredible father."

As my heart squeezed, glad she thought so, I leaned in and sealed those words with a kiss.

She sighed against my lips, relaxing completely into my touch.

Something about the way she eased against me, accepting everything I had to give, always made me want more, regardless of where we were or what was going on.

When I pulled back, to both our dismay, I pressed my forehead against hers to maintain as much of that contact as possible.

"Since we're on the same page, and we could both use a distraction, I'm going to plan a date for us," I told her, siphoning her affection straight into my veins. "You don't have to worry about anything. I'll let you know the place and time, and we can celebrate us privately. We'll be one-on-one without my mouthy siblings to interrupt."

"That sounds perfect," she hummed, embracing me in return with her arms around my waist. "I loved that restaurant from before. It seemed so romantic."

"Then I guess the place is taken care of. I'll contact my friend there and have him reserve us a table."

Glad to see her smile, I couldn't get over how perfectly it complimented her features, and how it made her glow. She was perfect in every sense of the word, and I needed the opportunity to show her just how much I cared about her.

"Right now," I murmured, slipping my hands to the back of her thighs to hoist her into my arms as she giggled to herself, "I have some time before work to do whatever I want with, and I have an idea of how I want to spend it."

Vivian clung to me with her pleasant aura, surrounding me with both her arms and her complete attention. "If I'm thinking what you're thinking, then I'd be happy to oblige."

"Let's find out, then."

While I intended on taking her upstairs, just looking at her lips was enough to pull that drive from me, and I settled for the couch instead.

I sat down and brought her onto my lap, pulling her as close as possible while our lips met once again.

I was immediately met with her returned enthusiasm, riling me up even more. Whether she was aware of it or not, it never took much for her to get me hard and in desperate need of her touch.

Most days, I found myself stuck in that familiar haze, daydreaming about when I'd get the chance to be inside her again, and when I'd get to watch her face tighten in pleasure. Her sounds of appeasement were so addictive that I couldn't wait to get my next fix, regardless of how recently we had sex.

She meant everything to me, and knowing she felt the same way about me made me even more eager to prove just how much I adored her.

Mutually holding one another as tightly as possible, we moved our lips with such sensual longing that I knew there was no turning back. I didn't want to stop, and neither did she.

At the brush of Vivian's tongue against my lower lip, I muffled a groan into her mouth and felt as it excited her from how she wriggled on my lap. Even the slightest movements of her hips were enough to cause a semblance of friction, getting me painfully worked up.

All thoughts of romantic candle-lit dinners and celebrating went completely out the window as sinful thoughts took over my mind, urging me to squeeze her hips and draw her impossibly close. While that would certainly come eventually, I was too fixated on having her and letting her know the exact power she held over me without even knowing it.

Growing impatient, I hummed against her lips as I hoisted her up again, turning us around so that she was spread out on the couch, looking up at me with those surprisingly lewd eyes, and her cheeks painted pink as she caught her breath.

Keenly noting how my self-restraint was crumbling with every passing second, I moved in, caging her against the couch as I latched my mouth to her neck, finding that sweet spot immediately.

Vivian let go of a breathy moan for me as I kissed down her neck, reaching the plunging neckline of her thin sleep set. The flimsy material was pushed up easily enough to expose her breasts, sending another wave of anticipation through me.

Cupping them both, I trailed my lips further down, leaving a teasing stripe against her left nipple before heading straight for the other. As my thumb stroked the former, I took the latter in my mouth and listened to how she was already falling apart, desperate for more.

Her quiet moans were all the encouragement I needed to keep going, and it became my personal goal to make them even louder.

I took great pleasure in pulling those breathless sounds from her with my ministrations, flicking with my tongue to make her back arch away from the couch cushions.

When I couldn't wait anymore, I popped my mouth off her and continued, catching her slight sigh from losing that contact.

*Don't worry,* I thought to myself. *Soon enough.*

Moving further south, I grazed every inch of skin I could find, making her wriggle out of desperation for more friction. As much as I just wanted to be inside her already, I wanted to make her come undone first. I wanted to maximize her pleasure as much as I could, even if it went to the point of overstimulation.

As my palms trailed down her thighs with my lips in tow, I lowered myself between them and felt right at home.

Vivian's breathing was already erratic as she waited for me to do something, anything. Not willing to wait any longer, I hooked my fingers in the equally flimsy bed shorts and pulled them down to reveal her more casual underwear underneath. Given her pregnancy, she opted for comfort over style, but I still found it sexy.

Especially because they so easily showed that lewd damp spot that made me harden even more, delirious at the thought of how turned on she already was.

"Ari, please…" she whimpered, nearly trembling from how needy she was.

"I said I'd take care of you, right?" I hummed, gently pressing a thumb against that tantalizing spot as she sucked in a sharp breath. "Trust me, sweetheart."

With her eyes already shut, Vivian leaned back into the couch, soaking in the light pressure of my thumb.

I continued with an almost wonder-like focus on her clothed sex, watching how she twitched from needing more. How she could hardly handle my teasing.

Feeling charitable, I ran a finger next to the lower hem of her underwear and snagged the material to pull it to the side.

Seeing how perfect and wet she already was for me, I couldn't hold back.

Whether it came from an honest place of wanting to help her feel release, or from my selfish desire, I wasted no time reacquainting myself.

I wanted to start slowly, to draw out her moans and listen to how they'd gradually grow in volume, but I couldn't wait anymore. The sight alone made me feral just to taste her again.

With one long swipe, I moved my tongue through the length of her, taking in her arousal. It triggered something almost primal within me as I wrapped my arms around her thighs and held her close, pinning her in place.

A moan ending with a cry of surprise left her mouth immediately, and it sent a shiver down my spine.

She was so perfect and she didn't even know it. Every sound and desperate little movement she made had my nerves frayed from how viscerally I needed her.

Even if my self-control was waning, I had enough left to please her first. To keep her pleasure at the forefront of my priorities.

Spreading her thighs apart to give me better access, I focused all of my desires and needs on caressing her clit with my tongue and exploring every inch of her, offering the occasional squeeze to her plush legs.

As Vivian's moans grew louder, my movements became even more intense, and I knew we'd both be reduced to sloppy, degenerate versions of ourselves sooner rather than later.

And I wouldn't change it for the world.

# Chapter 26 - Vivian

The afterglow of the intense sex we had lingered even after Ari hauled me into the bathroom with him to carefully wash me down before doing the same to himself.

It was easy to forget he still had to go to work, but with all the undivided attention he was giving me, I knew I'd be able to survive without it at least until he came back home.

The feeling of his hands gliding up and down my body while he gently provided ample aftercare still lingered throughout the day while I lounged around the house and did my best to keep busy.

Between naps and reading, I contemplated asking the driver to take me to the ranch, but I eventually let go of that idea when the ambition left me completely.

I felt incredibly loved even while Ari was away, but as much as I tried to cling to that bliss, I still couldn't ignore the worry that crept back into my mind.

Ari didn't want me to concern myself over what my brothers were up to, and I didn't want to either, but it was impossible to stop it the moment that seed was planted in my head.

I spent the rest of the day trying to push the anxiety away, hardly letting myself stew in those thoughts. But as Ari came home and let me know we were going out for dinner that night, deciding he couldn't wait until the weekend, I wasn't left much time to think about it.

To my relief, he was the distraction I needed as I got ready, heart full every time I laid eyes on him.

There was no mistaking that mutual love in our eyes every time we exchanged a glance, or each time his palm ghosted against my lower back as he leaned in to grab something and guided me out to the vehicle once we were ready to go.

I was so wrapped up in the romance of it all that I felt like I was walking on air, overjoyed by the prospect of our date.

As he said, everything was planned for us. We reached our table by six—a small booth tucked in a secluded corner so that we could be as handsy as we wanted, ignoring the fact that we were in public.

With the beautiful music playing in the background, the dim lighting that set the scene for us, and the alcohol-free champagne in our glasses, everything felt so perfect.

"Have you thought of any names yet?" Ari asked me as he cut through his steak and lifted a brow in interest.

"I've come across some interesting names in the books I've been reading recently, but I'm not completely sold on any of them yet," I replied, silently considering the top contenders.

"There's still lots of time to think of more," he murmured, giving me an encouraging smile. "I'm sure we'll stumble upon the perfect names soon."

"It's tough knowing they should sound good together. Maybe the shorter the better since we'll have two to keep track of?" I suggested, amused by the thought of getting the names confused or swapped while trying to get their attention.

Ari chuckled at that and nodded his agreement. "That's good thinking. We'll have to keep that in mind."

Even if we had fully established our intentions of being committed and raising the twins together, it still felt strange to be discussing the future so openly. Before, there was too much tension and resentment between us to have even remotely similar conversations.

But it was nice, and everything about the dinner was perfect.

While he didn't flaunt his wealth in a flashy, arrogant way, Ari knew how to flex it in the right way to make me feel like royalty. Between his plans and every thoughtful action like opening doors and pulling chairs out for me, I couldn't ignore his constant efforts.

As we ate and laughed together, I was more than happy to be there with him and appreciative of his idea to have one-on-one time out of the house.

The meal was incredible, and I couldn't have asked for a better time with the man I loved.

"Will you excuse me for a moment? I'll be right back," I said, feeling the need to visit the washroom before continuing.

Ari nodded as he reached for one of the menus. "Of course. I'll see about getting some dessert over here."

With a smile, I leaned over and pressed a grateful kiss against his cheek before shuffling out of the booth, catching the tender expression on his face. It made my heart squeeze to even think about it.

Making my way out of the main dining area, I followed the subtle bathroom sign and went down the indicated hall. I let go of a satisfied breath, finding myself smiling still.

Just before I could reach for the door handle, a rush of air behind me made my brows furrow.

Something clamped over my mouth as a pair of arms wrapped around me tightly, forcing the air right out of my lungs.

I had no choice but to breathe in, desperately searching for another gulp of air as panic spread through my system.

I tried to scream against the cloth covering my mouth and nose, thrashing and kicking as best as I could, but without proper oxygen coming in, I was immediately weakened and didn't stand a chance against the assailant. The cloth muffled my sounds, and nobody could hear me.

Even if it was useless, I fought anyway, hoping to give myself a chance at getting away—at running to Ari for help.

But that safety seemed so far away as my vision went bleary, and my pulse roared in my ears. I wanted to keep going, but that faint chemical smell was overpowering, and I could feel it burning within my senses.

As everything around me seemed to shift and lose all stability, I could feel myself slipping in and out like I hadn't slept in days, my eyelids refusing to stay open.

"Easy," the assailant muttered, gripping what was left of my consciousness with a cold hand.

That ever-fading awareness left behind only one thought for me to mull over as the hallway began to fade away, and I gave in to that seemingly endless darkness.

*It sounds like Dante.*

---

Pain roared in my head as pieces returned to me, building the scene before me brick by brick. As my eyes opened, those fragments became clearer, even as I blinked through that discomfort.

But while I worked through that grogginess, the aching slowly subsided, making way for the discomfort and fear that followed.

It was dark all around me, save the lit-up dash in the front, and the street lights that passed overhead. Music played quietly in an almost haunting way as I became more aware of my surroundings.

I shuffled in the back seat to sit up, only to find my hands were bound by thick ropes. Dizziness hit me hard, forcing me to blink through the discomfort until it cleared.

But when I opened my eyes again, I couldn't believe what I was seeing. I felt like I was dreaming—or, more accurately, having a nightmare.

My brothers were in the front seat, Elio driving, talking to each other.

More confused than when I first woke up, I couldn't understand what was happening, or how I got there. It had been months since the last time I saw them, and there they were, like nothing had changed.

The memories hit me at once: the restaurant, kissing Ari on the cheek before I left for the washroom, and never reaching it. Fighting to get away.

It was them.

With my hands bound and in the back seat of the moving vehicle, I felt more like a prisoner than a liberated captive.

"What's going on?" I asked, testing my voice despite how dry my throat felt. I was surprised they were able to hear the squeak I managed to get out when they both glanced at me.

Even if they captured me and hauled me away, I was hoping they'd show me some compassion. Something in me hoped it was some sort of misunderstanding, and that they assumed they were just saving me.

I wanted to believe they just wanted the best for me. That they cared about me.

But they never did that much growing up, and I had the feeling they would never change.

Their careless looks at me only affirmed that much.

Dante sighed. "I was hoping that would keep you out for another hour or so. Shitty product, I guess…"

"What?" I murmured, not understanding why that would be his first concern. "Dante, what's happening? Where are you taking me?"

Leaning his arm casually against the center console, he didn't even look at me as he spoke. "We finally got you away from that Levov dog. We've spent weeks trying to get through their defenses and trying to trace their steps long enough to piece together a suitable time to strike. Those bastards are good, I'll give them that. But not good enough."

"Aristarkh let his guard down, though. He didn't realize we caught on to his restaurant of choice, or that we managed to gain access to their booking system. So much for always being prepared," Elio added, focusing on the lefthand turn he took.

Guilt immediately trickled into my heart then, squeezing at the memory of suggesting we eat there again. If I had just let Ari think of one himself, there was a big chance I wouldn't be in that position.

"Why do I have the feeling you didn't do this for me?" I asked, recalling their usual disinterest in me.

Months had gone by, yet they only waited until now to take action. They could've tried anything then to save me if that had been their intention, but I knew better.

"Because we didn't," Dante snapped. "Unfortunately, you were the only real leverage our family ever had to make real progress. Dad always had money, but he used it frivolously rather than investing in the business or creating solid alliances in the city. Because of that, we had to get you back. Aristarkh thought he won, but now he has to face the consequences."

Blinking through my bleary vision as I silently panicked, I tried to keep my voice level. "What about the marriage license? Nobody will trade their allegiance for me when I'm already married."

Dante continued to look forward as he ran a hand over his face. "It doesn't matter. However we can, we're going to axe it. The marriage will be nullified, and it won't be a problem. You'll be back at home with us so we can keep an eye on you, and we'll get you married to someone more suitable for our needs."

A cold chill ran down my spine at that, hating the thought of not being married to Ari. I didn't know if my brothers' plan had any legs to stand on, but it was enough to make my pulse race.

The thought of being stuck in that house again, forced to sit idly by while my family pulled the strings behind the scenes to hand me over to someone else, made me feel sick. I didn't want to be trapped in that cage again.

I once thought Ari's house was another kind of prison, but with time, it proved to be the opposite. He showed me the life and future we could have together, and now that it was being threatened, I couldn't help but want it back more than anything.

To make matters worse, I was carrying his babies, and my brothers didn't know that. If they were to sell me off to another kingpin and he found out about the twins, I had no doubt I'd be in even bigger trouble.

I had to get away from them. I had to.

"I thought you didn't have any involvement in the business," I mumbled, struggling to keep myself together given the circumstances.

"A lot of things have changed ever since that night, Vivian. Dad isn't running things anymore," Elio said, gripping the wheel with a gloved hand. "We're making strides far bigger than he ever did."

"The Levovs tainted our name, but that won't matter once we take their place in the city," Dante said, focused on the road ahead.

Even if Elio was the oldest, it seemed Dante was the brains of the operation. He always had been the cruel one.

I should've felt some sort of relief, given how Ari had forced me into marriage and swept me into his life, but I didn't. Before, I would've gladly stepped back into my old place, left to wait and take that abuse. I thought Ari was as bad as they came, but I was wrong.

I knew then that my brothers were exactly that, and they had no intention of giving me a good life.

I didn't want to be separated from Ari. We were starting a family, and he made me the happiest I had ever been.

But of course, my brothers didn't care about what I wanted.

They wanted to trade me for their gain—nothing more.

# Chapter 27 - Ari

After sending the waiter off to grab us a few different desserts, I waited patiently in the booth for Vivian to return. Slowly sipping my drink, I considered how beautiful she looked, and how I couldn't wait to get back home.

As nice as the dinner was, I had a few ideas of how to close out our date, eager to pour my pent-up arousal into pleasing her.

When the waiter came back with several small platters as I had asked, I thanked them, but found myself wondering if she was alright. I expected her to be back at the table before the dessert came.

Soon enough, the ice cream melted down into a syrupy mess, and I glanced down at my watch.

It made me question if something was wrong. If she was in some sort of pain or going through something I didn't know about. If she was sick, I needed to know.

When I couldn't take it anymore and the time she was gone stretched even further, I got up from the table.

My mind was racing with concern, and whether it was from instinct or paranoia, I couldn't fight the dread as it sat heavily in my gut. I was sure something was wrong.

Locating the women's washroom, I strode over and knocked my knuckle against the door. "Vivian?"

I waited but heard nothing. "You in there?"

No response.

Mind running wild with the possibilities, my skin went cold, and for a momentary flicker of time, I didn't know what to do. I didn't know what to think.

But as that panic kicked my ass into high gear, I shoved the door open to find the swanky room empty. She wasn't there at all.

With concern gripping my throat like a vice, I immediately pulled out of there and looked down the hall, scanning the area for any sight of her. Every second that passed made that fear tighten even more, and it was nearly impossible to breathe.

Before I knew it, I was moving through the whole restaurant, looking for her.

A dreadful thought stung as it lingered in my mind—what if she finally left? If she got up and went out the exit door to never return.

I shoved that idea away, cursing myself for even entertaining it.

Vivian swore her loyalty to me. We were in love, and she was growing our children inside her. Everything was going so well, there was no chance she'd just throw it all away like that.

It had to be something else. Someone had to have done something to her.

With my senses completely frayed and my body full of adrenaline, I pulled my phone out and immediately dialed Lukyan's number as I went straight for the front door.

Catching the two guards, I posted outside, I couldn't temper my demanding tone. "Have you seen Vivian out here?"

They shook their heads.

"She excused herself and didn't come back to the table. Look everywhere—go!"

With curt nods, they hurried inside, leaving me to focus on the phone call as Luk picked up.

"What's going on?"

"I need you to tap into the live security footage and search it for any sign of Vivian. I can't find her, and I need to make sure nothing happened to her," I said, rushing my words out of fear of wasting even a minute.

Luk didn't hesitate as I heard him shuffling in the background. "Where?"

"Outside Dom's. Focus on the rear exit specifically," I told him, already heading back inside to find my men covering every inch of the place as Dom himself went over to question them, but they were too busy following orders to give him a proper answer.

He looked confused, but spotted me and came over, furrowing his heavy brows as he asked in a hushed tone, "What is going on, Levov? Your guys are tearing this place apart—"

"My wife is missing," I snapped, hoping he could see just how serious I was. "She got up from the table and didn't come back. Forgive me if this place is turned upside down. I have to find her."

Dom looked shocked, but he recovered, immediately filling with resolve. "My apologies. I'll have my staff do the same."

Giving him a gracious nod despite the fear gripping me tighter than ever before, I snapped back to it and continued searching alongside them, keeping my phone near my ear.

I could tell Dom and his employees were trying to maintain a level of calm throughout the place to not scare his patrons, but the longer it took, the more frantic I was becoming. Soon enough, it was evident she was nowhere to be found, and I couldn't contain my grief even as some of the customers watched me search the place up and down.

I couldn't let anything happen to my pregnant wife. She was vulnerable, and anything out of the ordinary could compromise the twins. The thought was enough to turn my stomach and quicken my steps.

For her, I was trying to keep my head level, but every passing second tested my patience. I couldn't ignore the sinking feeling that my worst nightmare was actively unfolding in front of me.

"Ari, I have something."

I perked up at the sound of Luk's voice through the phone and pressed it to my ear, aware of how hard and fast my heart was beating. "What is it?"

"A blacked-out Range Rover pulled up to the back about half an hour ago and two men stepped out. Five minutes later, they walked out carrying someone unconscious. It looked like Vivian," he said gravely. "Luckily, it's the same vehicle we've been tracking for weeks now, and they didn't bother swapping. The De Luca brothers came to collect, after all. I reached out to my guys for an approximate live location, and at least two full teams are already hunting them down. They should manage to intercept in about fifteen minutes if their course doesn't change."

Digesting his words, I could feel my entire body ringing with urgency, with desperate need to spring into action. If I didn't, I was sure I'd implode from that raw anger and adrenaline.

So that was their plan all along. It didn't have anything to do with our warehouses or trying to infiltrate our operations. They wanted her.

"I need that location," I said, gesturing for my men to follow as I headed for the door. "I want all of you there, too."

"I'm sending it to you and anyone available. I'll tell the others," he said, always good with following orders. "Don't worry, Ari. We'll get her back."

My phone vibrated in my hand as I received the message from my brother, pushing through the door and heading straight for my vehicle. "Thanks, Lukyan. Now get your ass out there. I'm going now."

With his confirmation, I ended the call, tossed the phone on my passenger seat where Vivian should've been, and I called over my shoulder at the two guards. "Follow me. We have a vehicle to intercept."

With their quick nods, they climbed into the SUV and followed as I brought my engine to life and hardly looked before pulling onto the highway.

Nothing could've prepared me for the pure agony of that drive. Of having to sit in that seat and operate the vehicle while I could only think about getting Vivian back, wondering if she was alright.

I knew I wouldn't be able to calm down until I saw her with my own eyes again—until her brothers weren't an issue anymore.

As a mercy, I'd wanted to leave them out of it. Their dad had been my target, but ever since they decided to step up to the plate, they became my problem. Because of the grave error they made in taking my wife from me, I had no intention of holding back.

Whatever it took, I was committed to doing exactly that.

So angry at the thought of anyone believing they had any chance of getting away with taking what was mine, I raced down the highway, passing whoever I needed to without care. Thankfully, we had connections in high places, and we were in enough pockets to keep the police off us.

Seeing the pinned location on my car's GPS felt like a taunt, yet a necessary one. Closing the gap in between us was the one thing I could focus on while I forced those unhelpful thoughts out of my head.

As easy as it was to get lost in wondering if she was hurt, or trying to understand what they planned to do with her, I couldn't let myself go down that slippery slope. I had to keep my shit together for Vivian and our children.

I was losing my mind without her, despite holding it all in.

We had come so far in our relationship, and the thought of her brothers trying to take that away was enough to push me over the edge.

Outside of the city, I pulled up to a hill, only to find a commotion caused by our vehicles on a side road, pinning the Range Rover in question. Even if they wanted to, they couldn't get away.

It seemed Lukyan had been right, and the interception time was bang on.

Pulling up, I didn't even turn the car off as I shoved my way out with tunnel vision locking me onto the scene ahead.

I could only hear the blood roaring in my ears as I pulled my gun out, walking through the crowd of our guys and locking them in place. Just as I did, my brothers rolled in and immediately engaged, pulling out their own weapons.

But I couldn't focus on them. Not while Dante and Elio stood there with guns pointed at Vivian.

Focused on how terrified she looked, my blood ran impossibly hot, and with Dante at the end of my pistol, I was prepared to do anything for her.

At the sight of me, Dante tightened his grip on his sister, not afraid to press his handgun against her head.

Ready to finally have it out, I called out to him, "Give me my wife back."

But he only scoffed. "You're in no position to be making demands, Aristarkh."

Though they were surrounded by our guys, the ball was in his court. He had Vivian in his grasp, and if anyone were to misstep, or if he were to decide he didn't have anything left to lose, she would go down with him.

I couldn't let that happen.

# Chapter 28 - Vivian

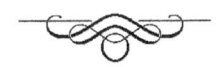

Dante was doing everything in his power to not give away just how terrified he was, but as he held me tightly in his grasp, I could feel how the end of his pistol trembled against my head.

I didn't bother trying to hide how scared I was. I was horrified feeling that cold weapon against my scalp, wondering when he'd pull the trigger and end it all.

Every time he squeezed me harder, I'd be hit by another wave of bitter anticipation, clenching as I braced myself for the final impact.

But the moment I saw Ari forcing himself to the front of that crowd, all guns aimed at my brothers, something in me couldn't help but feel sympathy for my flesh and blood. They had chosen their path and found themselves in a position that would surely only end in death.

Surrounded by Levov men, there was no way all three of us were making it out alive. That painful realization made me wish they had never engaged in this feud at all. I wished that didn't have to be the case, and we could come to some sort of agreement instead.

Whether it was the fact that they were my family alone, or perhaps because of the naive little girl in me who always longed to have a genuine connection with her brothers, I didn't want them to die.

I wanted things to be different. I wished they had been.

"Put the guns down and let Vivian go," Ari demanded. "I'm not going to say it again."

Despite the harsh clip in his tone, hearing his voice helped remind me I wasn't alone, and that he had come for me. He didn't plan on letting them get away with me. He was determined to fight for our future.

"No can do," Dante seethed, voice sounding so different without his usual confidence. "You wronged our whole family by pulling that stunt of yours. You disrespected our father, and you disrespected Vivian. Dad will never recover from that humiliation. In fact, he's given it all up because of you. Ever since that night, he put the family business behind him and couldn't even muster up the courage to get back in the game."

As he spoke, I felt every bit of forced determination emphasized through the gun as he tried to cover up his hesitation, the doubt that started to creep in ever since those vehicles circled us. Yanking me out of the Range Rover and aiming a gun at my head was all to mask that he knew they weren't going to get what they wanted.

"But even if he refuses to do anything to take back what was ours all along, or try to mend our family's honor, then I will," Dante continued, letting that pure rage fill his voice. But even through his anger, I could hear and feel his pain. He let out a bitter laugh. "With whatever resources we could scrounge up, we started digging into your operations to find a way in. We needed an angle, and to your credit, your defenses were pretty good. But I realized hitting your business was useless. Nobody can shake an empire like that from the ground floor. No, I had to go to the penthouse. I needed to get a little closer to home and take what we needed directly."

"So you managed to take her. But where did you plan on going after that?" Ari asked him, keeping his voice scarily calm, and his body unwaveringly still. "Surely you knew you couldn't outrun the greatest surveillance operation in New York. Or did you not think that far ahead?"

I just barely heard as Dante swallowed harshly, but his voice came out in a brutal rasp, "It didn't matter where we went, so long as we could nullify the marriage license. That was the missing piece."

Ari adjusted his grip on the pistol, looking like an impenetrable wall of pure muscle. "To sell her off to the highest bidder?"

Dante didn't say anything at first. Instead, he gritted his teeth, seemingly hating how Ari threw that question around like it wouldn't make or break his and Elio's future in the mob world. Then he let go of a subtle breath.

"If you want her to live so badly, then call your dogs off. Let us go, and Vivian will live another day. That's the only way she'll walk away from this," he proposed, laying it out on the table. "We will leave the city and never come back. You and your family can move on, and surely, you'll find someone else to marry."

I watched Ari for any signs of contemplation, afraid of what I might find, but he didn't waver for even a second. His eyes held every ounce of pure rage and disgust he had, focused on Dante.

Dante's idea made my stomach turn. He wanted to pass me on to the next man so he could capitalize on the opportunity that came with having a sister. He wanted to keep me as far away from Ari as possible.

But they still didn't know about the twins, and I couldn't tell them. That would create a new risk in itself.

Even considering living an abysmal life as some other man's wife and not getting to know my babies was enough to make tears burn in my eyes.

"Please, Dante," I managed despite how tight my throat felt. "I don't want this. I want to be with Ari."

I felt how his hold on me tensed.

"What did you just say?"

I sniffled and tried to maintain my composure. "I'm married to Ari, and there's nothing you can do to change that. Please just let me go."

"Shut the hell up," Dante spat, knocking the barrel of his pistol against my temple, sending a sharp pain through my skull.

As I winced, every Levov man cocked their guns, and fury burned within Ari's eyes.

"Enough!" my husband snapped, letting me see exactly what his enemies saw whenever they tried to cross him, proving to me why the world thought he was brutal. "Hit her again and your remains will be scattered on this road."

The entire area went quiet as his booming voice echoed around us, and while it should've scared me, I could only feel pride.

For our family, he wasn't going to pull his punches. He was determined to fight for us, to fight for me. Above all else, he wanted me to be safe, to get me back home.

"It seems that what we both want isn't lining up, Aristarkh," Dante growled, pressing his fingers into my arm with so much intensity that I knew it would bruise. "Need I remind you, I have her under my gun. Threaten me all you want, but so long as your precious wife is caught in this precarious position, there's nothing you can do."

"How can you do this?" I mumbled, unable to fully grasp how cold he was, and how he could threaten my life so carelessly. "I'm your sister!"

Dante sucked air in through his teeth and murmured with disinterest, "What's one life compared to the interest of the whole family? Tell me, Vivian. Would you sacrifice one of us to be with the Levov?"

Shaking in his grasp as I tried to fight off my tears, I already knew my answer, although I didn't need to say it.

All that sympathy I felt for him previously vanished, and I felt truly vindicated in my decision to turn my back on them. To put my complete faith and loyalty in Ari.

Even when given the chance to let me go, Dante would rather cling to his pride and threaten to take my life. For his gain and that of the family business, he was willing to kill me before allowing me to go back with the Levovs.

I was right to trust Ari over them. He cared about me, and he only wanted the best for us. He was willing to put everything on the line just to make sure we'd be there to watch our family grow and to get the chance to allow our love to flourish.

He wasn't my blood, but he treated me a hell of a lot better than my relatives did.

Stuck in that uncertain position, I couldn't stomach the idea of anything keeping me from Ari. More than anything, I wanted the chance to return to him and to feel his touch again. I needed to feel his careful arms around me and watch him become the father he always wanted to be.

There was so much left for us, and even if he had the upper hand in the situation, I felt just as pinned and helpless with my brother's gun against my head.

# Chapter 29 - Ari

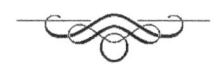

The longer we stayed locked like that, only going in circles as nothing changed, the closer I was to losing my mind. The more desperate I felt to have Vivian back in my arms.

I wanted nothing more than to gun Dante down and take her for myself, but I had to pull on every ounce of self-control I had left. It would be easy to let those emotions get the better of me, but I couldn't. Maintaining that calm facade was the only way I stood a chance of helping Vivian.

But as time went on and more of our men pulled up, vehicles kicking up dust, I could tell it was slowly breaking Elio down. Even if his gun was also aimed at their sister, he looked more hesitant than before.

Surely he knew it was over for them, even if Dante couldn't see it, or at least refused to acknowledge it.

We had far too many men against just the two of them, and despite that, Dante was right. They had Vivian.

Above all else, I had to get her to safety.

Realizing the heavy gun presence was making them both antsy to some capacity, I knew I had to make a choice.

"Guns down," I ordered, watching as I received confused glances from not only our men but from my brothers too. They didn't understand why, but I put a hand out to reassure them. "Do it."

At once, our guns came down in a wave of rustling, but mine stayed.

Dante glanced around, likely wondering if it was a trick. "What about yours, Levov? That doesn't look neutral to me."

"If you think about it, the scale is tipped in your favor," I said, pointing out the obvious. "Your two guns against mine, because that's what this is all about. You and me, Dante."

I watched as his brow furrowed, still holding my wife with such brutal strength I couldn't wait to take him down.

"You think this is supposed to help anything? All that power and influence has surely gone to your head," he growled, knocking the pistol against Vivian's head again, making me wince internally. "We wouldn't be in this mess if you could've just left things alone. But you had to flex that power of yours—you had to beat our father down all to prove a point, didn't you?"

"Don't forget it was your dad who hit us first. It was nothing personal, just business," I returned, aware that he and Elio were still new to the whole thing. If it weren't for me, they never would've found themselves taking over their father's modest empire. "But the moment you decided to hit back—the moment you took matters into your own hands and abducted my wife as if she doesn't share blood with you—that was when it became personal. That was your doing."

Dante scoffed before letting out an incredulous laugh. "If my sister hadn't let herself be used by a Levov, she would never have this false allegiance to you. Her Stockholm syndrome is so strong, she isn't even aware she's been brainwashed by you dogs! Now, why would I care about the blood she has tainted? She is a disgrace to this family, and the only way she can begin to redeem herself is by axing this sham marriage and being with someone whose ambitions line up with ours."

Even hearing him admit his plans was enough to make me see red, wishing I could cut the shit and knock him down already.

Forced to push down that rage, angered by how easily he could disrespect Vivian, I could hardly stand how it brought tears to her eyes.

He had a world of suffering waiting for him if only I could find my angle. If only I could fire without risking her life in the meantime.

"If that is how you feel about her, then just let her go, Dante. Let her be brainwashed. Forget all about her and never come back to this city. But only if you hand her over and leave. That's my one and final offer," I said, stretching that condition to him.

I caught Elio glancing between me and his brother with an uncertain gaze, surely tempted by the offer. From what I could tell, he had a stronger will to live than Dante. He knew there was no escaping our forces unless they took the deal.

But the younger of the two grit his teeth and refused, voice tearing through the space, "You aren't getting it, Levov! Without her, we have nothing. We have nothing to wager—nothing to propel us forward. Without her on the table, we have no leg to stand on with the other heads. All because of you!"

While he claimed to need Vivian in their lives, it wasn't so they could appreciate her or keep her safe. They wanted to use her as a means of tying themselves to another family, and one willing to follow through with a proper trade.

Confusing caring about his sister with the need to do business left him raging before us as the veins in his neck stood on end.

He didn't care about her, and he never had. Which was exactly why I needed to get her away from him.

If I were to let him go to ensure Vivian lived, he would fall back into old habits, or potentially treat her even worse than before. She would be miserable again, forced to be treated like an asset rather than a person.

An object instead of a sister.

The way he thought so lowly of her was shameful, and hell was too good for him.

"Listen, kid. Cut your losses now and get out of it while you can. Take your family and leave. Start honest lives somewhere else, and let the city forget all about you. If selling your sister off is the only way you can stay afloat, then you were never meant to make it in the first place," I said, hoping my calm tone would get to him eventually.

Only the most ruthless could make it in the city's underbelly, and given how he shook with anger and fear, he would never survive long enough to reap the benefits of handing Vivian over to someone else.

Dante shook his head hard as if forcing those thoughts away. Determined and stuck in his stubborn ways, he wouldn't let it go.

"That's easy enough for you to say from the top, Aristarkh. Taking Vivian from you wouldn't make a dent in your empire. But for us, she would make a difference. She would solidify our standing with the greats. She is a temporary blip in your world, but she would change ours completely!"

She was far from temporary to me, and that statement alone made me clench my jaw to hold my tongue.

Adjusting the pistol in my hands, I was itching to make him eat those words.

A wild glaze filled his eyes as he swung her around, loosening his hold with the gun balancing between them. "Don't you see? She changes everything! This whore will make the De Luca name rise in New York and beyond without even knowing it."

Seemingly drunk on his fear and reckless abandon, he was being careless with his hold on her, and with a cocky air, he pulled the pistol away as he held his arms out in a grand display, as if he was untouchable.

"The De Luca name will be infamous. Infamous!"

Time seemed to stand still as I locked eyes with Vivian, watching as her fear softened into comfort long enough to let me feel just how much she loved me. Then, her gaze filled with cold resolve as an idea seemed to strike her, like she knew exactly what needed to be done.

Elio looked hesitantly at Dante, as if questioning his manic shouting, and even allowed his gun arm to go slack.

That was our chance.

"I'm not a De Luca anymore," Vivian muttered, catching Dante's attention as his brow furrowed.

Before he could lift his pistol again, she swung back in a blur, clipping his face with her head before ducking again.

He staggered just as Elio, in a flash of confused momentum, instinctually grabbed Vivian's arm to pull her back.

Within half a beat, I aimed at Dante and squeezed the trigger as our men raised their guns against Elio, making sure he didn't pull a fast one on her.

But as Dante froze in place with complete shock stitched into his features, blood pooling into the fabric of his shirt, gleaming in the darkness around him, Elio dropped his gun.

In disbelief of it all, Dante coughed up blood as his pistol fell to the ground next, unable to fire at anyone. Then, as if the wind had pushed him just enough, he leaned too far to one side and hit the ground in a heap.

As everything came to a head, our men surrounded Elio with their rifles, forcing him onto his knees with his hands behind his head as Vivian was carefully moved out of the way.

Able to breathe again, I was with her in an instant, catching the dazed look on her face as I grabbed her arms and examined her.

"Are you alright?" I asked, concern gripping my heart tighter than ever before.

I was so afraid, not only for her, but for the twins, too. She had been through more than enough trauma, and I needed to know they were safe.

Vivian blinked back at me through her startled haze, eventually managing to nod. As the realization hit her that everything was over, tears filled her eyes as she pushed herself against my chest.

Instinctively, I wrapped my arms around her and held her close, breathing in the relief that my wife was just fine.

"You're okay," I reassured her, unsure if I meant it for her or myself. "I've got you."

She went through the motions as I pulled her away from the chaos behind us, eager to get her somewhere quiet again.

I could hardly fathom that she was back with me, and we didn't have to worry about her brothers anymore. While we still needed to check the state of our growing little ones, she was mostly physically unharmed.

But all the same, I was so grateful.

"I'm so sorry," I murmured the moment we were alone, unable to find it within myself to let her go. "I shouldn't have waited so long to take action. I should've put them back in their place before they could ever get the chance to find you again."

With a sniffle, Vivian shook her head and pulled back just enough to look up at me. "Please don't blame yourself, Ari. You're here, and you kept your promise."

Managing a small smile for her, I stroked her hair out of her face before caressing her cheek. "I told you I would, and I meant it."

I could've looked into those damp, yet crystal-clear eyes of hers all day and soaked in her beauty, but our attention was snagged away as orders were given, and a shuffle of movement came from them hauling Elio away.

With ample gun power against him, he had no choice but to be cuffed and led toward one of our blacked-out vehicles to be sent elsewhere. His face was mostly blank, but the last glance he made in Vivian's direction gave away the slightest fear. The regret.

"Please spare him."

My brows furrowed in confusion as I looked back down at her. "What?"

"Please," Vivian insisted, looking alarmed at the thought of not knowing what was next for her brother. "Punish him as you must, but let him live."

I still couldn't believe what she was asking of me after it was all said and done.

"But why? He had a hand in this, too," I reminded her. "He also had a gun pointed at you."

"I know, but Dante was the one orchestrating everything, and Elio was going along with it for the benefits. While he wasn't always the best to me, I could tell he was fighting between who he was and who he thought Dad wanted him to be. He was neglected, too," Vivian explained, showing me her sincerity through her determined gaze. "Elio may have assisted him, but Dante was the worst of them. I believe Elio can learn a different path if he's given the chance."

Taking her in completely while I considered her words, I knew I couldn't say no to her. Instead, I sighed and nodded.

"So long as he's as far away from you as possible, and you believe he isn't completely rotten, then fine," I said, honoring her request. "I'll make sure he lives. But for now, I need to get you home and have a nurse swing by to check on you."

With a faint smile, Vivian nodded and moved back in for another embrace. "Thank you, Ari."

Holding her close, it took everything in my power to not get emotional in front of the others, even if we were some distance away from the scene. "I was scared out of my mind that something might happen to you, but you're safe now, and we don't have to worry about anything. You were brave out there, and I can't tell you enough how glad I am to hold you now."

"I could only think about how much I wanted to be back home with you and live out the rest of our lives together," Vivian murmured against my chest, letting me feel her warmth. "I love you, Ari."

"I love you more," I said, cradling her like I'd never get the chance to again. But knowing that wasn't true, I let a content smile settle on my lips. "Let's go home, sweetheart."

# Chapter 30 - Vivian

After everything went down with my brothers, Ari followed through with his word and had a nurse come by the house nearly as soon as we got there. To our relief, no harm had come to the twins, and they were still just as happy despite the spike in my blood pressure I had endured.

Ari did everything he could to make me feel safe and comfortable moving forward, including staying home from work for a week to make sure I was doing all right. Even in wake of what happened, that time for just us was everything I needed to feel better again. Everything I needed to feel so completely adored and appreciated by him.

Behind the scenes, Lara and some of their cousins worked together to plan a baby shower for us, and on that beautiful day, the back yard was full of Levovs as they gathered to celebrate our little ones.

By then, I was more noticeably pregnant, much to Ari's delight, and there was no doubting just how big my belly was getting. It made it easier for me to hold my bump lovingly, and to offer our babies as much comfort as I could.

Of course, Ari was never too shy to do the same. Every night, he'd caress my stomach and whisper his feelings, letting them know how much he loved them already. Those words would be directed to me afterward, affirming the work I was putting into growing our sweet twins.

With most of his family there, I spent the first part of the afternoon getting to know everyone, finally able to place the names I heard in passing to faces.

It was easy to see just how much they all cared for each other, with that sentiment going beyond just Ari and his siblings. Regardless of how intimidating most of them seemed, I came to realize they were all just hardened masks used while they did business. But underneath it all, they were rambunctious and caring, and they took pride in teasing one another.

There were endless streams of congratulations for the two of us, along with a sea of more gifts than we could ever use.

"You've impressed me, Vivian," Anastasia said as she stood with her slice of cake in hand. "I never thought anyone could get through Ari's macho exterior, but you've done the impossible."

"Eh, we've all known he's soft under there, he's just too embarrassed to show it," Lukyan teased with a knowing grin.

As he and the others laughed, Yaro came up from behind and hooked an arm around his neck playfully, ruffling his hair. "Says the softest one here, kid."

"You've got me all wrong," he said in defense of himself. "I'm just hoping that if I follow Ari's lead, I'll snag a wife of my own."

"It doesn't get softer than that," Ari said with a chuckle, putting an affectionate hand against my waist. "But I'm waiting to see who manages to whip Benedikt into shape. Any luck at the clubs yet?"

With a scoff, Benedikt rolled his eyes. "It might be your day today, but you're still not allowed to say 'I told you so.'"

Amused by how they always seemed to end up in a constant roll of banter, I was glad to witness it for myself.

Despite everything we went through, I finally felt at ease. That lingering dread in my stomach went away after our worries were taken care of, and all that remained was the chance to truly explore our connection.

Ari had been dedicated before, but after it was all said and done, he became the best husband I could ever ask for.

We were closer than ever, and there was no doubt in my mind that we would be just fine.

He was everything I wanted and needed, and I could put my complete faith in him.

Making the deal even sweeter, I felt like I had a place in his family, as his siblings and cousins accepted me without hesitation. Even if I had been a reluctant outsider before, I felt like one of them, and I never got sick of being around them.

While they had made me nervous initially, that hesitation went away as I warmed up to them and realized they weren't as intimidating as they seemed.

"All of that aside," Lara began, throwing her brothers a warning look as she steered everyone back on track. "I just want to say to Vivian that I'm still so glad to have you here with us. Not only do you give me a break from these idiots, but you bring out the best in Ari, and I know you two will make incredible parents."

My heart swelled at the acceptance as the others smiled.

"A toast to Ari, Vivian, and the twins," Benedikt proposed, lifting his glass flute full of punch in the air.

Everyone joined in, offering us another wave of congratulations. Even the children who had spent the whole time running around and playing joined in with their enthusiastic cheers.

My cheeks started to ache from smiling as Ari held me close to his side and gently clinked his glass against mine, mirroring his happiness back to me.

"So where to?" Lara asked, looking at us through her stylish sunglasses.

"I found a great place for us in Costa Rica. We'll be there for a week before heading to the Keys," Ari said, sounding just as excited as I felt for our baby moon.

"Don't tempt me into booking a flight," she added, smiling at the idea.

"No offense, Lar, but I don't think they want any visitors on this trip," Kir murmured with a mischievous grin.

Lara threw him a look of repulsion at the idea as she playfully swatted him away. "Gross!"

The others laughed as I tried to push away the heat creeping up my neck at the implication, well aware of how we intended to pass the time together.

Eventually, the celebration came to a close, and everyone saw us off. With our bags already in the back of the car, Ari pulled away from the house as evening set in, holding my hand all the while.

We finished the wonderful day spent with his family by catching our flight to Costa Rica, prepared to continue the celebration on our own.

"The honeymoon we never got to have," Ari murmured to me as he kissed the back of my hand while we sat together in the private jet, overlooking the world beneath us.

I smiled at him, grateful for it all.

After everything, I couldn't wait to relax and focus on the two of us in the warm weather, soaking in the sun and the fresh air.

Realizing he was right, I knew the trip was going to be even better than I had anticipated.

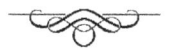

---

The suite was even more perfect than I could've imagined, in awe of the resort choice Ari had made for us.

Surrounded by glimmering water, we were practically staying in a mansion on a pier connected by boardwalks and short bridges. Outside every window was a view of the ocean, along with the beautiful scenery.

The lush interior felt so open and airy as the white curtains billowed in the light breeze, immediately offering us pure comfort and relaxation.

I breathed in that salty air as Ari wrapped his arms around me and pressed a gentle kiss against my neck.

"You like it?"

"Of course," I hummed, putting my hand over his where it rested against my stomach tenderly. "It's incredible."

"Good. Make yourself at home for the next week," he said, pressing a kiss against my neck that made me smile. "I have a relaxing itinerary you can take a look at, and dinner will be brought to us shortly. But in the meantime," Ari hummed, carefully turning me around to face him, "I was thinking we could break this place in."

Catching on to his real meaning, my heart thrummed, and my skin was already warm all over.

"I wouldn't complain," I murmured in return, looking up at the gorgeous man I had the privilege of calling my husband.

Pleased by my confirmation, his hands were already ghosting my waist and hips—a telltale sign that he was already turned on and growing more restless by the minute.

"I'm glad we're always on the same page," he returned quietly as he leaned in, capturing my lips with his.

It didn't matter how many times we kissed, it always felt just as intense as the first time, and it always left me wanting more. Thankfully, he seemed to be thinking the same thing, as he didn't break the kiss to nudge me back, guiding me toward the bed.

"You don't know how worked up I've been all day," Ari mumbled as the mattress connected with the back of my legs, and he carefully eased me onto it. Pushing my hips back and guiding me to a lying position, he sank to his knees as he pressed kisses down my legs. "Seeing you in that dress, walking around and looking so pregnant—fuck..."

Excitement scurried through me at his confession, still just as glad about how much it aroused him to see me that way, knowing I was carrying his children.

"Now I don't have to wait," he continued, moving between my thighs as he made his way closer to my throbbing heat and pushed the hem of my dress up to expose more of my skin.

Sucking in a deep breath the moment he hooked his fingers into the hem of my underwear and pulled it down, not bothering to tease me beforehand, I let go of it the second his tongue brushed against my clit.

Breathlessly, I moaned for him, melting as his tongue ran through my folds, eagerly collecting my arousal.

He hummed into me as he gripped my thighs, taking so much pleasure in exploring me that I couldn't help but wonder if it was borderline more for him than for me. Losing himself in it, Ari moaned into me and devoured every inch, not letting it go to waste.

As his saliva mixed with my arousal, creating the perfect concoction between us, my thighs started to shake, my belly already tightening from his enthusiasm.

Arching my back slightly off the bed, I let myself soak up that addictive attention, beyond grateful he took so much pride in making me feel good. It seemed like a bonus that his pleasing me turned him on with absolute ease.

Before long, I was moaning out for him, practically begging for more, and to my relief, he was too desperate to tease me any longer.

Leaving a final kiss on my clit, he pushed the dress up and over me as he hovered above, reaching to free my breasts from over the top of my bra. Urgently, he leaned down to kiss me, dragging his cock through my folds.

He moaned into my mouth, catching my own as I shuddered from the feeling, aware of every pass he made over my clit.

Sinfully, he slowly moved his hips, slicking himself in that damp combination of fluids between my legs. His whole body tensed at the sensation as he supported himself above me, dropping his head as it coursed through him.

Head already foggy from just getting started, I reached up for him and gripped his back, prepared to stabilize myself through the bliss he was about to feed me.

"Christ, you're too much," Ari managed to say, voice gruff as he parted my legs further and lined himself up.

Given how wet I already was, he faced no resistance as he slid inside, making us both gasp at the sensation.

I had grown used to Ari's size and knew what to expect, but every time he entered me, it felt just as intense. His girth made me pause to accommodate him and to revel in how much it completed me.

Surrounding me and filling me so completely, I could only grip him tighter, letting my nails sink into his skin as he started to move.

No matter how hard he tried to hold back his moans or how he attempted to resist how tightly I clenched around him, Ari could never keep those sounds to himself. His rigid body always made it clear just how much it was affecting him, and how eager he was to move within me.

With one hand on the mattress to prop himself up and the other on my hip, he started at a slow pace, jaw clenching from that sheer bliss.

Moaning for him, I felt every second of pleasure, and every inch of him as he dragged himself in and back out again, letting us both hear just how aroused we were. He did it several times, driving me crazy every time he entered me again.

As lust darkened his eyes, Ari couldn't keep up that deliberate pace as he thrusted into me harder, building a rhythm that had me squirming for him.

Encouraging him on, I knew it was no use swallowing back my moans. Instead, I wanted him to know just how much I loved it, and how he could push me closer to release every time.

Zeroing in on his movements, Ari snapped his hips harder, digging his fingers into my skin all the while.

I couldn't complain, not while I did the same to his back, clawing at him and clinging as much as I could. He was the only thing I could anchor myself to as he pulled those groans from me and made me take that endless intensity.

Mindlessly murmuring how much I was enjoying it, those words seemed to come out more like a chant for him. Useless babbling was all my hazy mind could come up with, but as far as I could tell, he didn't mind it for a second.

Instead, Ari let go of his shaky moans and drove his hips into mine. That sickeningly addictive slap of his skin against mine echoed throughout the room, only making the whole thing more alluring.

The closer he moved his body to mine, the more muted that sound became, and the deeper he thrusted into me.

As my throat went dry from moaning, those sounds cracked and fragmented as I took more of him, so overwhelmed by the fuzziness filling my system.

His size alone was enough to push me over the edge, but pairing it with his relentless speed, depth, and perfect sounds, it was all too much.

Dropping his hand between us, he circled my clit, immediately lighting fire across my entire body with how intense it felt. With the added stimulation, everything mounted at once, building and building until I couldn't keep it in.

Letting go of a choked groan, I crashed into my release as I clenched around him, and my vision went black. My lower belly tightened when my orgasm hit me, and it was all I could do to hold on.

Ari's thighs quivered as he groaned, stilling against me as he released inside me, filling me with his warmth. He gripped me as his head tipped back, bliss cloaking him, looking like a god through my haze.

Panting, he supported himself above me as he swallowed back his relieved moan before relaxing next to me. Ari draped an arm lazily over me as we both collected ourselves, staying as close to me as possible.

"I love you," he whispered, nuzzling his face into my neck.

Reaching for his hand, I laced our fingers together and soaked up my relief, unable to deny how complete I felt. "I love you too, Ari."

There was no telling how long we stayed like that, blissed out and not missing a moment of our shared time together.

We were both at ease, not needing any words to fill the silence. It was more than perfect, and I knew I couldn't ask for more.

Eventually, there was a hesitant knock at the door, and I looked at him in confusion.

Recognition filled his eyes, and Ari chuckled. "Must be dinner. What good timing."

Laughing at how absurd it was, I fell back on the bed and felt as his arms pulled me close, not letting me go despite the employee waiting outside the door.

"Just a minute!" he called, not making any move to get up as he pressed a kiss against my skin. He murmured into my neck, "My wife currently has my full attention."

My heart clenched at his words, reminding me of the simple fact that was always so difficult for me to believe.

Despite everything, it turned out that being Ari's wife was the furthest thing from a curse, and he was everything I ever needed, wrapped into the most perfect package.

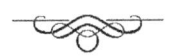

# THE END

# About Deva Blake

Deva Blake writes from her study room with garden view in her Californian home. She loves having a cup of mint tea as well as a rose candle burning next to her while working. Deva writes dark mafia romance about the type of guys that your parents warned you about but that you end up falling for anyway, because they're just too irresistible. When not buried in her dark imagination, she enjoys baking cakes for her son and husband.

# Books by Deva Blake

**"Levov Bratva" Series**

The Bratva of New York are the most ruthless, merciless and possessive mobsters of the city. They take what they want, break what they please, and heal what they deem worthy. But will they take the biggest risk of all: open their heart for the one they've claimed?

**The Bratva's Kidnapped Bride**

**The Bratva's Secret Baby**

**The Bratva's Pregnant Bride**

**The Bratva's Hostage**

**The Bratva's Forced Bride**

**The Bratva's Surrogate**

**The Bratva's Used Bride**

**The Bratva King's Twins**

---

**"Dubrov Bratva" Series**

The Dubrov Bratva are the ruthless keepers of the city, the cold protectors of the women they claim, and the gentle daddies of the babies they make. Love them or hate them, you have no choice but to obey them the minute they decide that they want you for life.

**Brutal Bratva Boss**

Pregnant Bratva Prisoner

Kidnapped Bratva Bride

Forced Bratva Bride

The Bratva's Kidnapped Bride

Printed in Dunstable, United Kingdom

# THE HARD WAY HOME

**ALLAN ROBERTS**

with Paul Greenway

JoJo
PUBLISHING

*The Hard Way Home*
Allan Roberts

Published by JoJo Publishing
First published 2014
'Yarra's Edge'
2203/80 Lorimer Street
Docklands VIC 3008
Australia
Email: jo-media@bigpond.net.au or visit www.jojopublishing.com
© Allan Roberts

All rights reserved. No part of this printed or video publication may be reproduced, stored in or introduced into a retrieval system, or transmitted, in any form, or by any means (electrical, mechanical, photocopying, recording or otherwise) without the prior written permission of the publisher and copyright owner.

JoJo Publishing
Edited by Julie Athanasiou
Designer /typesetter: Chameleon Print Design
Illustrations by Bill Wood
Printed in China by Inkasia

National Library of Australia Cataloguing-in-Publication entry

| | |
|---|---|
| Author: | Greenway, Paul 1960- author. |
| Title: | The hard way home / Paul Greenway. |
| ISBN: | 9780987587909 (paperback) |
| Subjects: | Greenway, Paul 1960---Travel. |
| | Motorcyclists--Biography. |
| | Motorcycle touring--Biography. |
| | Motorcycle touring--Personal narratives. |
| | Travelers--Biography. |
| Dewey Number: | 910.4092 |

*In the end it will be alright,
and if it's not alright it's not the end.*

*Why?*
It seemed a reasonable question.

I could answer *how* — on my Honda Africa Twin 750cc motorbike — and *when*. I could usually (but not always) answer *where*. But as kids in Africa sometimes asked me, "What is your mission?"

I would ask myself this while I was lying in a malarial fever for three days on the concrete floor of a police station in Angola or spending more than 10 days trying to cross the border from Mongolia to China or finding maggots growing inside my leg.

Why did I start?

It was on a particularly bad day working as a commercial diver along the remote Western Australian coast that I was enticed by a mate, Clint, to join his jaunt around Southeast Asia. Impulsively, I quit my job, drove back to the family farm in Victoria and bought a one-way ticket to Singapore. I never imagined that I wouldn't be home for over five years or that I'd be returning on a motorbike. Thoughts about this adventure blossomed while I was in Thailand — until I ended up in hospital. But that's another story…

I wanted to ride from London to Cape Town via the Sahara and Timbuktu. If my backside wasn't too sore and wallet wasn't too empty, I then planned to head north along East Africa to Yemen. From there, it was through all the '-stans' of Central Asia, Russia, Mongolia and China before heading to Southeast Asia. A detour to ride the Abu Dhabi Desert Challenge rally in Dubai wasn't in the original itinerary, but that's also another story…

My trip was planned before two 'celebrity riders' started theirs. Ewan McGregor, the famous Scottish actor, and his mate had an office with staff working full-time for four months and a guaranteed publishing and television deal. I didn't attend courses in fitness, mechanics, first aid and 'hostile environment situations'. Of course, motorbike sponsorship and free equipment never entered my mind. They could afford a medical officer and security guard to accompany them as well as support vehicles carrying fuel, equipment and spare parts. And *my God* what I would've given for a 'fixer' to sort out visas for me and paperwork for my bike at the innumerable border crossings across Africa and Asia.

So why did I continue?

The answer was obvious while following gorillas through the mountains of central Africa or watching a cow-jumping manhood ceremony among remote tribes of Ethiopia or playing *kok boru*, a bizarre game of horse polo with a headless goat, in a country I still can't pronounce (Kyrgyzstan).

But I also *wanted* to go home. And I *needed* to see if it was possible to travel over 100,000 kilometres — about six times further than travelling by air — through 59 countries across four continents.

I had to do it the hard way.

**ALLAN ROBERTS**

Born and bred in the Mallee region of northern Victoria, Allan's love of adventurous travel was sparked by the numerous camping trips across Australia he took with his father, who also bought Allan a motorbike when Allan was five years old. After finishing school, Allan worked for the Royal Australian Air Force as an aircraft technician in Adelaide. Tired of the rigidity of the military, he moved to Japan to teach English before returning to Australia and training as a construction diver.

Allan worked as a diver on tuna farms in Port Lincoln as well as Broome and Perth, but the lure of travel was again too much. After backpacking throughout Southeast Asia and trucking through the Middle East, Allan chased a girl to London, where he worked as an engineer fixing trains. After two-and-a-half years, Allan wanted to come home, but — forever a dreamer — he wanted to ride a motorbike and do it the hard way.

**PAUL GREENWAY**

Paul worked at Lonely Planet for nine years, writing and co-writing 30 guidebooks, including guides for the countries that Allan knew so well, such as Botswana, Iran, and Mongolia. He also happened to be living and working in Indonesia while Allan travelled through that country. Paul's other professions include working as an intelligence officer in Sydney, Canberra and Darwin and working as an Indonesian teacher at a South Australian high school.

Now a full-time writer again, Paul's recently-published works include a novel *Bali & Oates*, the first of a trilogy (through JoJo Publishing); the *Tuttle Travel Pack: Bali & Lombok* (Tuttle Publishing); and a photo-book, *Journey Through Bali* (Periplus).

Neglecting to get married, he now lives in Adelaide without any wives or children and currently spends his time either writing or not writing.

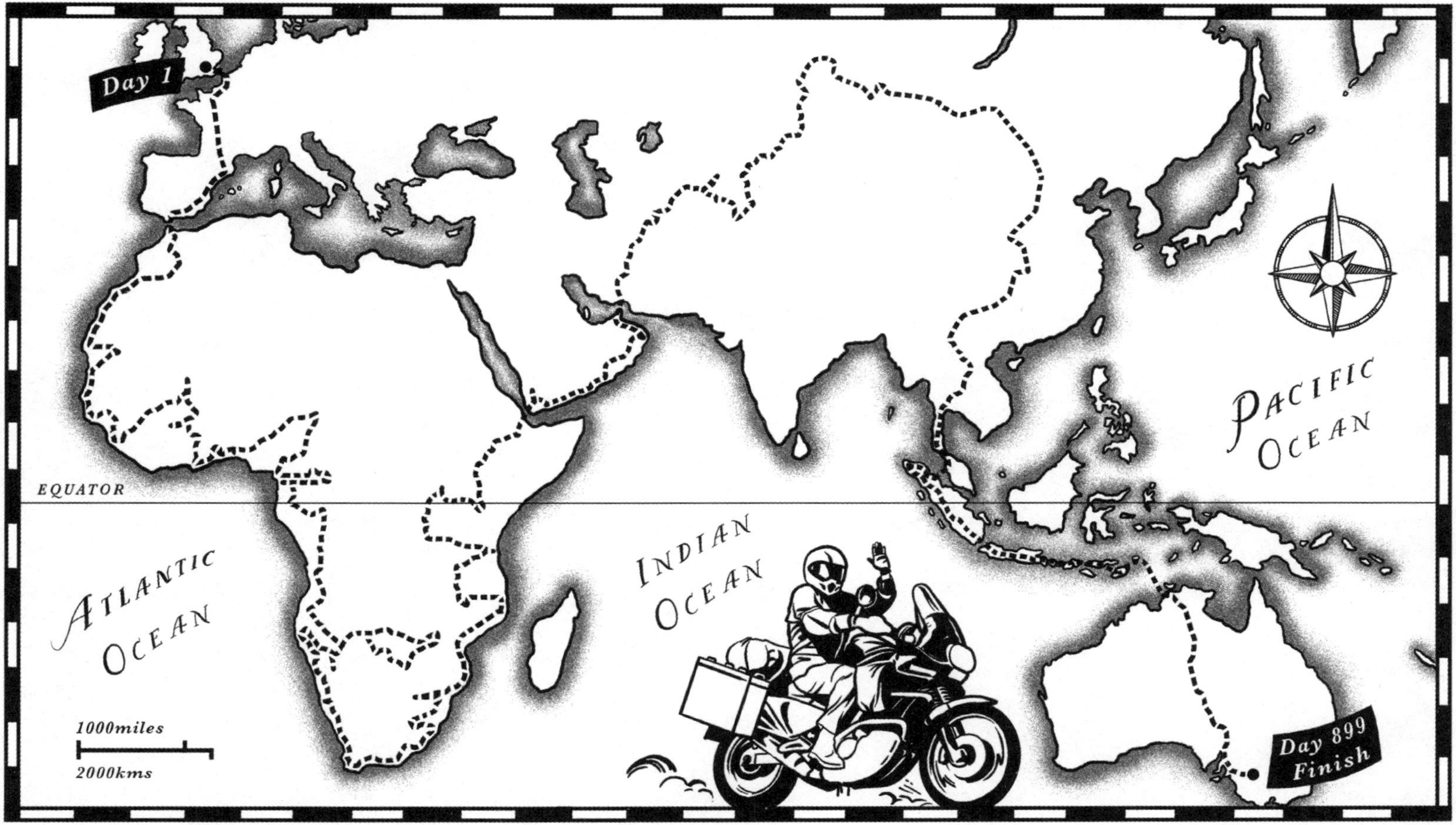
Day 1
Atlantic Ocean
Indian Ocean
Pacific Ocean
EQUATOR
1000miles
2000kms
Day 899
Finish

# CONTENTS

**PART ONE**     1

**Chapter 1: Europe**     3
*England to Gibraltar: 19 days*

**Chapter 2: Northern & Western Africa**     13
*Morocco to Nigeria: 139 Days*

**Chapter 3: Central & Southern Africa**     69
*Cameroon to South Africa: 207 Days*

**PART TWO**     117

**Chapter 4: Eastern Africa**     119
*Mozambique to Djibouti: 126 Days*

**Chapter 5: Middle East & the '–Stans'**     165
*Yemen to Russia: 206 Days*

**Chapter 6: Asia**     203
*Mongolia to Indonesia: 171 Days*

**Chapter 7: Home**     257
*Darwin to Turriff: 31 Days*

# PART ONE

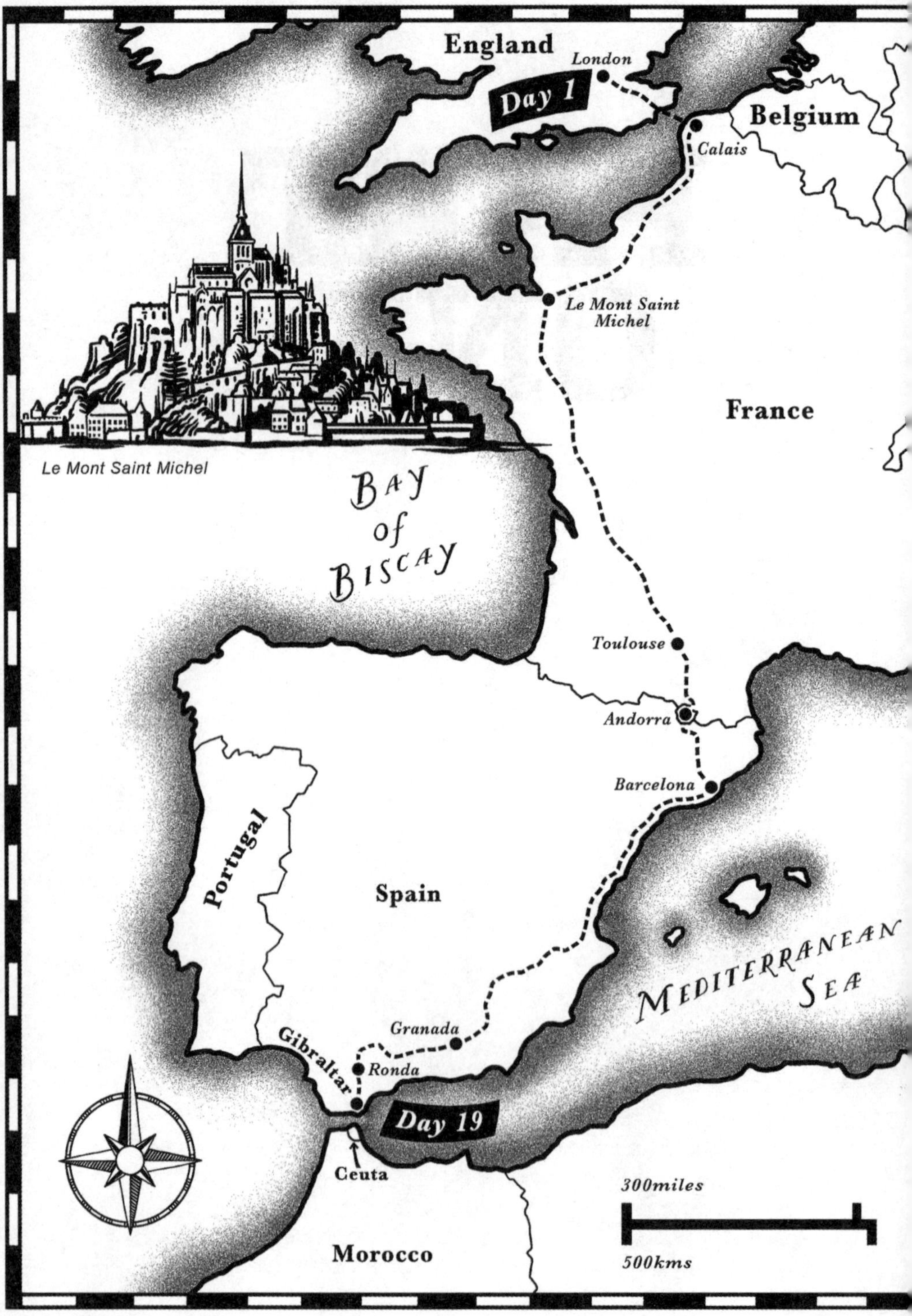

England
London
Day 1
Belgium
Calais
Le Mont Saint Michel
France
Le Mont Saint Michel
Bay of Biscay
Toulouse
Andorra
Barcelona
Portugal
Spain
Mediterranean Sea
Granada
Gibraltar
Ronda
Day 19
Ceuta
300miles
500kms
Morocco

CHAPTER 1

# Europe

*England to Gibraltar: 19 days*

**ENGLAND**

Somehow I'd packed everything (from the tubes of Vegemite to a French dictionary) that lay across the floor of my flat on and around the bike, and the little Aussie flags and stickers were now attached to it. Most of my friends and housemates for the past 27 months had come to say goodbye over a typical English fry-up for breakfast, but my nerves prevented me from eating too much before I went. My anxiety increased further as I turned a corner and stopped at a traffic light after only 50 metres.

Working in London had enabled me to travel to places I had only ever dreamt of, such as Iceland and Bosnia, but I soon become bored. My two passions have always been motorbikes and travelling, so it seemed logical to combine the two for the ultimate adventure: riding the hard way home from London to the family farm in the heart of the Mallee region of Victoria.

I glanced across at Amy, who I'd met about three years before in Bangkok while convalescing. Sitting at a breakfast table at a hostel a short walk from the hospital where I was getting treatment, I noticed a girl with an Asian appearance walk in and say, "Good morning" in a broad Australian accent. Born and bred in Brisbane, Amy's parents emigrated from Hong Kong, and over the next few days she and I ran into each other and swapped travel stories. She'd just finished her degree as an occupational therapist and was on her way to live and work in England for two years.

I was soon smitten; she had an adventurous spirit and an infectious willingness to try different food, see unusual places and experience new cultures. We spent a few precious days together exploring Bangkok, and I knew I wanted to see her again. But she soon continued her plans in London, and I resumed my travels across Asia alone. Before heading to Gallipoli in Turkey for the Anzac Day commemorations, I travelled to England to see Amy again. We spent three weeks together, and our relationship grew. After travelling on a truck through Turkey, Syria, Jordan, Lebanon and Egypt, I came back to London once more to find a job and, more importantly, be with Amy.

As well as the traffic, the other thing I would never miss about England is the weather, but the rain did clear for our ride to the renowned white cliffs of Dover, the departure point for the ferry to France. As the sea gusts blasted our faces, the tension that had built over months of arduous preparation had finally lifted from our shoulders and our relief about finally starting the trip was palpable. Now, after I'd been planning this trip for the past year or so, the day had finally come. The trip would be very long, extraordinarily difficult and frequently fraught with danger, and I knew that success was reliant on my mechanical knowledge. It was also obvious that I'd be out of communication range for long periods of time and would need to rely almost totally on my own instincts and resources. There could and would be any number of major problems.

Not least the fact that Amy had barely even ridden a motorbike before.

**FRANCE**

Our first overnight stay was at a campsite on the beach in foggy Calais, on the French side of the Channel crossing. We'd only covered 180 kilometres, but it was a long day — the first of hundreds more. Dinner was typical (sardines cooked over a portable stove), but not so the wine. We met the first of a seemingly endless number of other adventurers — this time an English couple, Bunny and Sorel.

Along the roads that hugged the English Channel, it was windy and the weather was glorious. When the sun shined and I leant into a bend with the gorgeous countryside all around, I felt so free. The landscapes were extraordinary and varied, and pitching our tent among the mostly-empty camping grounds in the sleepy villages was a joy. We tried to avoid motorways so we could travel through the picturesque French countryside and stop and admire the historic buildings and villages. It was all so beautiful, but the weather was often not. And Amy's boots were impractical; they were like big sponges soaking up so much water.

We visited the Valley of the Somme in the sort of dreary mist I would've imagined was common during the battles that raged there nearly 100 years ago. The site of the Battle of the Somme, one of the most tragic of World War I, is where many visitors, including Australians, understandably feel the tragic waste of life in a lush part of the French countryside where tens of thousands of young men died fighting for Britain and her allies.

Another highlight was La Mont Saint Michel, an amazing *chateau* (castle) with a majestic spire perched on a rocky islet. This Gothic-style Benedictine abbey built between the 6th and 7th centuries is set in the midst of vast sandbanks exposed to the powerful tides and surrounded by a village. Dedicated to the archangel St Michael, the abbey is a technical and artistic masterpiece. We camped nearby, helping ourselves to apples from a tree in the camping ground, and wandered about the next morning when the weather had improved. But the tide was out, so the setting was less spectacular.

Amy's abilities and determination never ceased to amaze me. She'd had to leave London after her two-year visa expired, but I stayed and worked, planning my trip. I'd always intended to take the trip alone, but in the six months before my departure, things got tough for both of us. With the prospect of me riding around the world for a year or more, Amy called it quits on our relationship a few weeks before I left. I couldn't blame her, but with the thought of losing her I panicked and pleaded with her to join me.

"But I am not sitting on the back of your bike all that way," she said.
"No. You'll ride your own bike."
"But I can't ride a bike!"
"Then I'll teach you."

So, three weeks before my planned departure, Amy flew back to London from Brisbane and bought a motorbike, and I taught her how to ride. All my plans had dramatically changed, but I was so glad she was with me.

Except perhaps when she got lost, such as in Toulouse, when her ticket for the toll-way didn't work and I couldn't stop (but she eventually caught up). And she did have a little mishap with the bike, which we simply nicknamed 'The Baja' (because it was a Honda XR250 Baja): She dropped it while pulling up, but again there were no problems. Remarkably, Amy showed no signs whatsoever of nerves or anxiety while on her bike.

Continuing through the hills and over the mountain ranges, we followed the gushing rivers and lofty trees that lined the roads and created welcome shade and amazing shadows. I'd been to Paris but not the rest of the country, and I quickly loved everything about France: the affable people and the food, especially the baguettes *au jambon* (with ham) that we seemed to live on. It was very unusual to pass through a country without having at least one bad experience, but we had none.

Starting each day early meant that we'd witness the energy of the country folk as they began their own morning activities. They always had time to stop and stare as we passed through each village and town like we were in a parade. No doubt they were forewarned by the *thump-thump* of my Africa Twin XRV750, which I nicknamed 'The Mothership'. We waved at farmers on tractors and old people sitting and watching the world, including us, go by. Clearly, they had no idea what we were doing and where we were going (but neither did we sometimes).

But France was only ever a thoroughfare, and we were keen to reach Gibraltar and catch the ferry to Africa.

**ANDORRA**

Breakfast in France. Lunch in Andorra. Dinner in Spain.

Six hours was enough in this tiny principality squeezed between France and Spain but without the charms and attractions of either. The ride along the switchback roads across the 2000-metre high Pyrenees was spectacular, but Andorra was not; it was cold, and the bikes were chugging in the thinner air, especially The Baja, which sounded like it was suffering from a severe case of asthma. Perhaps it was because Andorra is a tax-free haven, but the people seemed strange, and we were glad to get out quickly. The capital, Andorra la Vella, looked so out of place amongst the lovely mountainous scenery, with its bizarre modern buildings and congested streets lined with upmarket shops designed for one only thing — the sale of duty-free goods.

**SPAIN**

The landscape was drier and rockier in Spain than in France and the weather certainly warmer than Andorra, but the scenery was still superb, with colossal mountains and immense valleys. However, the Spanish didn't seem as friendly as the French (although I'd assumed it would be the other way around).

Braving the insane traffic, we dashed into Barcelona, where Amy almost ran out of fuel. We visited *La Sagrada Familia*, a hideous-looking temple with numerous spires that has been under construction since 1882 and was not expected to be completed for at least another 30 years. Controversy continues about the construction because of new materials that some felt the architect, Gaudi, would not have used. While impressive, the masses of tourists and frenzied pace of Barcelona reminded me why we were speeding through Europe and heading to the open spaces of Africa.

From Barcelona, the road twists alongside the Mediterranean coast. The camping grounds seemed to be all or nothing — either overcrowded 'mini-cities' with too many people and facilities or the complete opposite. So we were often consigned to charmless 'Legoland' grounds with amenities like hair salons and supermarkets, whereas we preferred to pitch our tents on grassy patches (which often turned into muddy swamps, of course). One benefit of such places was the chance to fling a load of dirty washing into a machine (never underestimate the joy of clean, dry socks), and the pleasure of a hot shower, especially as we knew that washing our clothes and ourselves would be a rarity across Africa.

The rain persisted, so we rested for a day, which I needed anyway because my back was a little sore — probably from camping on thin mattresses each night — and I'd developed a sharp pain in my shoulder blade from riding all day. The camping ground with the launderette quickly lost its appeal, so we tried to find a more appealing place to pitch a tent inland where the skies seemed clearer.

The rain was incessant and our fuel tanks almost empty as we rolled into a village. We were lost but eventually pointed in the right direction. However, we decided to fill our tanks and head back towards the coast, so our previous attempts to move inland and avoid the rain had failed miserably. We stopped at a roadhouse to dry out Amy's boots and gloves with a hand dryer in the toilets and then continued to the coast, wet, cold and tired. We were forced to stay in a camping ground just north of Valencia that was even less appealing than the one with the launderette; in fact, it was our most unpleasant yet. The news on the TV in a bar reported what we already knew: Spain was experiencing abnormal rainfall and widespread flooding.

With the sun finally shining, we again tried to head inland and were glad we did. The mountains were dramatic and fields smothered with orchards of olive trees. We passed through villages that seemed so backwards in time with their old buildings, small cobbled streets and little old cars. Locals strolling along narrow, cobble-stoned lanes would stare as we passed; it wasn't every day they saw crazy people like us riding through with overloaded motorbikes.

In one village square, a tiny old man got out of his car and started speaking to us — in Spanish, of course. He wasn't angry, just chatty. All I could do was point on my map and say 'Iniesta' — our next destination. He grinned, provided incomprehensible directions in his language, hopped back into his antiquated car and drove off.

As the rain returned in the south, we avoided the longer, scenic routes and chose the quickest way, but the rain was another reasonable excuse for staying in a *pension*, while in Granada, which was basic accommodation but with a dry bed and hot shower rather than a saturated tent. Located where the Sierra Nevada mountains meet a fertile plain, Granada is a typical Spanish city with a variety of churches and museums, but it is most famous for the Alhambra.

The Alhambra is a massive castle constructed over many centuries which consists of the gardens, fountains and palaces that were the home of Arabic sultans who once ruled the Iberian province. The history, architectural designs with intricate carvings, and setting high on the edge of a steep hill were superb, and I tried to imagine what life would've been like in the Islamic region now known as Spain. As an apparent attempt to create 'Heaven on Earth' in accordance with the Qur'an, Alhambra is Spain's most visited monument — and, therefore, also packed with the sort of people I wanted to avoid.

We rested for a day to dry everything out, but the spare time allowed me to become more anxious about heading to Africa. Europe was a safety blanket: There were motorbike shops, and if anything goes wrong, there was always a way out — but not so in the Dark Continent. In Africa, it would be up to me to sort out any problems, and there were now two bikes to worry about. I would continually have to check them, but both Hondas had been pleasingly reliable so far.

It was probably the thoughts of home that made me want to stop at Ronda so I could tell my mother that I'd visited a town with her name (albeit with a different spelling). Ronda retains much of its historic charm, and the setting across a plateau on a cliff's edge is stunning. Ronda (the town, not my mother) is also famous for bull-fighting, as evidenced by the stadium in the town centre. We even found a lovely camping ground with a view of everything that Ronda has to offer. We were enjoying the Spanish cuisine and would miss the *tapas* and *paella* when we reached Africa.

Our last memory of Spain (or so we thought) was the breathtaking road to Gibraltar, a windy road that climbs up and over a mountain range through arid and rocky countryside — probably the most spectacular scenery we'd seen so far. The massive gum trees lining the roads and following the dry riverbeds reminded me of the farm in the heart of the Mallee of northern Victoria, where I grew up with my parents and elder sister. This was where my passion for motorbikes was born. My father bought me my first bike, a Honda Z50, when I was just five years old, and I have almost always had a motorbike in my life ever since.

Now the motorbike *was* my life.

### GIBRALTAR

We sped over the crest of a hill and there it was: the rock of Gibraltar. Soaring skywards from the Mediterranean Sea, Gibraltar is a municipality squeezed between Spain and Africa that's controlled by the British and is a strategic base for British armed forces and navy. In this incongruous slice of England, complete with red telephone boxes and fluttering Union Jacks, I ordered a surf 'n' turf (seafood and steak), a real treat on what we assumed was our last night in Europe. The frontier of Africa beckoned us from across the strait. I was excited and nervous but not really sure how I should feel. I'd never done this before, of course, but I felt prepared — at least as much as I could be.

Amy didn't share my excitement about visiting Quick Fit and replacing the tyres on our trusty steeds. We parked our bikes along the street so I could take the wheels off myself, hoping to save some time and therefore cost at the motorbike shop. I also wanted to check the bikes one final time before catching the ferry to Africa tomorrow.

But I quickly discovered a broken fork seal on my bike. Oil was leaking badly, and the fork seal was one spare part I had not brought along. I was carrying spare wheel bearings, levers, cables, filters and even spokes, but no freaking fork seal.

## SPAIN — AGAIN

So, with nice new tyres but a stuffed fork seal, we had to head back into Spain. In Algeciras, we found a bike mechanic, Antonio, who could help, but it was 2pm — siesta time, of course — so we had to return at 4pm. It was Friday, and I started to realise this problem was not going to be fixed any time soon, so we were not going to Africa today or any time over the next two days because everything would be shut over the weekend. Disappointed with another day lost, we could see Africa from across the water but were no closer to getting there.

With the help of Antonio's mate, Frank — who knew a little English and took us to an authentic Spanish bar for some superb local cuisine — we drove all over Algeciras in search of the required fork seals. Eventually, we realised none were available, so the only option was to order them. They wouldn't arrive until Tuesday, so another four days would be lost. We agreed to meet Antonio again on Tuesday at 4pm — after his siesta, of course.

There was nothing to do but wait. Algeciras is an ugly port town from where the ferry leaves for Morocco and not a place to hang around. Frank recommended that we head 20 kilometres along the coast to a little place called Tarifa at the southernmost tip of Spain. We found a great camp ground only 50 metres from the beach and met a Dutch couple, Marcel and Monique, and their dog Woody, a beautiful Husky cross that Amy fell in love with on the spot. During those four days, the beer flowed and the muscles relaxed. The enforced stop was just what we needed; we went swimming in the Mediterranean during perfect weather, read books and played chess. Yet the sight of the African coastline only 14 kilometres away was so tantalisingly close.

The bike was fixed — after siesta, of course — for a small fortune. The front suspension felt different due to the overhaul, but I hoped I'd get used to it.

I'd grown to love Spain and was again getting anxious about what to expect across the Strait of Gibraltar. At the camping ground in Tarifa, we'd met two guys and a girl from France who planned to travel like us to Ouagadougou (the capital of Burkina Faso in Central Africa) — but on Vespa 125cc scooters. I figured that if they could do it on scooters, we could on The Mothership and The Baja.

300miles
500kms
Day 20
Ceuta
Fes
Morocco
North Atlantic
Tan Tan
Western Sahara
Algeria
Libya
Atar
Nouakchott
Mauritania
Mali
Timbuktu
Niger
Chad
Dakar
Senegal
The Gambia
Bamako
Burkina Faso
Day 158
Guinea-Bissau
Guinea
Abuja
Benin
Ghana
Ivory Coast
Nigeria
Sierra Leone
Liberia
Lagos
Togo
Cameroon
Central African Republic

CHAPTER 2

# Northern & Western Africa

*Morocco to Nigeria: 139 Days*

I was nervous, and it was a very strange feeling. This was it: Africa. Everything I'd planned for. I'd departed Spain and left the security of Europe behind. I'd dreamed for years about the day when I'd roll my bike off the ferry and head into the Dark Continent. As I sat at the back of the ferry and saw Tarifa, where we'd camped for the previous four days, and the rock of Gibraltar soaring into the blue sky, I realised Africa would soon fill my horizon.

**MOROCCO**

In fact, I didn't have much time for reflection; the journey from the European coast to the African shoreline only took 35 minutes, and we didn't actually arrive in Africa at all, but the Spanish enclave of Ceuta.

Getting into Morocco proper was the first of *many* long, tedious border crossings across Africa. Two officially-dressed men waved for us to park in a particular spot. They were 'official touts' who would help out with everything, such as getting forms signed and stamped, and show us where to go. As Muslims, they typically gestured for me to work with them while Amy looked after the bikes. We strode from office to office to get our visas and a green card that covered insurance for our bikes while in Morocco. After an hour of people yelling and cars tooting, we made it into the country — and Africa.

Immediately, everything was different to Europe, from the mountainous but treeless landscape to the people — and, of course, the toilets (squat-style and bring-your-own toilet roll). Our first night on African soil was at Chefchaouen, about 100 kilometres south of Ceuta. On the way, plenty of kids waved, but they hadn't yet thrown any stones (a habit I'd heard the Moroccan kids enjoyed). Everyone else just stared at us, while young men tried selling hashish, which grows in nearby fields along the Rif Mountains. Not surprisingly, the camping ground that night was full of pot-smoking hippies.

This was where we first meet Olly Vine, a locations manager from London who'd ridden his motorbike alone across to Morocco on the spur of the moment with the full blessing of his understanding wife. Olly liked to travel in style, with all the gadgets, but also roughed it like Amy and I. He had an open-faced helmet with pilot-style glasses which gave him an increasingly redder face at the end of every day from the sun and wind. He was a really genuine guy who mixed in high circles (the famed singer Jamiroquai had bought him his CBF1000 Honda), but nothing had gone to his head.

Chefchaouen is a charming Berber town, where the tiny streets hug the rugged, arid mountainside and every house is brightly painted. But our first major stop was Fes, deemed to be the 'world capital of hashish'. About every 100 metres men aged from 15 to 50 stood alongside the road waving for us to stop — and if that didn't work, they whistled, begged and yelled, "Hashish! Hashish! Hashish!"

It wasn't long before the first stone was thrown at us. The kids waited until we'd ridden past before throwing the rocks, but luckily they missed. That was how they amused themselves, and there seemed little else to do in these dry and harsh mountains.

By Moroccan standards, Fes is a large city. The old *Medina*, or city centre, is a labyrinth of narrow alleys, a giant maze with all sorts of things for sale and all kinds of weird and wonderful smells (but often more weird and rotten than wonderful and appealing). There were shoe cleaners, tea traders and hashish sellers, of course, but the only thing Olly bought was a live chicken (for our dinner that night), which was killed, plucked and handed to him in a bag, still warm. Morocco was full of highs and lows: One minute I was enthralled by the exoticism of the Islamic architecture, aromas of the markets and sounds of the *muezzin* (call to prayer); the next, kids were throwing stones as I rode past.

The timing wasn't perfect, either; we travelled through Morocco during the holy month of Ramadan, so locals were fed up and tired from fasting. Food was hard to buy and even find during daylight hours, and eating or drinking in front of a Moroccan was very rude. Sadly, most Moroccans we met were unscrupulous and money-hungry, and occasionally they stole stuff, such as the handlebar padding from a mate's bike and a little gecko I'd stuck to my tank — nothing of value, but it was disappointing and annoying nonetheless.

Heading south (of course), we headed inland to an area supposedly renowned for its wild Barbary Apes, which seemed more like monkeys, but it was our first taste of African wildlife. This was when the first trouble with the bikes started. The Mothership coughed and spluttered, but cleaning the air filter didn't work, and riding along gravelly goat tracks didn't help either.

The next day, my bike got worse, so I replaced the spark plugs, but again, it was no better. We had no choice but to limp out to the main road and hopefully find another biker who could help. With enormous luck, we soon met Mike, who was riding a motorbike similar to mine and carrying a manual that covered my type, the Africa Twin. That night, as we camped together and with my bike in pieces, I discovered the problem: The choke plunger had rusted and was stuck on, so the bike ran as if the choke was always on.

Happy again, after fixing the problem we set off to where Morocco meets the Sahara at Erg Chebbi. We pulled up alongside the fantastic 200-metre-high sand dunes and rested while admiring what seemed like scenes from another planet. Again, we met up with Olly and several other bikers, including some Spanish guys on quad bikes, who let us ride their machines up and down the dunes, which was great fun.

It was about this time we both had our first stomach aches and attack of the runs. Amy suffered so much that she fainted. Luckily, we were staying somewhere nice (with acceptable and convenient toilets) and she recovered quickly. Soon, we were fit enough to continue with two Germans, Axel and Andy, on our first *piste* (French for 'track', which means going off-road). The scenery was absolutely amazing, but the roads were really tough. I was okay because I'd been riding for years, and Amy did an amazing job.

Houses in the villages across the rocky Atlas Mountains are made from mud. The children would sprint down the road, waving and giving us high fives or asking for money and sweets. The kids could be annoying at times, but at least they weren't throwing stones. And we had to remember that they had nothing to do, and we were creating vast amounts of dust riding past their homes.

By the end of that day, Andy had broken his gear lever and Amy had grazed her knee and broken her mirror. Olly had made it along the *piste* for one day by lashing a small metal camping table that acted as a bash plate to protect the exhaust pipes, but he was on a road bike and couldn't continue with us, so we bid Olly a fond farewell.

Now we were prepared for *real* desert trails: a variety of *pistes* covering over 1200 kilometres from Merzouga to Touganite. The *piste* from Tinghir to Alnif was an easy warm up. There were lots of rocks and a little sand, but we all got through okay, and Amy did very well. As we arrived in Alnif, the wind started blowing hard, and as we rode towards Merzouga, we headed straight into a sandstorm. I was worried about the air filters on the bikes, but we couldn't stop and we had no idea how long the storm would last. There was so much sand blowing across the road and into our mouths that when I licked my lips I felt like I was eating the desert (not dessert).

In Rissani, we loaded up with enough fuel, food and water for three days. I was nervous: I knew I could do it, but I was concerned about Amy and the remoteness of the area. We set off down the highway as the sandstorm continued. In the shanty town of Touaz, the locals simply waggled their fingers at us and said we wouldn't make it because our bikes were too heavy. We weren't deterred.

But perhaps we should've listened to their warnings. Within a few kilometres, we took a wrong turn in the eye of the sandstorm and ended up in a river bed, thankfully dry like those in central Australia, but also several kilometres wide. The sand was so deep that Amy fell off. We were forced to let out air from our tyres so we could head for higher ground. The *piste* was exceptionally tough, and wrestling my fully-loaded 250-kilogram bike was exhausting. According to the GPS, the correct track was less than one kilometre away, but between us and the track was a mountain about 800 metres high. We followed a rocky track that ended at an abandoned mine, where we gave up and camped for the night.

Most of Africa is highly populated, so it was a challenge each evening to find a campsite in the wild that would not be found by locals gathering wood, looking for water or just walking around. We would normally pull up about an hour before sunset and pitch the tent together. I'd check over both bikes, oiling the chains while they were still hot and checking all the nuts and bolts, while Amy would start preparing our evening meal. Other chores included washing plates and ourselves, if possible, and collecting water through our purifier if we were near a river or well. After dark, there was no option but to retreat to the tent, where I'd often write in my diary with a head lamp on. But often crowds would gather before the sun set, and every single thing we did would be watched and discussed among the onlookers.

The next morning, when the storm had receded, we noticed that Touaz — where we'd started the day before — was only about 1 kilometre away. Andy, who was a doctor (and a useful companion), decided not to continue and returned to Touaz because he'd damaged his ribs during a previous fall, but Axel wanted to go on.

We did eventually find the correct track, but locals warned us again about the conditions ahead. Once more Amy, Axel and I ignored them, and once more we fell off our bikes — this time all of us in the dry Oued Rheris riverbed. I wouldn't have been able to pick up my bike again without the help of some local kids who were following us with great delight and some Spanish guys in a 4WD vehicle who happened to be right where I fell off.

We continued to wrestle our bikes through the impossible sand for another 30 minutes, and Amy and Axel dropped their bikes but we'd only progressed about 500 metres. We accepted the inevitable and asked a young boy to lead us out of this hell. He was floating on top of the soft sand beside us on a *peddlo* (a locally-made, half-motorcycle half-bicycle that could go anywhere).

We followed him, zigzagging our way across the sand, alongside the riverbeds and up and down the steep banks before he stopped and pointed in the direction of the track. Again, the sandstorm was blowing steadily, and again the GPS indicated that the track was only 300 metres away, but once more what stood in the way were impassable sand dunes. But we were stubborn, and after getting bogged again and again and *again*, we navigated the dunes and sandstorm and found a decent place to pitch our tents.

The following day, we managed the final 70 kilometres of the *piste* to Tougnite, which was comparatively easily despite the intense wind. Doing this *piste* was one of the most amazing things I'd ever achieved, and I loved travelling with the great team of Amy and Axel.

But we weren't finished with these desert trails quite yet. Once more, the locals warned us that our bikes were too heavy and that there was too much sand. Needless to say, we ignored them. This *piste* was shorter ('only' 148 kilometres) and the sand more compact. At one stage, we breezed across a 10 kilometre-long clay pan at about 100 kilometres per hour compared to the normal 20-30 kilometres per hour for the past few days. It was as hot as hell when the wind died down, but that did mean there would be no dust or sand (which had already damaged our camera). Later, the GPS indicated that at one point we had drifted about 1 kilometre across the unmarked border into Algeria.

There were scary sections made of rock, but we arrived at Forum Ziguid unscathed with another amazing adventure under our belts. We said farewell to Axel and Andy (who had ridden the previous few days the long way around on sealed roads). Not soon after, we met up with an Italian couple, Carl and Sylvia, who were driving a Land Cruiser. We decided to head off together to Ourzaratte.

After a refreshing swim at a waterfall that some local kids showed us, we camped at another spot, where I suffered my first (but not last) bout of fever. I woke up freezing and, despite being fully dressed and with both my and Amy's sleeping bags wrapped around me, I shook uncontrollably for about two hours. Eventually, I fell asleep but awoke again an hour later, boiling hot. The fever soon passed, but the runs did not.

Despite my gastric problems, I was up for another *piste* called The Mill. It was only 70 kilometres long and featured an amazing gorge with very steep walls and thousands of date palms below. The air was far cooler, and there were so many sounds of birds. Along a particularly steep ascent, Amy's bike lost power and stalled; then it started spluttering black smoke. It seemed to clear itself, however, and The Baja climbed the pass and onto the plateau. Then I got a flat tyre — my first of many, *many* more.

Somehow, it felt more civilised along the coast, and we even found a modern supermarket in Tiznit, although we stayed further south at Sidi Ifni. This was the sort of place where we liked — and needed — to rest sometimes. We ate well and relaxed, and I repaired the bikes and updated my blog, which my friends and family seemed to enjoy reading.

I was so glad Amy was with me. I wasn't sure what it would be like travelling on my own. No doubt very lonely — a feeling I'd have to get used to because Amy planned to go home to Australia when we reached South Africa.

Our next stop was Tan Tan, the gateway to the Western Sahara. The *piste* started well but quickly turned bad. We stopped to admire the shipwreck of *The Zahra* and went swimming along a beach all to ourselves. We tried riding along the beach, but again my anger erupted as I had to wrestle The Mothership between car ruts, and we couldn't stop in case we got bogged. Eventually, we made it out, found a road, and decided never to ride along any beach ever again. Beaches, however, are ideal places to pitch a tent (and the sea is perfect for washing ourselves), and we found a wonderful resting spot past an abandoned fort and overlooking another shipwreck.

Sleeping under the stars can be problematic at times, especially when the wind starts blowing. Sand blanketed our hair, got into our eyes and sleeping bags, and then hid the track we needed to find the next day. With still another 50 kilometres to Tan Tan and using my reserve tank of fuel, we followed the most direct route according to the GPS, but there was so much sand at one stage that I could only see about one metre in front of me — and I couldn't see Amy anywhere.

Now she was down to her reserve tank too. We thought she could reach Tan Tan, buy fuel for me and come back, but it would be too easy to become lost in these conditions. Ensuring maximum fuel efficiency by being easy on the throttle, we got to within nine kilometres of Tan Tan. Then we got within six. Soon, the GPS indicated it was only four kilometres away; then three. Suddenly, we joined a lovely bitumen road and made it to Tan Tan with about one-quarter of a litre of fuel remaining in my tank.

We met up again with Carl and Sylvia. The rain came bucketing down, which was a welcome relief from the dust and sand.

### WESTERN SAHARA

The next day, after fixing another flat tyre, we travelled with a German couple we'd met at the camping ground, Natasha and Chris, who were heading to Dakar (in Senegal) on their F650 BMWs. The long, boring roads that lead about 1000 kilometres towards

Mauritania start in a region called the Western Sahara, which is claimed by Morocco despite condemnation from some countries and independence activities from some locals. This meant frequent checkpoints along the highway, sometimes only 5 kilometres apart.

At one checkpoint, I was told to enter a hut and sit on a bench next to three fat policemen, who again asked the usual questions about my occupation, destination and motorbike type. I soon got sick of all these questions and said, *"Oui"* when asked if I was part of the Paris to Dakar car/motorbike rally. It worked: The questions stopped, and they waved us through. (The silly buggers didn't know the rally wouldn't be held for another few months.)

A few days later, I printed out logos of the Paris to Dakar Rally at an Internet centre and stuck them to the front of our bikes. I showed these pictures to the police at each checkpoint, and they continued to wave us through. We were never asked any more stupid questions.

The coastal road is spectacular, with cliffs reminiscent of the Great Australian Bight, as well as superb beaches and occasional shipwrecks. The traffic included wild camels and Arabs seemingly walking in the middle of nowhere. The weather was perfect — sunny, with cool air for the bikes — but one night we were woken by torrential rain while camping on the edge of the Sahara Desert. My amazement, however, was tempered by another flat tyre the next morning. Natasha took a fall and hurt her knee while pulling off the road, making Amy (and I) realise how much better Amy had become at riding. Amy now rode with remarkable confidence.

As we approached the border with Mauritania at Dakhla, we noticed a lot more soldiers and UN vehicles. (This border was particularly touchy.) I gave our bikes another complete once-over, which I enjoy doing. My bike was my life-line and the better I treated it, the more likely it would get me to South Africa and beyond. My father loved packing the family Land Cruiser for camping trips when I was growing up, and like Dad, I'd have a place for everything in my panniers.

While stopping along the road to admire the ocean views, we were approached by Blair (who was from New Zealand) and his German girlfriend, Kati, who'd met Carl and Sylvia a few days before and had therefore known about Amy and me. They were looking for people to accompany them on a *piste* in Mauritania, but it was 540 kilometres long and impossible without a support vehicle carrying extra fuel. Luckily, they were travelling in a Mitsubishi Triton dual cab diesel utility vehicle.

## MAURITANIA

The few kilometres of no-man's-land between Western Sahara and Mauritania is completely empty, and for good reason: It used to be riddled with landmines. Although most have been removed, some still remain, so we picked our routes cautiously between the two borders and carefully followed the best of the many car tracks. We were told that vehicles which had strayed slightly off the path had been blown up, and only a few months later we heard about two French people in an overland truck being killed by a landmine at this border crossing.

We waited three hours to cross the border at Fort Gaugarat, but like everyone else in the line of cars and trucks, we weren't sure why. We had to endure four checkpoints: one to get out of Western Sahara, another for a Mauritanian visa, one more to acquire insurance for our motorbikes, and the last to finally enter Mauritania. While waiting, we witnessed the extraordinary sight of a two-kilometre-long coal train passing by with a single camel on a wagon.

Mauritania is the start of 'Black Africa', and although most of the people there are still Muslims, their skin is far darker than the people of Morocco and Western Sahara. Our first stop was the chaotic border town of Nouadibou (pronounced *noo-adi-boo*), where the streets were filled with cars, dust and more goats than people. I felt we'd reached another part of Africa, and I loved it.

We decided to go on that *piste* with Blair and Kati as far as Atar — despite the sign at the beginning of the track that greeted us with 'Danger de Mort' (French for 'Danger of Death') in reference to the land mines. The first 60 kilometres were along a highway until we turned east and followed a train line for 430 kilometres before turning toward Choum (430 kilometres). The *piste* heading back into the Sahara was really long and very sandy, and we couldn't have done it without Blair and Kati carrying extra fuel for us.

After less than 100 kilometres of the 540-kilometre trip, The Baja wouldn't start, and due to a persistent afternoon sandstorm, we decided to camp. The following morning, I panicked when I found some damage: A bracket where the seat was bolted at the back and the soft pannier bracket were broken. With some steel putty, Blair and I temporarily fixed the brackets but then found that The Baja's carburettor was full of grit.

At this point, a couple of 4WDs with some elderly French couples pulled up to check if we were okay. I asked if they had a stocking and *voila*, one of the nice old ladies produced one, which I used as a makeshift air filter for the carburettor breather. The Baja was back in action, but it was now about 40 degrees Celsius, so we stopped at a village to douse ourselves with water from a well.

We slept that night without the tent on a dune with the moon so bright I could almost read a book; this was followed, as usual, by another magnificent sunrise. The next morning was the same routine: We'd get up early, often at or even before sunrise because the day was already starting to get very hot and I didn't fancy lying on my thin mattress any longer than necessary.

Breakfast often consisted of bread and cheese, but soon I'd get addicted to Quaker oats in the future mixed with powdered milk and plenty of sugar, so I'd have to start up the tiny Coleman stove. We were usually up, packed up and gone within 30 to 40 minutes, often with a larger crowd of onlookers than the evening before.

The *piste* to Choum, which we shared with wild camels and their calves and camels herded by nomadic tribesmen, was flat with some sandy bits but reasonably good, although I got another flat tyre not long before Blair and Kati got bogged. We all helped each other with the digging and pushing — another reason to do these sorts of trips with plenty of company.

We passed Ben Amera, the second largest monolith in the world (after Uluru/Ayers Rock in Australia), but disappointingly it was just a rock, albeit a very large one, sticking out of the ground. This section of the *piste* ran directly alongside the border between Western Sahara and Mauritania, so it had been plagued for decades by war. I saw what looked like the end of a mortar sticking out of the desert, but upon closer inspection the mortar was spent — just another used weapon from a conflict long gone.

The sand dunes we had to traverse never seemed to end. With the train line to our left, but also following the GPS, we often made our own tracks, and sometimes the sand was so deep and soft that The Mothership would sink fast. I would go down a gear and screw the throttle, and the deep V-Twin engine thumped harder, but once I was stuck completely. Luckily, the others could help push me out; it would've been impossible on my own. Amy had the same problem with the deep soft sand and was thrown over the handlebars. But she just got up, picked up her bike, and soldiered on.

We used up the fuel in our tanks and had to use the reserve supplies carried in Blair and Kati's vehicle. We eventually reached Choum and then headed south (our normal direction) to Atar. The corrugations were very bad, and I was travelling fast. That fateful combination ensured that I skated all over the road and at one point right to the edge, where the bike dug into the ground and my right pannier hit a rock and dented the corner. Eventually, we climbed high onto a plateau and soaked up the final 20 kilometres along the glorious tarmac.

After four days, we had made it to Atar. We enjoyed the comfortable chairs and hot showers in the camping ground as well as the strange Mauritanian music fading in and out from the town centre and a meal of camel steaks.

Traveling along a *piste* can seriously damage a bike: On Amy's, we had to replace the mirror and weld the lugs holding the seat and pannier bracket. I also straightened out my pannier after hitting the rock the day before and put some sealant on it to make it waterproof again. The repairs took two days, but the bikes — and their riders — needed the rest.

While Blair and Kati went onward to Nouakchott, the Mauritanian capital, Amy and I headed further into the desert along yet another *piste*. It was short and beautiful but the hardest yet, with impossibly steep passes. At one stage, the road basically disappeared and headed straight up a steep section of mountain called the Amougha Pass. It was almost impossible to determine the route of the *piste*; it seemed to be just one huge boulder after another. I couldn't believe that my huge Africa Twin could traverse the boulders. I'd never ridden over anything that difficult.

Another time, my bike and I were thrown up into the air and landed onto the other side of the track. After picking up the bike, I accessed the damage: mostly a dented bash plate (which protects the bottom of the engine and frame from damage). Amy did a superb job getting The Baja through the *piste* too and only dropped it once. As we reached the top, exhausted, I decided I was beginning to tire of off-road tracks.

Not long after, I seemed run down, perhaps from not eating properly, and I developed cold sores along my top lip. I could hardly talk. We stopped at Chinguetti, the seventh holiest Islamic place in the world, and visited one of the 12 ancient libraries. That night we stayed at what could be called an oasis, but added to the pain of my cold sores was an invasion of ants in our food supplies.

The road to the capital, Nouakchott (pronounced *noo-ak-shot*), was long and straight, but there was enough to keep it interesting, particularly the numerous donkeys, camels and goats we had to avoid hitting. Although a decent highway, it was in the middle of nowhere surrounded by sand dunes and affected by strong cross winds. By now, our supplies of petrol (and local currency) were dangerously low. Amy ran out of fuel, so I tipped in two litres from the five-litre jerry can in my pannier. Then I ran out of fuel.

I switched to my reserve tank, and we both ducked to reduce wind resistance and therefore fuel consumption. With about 70 kilometres to go, I put two more litres in my tank from the jerry can and another one in Amy's bike. This was all the fuel we had left. About 30 kilometres from the capital, I had to tow Amy until I ran out about 10 kilometres later. With about one litre between us after rocking and tilting the tanks, we got to within two kilometres of the Auberge Sahara, where we planned to stay. We eventually found a petrol station but only had enough *ouguiya* (the local currency) to buy less than one-third of a litre.

The bike insurance we bought at the border with Western Sahara expired on the day we applied for visas to the next country at the Senegalese Embassy in Nouakchott. We went all the way to the Mauritanian capital for these visas, hoping to receive them the next day. But our hopes were dashed; we had to wait until Monday morning, and it was only Thursday.

We went back to the Senegalese Embassy to confirm the exact time and cost (which we weren't sure of because of the language barrier), but this was a mistake: the price was correct, but the time for collection was 4pm on Monday. We were clearly unused to this visa run-around, and we weren't even sure if we were going to receive a multi-entry visa allowing us to enter the sliver of Gambia, which is surrounded by Senegal.

So what to do for a long weekend in Nouakchott? We relaxed by swimming and playing chess as well as preparing the bikes and ourselves for the trip ahead. We also received some free language lessons from a French couple who had no language barriers in Francophone Africa and met some truly crazy people riding *pushbikes* from Paris to Dakar (Senegal).

We also went to a concert at the Olympic Stadium, where thousands of locals enjoyed some infectious music despite baton-wielding riot police hitting anyone who stormed the barrier. It seemed incongruous that there was such a distinct lack of structure and rules in the country, yet when the public stepped out of line they'd be beaten. Despite this, I loved this part of the world and felt that I'd like to work or live in Africa for a while.

But the paperwork would drive me mad. We went to the Senegal Embassy on the Monday after packing up our bikes, but the official told us to return at 5pm. At the appointed time, we entered his office, which had little more than a desk and ceiling fan. We handed over 3000 *ouguiya* (about 5€) each and watched as he painstakingly glued the multi-entry visa stamps into our passports. We were anxious to leave before dark but unwilling to hurry him up.

As we approached the Senegalese border the next day, the deserts of Mauritania disappeared and the landscape became greener and trees lined both sides of the road. By now, there were so many camels, donkeys and goats all over the road that we often only just avoided colliding with them.

Then the inevitable happened.

Only 20 kilometres before the border, we were asked at the final checkpoint about our bike insurance. I pretended not to understand and tried stalling in case he would forget about it. *What was I thinking?* He continued to ask for our insurance, and he had our passports, so I lied.

This was another mistake. "Ah. Yes insurance," I said. "We have."

I pretended to search anxiously for documents 'proving' valid insurance we didn't have. I 'searched' for about 10 minutes hoping he would give up, but no such luck. I even tried getting a pen to change the date on the insurance documents, but that wouldn't work either. Eventually, I gave up and handed him the out-of-date papers.

As he told us the obvious, we played dumb (again) and expressed amazement at the papers which were clearly 'wrong'.

"I know it says 10 days," I exclaimed, "but we paid for 20 days!"

He told us to ride back to Nouadibou, the main town on the border between Western Sahara and Mauritania, and buy more insurance, but this was not an option because the town was 700 kilometres in the opposite direction. Worse, we had very little Mauritanian money left and even less fuel — and there were no petrol stations from where we'd just arrived. We explained our predicament and pleaded. Soon, we realised there was an obvious alternative.

"You pay me 10 Euros each, and I close my eyes," he said.

In case we didn't understand, the customs officer placed his hands over his eyes. We quickly agreed, paid, and hurriedly got on our bikes, but his colleague had other ideas. This resulted in an argument between the two officers, but we eventually got our passports back for 10 Euros each and sped off hurriedly.

We'd been warned to avoid the border crossing at Rosso and quickly understood why as we were swarmed by touts while buying fuel. Assuming we planned to cross at Rosso, police asked to see our passports, drivers licences and registration papers, while everyone else claimed the alternative border at Diama was closed.

We assumed they'd said this so we would cross at Rosso and get fleeced by the corrupt officials there, so I was firm. "No Rosso. No Rosso," I said. "We go to Diama. Diama."

The officers understood, handed back our documents and gestured for us to go. Thankfully, we weren't asked about our insurance (or lack thereof). We followed the Senegal River along a dirt track through flood plains choked with birdlife such as pink flamingos and detoured around a dead warthog with massive tusks in the middle of the road.

After about 80 kilometres, we arrived at the Mauritanian border of Diama, which was *not* closed. We paid the normal custom duties for the bikes and showed them our passports, but we refused to pay another 10 Euros each for unspecified 'stamps' to leave Mauritania. Instead, they begrudgingly accepted our remaining 800 *ouguiya* (less than 3€).

Across the bridge at the Senegal border post there were more hassles and more rip-offs. But what could we do? We were charged 15 Euros just to cross the bridge and another 10 to get our *carnet de passages* stamped; surprisingly, this was the first time we needed to show those documents.

(A *carnet* is basically a 'passport' for motorbikes. Owners must put up money or pay an insurance premium in the country of registration — in our case, the UK — to stop them from riding into the country and selling the bikes. It was always essential to get the *carnet* stamped in and out of each country to prove you'd taken the bike out. It was a headache, of course, but some countries flatly refused entry without one.)

All we needed now was a stamp on our Senegalese visa, but the sign on the Immigration hut explained that it was closed for lunch and wouldn't be open for another two hours. We felt better while chatting to some French people who'd been waiting all day due to some complicated Customs problems with their vehicles.

**SENEGAL**

We relaxed for a few days at a camping ground called the Zebra Bar about 15 kilometres south of Saint Louis, the first major stop inside Senegal. Already at this shady hangout were those crazy cyclists doing the mock Paris to Dakar Rally on their bicycles as well as some Germans on a charity drive. We loved the chance to unwind at these sorts of places, where we could swim, read books, check our bikes, swim again, double-check our bikes, eat well and splurge on the occasional beers.

It was also at places like the Zebra Bar that we'd meet some amazing people, such as an English couple our age (James and Katrina) planning to write a guidebook to Sierra Leone, which had been in the throes of a civil war for a long time; and in contrast, a retired German couple, who taught Amy and me how to wind surf. We also met an English guy, Frazer, on a BMW 650 Dakar, who was one of those people I believe I met for a reason. Before becoming a pilot for Virgin Atlantic, he flew helicopters, which is what I want to do — correction: what I am *going* to do. I asked him so many questions and, for the first time, he was someone who gave me positive ideas and encouraging information about having a career as a chopper pilot.

Soon word got out that many crazy foreigners were at the camping ground, so half the people from the nearby villages (or so it seemed) turned up to watch us, especially the children, who seemed endlessly fascinated by simple things such as my writing in my diary. We were even invited by a teenage boy into a local home one evening for a meal. Sitting on a woven mat in a circle on the floor of a mud hut, the family, Amy, and I ate crushed maize and a sort of salty fish with our hands. The language barrier was difficult, but we smiled a lot and used what little French we knew.

We travelled with Frazer towards the capital, Dakar, where we hoped to get visas for Mali and Cameroon. On the way, we were stopped at a checkpoint because we hadn't used our indicators when the cop told us to pull over, and for that heinous crime he wanted 2000 CFA Francs (about 3€) from each of us. We tried reasoning with him, but these sorts of people are completely unreasonable and totally corrupt. And they had the 'upper hand': our passports.

But I'd had enough. I'd spent six years in the Australian Air Force as an avionic engineer before training to become a commercial diver. Fortunately, I still carried (although I shouldn't have) my defence passport with the magic words 'Official Passport' printed on the front. I showed this other passport to the checkpoint official, who immediately smiled and waved us through.

Lac (Lake) Rose was the finishing point for the famous Paris to Dakar Rally (before it was moved to South America because of threats against cars crossing West Africa). This seemed as good a reason as any to try another *piste*. Although only 16 kilometres, it was all sand, so Frazer turned around and took the easier option along the highway. But Amy and I wouldn't give up that easily. At one stage, my bike dug in and turned sharply. I put my foot down to hold the bike up and it dug further into the sand. My foot jammed between the pannier and ground and twisted, causing me great pain.

We passed several villages where kids ran away from us in terror while elders looked at us with amazement. Amy soon became weak from falling off her bike and having to pull it back up so often, and I felt helpless; I couldn't get off my bike because of the sand, and my ankle was now swelling up inside my boot. When we eventually reached the highway, we decided not to do another *piste* — except when really necessary. The exhausting day ended at a camping ground at a resort with a swimming pool and a view of the sand dunes and Lac Rose.

The congested road into Dakar was full of obstacles, particularly people, goats, buses, and worst of all, massive speed humps. We only needed to go to the Senegal capital to get onward visas, which invariably involved the laborious process of finding the embassy, filling out the paperwork and explaining what we wanted and why we were travelling on motorbikes — all with the usual language barrier. Additionally, visas are often ridiculously expensive and eat into our budget: for example, a visa to Cameroon cost us 50,000 CFA each (75€).

Our excitement about getting a Cameroon visa here (avoiding the horrors of getting one in Lagos, the appalling former capital of Nigeria) and picking it up within 24 hours was soured when we realised our hotel was really a brothel — and a busy one. Getting a visa at the Malian Embassy involved waiting from 10am to 2pm only to be told that the relevant embassy official was 'out' and then having to wait again for hours the next day. Our attempts to buy a new camera to replace the one damaged by dust, sand and ongoing problems with the electrics in The Baja didn't improve my mood either.

As we continued south, the landscape started to change; it was now greener, with huge Baobab trees everywhere, each with massive, cylindrical trunks and thick tapering branches. We rode from one village to another while everyone stared at us with astonishment, but unlike in Morocco and Mauritania, we didn't receive many waves (or, thankfully, stones).

**THE GAMBIA**

Gambia, which is often preceded with 'The', is a narrow slice of English-speaking colonial lunacy completely surrounded by French-speaking Senegal.

For a change, the border crossing was a breeze — no bribes and no hassles — or so we thought until we started to ride away and a man blew a whistle and yelled, "Stop! Stop!" He explained that it was 'National Clean-up Day' and no-one was allowed on the road for the next hour. I expressed some understandable astonishment, but some locals confirmed that it was true: The road was closed for one hour every month (at the exact time we planned to use it). Of course, once vehicles were allowed back on the road, the traffic was chaotic.

Across Gambia, the landscape was even greener, potholes deeper and activities more unusual: Ladies with huge buckets were trying to catch something with long poles which they used like crowbars to break up the ground, and men slashed and stacked high grass alongside the roads.

The ferry to Banjul, the capital, was our first taste of the madness that is African public transport. A truck scraped the side of my pannier, which prompted Amy to yell at the driver, but to no avail; in any case, everyone else on the ferry was yelling and screaming too.

I knew something was very wrong when I woke up in the middle of the night feeling really cold. My body was sore, and my joints started to ache. I'd experienced these symptoms before in Morocco, and they soon passed, so we decided to see if my fever would do the same. A few hours later, I started shivering and getting hot flushes. Amy was worried enough to find the night-watchman and ask about a hospital. He confirmed that there was one in the city centre but that no taxis would be available at 2am.

By daylight I was no better, so Amy organised a taxi and rushed me to the nearby medical clinic instead. There were syringes on the floor and rubbish everywhere, but I had to get medical attention quickly. They did a blood test by pricking my thumb and tested me for malaria, but the result was negative. Then I rushed towards the toilet with an extreme case of the runs. (Sadly, I didn't make it in time. No more details are required.)

The medical staff didn't know what was wrong, but they decided to treat me for malaria anyway. They told Amy to buy me a Fanta, which — given the number of people in the waiting room holding the orange drink — seemed to be the prescribed medicine for every ailment, including whatever I had. I did get some pills for the diarrhoea, but after an hour or so my fever hadn't subsided.

I still felt like hell, so they injected something else into my backside and gave me more pills. (Luckily, we had brought our own first aid kit and could use sterile syringes and needles.) Things got *really* bad when I started vomiting uncontrollably. Surrounded by babies and mothers in more pain than me, I soon realised I was in the maternity ward. It was time to get to the larger city hospital.

With the siren blaring, the ambulance (a trusty Land Cruiser troop carrier for which we only had to pay petrol) bounced along the road while I bounced out of my stretcher with Amy holding me down. The city hospital was larger, and it did at least have a qualified doctor, but the facilities still looked pretty grim. My confidence in a speedy recovery (or any sort of recovery) wasn't helped when I noticed the large number of coffins lined up outside. The nurses took more blood, tested me again for malaria, and came up with the same negative result. But again, they treated me for malaria anyway. And once more, I didn't improve. (They didn't suggest I drink a Fanta.)

They lay me down again and inserted a drip. For the next four hours, I lay there in pain but still didn't feel any better. There was nothing else they could do, so they sent me back to the camping ground in the ambulance to rest and eat. As I walked outside, I vomited violently again, but no one paid much attention. Amy was amazing; she cared for me and sat beside me the whole time as I could hardly function. I couldn't imagine how I would've survived without her.

I did feel a lot better after a long sleep and some food and water. I was still tired and sweating, but my body seemed to recover enough after two days for us to continue on our next quest: getting visas for Guinea Bissau and Guinea. (Yes, they are two different countries.) It took us two hours in the nearby town of Serrakunda to find the Guinean Embassy; even the taxi drivers didn't know the location.

Then it was off to buy some 'Brown Card Insurance' for our bikes; we didn't want to take any chances, especially after the drama in Mauritania. (Apparently, we needed 'Brown Card Insurance' because it included all the countries in the region, whereas the policy sold to us in Senegal was possibly okay for West Africa but no specific countries were listed on the document.)

Thankfully, everything just clicked. We collected our visas for Guinea on time and without hassles, bought a new camera online (far cheaper than buying one anywhere in West Africa), which would be couriered to us in Guinea, and picked up a spare tyre Frazer had left for me. After all the crap with my illness (which still hadn't been diagnosed), it was a relief when some things went smoothly.

**SENEGAL — AGAIN**

The road towards Senegal was disgraceful, with too many potholes, but again the border was pleasantly hassle-free. Crossing into Senegal meant better roads and people speaking French. (They speak English in Gambia.) The thin, southern section of the country, known as the Casamance region, is beautiful and green with enormous trees everywhere.

This region was colonised by the French and Portuguese, and influences from both cultures are still evident in the food, language and names. The area has also been a source of conflict for decades as many southern Senegalese seek independence from the north.

We headed down a track to Affiniam, where we stayed in a *pluvium*. This is a huge round building (shaped like a donut) with rooms all around, to which a whole village would retreat in times of danger (which usually meant war). Tourism had replaced terrorism, and the *pluvium* had been converted to a guesthouse (although it still looked more like a rundown jail). On the way to Ziguinchor along the southern border, we did see an army tank with soldiers and stopped at another police checkpoint, but nobody bothered us at either place.

The highway crossed the floodplains of the Casamance River, and at one stage the road had sunk so much from the weight of vehicles that streams regularly crossed it. In Ziguinchor we got some cash from the bank, loaded up on the sort of supplies we thought would soon be limited, bought more Artiquin tablets for my (undiagnosed) malaria and cannulas for IV drips, and tried (unsuccessfully) to contact the English couple (James and Katrina) to see if it was safe to visit Sierra Leone.

**GUINEA-BISSAU (GB)**
Again, the border crossing was uncomplicated, which was just as well because in GB they speak Portuguese. This was the first country we visited that had so obviously been affected by civil war. GB was only just recovering, and people would stare at us as if we were from another planet.

The police at our first stop, San Domingos, told us the road to Verala was bad, but we'd heard warnings like that before. The road was bearable, but the final 50 kilometres did take a few hours. Later, we knew what the police had meant: We came to a bridge where a truck had fallen off and the bridge had collapsed five months before. The river looked impassable and the bridge irreparable, but a man told us to wait. We were highly dubious until an ingenious alternative was quickly created.

The workers laid planks down for us to get across. Along the planks construction workers had laid out for us across the river, we pushed our unloaded bikes with their help. I had to sit on The Mothership, which weighed 250 kilograms, to maintain its balance while one man directed the front wheel and two more at the rear pushed and directed the back wheel. My heart was in my mouth at times. It was a huge relief when both bikes reached the other side and didn't join the truck still visible under the water.

The lovely place where we camped right above the beach on a cliff at Verala was ideal for more repairs. I tried to pull apart The Baja and fix the wiring so Amy's speedometer would work, but to no avail, so we just went swimming instead.

After again crossing the same river in the same way, but with more experience this time, we rode towards the capital, Bissau. It was a superb ride with almost the entire road to ourselves, infrequent checkpoints and flat tarmac.

After some incredible running around, which involved Internet searches, asking a local German couple and then an American, and a phone call from a hotel reception, we found the names and telephone number of some friends of friends. Cassandra (an Australian) and Steve (a Brit) took us out for a well-earned beer (or two) — certainly enough to get a hangover the next morning — and kindly let us stay with them. We felt secure with our bikes locked in their garage.

They are a great couple and shared some fascinating stories. Steve worked at a demolition range which involved the disposal of bombs left over from the Guinea Bissaus civil war from years gone by. We watched as he trained locals to stack the mortars, warheads and other bombs into huge ditches, place explosive charges around them, and cover everything with sandbags. We retreated while they set the detonator and wired the fuse. Even from the bunker one kilometre away, the sound of the explosion was loud enough to make Amy jump. Returning to the spot where the mortars and warheads had been detonated, we could see the mess, with sandbags and debris strewn across the ground and trees.

In contrast to other African cities, Bissau is quiet but more hectic at the harbour with its fishermen and market. With Steve and Cas, we splashed out on some pizza, tried Portuguese custard tarts and lapped up an ice cream. We also received some good news: James and Katrina said that Sierra Leone was safe (after years of war), so we decided to detour there.

As we continued south from Bissau and looked for somewhere to camp, we spotted a vulture attacking a carcass on the road. Nearby, two boys painted head to toe with a white powder and carrying what looked like a bowl of food were doing a song and dance. (From what I read later, they were probably going to an initiation ceremony where a 'boy' becomes a 'man'.)

Later, we came to a village and asked for somewhere to camp for the night. Within minutes, everyone from the village was watching us erect our tent; Amy counted 35 kids among the crowd. A lady in the background was chopping wood with her pancake boobs swinging in the breeze — such a typical African scene — while we sat around a campfire surrounded by dozens of kids who were amused by our tricks and noises. Luckily, they disappeared when we went to sleep.

We had pitched a tent in someone's backyard, so as expected, we woke early to the sounds of roosters crowing and chickens scratching. But there was another strange dull sound all around — *thump… thump…thump*. I peered out of the tent and saw ladies crushing maize using something like a huge mortar and pestle with the help of little girls. The women seemed to do all the food preparation, usually with babies strapped to their backs with a material that looked like a towel. Of course, when we got out of the tent and started packing, the crowd of onlookers returned.

One man beckoned a small child to fetch something, and the child returned a few minutes later with a shotgun. The man loaded the gun, pointed it at the tree — *ka-boom!* — and out fell a hawk. In fact, it was the first time Amy had seen a gun fired. We gave the kids some coloured dot stickers and one man a purple T-shirt that Steve had given us. They never actually asked for anything in return for letting us camp in their yard (which was a nice change). The kids came to say goodbye with dot stickers all over their heads and hands and ran beside us as we left the village.

**GUINEA**

Guinea-Bissau had left a really positive impression on us, and we were sorry to leave. Not once had anyone asked for or demanded anything — and that included border officials. We were unsure if Guinea would be the same, however, because we'd heard conflicting stories — mainly from citizens of neighbouring countries. (None of the people in West Africa seemed to like any other country.)

Throughout this part of Africa so far, the roads were still mostly dirt. People stared at us with amazement, and there seemed more cows on the road than cars. At creeks alongside the roads, women bashed clothes on rocks to wash them, kids jumped about, and men sat under trees doing very little. It was the dry season and *everything* seems covered in dust, including the trees, bikes and us.

The first stop was the quiet town of Kondara, where the streets seemed even more dirty, dusty and bumpy. The petrol station had run out of fuel, so we had to use the black market, but first we had to change enough CFA Francs into Guinea Francs. (Most of West Africa used a common currency called CFA, but some countries, such as Guinea, had their own currency.) We also changed money on the black market, which involved an arduous negotiation in a room choked with sacks of rice. I was anxious to get the money, buy fuel and leave, but we got a good rate thanks to Amy's persistence. With 200 Euros exchanged for 1.6 *million* Guinea Francs, my money belt bulged to a thickness that was difficult to hide.

With our black market cash, we had to buy some black market fuel. A man pointed to a teenage boy who gestured us to follow him on his mountain bike. The boy rode over a bump, dislodging his bike seat, so he just took off the seat and sat along the pole. (And I thought we travelled rough sometimes.)

The boy took us to a house where a man with a bandaged finger produced containers of fuel for which he charged about 30 per cent more than the normal rate. We had no other option but to accept his rate, so he siphoned 25 litres into our tanks. Shaking hands with us later, he smiled and revealed a golden tooth, so the black market fuel business was clearly profitable.

At a campsite south of Kiyama about 20 monkeys scurried into the trees, and we slept to other strange animal noises from the jungle nearby. In the middle of the night, I heard a familiar crackling and snapping sound like fire that was moving closer but then seemed to pass by and move on. The soot all over our tent the next morning proved me right. A fire had crept through the jungle during the night, but it was small and simply burned anything that was dry (which wasn't that much). We had camped in a clearing, so there was no real danger.

As we continued south, Amy had a few near misses along the dusty roads. On the Fouta Djalon Plateau, she fell off while turning a corner but was fine. Later, a car cut her off at a bend and only just missed her. (But worse was to come.)

At Doucki, a town that a friend had previously recommended, we were lucky to meet Hassan Ba, the owner of the main camping ground, which was really just a collection of mud huts. We stayed there for a few days, enjoying Hassan's hospitality and trying out local food such as 'fat cookies' (dough balls) which Hassan cooked for us. Each day we went for lovely walks. One was to Vultures Rock (named after the numerous inhabitants), which also boasted a waterfall and swimming hole, but we were a little more hesitant about walking to Hyena Rock. The rest of our time was spent clearing out all the dust that had accumulated in and around the bikes' engines.

We reluctantly left Doucki for Conakry, the capital, to organise visas for Mali and Sierra Leone and to (hopefully) collect our new camera. The road was bumpy and dusty, as usual, and often washed out, while rocks, cows, chickens, children and every other conceivable obstacle hindered our ride. But the countryside through the Fouta Djalon Mountains was superb. A huge snake slithered across the road (and we hoped it wouldn't go into the creek we later stopped at for a swim), and boys carried huge stacks of grass on their heads. Every one of them stopped like statues and stared at us, but when Amy slowed down to take photos of two boys, they fled into the bushes in terror, leaving their bundles in the middle of the road.

At a checkpoint just before Kindia, the police demanded money, but we steadfastly refused until they reluctantly waved us through. Nearer to Kindia, the road turned into tarmac *at last*. During the five minutes it took Amy to buy bread and tomatoes for dinner, about 100 people appeared from nowhere and crowded around me and the bikes. Amy had to literally push her way through the five-metre deep crowd to find me.

We often set up camp in the fading light of dusk and near thick, tall grass. At about midnight, we woke to a frightening noise that continued to get increasingly louder. Accompanying the noise was a massive, bright light beaming directly into our tent. For a moment, I was confused and couldn't work out what was heading towards us in the tent as the light grew frighteningly large. At the last moment, the light turned when it seemed only metres away. We hadn't realised that we'd camped right alongside a train track, and it felt like the train would go straight through our tent. During the night, another four trains roared past, so we packed up quickly and rode off at dawn. The ride was fantastic, with the bright-red sun rising across the cool, misty mountains.

Chaos returned as we reached the fringes of 'civilisation' at Conakry. As we weaved around and through the traffic, it became increasingly hot and oppressively humid. Suddenly I heard a bang, and Amy started tooting frantically behind me. I turned around to see her slowing down and grimacing. The Baja had stopped, so I pulled up alongside the road and ran back to her, with my bike still running. She was obviously in pain, and I could see that the pannier on the right side of her bike was at an unusual angle and the left pannier had disappeared.

"What happened?" I yelled.

"A car just hit me."

"Shit!"

"And I think I broke my ankle."

Amy was still sitting on her bike as cars sped past. A fat policeman arrived and helped lift her from the bike. I then noticed that a car that had stopped behind Amy had something jammed under the front. It was the missing pannier. I lifted Amy across a drain about a metre wide and a metre deep and lay her on the ground.

As usual, a crowd was now forming, and more police had arrived. Down the road about 20 metres, my bike was still running, so I ran back and switched it off, at the same time telling the fat but helpful policeman in panicky 'Frenglish' not to touch Amy.

Rushing back to help Amy, I saw a man dislodge the pannier from under his car with great force and throw it into the bushes. I loosened her laces, removed her shoe and sock, and immediately saw the bruising. It seemed her ankle wasn't broken, but there was severe swelling near her little toe, which also seemed to have turned black. Amy could move her toes, so we concluded nothing else was broken but it could still be fractured. (After a few days rest, the swelling subsided so there was no need to go to a hospital for X-rays.)

Another man (not the driver who hit Amy) approached us, carrying the pannier, which I hadn't had time to fetch from the bushes. More police soon arrived, and a crowd of about 50 had now surrounded us. The police asked questions of us and the witnesses about the accident, but no-one could provide any licence details about the car. It was a hit and run.

The pannier was a mess: The two straps that connected it to the seat were completely torn off, and there were holes in it from being dragged under the car. I loaded her panniers on to my bike, and we quickly left the scene. Thankfully, Amy wasn't seriously hurt and there was no serious damage to the bike, which she could still ride. She was amazingly tough.

Our impressions of Conakry did not improve. We found the Malian Embassy and dropped off our passports, for another visa and entered the Catholic mission where we hoped to stay. Amy's foot was still very painful, and by now my temper was beyond boiling point. When a policeman on a scooter pulled me over for some minor traffic infringement, I let him have it.

"Don't you fuck with me! I've had it with these crazy fucking drivers."

Dripping with sweat and covered in dust, I explained about Amy's accident. I took her panniers from my bike, threw them to the ground, and showed him the damage. He quickly realised that he'd met his match, so after a perfunctory glance at our documents, he sheepishly disappeared. (Of course, I'd conducted this curse-filled rant on the grounds of a church.)

At the mission, a priest called Jean Claude helped pack Amy's foot with ice and offered any assistance we needed. Under a huge tin shed in which about 30 people used old-fashioned trundle-style Singer sewing machines, I found someone to fix the pannier (which he did superbly) and sew the straps back on. Above the repair man, a snakeskin was dangling, and nearby an albino Guinean repaired someone's shoes. I sat watching them for an hour while reflecting on the day's events.

Amy's foot quickly improved, but our collective mood did not when we were charged US$100 each for a visa to Sierra Leone. Our detour to Sierra Leone also meant we had to visit the local Ministry of Interior and change our visa status to 'double-entry', allowing us to return to Guinea and then continue to Timbuktu in Mali.

The Ministry building was swarming with men in police and military uniforms, and many inspected our bikes; they didn't want to see any documents, just admire our machines. One beckoned us into a shed, which he opened to reveal a fleet of BMW R1200 road bikes used to escort the President and other VIPs. He revved one up, switched on the siren and delighted in showing off the bikes. By the amount of dust on them, however, the President didn't seem to get out much.

While waiting for our double-entry visas, we went to the 2nd of October Park (named after the date in 1958 marking independence from France). From the front row, we watched an amazing African drum dance troupe in rehearsal. The drummers dripped with sweat as they beat their drums by slamming down their hands on the pigskin. Their bodies were so lean, and their endurance was amazing. Apparently a famous African drummer was watching, and they wanted to show off their prowess. Whenever someone made a mistake, a lady in charge would yell out in disgust and make them repeat it again and again until they got it right.

## SIERRA LEONE

The border crossing on the Guinean side was smooth, but not so in Sierra Leone. The immigration officer asked all sorts of stupid questions but finally gave us the stamps we needed, and eventually someone from Customs turned up to sign our *carnet de passages*. It was dark by the time we finished, so we slowly rode down a dirt road and then along a worse track deep into the dense jungle. We set up our tent about three metres from the track and backed our bikes into the long grass for cover — and maybe for a quick get-away.

We were now in Sierra Leone, which was not that long ago regarded as one the most dangerous places on earth because of endless civil wars, and we just did not know what to expect. After all, the Australian Government had issued warnings on their website for people to defer all travel to Sierra Leone unless absolutely necessary and to avoid all border regions *at all costs*.

Unscathed, we quickly left the campsite before sunrise. At daybreak, we appreciated the beauty of the countryside with its abundance of palm trees, and to our surprise the road continually improved and became as good as any autobahn in Germany. Of course, the people still stared at us with incredulity as we approached the first town, Port Locko.

About 30 minutes from the capital, Freetown, we approached a checkpoint with great apprehension. Inside the straw-roofed hut, the policemen and other military personnel with SLR rifles asked us loads of questions — in English, the official language, so we couldn't feign any incomprehension. But they were just curious about our travels.

One of them dashed off and came back with *poyo*, the local palm wine, which they insisted we drink. I explained that we had to ride our motorbikes, but they still insisted we drink a pint of the lethal concoction. We sipped a little before they eventually let us go (but we would probably have to repeat it all over again when we returned to Guinea a few days later). From another checkpoint, some policemen escorted us into Freetown while taking great pride in making a path for us by clearing the road of people and cars.

Our first intention was to find James and Katrina, the two British journalists we'd met at the Zebra Bar in Senegal and who were writing a guidebook to the country, but they wouldn't be back in Freetown for a few more days. We quickly attracted a crowd of about 50 inquisitive locals, and I couldn't ignore their endless questions because we shared a common language. We found a hotel by the beach, which we thought might've been a brothel. This was confirmed during the night when we heard a woman crying outside our window and men hassling her. The red lights outside probably should have warned us, too.

Built high among hills, Freetown is dirty and packed with beggars often missing arms or legs that had been hacked off by rebels during the civil wars. But the people were friendly enough — certainly inquisitive with their excellent English — and we never felt unsafe. The beaches nearby were also appealing, but we decided to press on, particularly because we didn't like big African cities. We also wanted to catch up with Blair and Kati at Bamako in Mali, and we needed to allow ourselves enough time to visit Timbuktu, a major detour.

Frustratingly, there was *still* no sign of the camera I had bought online and hoped to have couriered to us in Freetown. (The camera never came. It was to be originally couriered to Conakry, but the seller on eBay had closed his account, so I also lost the £200 I'd paid for it. Later, I bought another camera online, which was sent to a friend in London, who forwarded it to Leo's girlfriend in Spain, who then bought it out with her to Africa.)

The peninsular road out of Freetown was rough for the first 30 kilometres but turned into another amazingly smooth ride. On the way, we passed three boys aged from about six to eight. One threw a rock but missed us by a mile. I'd had enough, so I slammed on the brakes, spun around and followed them as they scattered back to their houses. An elderly man asked what was happening, so I told him.

After discussions between elders in the local language, an old lady with pancake boobs down to her waist tore off a branch from a tree and stripped the leaves. The man grabbed the boy who'd thrown the rock while the woman started whipping the boy's legs. I wanted the boy to be taught a lesson, not flogged to death, so I asked them to stop. I explained to the old man and woman that we were visiting Sierra Leone and only wanted a positive experience, which did not include having rocks thrown at us. They understood and stopped flogging the boy, and we left among much shaking of hands.

Continuing inland towards Makeni, the road improved again and we passed some stunning mountainous jungle and stopped at a beach fringed with palms. But every time we stopped, about 50 people would appear from nowhere and swarm all around us, which could be quite daunting at times. We also passed through the same checkpoint from earlier, but we didn't need to drink any more palm wine.

The road from Makeni to Kabala disintegrated as we ploughed through water crossings, over makeshift bridges, around enormous potholes and over giant boulders. Again, we thought we'd found a great place to camp only to find out later that it wasn't; our tent and bikes were next to a well-used path, which meant plenty of guests watching us throughout the evening.

Our plans to leave the next day before dawn to avoid more onlookers were thwarted as they started arriving at 5am! The going was again slow as we rode through more thick jungle and stopped at more checkpoints, but the air was refreshingly cool. We finally reached the border with Guinea and got our passports stamped out, but we were then told by the immigration officer to return to Kabala (70 kilometres back) to get processed by Customs. We asked if the immigration officer would stamp and sign our *carnet de passages* instead.

But he couldn't, or wouldn't, which was understandable, so I had no choice but return to Kabala while Amy stayed at the border crossing. (It was pointless for both of us to go as we had to conserve fuel.) A soldier asked for a lift to the Customs post. I'd learnt that it was never wise to say "no" to anyone with a uniform and gun, although I did suggest nicely that he couldn't take with him the chicken he'd tucked under his arm. Our departure, of course, was a source of great amusement for the increasingly large crowd, which then focussed their attention on Amy as the soldier and I left.

The immigration officer had told me the Customs post was about 32 kilometres away. We continued along the rough road, passed our old campsite, rode through herds of cattle, and found the post after 70 kilometres. It then took less than five minutes to get the *carnet* signed and stamped before I started the two-hour ride back — albeit minus the soldier.

Along the way, the suspension was getting a real workout and some of the potholes made the bike shudder. Anxious to rush back to Amy, I rode too fast over a bridge and hit one of the many large, deep potholes on the other side. I bounced up and could immediately see that I was about to land in another pothole. All I could do was hang on to the bike and give it more throttle. I knew this was going to hurt — both me and the bike. The bottom of the Africa Twin struck the edge of the massive pothole and bounced across the row of potholes to the end.

Then I heard a noise from my bike — a new one. A bad sign. The rubber stop on the centre stand had smashed off, and the chain was now striking the metal stand as it rested higher than usual. I couldn't fix it then, so I continued back to Amy with the annoying sound of chain running over metal. Finally, after about four hours to get our *carnet* stamped, we could leave Sierra Leone.

## GUINEA — AGAIN

To reach Mali and Timbuktu, we had to go back into Guinea. Once more the immigration procedures were smooth, and once more the customs officer was absent, so we had to get the *carnet* stamped in Faranah, 40 kilometres further on. But to get there we need fuel. At a petrol station, the manager said there was none, but after we ate lunch he suddenly announced there was some fuel after all. The customs officer completed our paperwork and provided an escort further along to Dabola.

Later, we stopped at a village to refill our water bottles by using a well with a hand pump. This activity almost caused a stampede of kids looking on. Nearer to the border to Mali, we rounded a corner and came across some soldiers dragging trees onto the road to create a roadblock. We'd heard that sometimes 'soldiers' were simply thieves dressed in army clothes and holding guns to stop and rob people. I slowed down quickly so that Amy could come up beside me. While staring at one soldier aiming an AK-47 rifle at us, I told Amy to follow what I did, which involved gulping, smiling and shaking hands. They waved us through without any hassles.

## MALI

Crossing into Mali was painless, and we reached the capital, Bamako, by mid-afternoon. We were now heading north for the first time since leaving England. Staying in any capital city in Africa allows us to complete (or, at least, attempt) two important chores: repairing the bikes (in this case, Amy's pannier rails) and buying more visas for more countries (in this case, Burkina Faso and Nigeria). We also caught up with Blair and Kati, who were staying at the Austrian Consulate after selling their car to the Ambassador.

With some new biker friends, including Leo (from Spain) and Del (from England), we decided to replace our old tyres, which sounded easy but wasn't. Leo and Del pinched the tube when putting it in, so we had to patch it up again — and again and again for the next seven hours because they kept pinching the tube when putting it in the tyre. After all this fixing of flats and changing of tyres, one of my tyre levers went missing. Assuming, it'd been stolen, I offered a 'reward' of US$20 (a lot of money for Malians) to whomever could find it.

Many locals frantically searched for it, but the lever couldn't be found. The next morning I awoke to find that my tyre was flat again, which I fixed, and then I noticed a nail in Amy's rear tyre, which was another headache, especially with one of my tyre levers missing. In total, I repaired our tyres about a dozen times over two days. My hands were sore, and I was exhausted.

We always met such fascinating people. Leo was an architect riding from Spain to Cape Town who'd met and teamed up with Del in Morocco. I admired Leo: he knew nothing about motorbike mechanics and was undertaking his trip on an old BMW R8. He had a great sense of humour and was willing to learn about mechanics from all the time I spent fixing their bikes. He also spoke French, which was very useful in Francophone Africa. Del (Derrick) was 50 and still limped badly from having polio as a child. He'd sold a few shops he owned and operated and rode from New York to Tierra del Fuego, the southernmost tip of South America. Now it was across Africa, but he still hadn't learned how to ride his bike properly.

It was Christmas Eve, and we were still in Bamako but keen to head to Timbuktu with Leo and Del. Just out of Segou, the inevitable happened: Amy's back tyre went flat again. After fixing it, we had lunch, and then it deflated once more. These constant repairs and the heat were really killing me. I repaired the hole, and another patch failed. There were now too many patches on the tube, so Del offered to give us his new spare rear tube. We headed down a *piste*, where we camped alongside the Niger River. That afternoon, we went swimming and cooked fresh fish bought from a man in a *pirogue* (wooden dugout).

Christmas Day conjured up thoughts and images of home, of course, but it didn't start well. It should've taken about two hours to reach Djenne, but we were given bad directions at a village and went the wrong way. Along a narrow sandy track, Del fell off several times, and he seemed slower to get up each time. Constantly waiting for him was tedious.

When we did find the correct road and took a break under the shade of a huge tree, I circled the bikes to check them out. I noticed something sticking out of Del's new front tyre — it was my tyre lever! No wonder he was falling off, because of the huge imbalance in his front tyre. After laughing about this for a while, it dawned on us that we couldn't actually fix the problem. Luckily, a man passed by on his scooter, so we asked him to take Del's rim and tyre to the next town and get it fixed. While waiting, we enjoyed Christmas lunch: the usual combination of stale bread, tinned tuna and tomatoes from a market we'd passed earlier as well as water and dry biscuits.

Along the way to Djenne, we passed many villages with mosques made from mud. We entered one, which angered a local Muslim man, and took some great photos. Djenne boasts the largest mud-brick building in the world. This mosque, built in 1907, is the town's centrepiece and one of the most recognised landmarks in Africa.

Stopping at Djenne was also a chance to eat properly at a restaurant, enjoy a shower, and top up with supplies of food and petrol. But to find a campsite, we had to cross a river by ferry. My enjoyment of travelling with Del and Leo was tempered by a case of haemorrhoids — one of the worse afflictions possible for anyone travelling by motorbike across vast distances along rough roads.

The next morning, Boxing Day, Del checked his oil. The oil sight glass on his motor was a white-milky colour, which could mean only one thing: water in his engine. Not good at all. After some discussion, we decided to drain the oil/water mix onto the ground, refill it with what clean oil we had between us and change the oil at Mopti (about 40 kilometres away). This worked out okay, but we had to watch his temperature gauge very closely along the way.

For another 120 kilometres, we filled the engine with new oil but didn't put water in the radiator until the 'over temperature' light came on. Then we had to stop, fill the radiator with water and ride (perhaps another 30 kilometres) until all of the water had drained into the engine. And then we had to repeat the process until we reached Douetide. That night I pulled the head off Del's KTM and, as suspected, the water pump seal had failed. Del would have to organise spare parts and wait for them to come from Europe.

So, Amy, Leo and I headed to our prime destination — Timbuktu. For some reason, the name Timbuktu — a city with a lengthy history as a trading outpost linking West Africa with Arab and even Jewish traders — filled us with excitement, but not so the corrugated road which shook us and the bikes uncontrollably. We were now back in the desert after weeks along the coastal regions of West Africa, and it was hot and dry, but there wasn't as much sand as I'd imagined. We made it to the Niger River, which was green and cool, and waited for the ferry. The final 15 kilometres turned into a highway as we approached the legendary town.

Many homes in Timbuktu are made from mud-brick, while others are Berber-style tents. Brightly-dressed Tuaregs in indigo veils, named the 'Blue Men of the Sahara', lead their camels along the sandy streets, but the town is also poor, with raw sewage flowing down some alleys. (I never saw any flushing toilets or plumbing.)

We looked up friends of Blair and Kati's — some South African pilots — and one of them, Feltus, offered us a room. Staying in a house meant we could enjoy some luxuries, like ringing Mum at home and watching TV. Timbuktu is comparatively developed for tourism, so we enjoyed nice meals and some nicer beers. We even got our passports stamped (unnecessarily) with the word 'Timbuktu'.

Soon we had to start heading south again. We shared the ferry across the Niger with about ten sheep and found a campsite in the desert. Because the ground was layered with prickles, we needed to clear an area for the tents by burning some dry grass. In the process, Leo's shoe caught fire for a split second amid much laughter. The roads in this area were even more corrugated than before, and the only way to cope with the corrugations was to ride really quickly. And to make matters worse I was getting sick.

We met up again with Del. His bike was temporarily fixed (we hoped) after I put some sealant around the water pump seal, and we headed along some more terrible sandy roads. Amy and I were experienced, but the others fell off a few times. Del really struggled but had a great sense of humour about it; Leo sped around the corner and spun out, but he was fine too. Later when I looked for Del, he was angrily cursing his bike, which lay on the ground. The fuel tap had broken, and petrol would gush out whenever he removed his finger from the hole. This was obviously not good, especially as fuel was such a rare commodity out here. We never knew where the next supplies would be, and running out of petrol could be a matter of life or death in the African desert.

We drained the remaining fuel from Del's bike into my jerry cans and fixed the hole with a rubber plug I cut out and clamped on. At one stage, I had to lie down in the shade because I was feeling so ill, but we continued into Dogon country, a mountain range of ancient villages that seemed like they were from some fantasy book.

I still felt terrible as I rounded a corner and to my surprise was met by a group of westerners, mostly French, who were undertaking an ultra-marathon of 100 kilometres. One of them, Frank, was — believe it or not — a motorbike mechanic with one leg. (He was even doing the marathon with his titanium leg.) Frank helped repair Del's bike as best as he could, while a doctor (who was also part of the support crew) gave me some pills.

I awoke the next morning feeling better, but Leo's bike was in bad condition: The swing arm bearing was blown out. (A swing arm on a BMW is single-sided, with a drive shaft opposed to a chain and sprocket setup. The swing arm pivots from the engine as the suspension soaks up the bumps.) Luckily, I had some spare Honda wheel bearings which were an exact fit. Frank hobbled over to help us, and the problem was sorted out in no time. I was concerned about the hairline crack that had formed from the movement around the failed bearing, but there was nothing more we could do at that time.

Amy, Leo, Del and I spent New Year's Eve camped in the desert of the bizarre Dogon country in the middle of Mali with a bunch of Europeans we hardly knew. While a dust storm was brewing, the four of us shared a can of grapes brought by Leo all the way from Spain and took part in a strange Spanish tradition. This should've involved us eating six grapes — one every second at midnight, but we only had three each and did it at 10pm instead. The tradition is meant to bring good luck, and Del could've used some because water was again leaking into his oil.

The dust storm continued all night while we slept — or at least tried to — on the ground in a little open-air straw-roofed area; we awoke covered in dust from head to toe. We organised a walk into the Dogon region with a guide, Gadibou. (I nicknamed him Gary Baldy because when he said his name, I was reminded of an incident that made headlines when I was young about a company called Garibaldi in South Australia that produced meat with salmonella. The guide never did understand my choice of nickname.)

Gary Baldy explained that the Dogon people came to the region about 600 years ago from elsewhere along the Niger River but refused to convert to Islam. He took us high onto a plateau and through traditional villages with tiny granaries (for storing cereals) with wooden roofs shaped like witches' hats. The most extraordinary sight was a huge tortoise under a shady bush. I couldn't believe that it could live on the edge of the Sahara, but Gary Baldy poked it to prove that it was alive. He said the turtle was over 90 years old.

In one village, we heard and then saw many people wailing for a boy who'd died during the night. Throughout the funeral ceremony, a man loaded an old gun, which sounded like a cannon, and fired it continuously. We watched from afar as another man carried the boy, wrapped in cloths, on top of his head toward a burial ground in caves among the cliffs. The boy had been ill, like we'd been many times before, but there were no medicines in this remote area. His only fate was death.

*All shiny and clean, ready to pack the night before leaving London*

*15 September 2006 outside our address in London*

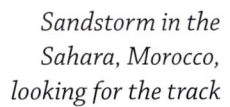

*Sandstorm in the Sahara, Morocco, looking for the track*

*Beautiful scenery of Morocco and crazy roads*

*The beach Amy and I went to relax at whilst waiting for our visas in Nouakchott, Mauritania*

*The famous Djene Mosque in Mali*

*Local Butcher in Fes, Morocco*

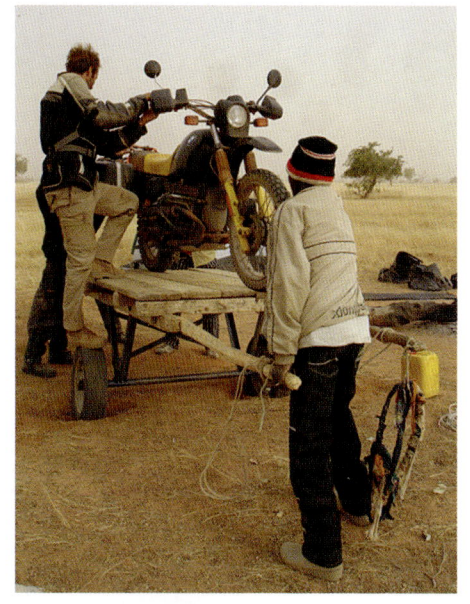

*Loading Leo's BMW onto the donkey cart in the desert, Mali*

*On our way to Timbuktu — Leo, myself and Amy*

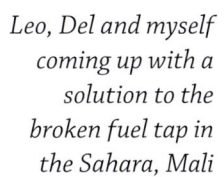

*Leo, Del and myself coming up with a solution to the broken fuel tap in the Sahara, Mali*

*Making it to Timbuktu — Del, on the left, myself and Leo*

*An inquisitve child — waiting for the ferry to cross the Niger River to Timbuktu*

*Frank on the left holding Leo's swingarm, Leo on the right in the desert, Mali*

*Waiting for the bridge repair in Guinea Bissua — the yellow thing on the right is the truck that fell in*

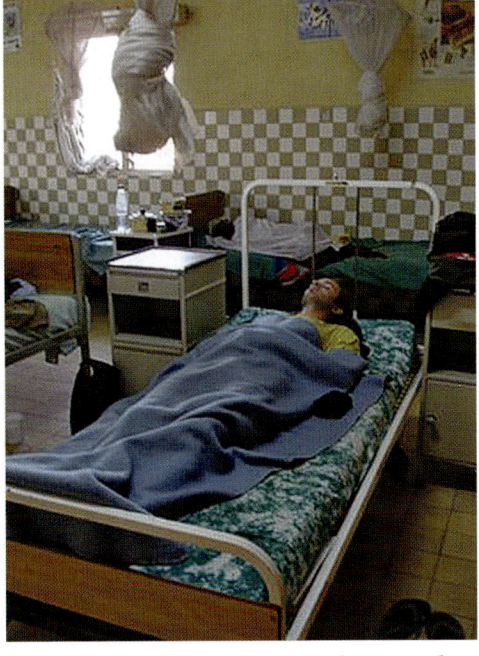

*Very sick in a maternity ward in Banjul, the capital of The Gambia*

*The friendly elephant drinking from the pool at Mole National Park, Ghana*

*Amy came in handy to act as a 'weight' to weigh down the rear end when I needed to change the front tyre*

*Helpful Nigerian soldiers giving Leo a push-start*

*Del dropping his KTM into this puddle, destroying all his camera equipment, DRC Congo*

*A landmine lay in the middle of the road, uncovered by the rain, number one highway, Angola*

*Maurice the Cameroonian walker
I met along the road high on life*

*Bush meat, Cameroon*

*This soldier in Seirra Leone wanted a lift but I told him to lose the chicken*

Afterwards, we rested and then set off into another sandstorm along another sandy track. We hadn't covered more than six kilometres when there was another major problem — so much for the good luck tradition the night before. The drive shaft on Leo's bike had snapped in half around the bearing when he went over a bump; the hairline crack I'd noticed before had reared its ugly head. He couldn't go on, so we set up camp in the howling wind.

I started to take Leo back to the village, but on the way we came across a man leading his donkey. We asked if he would take Leo's bike to Madagou (about 30 kilometres away) on a donkey cart. He demanded an outrageous 50,000 CFA (about £50), so we tried to get a cheaper ride from Gary Baldy. He said he had no donkeys (although I counted nine nearby), so we followed him on his motorbike to his brother's village. We ventured further into the dusty desert as it got dark. Gary Baldy's dilapidated motorbike ran out of petrol, so I siphoned some from my tank into his.

In the village, he offered us some smoked meat (which was delicious) and something else (which was absolutely disgusting). We also met one of Gary Baldy's wives (he had two) and all of his ten kids. Eventually, his brother agreed to take Leo's bike into Madagou by donkey cart for 20,000 CFA.

The next morning, there was the ludicrous scene of two Africans loading a modern 3000 Euro BMW motorbike onto a wooden cart drawn by two donkeys. We packed up camp, shared Leo's gear amongst us, and rode into Madagou to wait for the donkey-cart to arrive. Leo then chartered a vehicle that resembled a utility vehicle to take his bike and Del's (with the watery oil) to Koro, a larger town with potentially better repair facilities.

We all stayed overnight in Koro at a camping ground during a dust storm that unfortunately didn't disperse the swarms of mosquitoes that attacked us. The two bikes couldn't be fixed in Koro, so they were loaded onto a trailer and taken to Ouagadougou, the capital of Burkina Faso.

## BURKINA FASO

The ride to Waga — short for Ouagadougou (pronounced *waga-doo-goo*) — was very dusty, but border formalities on both sides were painless. One official did spin some story about it being a public holiday in Burkina Faso, so he wanted us to pay him 3500 CFA each (about 5€). I explained that I was an 'important government official' and showed him my old Air Force passport to 'prove' it, so we only paid extra for Amy's bike.

At first, there seemed to be only two places to stay in Waga — a Catholic Mission, which was closed, and the Charles Dafour Orphanage, which was horrible — so we stayed somewhere else that was a little pricey. Amy had become ill by now, so we rested up here for a few days and met up with Del and Leo, who'd arrived at about 11pm by bus. Del stayed with us, but Leo quickly boarded a bus to Lome in Togo to meet his girlfriend (who brought with her a new swing arm for his bike and the camera I'd couriered to her).

Another capital, Wage, and another visa — this time for Ghana. The bad news was that the visas wouldn't be ready for four days; the good news was that the spare parts for Del's bike had arrived by courier from Europe, so he could fix his bike (if and when it arrived from Mali).

Waga wasn't so bad — nothing much to see or do but a nice enough place to relax and repair. I changed the oil on both bikes and cleaned my air filter, fixed Amy's front sprocket retaining clip that was missing a bolt, and paid a pittance for someone to wash the bikes. Leo's and Del's bikes finally arrived by trailer from Mali and were fixed by a fat, funny Frenchman called Fredrika.

I had a long crack on a pannier that needed fixing, but I tried to explain to the guys at the repair shop that the pannier was made from aluminium and couldn't be welded. Nevertheless they insisted, and at one point they were trying to melt a spoon into the crack to fill it. Subsequently, they burned holes into the precious pannier worth £300. After several hours, they agreed with my angry protestations and covered the crack with a metal patch, which was what I wanted them to do in the first place, but they didn't have a drill and used a bolt and hammer to make the necessary holes. Clearly, this wasn't going to work, so I stormed out as they started their prayers.

My pannier box was now a mess, and one spot was distorted from the heat. I was so angry. I didn't go back to the repair shop the next day, so they didn't get paid. I just covered the holes with duct tape and hoped for the best.

Leo arrived with his girlfriend, Gabriel, from Lome after a horrible bus trip that included break-downs and a closed border crossing. Amy and I were keen to get going, especially as we had to arrive in Cameroon by February 23 as specified in our visas, but Del couldn't join us because the starter on his KTM bike was now stuffed (which he could get repaired in Lome), and Leo (and Gabriel) headed back to Togo as well. They all planned to meet us again at the Mole National Park in Ghana in about one week.

Feeling quite smug on our (almost) faultless Hondas, with new oil and chain wax and clean air filters, we left Waga and camped at the Deux Bale Forest National Park in Boromo. We hoped to see wild elephants and photograph them with my new camera. We spotted plenty of birdlife around the tranquil riverside camping ground, but nothing large, grey and with a trunk.

I awoke early the next morning to see Amy sitting on the camping ground decking, wrapped in her sleeping bag. She was watching out for elephants but was again disappointed. We organised a guide to take us further inside the national park, but yet again there were no elephants. The location was beautiful and relaxing, however, and the birds were always singing, but the insects were voracious, and Amy had bites all over her forehead.

At about this time, I started studying my maps and thinking about the route from Ethiopia to Yemen and across to Iran, Turkmenistan, Uzbekistan and Kazakhstan and then south to Australia through Russia and Mongolia. This part of the trip was still just a plan — a dream — but one that I'd have to make on my own.

Amy was still determined to finish in South Africa, and I was stubborn. I was always going to do the trip myself and felt that I still wanted to do part of it on my own — if only as some sort of test. It was easier travelling as a couple, but I always wondered if I could do the trip on my own, so I never really asked Amy to stay on. Perhaps she had wanted me to ask her, but she'd always felt that I'd asked her to join me on the trip for the wrong reason (so she wouldn't break up with me) — and this was true.

Her practical side was still calling her home from South Africa. She needed to get on with her career and pay off a university debt and was less keen to spend all the money she'd worked and saved hard for in the UK. Additionally, she would've achieved what she'd set out to do in the first place: ride by motorbike from London to Cape Town.

Also, at times she felt there was no romance. The trip consumed us completely; it was a full-time job — logistically sorting visas out when and where to get them and physically — just to find food, purify water from rivers and wells, repair the bikes, ride, find campsites and so on. I felt that riding a motorbike across Africa was romantic enough, but as lovers we started drifting apart. As best friends, however, we were tied to helping each other more than ever. We worked so well as a team, but I still wanted to test myself and go all the way home alone.

The next morning, there were still no elephants, which was so disappointing after two South Africans we'd met said they saw them every day. Assuming we'd see some further south anyway, we packed up and rode to Bobo Dioulasso. This place was meant to be nice and relaxed (and perhaps it once was), but we decided to continue towards Banfora. Along the way, we met a Latvian guy, Casper, riding a massive BMW 1150 motorbike and a German riding a tiny Saxy 45cc, and then we camped at Lac Tenguela, where we hoped to spot some hippos.

After the disappointment about the elephants, we woke up early, walked to the lake and chartered a *pirogue* (wooden canoe). We were quickly delighted to see two groups of hippos frolicking in the water. This was followed by another breakfast of oats and sugar, which I'd become addicted to. But then the day got worse.

We'd met a Belgian couple a few days before who gave us a list of places to go and the name of a reliable guide in Sindu. Somehow our information got mixed up, so we decided to go to Negunie instead, which we thought from their information had something interesting to see. (It didn't.) Along the way, Amy had a small spill and thought there was something wrong with the front end of the bike.

We continued along the road, which turned into a walking path, and reached a dry sandy creek. We'd negotiated something similar before and I got through, but Amy ended up crashing into the bushes. I rushed back to pick up her bike while she rested in the shade. Amy was shaken, bruised and winded but seemed okay. It was her worst crash so far.

I decided that it was too risky going to Negunie and that we couldn't risk damaging the bikes and injuring ourselves in such a remote place; Amy's spill reminded me how vulnerable we were out here. I checked Amy's bike, which seemed okay although she still thought there was something wrong with the front end. It was as difficult for me to fix the problem as it was for her to explain it — after all, she'd never grown up speaking 'motorbikish'.

We stopped at a village where the locals told us there was nothing to see at Negunie. Amy was in no shape to go hiking anyway, so we headed back 40 kilometres to Sindu. Arriving back unscathed, we found out that we hadn't been that far from some amazing villages, but we agreed that we weren't going back. Instead, we returned to Banfora, home to the magnificent Cascades Kifugella waterfalls, where we dipped in the freezing pools and bought some supplies. We also visited the Domes de Fabedougou, an amazing rock formation like the Bungle Bungles in Australia.

As we sped towards the Ghanaian border along a decent road, which turned into a goat track, Amy again said The Baja had problems. Once more, I checked the front wheel bearings (which were okay), greased the axle and replaced her brake pads, but couldn't find any problems. The next day, however — after I'd fixed her flat tyre again — The Baja started making a horrible noise. Taking the front sprocket cover off, I could see that the chain was hitting the swing arm as the rubber chain slide had worn through. My concerns about how to get the problem fixed weren't helped when the pain in my elbow flared up.

Three years before in Thailand, my mate Clint and I headed for the infamous full-moon party on Koh Phangan Island, an amazing event where thousands of revellers from all corners of the globe scatter along the beach to party. Activities included drinking 'bucket' cocktails of Thai Whiskey, lemonade and Red Bull; being photographed with sea eagles, massive iguanas and even pythons which locals carried around; and jumping through giant rings that were wrapped in cloth, soaked in kerosene and set alight.

Clint and I had to try the latter, of course. Encouraged by cheering onlookers, we ran and dived through the burning ring a few times and landed in a heap on the hard sand. I soon got bored of this, so I decided to do it again — but naked. With Dutch courage from another cocktail, I ran, dived and crumpled on the ground again, but this time with excruciating pain: my elbow was completely dislocated at a sickening angle. Oblivious, the onlookers cheered and Clint brought me my clothes. He saw my injury, panicked and raced off to get help, still holding my shorts.

He soon came back and dressed me. We rushed to a hospital in a taxi, which was really just a small truck that collected passengers along the way. We paid the driver 10 times the normal rate and went directly to hospital. It was about 2am, so we had to wait an hour before the doctor arrived and took some X-rays. About 30 minutes later he came back to tell us what we already knew — "it is dislocated" — and what we didn't want to hear: "I no fix."

We would have to transfer to a larger hospital on the next island, Koh Samui, but the first boat wasn't until 8am the next morning. I begged for painkillers, but he wouldn't give me any. Lying in the hospital bed, I moved my leg and a massive pain shot up from my calf muscle. When I raised my leg, it was stuck to the sheet. With no sympathy, the nurse ripped off the sheet to reveal a huge burn on my calf. Obviously, I hadn't felt that pain yet because of the dislocation of my elbow.

The next morning, I was loaded into an ambulance and driven to the jetty. (I'd lost Clint by then while he tried to find some money, but he left me what cash he had and also gave me his credit card.) It was just the regular public ferry — crowded and slow. Two more hours of agonising pain and I arrived in Koh Samui, where an ambulance was thankfully waiting. At the hospital, the nurse still would not give me any painkillers in case I needed an operation. Then, a large Thai doctor in a floral shirt announced he was going to "fix me now because waiting for an anaesthetist could take hours."

I did not want to wait for another second, let alone "hours", so I reluctantly agreed to get fixed there and then. The nurse rolled up a hand-towel and placed it in my mouth. She then climbed onto the table and sat on my right shoulder while two other nurses put their body weight across my hips and legs to keep me still. I turned away as the doctor lifted up my left arm, which had been motionless for nearly 12 hours and was now the size of a football from swelling, and began trying to relocate the joint.

The pain was *utterly* indescribable. A wave of coldness shot through my body, but I was sweating. The towel in my mouth helped muffle the screams and stopped me from biting my tongue. The doctor worked the joint back and forth, pulling and pushing with all his strength, while the three nurses struggled to keep me pinned down. I hoped I would pass out, but I didn't.

After what seemed an eternity but was probably only about one minute, he placed my arm back on my chest. As I let out a huge breath of air, he made an announcement: "I can't fix it. We operate."

It was another hour before they wheeled me into the operating theatre. As I lay on the table, staring at the ceiling, I watched a gecko crawl up the wall. I could hear ladies eating food in the next room, and one of them emerged with dirty plates and began cleaning them at the end of my bed. By now, I was desperate enough for them to chop my arm off — even with a kitchen knife. An orthopaedic surgeon and anaesthetist arrived, put me under, and operated. I woke up later with plaster up to my armpit. About three weeks later, I made my way to Bangkok for physiotherapy and stayed at a hostel near the hospital.

And that was how and where I met Amy.

## GHANA

Along the dusty roads through towns called Kelesso, Diebougou and Ouessa, we reached the border with Ghana. Once again, immigration and customs procedures were straightforward, which was just as well because Amy was getting tired — of constant bribe attempts by border officers, problems with the bike, and perhaps my lack of romance. She was deflated at times, and it was often hard to keep her spirits up.

We travelled about 400 kilometres in one day to reach the Mole National Park, where we planned to meet up with Leo and Del again. The final 50 kilometres was a terrible dirt road, and to avoid eating any more of the dust caused by Amy in front, I sped past her and went ahead.

A few kilometres further on, I glanced off the road and there were six huge elephants grazing in the forest. I slammed on the brakes, parked the bike and grabbed the camera. I was running down the track with camera in hand by the time Amy came zooming up. She wondered what I was doing until she saw the magnificent beasts too. After the previous disappointment at the Deux Bale Forest National Park in Burkina Faso, Amy was ecstatic. It was the perfect pick-me-up she needed to lift her morale.

The Mole National Park was superb, with a motel high above a waterhole where all sorts of animals came to drink. Very soon, we spotted even more elephants, and loads of warthogs were running around the motel grounds. The next morning, we awoke with the grunts of warthogs outside our room and then wandered to within about 50 metres of a muddy lagoon to watch the elephants graze, play and swim; despite their size, they seemed so graceful. And in the local village, warthogs and wild baboons seemed to casually walk about, almost mixing among the people.

Of course, it wasn't all rest and fun: On The Baja, I had to fix another flat tyre, change the front sprocket around to stop it from deflecting the chain into the swing arm, and wind up the suspension a little. Del and Leo were still in Togo waiting for spare parts for their bikes, but they eventually arrived together on Leo's BMW. It was great to see them. We bragged about our wildlife sightings and took them to see the elephants at the lagoon.

Later, our guide, PK, dressed in a khaki uniform and wellington boots, took us really close to the lagoon while the elephants frolicked in the water. But PK became very anxious when another massive elephant approached the lagoon, so he told us to move back slowly. He threw several branches and sticks at the elephant, which only made it angry. The elephant started circling us, so PK and I frantically threw more sticks. We were soon cornered, and behind us was the lagoon already filled with five elephants — as well as crocodiles.

The elephant was now flapping its ears as it started to charge us with trunk erect. PK immediately gave up throwing any more sticks and fired a shot over its head from his 375-millimetre rifle. The deafening noise startled us and the elephant, which turned and fled with its tail in the air. Our adrenaline was pumping, and even PK was sweating, so we thought it time to leave all the elephants in peace.

Over a beer that evening, PK admitted that it was the first time in 20 years he'd been forced to fire his rifle to scare off an elephant. Incredibly, a few days later, one of the friendly elephants from the lagoon approached the motel, leaned over the ridiculously-low brick wall and casually drank from the swimming pool — while I was in it.

As we headed further south through Ghana, still with Leo and Del, we appreciated the greenery and lack of dust and were looking forward to the beaches. We had to endure several long days of travelling because we found it hard to find places to camp that weren't crowded and there seemed few attractions worth stopping for and exploring anyway.

In one day, we rode about 450 kilometres to reach the crater lake at Kuntansi. The lake was high up, and therefore cooler, but we couldn't see much among the misty clouds. It didn't seem too appealing for a swim, either — more like a tacky, run-down destination for Ghanaians on weekends and holidays.

The roads through Ghana were pretty good most of the way, and The Baja was running smoothly, but the four of us weren't so interested in using these sorts of easy, direct roads. We seriously considered an unused route east, which involved taking a boat up through the Democratic Republic of Congo and reaching Uganda through the real Heart of Africa. Nobody had done this route before (but we ended up not doing it either).

Along the hot and humid Gold Coast, we saw evidence of Ghana's tragic history of slavery, such as the restored white Elmina Fort. Built by the Portuguese in the late 15$^{th}$ century for legitimate trading purposes, it is now the oldest sub-Saharan building constructed by Europeans. But back then it was later used for the gruesome slave trade, especially by the Dutch who seized the fort from their rivals. We were happy to stay a few days at the beautiful Green Turtle Lodge near Dixcove, a perfect place to swim, play cards, eat well, boogie-board along the deserted, palm-fringed beaches — and, of course, fix the bikes. Another patch on an inner tube had lifted on The Mothership, so I fitted a new tube that already had two holes in it.

I nearly broke my neck as one wave picked me up high and dumped me straight down, head-first into the sand, and bent my head back so far I swear my skull touched my shoulder blades. That night, I awoke with the worst earache of my life, which was probably somehow connected to the dumping.

We couldn't stay long because we had to enter Cameroon soon. By the time we reached the Kakum National Park on Australia Day (26 January), it was dark but still hot and steamy. A guard, who told us his name was Still Alive, said we had to walk two kilometres to the town and ask his boss if we could camp within the park. We walked and asked but decided to free-camp instead behind a tin shack with our tent set up on the one dry spot we could find: on top of a septic tank. The next morning, we staggered across an extraordinarily long and narrow rope canopy strung between two trees high above the thick jungle.

With so many visas required (and most visas using up one page each), Amy started running out of pages in her passport, so we visited the Australian High Commission in the capital, Accra, the most modern African city we'd visited so far. We had to wait three days for the High Commission to open because it was celebrating the Australia Day holiday weekend, so we stayed with Dan and Gacelle, whom we'd met at the Mole National Park. Dan worked at the American Embassy, so they lived in a huge house in a flash compound with a guard and swimming pool, which was a real treat for us.

When we returned to the High Commission, it felt so strange seeing pictures of the Australian Prime Minister and the Queen along the walls, but it was a waste of time: Amy couldn't get a new or extended passport.

Heading north along a pretty decent road, we met a policeman who'd served in East Timor and visited Darwin. Later, we saw plenty of wild baboons before we camped alongside a lake filled with thousands of frogs that croaked all night. We never seemed to get used to the extreme heat and severe humidity, even at night, and I always found it so hard to sleep in a tent and sleeping bag; I much preferred kipping down in a swag in the open-air.

Dam Akosombo, which produces much of the hydro-electricity for Ghana, was pretty uneventful, but we had great fun swinging into the water from ropes hanging among the trees and relaxing in hammocks. We rode on to the impressive Wli Waterfalls, the highest in West Africa. We didn't swim, but we stood under the refreshing falls.

We needed to move on quickly through Togo, Benin and Nigeria in the next couple of weeks in order to enter Cameroon by February 23; if we didn't, we were stuffed. And we needed to find new tyres along the way — probably in Lome, the capital of Togo, where there was a KTM dealership, the first 'real' motorbike shop since leaving Spain.

## TOGO

By the time we crossed the border into Togo, it was absolutely sweltering. Remarkably, this border didn't issue visas (most did, but not the one we chose). Thankfully, a muscled army officer let us through as long as we got a visa in Lome, which we did later. Also, the *carnet* couldn't be stamped at this border either, but it could be at Badou, the first town past the border.

Togo is very thin, maybe 120 kilometres from west to east. We sped over a mountain range and headed south to Kpami Falls. After returning from a swim at another waterfall, we noticed that a guard/caretaker had stolen Leo's boots. Our guide found the boots, returned them to a grateful Leo, and started a yelling match, which was quite comical, with the guard/caretaker.

We rode on to the Togolese capital, Lome. Our first stop was the legendary Toni Togo, a KTM dealership and workshop where we checked out some new tyres. Our second chore, as usual, was to drop off our passports at various embassies for the next bunch of visas we needed.

While staying at the Chez Alice camping ground for a few days, we met some other bikers: two Swedish guys on KTM950 Adventures waiting for new fuel pumps; the Latvian guy, Casper, whom we'd met in Bobo, Dioulasso; and a Swiss man on a XL600R Honda with panniers made from jerry cans. I felt so relieved when we fitted new front and rear tyres for The Mothership and a new rear to Amy's Baja. I hoped they'd last us until South Africa.

## BENIN

We skipped through Benin quickly because, like Togo, it's very narrow and there wasn't much to see. Also, we only received a 48-hour transit visa allowing us to speed through and continue to Nigeria.

As the heart of 'Voodoo Country', the religious beliefs across Benin are very strong, whether practising black magic or selling Catholic symbols alongside the road. While waiting for Del to sort out some insurance problems, we were, of course, surrounded by children. As we took their photos and showed them to the children (something they'd never seen before), we noticed the children's protruding belly buttons. It was due to the way their umbilical cords were tied at birth, and some kids even used the protrusion to hitch up their loose, beltless pants.

## NIGERIA

Despite all the horror stories we'd heard about Nigeria, the officers at the Nigerian border were some of the friendliest we'd met so far; one officer even offered his sister as Del's wife. From the border, we had to stop at about a dozen checkpoints where soldiers with machine guns checked our passports and demanded answers to the usual questions before we reached the first major stop at Ibadan.

We stayed with Alessandro, an Italian friend of a friend, and his English wife Bernie. Sandro had lived in Nigeria for 20 years, was managing director of a building company, and was very successful judging from the two XRs, XL600 and Dominator bikes in his garage. We stayed at his spare house in a compound with a three-metre-high fence guarded by a man with a machine gun and fierce-looking dogs that had to be restrained every time we entered. Olly (who we'd met back in Morocco) had sent me a new Thermorest (a self-inflating sleeping mat) to the house, which was very welcome.

We'd stayed in Ibadan to avoid the hassle of going to Lagos, which we didn't need to visit because we already had Cameroonian visas. Del and Leo did not, however, so Sandro's driver, Agebola, drove us to Lagos for the day. The 150-kilometre-long, two-lane freeway from Ibadan was littered with destroyed or crashed cars, trucks and vans so horrifically smashed that all occupants would've died.

In Lagos, Agebola took us through the craziest and most suicidal traffic I'd ever seen. At times along the expressway, cars would suddenly appear from nowhere on *our* side of the road, coming towards us at 120 kilometres per hour because of an accident on their side of the highway further down, forcing us to constantly swerve to avoid becoming more highway litter. I was so glad we weren't riding our bikes. Agebola was eventually able to find the Cameroon High Commission despite the sign outside, which read: ...MEROO...IGH...COMMI...SIO...

The next day, the four of us took off the panniers and other gear from our bikes and did some trail-riding in the bush with Sandro. He also took us to the beach, where we feasted on freshly-caught seafood. We felt like kings eating so well, and as Sandro was a true Italian, pasta was on the menu most nights. We drank beer and spirits with our gracious hosts while being waited on hand and foot by his staff and were then driven back to our own private house every evening by Agebola.

Reluctantly, we had to keep going as that Cameroon entry date loomed. We also needed to head to Abuja (the newer Nigerian capital) for visas to Angola (we hoped) and maybe Congo. Along the way, we camped overnight on the football pitch of a village school, which was a fun way to wind down after the crazy traffic and endless checkpoints with machine-toting soldiers.

At these checkpoints, we'd become a little complacent and would just slow down, wave at the officials, and ride straight through. I did this again at one checkpoint but did decide to stop when a soldier about 50 metres in front of me stepped into the middle of the road and raised his machine-gun towards my head. But these military guys weren't all bad; some even gave Leo a push when his bike wouldn't start.

For once, the timing was perfect: The Angolan Embassy in Abuja only issued visas on three days a week, so we could get ours quickly, as we arrived on one of those days. Meanwhile, Amy and I tried again at the Australian Embassy to do something about Amy's passport, which was rapidly running out of blank pages. But we got the same response as in Accra, Ghana: We'd have to wait 10 days for a new passport (but we only had seven days to get into Cameroon).

This inconvenience was offset by getting a visa for Congo on the spot. This efficiency was unheard of, but it did take up another full page of our passports, of course. (The Angolan visa didn't stick very well, however, so we peeled it off and stuck it to a page already full of stamps, thereby creating one additional free page.)

With our visas obtained, we were keen to escape the ugly city, but as we waited outside an Internet centre, a Nigerian singer, Amenia, approached us. Speaking with an American accent, she explained that her mother worked for the Nigerian Television Authority, and they wanted us to appear on a national sports channel. A very attractive reporter (whom Del couldn't stop ogling) explained that she wanted us to ride into a courtyard and pull up in a semi-circle. We then sat around on a couch while the beautiful reporter asked us questions about our journey — where we'd come from, what things we'd encountered, what we thought of Nigeria and so on. It was great fun, with plenty of laughs, and we saw the report that night on TV in the room they gave us for the night.

We eventually got away the following morning and reached Yankari, home to the fantastic Wikki Warm Springs with its crystal-clear waters, but the springs were warm and a little less welcoming for a swim in the intense dry heat. On our last night in Nigeria, we camped along the flood plains of Lake Chad. After dark, we heard some very strange and loud noises, which we soon realised was about 50 cattle being herded past our campsite by three shepherds. The following morning, we visited a nearby village with large, round wooden huts and corrals made from tree branches to keep in the cattle. It was a far cry from the chaos of metropolitan Nigeria.

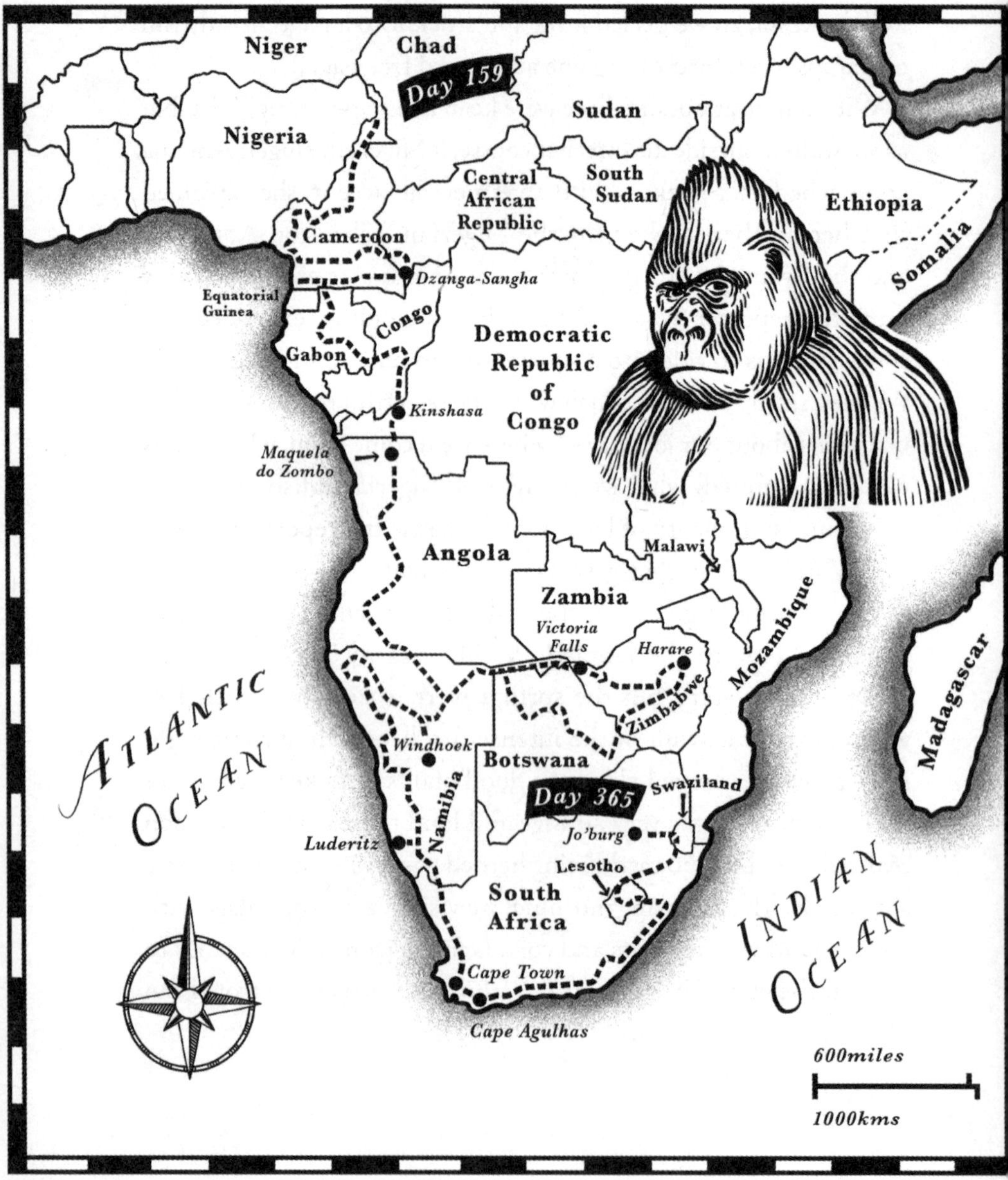

Niger
Chad
Day 159
Sudan
Nigeria
Central African Republic
South Sudan
Ethiopia
Somalia
Cameroon
Dzanga-Sangha
Equatorial Guinea
Congo
Gabon
Democratic Republic of Congo
Kinshasa
Maquela do Zombo
Angola
Malawi
Zambia
Mozambique
Victoria Falls
Harare
Madagascar
Zimbabwe
Windhoek
Botswana
Atlantic Ocean
Day 365
Swaziland
Namibia
Jo'burg
Luderitz
Lesotho
South Africa
Indian Ocean
Cape Town
Cape Agulhas
600miles
1000kms

CHAPTER 3

# Central & Southern Africa

*Cameroon to South Africa: 207 Days*

**CAMEROON**

It was incredibly hot by the time we crossed the border into Cameroon — an intense, dry heat that sucked the life out of us. After the smooth border crossing along some fantastic roads, we rode to the Waza National Park in the far northern edge of the country.

We got up at dawn the next morning and went on a safari in the back of an old Toyota truck in search of giraffes. As expected, the park roads were very bumpy, but after about four hours we'd still seen nothing. Then, finally, we watched and grinned as we came upon giraffes drinking from a waterhole, crouching awkwardly with legs splayed while craning their necks to the water.

From Waza, we rode to Maroua, a likeable town where we rested for a day, and then onwards through some gorgeous mountain ranges to the main northern town of Goura. Approaching Goura, Leo's bike stopped completely, but luckily, it stopped right outside a mechanics shop. Almost immediately, about 100 people emerged to watch us. As it was getting dark, Del, Amy and I left Leo to the crowd and searched for somewhere to stay. A few kilometres further on, Del got a puncture in his back tyre.

At this stage, Amy and I decided that we couldn't wait any more for Leo and Del to fix their bikes; we wanted to keep going and travel by ourselves. It was fantastic riding with them, but they travelled differently to us. Amy and I worked so well as a team and knew what the other was thinking, so when we consulted each other the decision was reached very easily, but in a group it was much harder; everything from getting fuel and crossing borders to deciding where to camp took longer.

So the following day, alone together for the first time since Ghana two months ago, Amy and I left the boys and took the road into the highlands of Cameroon. Thankfully, the temperature dropped a few degrees, but it was still stifling hot. Among the highlands, we saw piles of wild baboons and chameleons as well as many traditionally-built homes made from mud and thatched roofs. We were happy not riding in a group anymore, and Cameroon was a pleasure. The people were really pleasant; they didn't crowd much when we stopped and were more reserved.

And the roads were fantastic; even the off-road *piste* tracks were good — dusty, but doable. By late afternoon one day, we camped alongside a ridge with superb views but also loads of flies and ants. When a thunderstorm started, we had to take the mosquito net down and erect the tent, but it only drizzled for a short while. The morning clouds brought relief from the heat, and the rain had settled the dust.

The scenery in northern Cameroon never ceased to impress: rolling hills and winding roads with villages scattered throughout. The country gave me a new lease of life, a renewed enthusiasm for the trip. Leaving the deserts of Northern Africa and the hassles of places like Nigeria well behind, I was really enjoying the trip and looking forward to what Central Africa had to offer.

In Tibati, official supplies of fuel had run out, so we bought some on the black market, although it looked like water. Further south in Banyo, we met a policeman who'd been trying to kill an armadillo so he could take it home to show his children (who'd never seen one). The poor beast was covered in blood and barely breathing.

"It is so tough," the policeman said. "I have tried, but it's so tough."

Amy was upset, and I tried to stop him, but it was far too little, far too late.

The glorious days heading south continued with the perfect combination of great roads, amazing scenery and cool weather. There were a few hiccups along the way, as usual, with the wiring in my ignition, speedometer and dash — annoying, but nothing major — but the scenery seemed to get more spectacular by the day. This was especially so along the roads marked in the Michelin map as 'scenic' that rose to about 2000 metres.

At times, the countryside reminded me of Australia with its eucalypt trees; then, just as quickly, the road descended into tea plantations that smothered the hills like a green patchwork quilt. Once, when we stopped and the usual crowd gathered, we noticed a girl about three years old with nasty sores on her legs. All we could do was place some antiseptic cream on the sores and a Band-Aid on the worst of them.

The road deteriorated after Nkambe and sometimes turned into a trail with steep rocky parts that make the bikes and riders bounce all over the place. These tracks snaked around hills and through water-filled gullies that we had to ride through slowly. As we passed occasional villages of thatched-roof mud huts, some people stared blankly while others waved. Some nights we would find a perfect spot to pitch our tent, maybe atop a hill, where the views were priceless and the air was fresh, or in the middle of a rubber plantation.

We also saw something so unusual that I had to stop: a man dressed like an Olympic walker with running shorts, a colourful athletics top and socks pulled up to his knees. I asked what he was doing. He introduced himself as Maurice.

"I love walking, and I love life," he explained. "And it's a beautiful day, isn't it?"

I agreed and told him that I'd never met such a proud person. I asked for a photo, and Maurice obliged before walking on.

The road improved towards Wum, where we loaded up with fuel, and was even better on the way to Bamenda, a lively, likeable city. Along the way, we stopped at an enormous waterfall with a thunderous roar and passed through a village where about six masked men with long dreadlock wigs were involved in some kind of *juju* act of voodoo. Taking themselves very seriously and looking quite evil, these men walked along the road, waving sticks with material on the end at each house. It wasn't an act; they were in some kind of trance while banishing spirits from the houses.

I awoke on my birthday (February 27) with the realisation that we'd been eaten alive overnight by midges. Poor Amy's face was covered with bites, and my forearms were plastered too — but, surprisingly, the rest of my body was midge-free.

To make matters worse, the road the next day was horrendous: a combination of bitumen and gravel with huge potholes that forced us to ride very slowly. Travelling via Mount Cameroon, which we couldn't see because of clouds, we eventually reached Limbe, a relaxing resort town with black-sand beaches.

We camped at a seaside hotel with a swimming pool, where we met Guy (from England) and Maria (from the US). The four of us celebrated my birthday with fresh fish, a few beers and great conversation. We relaxed at Limbe for a few days, doing chores (eg. uploading photos and completing blogs), and visited a wildlife centre where we were guaranteed to see gorillas and chimpanzees. This whetted our appetite to see these creatures in the wild at the Odzala National Park in Congo, although we were still unsure because it would involve mountain trekking. (We found out later that a lot of gorillas had died from an Ebola outbreak, so the park was closed anyway.)

We headed to Buea to find a reliable guide and pay the appropriate fees for a hike up Mount Cameroon. We originally planned on a two-day trek but were soon persuaded by staff at the small tour agency to see more of the park and its inhabitants over three days and two nights. We were happy with the price: 70,000 CFA (about £35) each for a guide (Tom) and the porters (Samwell and Frances

Escobar) who carried most of our food and water — and what they were able to carry was amazing.

During the first day, the landscape quickly turned into jungle, as expected, then plain savannah and eventually rockier terrain. It was *really* rough going — hot and sweaty work. We reached Hut 2 at about 4.30pm and camped there for the night. It was freezing, and a rowdy group of Cameroonian students kept us awake all night, but the porters and guide barbecued some tasty (but unidentified) meat in a marinade for us.

The second day was even tougher, but the porters made it look easy. We snacked on chocolate bars for energy, and the air became thinner, so we had to stop regularly to literally catch our breath — initially every 50 steps, then every 25, then 20. Soon, all I could manage was 10 steps before needing to sit down, recuperate and breathe in more oxygen. After about five hours of hell, we reached the summit of 4095 metres. It was so windy and cold that we huddled together. The view was unspectacular because of the clouds, but to reach the peak was worth the climb.

After five minutes, however, we'd had enough of the wind, cold and clouds, and we started our descent. We passed old lava flows and craters from an eruption only eight years before, and at times it felt like we were walking on the moon. We camped in a grass hut near a spring, which was far from the greatest place in the world to contract a terrible case of diarrhoea and stomach cramps.

But we did have a lot of fun chatting around the fire with the other porters, such as 'Diesel' (self-penned because he proudly said, "I am strong like a motor"). He carried the bag of one trekker on top of his head all the way up and down the mountain, wearing only socks, because the only sandals he had were too small. None of the porters had proper boots.

Day three was comparatively easy, but of course our muscles ached, and my left knee exterior cruciate hurt a little. We gave each of the porters and the guide a tip, and I bestowed my Merrells (sandals I'd had for three years) to Samwell because his sneakers were useless.

We returned to the beach town of Limbe to rest for a couple of days. We caught up again with Del and Leo, who had finally made it with a few of their own stories: For example, Del had fallen and hurt his leg badly, while Leo's bike had broken down a few more times. While Leo did the same trek as us, Amy and I rode to another beach further along the coast where more lava flows from the 1999 eruption of Mount Cameroon had covered the road.

We were all packed and ready to go to Yaounde, the Cameroonian capital, to get more visas (of course), but Amy's bike would not start. I did the usual checks: The spark plug was fine, and I cleaned the carburettor and air filter but, again, no luck. The day was disappearing, and with it the chance to apply for some visas, and I still had no idea what the problem was. I took The Baja's carburettor to a mechanical repair shop and blew it out with an air compressor. More gunk came out, but still it wouldn't start, and by now the battery was running low too. I found a mechanic called Elvis, who suggested we give The Baja a push. *Surely it couldn't be that simple?* But it worked a treat.

We rode on for a short way and camped that night on an old football pitch. The next morning, we were all packed and ready to go to Yaounde once more, but once again Amy's bike wouldn't start. I checked the spark plug again — and scratched my head again — and then took Elvis' advice: We pushed Amy's bike down the hill until it eventually started.

Our first stop in Yaounde was the Gabon Embassy, and our worries about the bikes were offset by being able to collect our visas that afternoon. But then we had trouble finding somewhere to stay. The hotel recommended in our guidebook was awful, and the next option, the Catholic mission, wasn't much better either: At night, the priest indulged in the 'devil's drink' and yelled obscenities. Later, we saw Chris and Valkmer, whom we'd met at the Mole National Park in Ghana, and then Amy and I were forced to wait an extra hour for our visas to be processed as 'punishment' for my wearing shorts into the embassy. Our typical day of ups and downs and highs and lows finished with a delicious Chinese meal and some welcome beers.

Despite the major detour — an extra 900 kilometres one way over terrible roads — we really wanted to visit the Central African Republic (CAR) in search of gorillas, so the next morning we headed to the CAR Embassy. Remarkably, we got our visas within a few hours, but Amy now had only one or two blank pages left in her passport, which was just enough to get a visa for Congo. Being in a major city also gave us the chance to repair and clean the bikes and contact family and friends by email.

Roads to the borders across Africa are often atrocious because no country is willing to build and maintain a road that only goes to or from another country. The route to the CAR border is no exception: just one long, dusty, corrugated track choked with logging trucks. At one stage and, maybe for the first time on this trip so far, I really started to wonder what the hell I was doing out here instead of working, making money and settling down. But I knew if I had settled down, I'd want to be in Africa — though perhaps not skidding along a corrugated track and breathing in clouds of dust.

This road, and the thousands of other kilometres of similar tracks we'd crossed, was taking its toll on both bikes. Africa is a *very* tough place to travel, and The Baja and The Mothership were starting to fall apart. Part of Amy's chain rubber was held together with glue, and the crack in my pannier was patched up with duct tape.

**CENTRAL AFRICAN REPUBLIC (CAR)**

We knew nothing of CAR except that it was supposed to be one of the most dangerous, corrupt and lawless countries on earth — a real 'no-go' area for travellers. But we thought we'd be okay, because we were just nipping into the south-west corner and out again quickly.

The border crossing on the Cameroonian side went smoothly, but the CAR side was indicative of what to expect throughout the rest of the country. At one checkpoint, we had to show our passports, then yellow fever certificates, then passports again, then *carnet de passages* and finally our passports once more. The customs officer kept us there, obviously wanting money, but we refused and continued to the Immigration post. This started well, but the immigration officers soon made their demand: 4000 CFA (6€) for some 'stamps'. We assumed it was some sort of bribe, so we found and talked to the boss, a fat brute. He became very angry very quickly (and Amy snapped at him), so we demanded to know his name and threatened to report him to the Immigration Office in Bangui, the capital (which we had no intention of going anywhere near). The fat boss reluctantly returned our passports and told us to leave, without a bribe.

An hour or so later, we were gestured to stop at another checkpoint by another policeman who no doubt wanted another bribe. But I just waved and kept going and hoped Amy would do the same. (She did.) From behind, I heard the policeman blow his whistle frantically, but he didn't follow us.

By now, we were physically and mentally exhausted and Amy's bike was not breathing well due to all the dust, so we found a friendly village to camp in about 50 kilometres from the border. Despite all the hassles, in this case caused by CAR officials, it was amazing how quickly a simple dinner could revive our spirits.

We had two pots, one fitted inside the other, and I'd always make sure the Coleman stove had petrol, which I got from my bike. Every evening was a routine of boiling water for the pasta and then putting it aside while using the second pot to cook the tuna or sardines, often with anything we could buy along the way, such as garlic, chillies and tomatoes. Then we'd mix the contents of the two pots and scoff it down. It was simple and created minimal washing up, but I did get sick of the same thing night after night.

On our first morning in CAR, we awoke early as the elders and kids gathered to watch us as usual, and in this part of Africa many of the villagers are pygmies, a very short people with a full grown male only coming up to Amy's shoulder. The roads became even dustier, so we didn't bother changing or washing our clothes because they would simply get dusty again immediately. We also became really sick of checkpoints. At one, a policeman demanded to see our passports and wouldn't give them back without a payment; he then wanted us to take him to the head office in Berberati to see the boss, so we told him some crap about our insurance not covering us if we crashed and had a passenger on board, and it worked. We got our passports back and were allowed to continue.

To add to our dislike of CAR, petrol is diabolically expensive, at 758 CFA (US$2) a litre, and the rainy season was about to commence. After some more slippery roads and checkpoints (at which we continued to refuse to pay any bribes), we reached the 'Checkpoint from Hell.'

It didn't start so well when we noticed that one of the officers was drunk and waving a gun in our faces while demanding that we get down from our bikes. He told us to sit under the straw-roofed hut and then started rambling away in good English while someone else wrote down our details. I tried explaining where we were headed.

"Shut ya mouth," he suddenly said to Amy and I with a slur.

He became even angrier when we refused to pay any bribes, so I tried a tactic that had worked before. I handed over my 'Official Passport' and told him that I worked for the Australian Embassy.

"Shut ya mouth," he stuttered again.

The others weren't impressed with his behaviour, but no-one was willing to stop him either, except for one man who came forward and took away the AK-47 from the drunken officer's side. Now that he wasn't armed, I felt more confident about telling him how drunk and rude he was and reminding him that we were not going to pay any bribes. Amy showed her (expired) credit card to 'show' that we don't carry cash but use credit cards for payments instead. They examined the card, holding and rotating it as if they'd never seen one before. (Perhaps they hadn't.) This seemed to have some effect, and we eventually escaped with passports intact. Amy was shaking for a while afterwards.

While the police we met in CAR were obnoxious, the scenery was gorgeous. The jungle was lush and tall along both sides of the road, and among the muddy patches thousands of bright-yellow butterflies soared about aimlessly. Pygmies lived alongside the roads in traditional huts made from leaves and shaped like igloos.

We arrived at the Doli Lodge in Dzanga-Sangha National Park as the sun was setting. The location was quite surreal, set among dense rainforest and next to the Sangha River, along which so many *pirogues* (wooden canoes) would glide past.

All the hassles that CAR had thrown at us so far were forgotten when we saw the Western Lowland gorillas in the wild. To avoid renting a car for 100,000 CFA (US$250), we convinced the head of the Lodge to allow us to ride our bikes into the camping ground, from where we would hike into the Park to see the gorillas. Of course, we had to take guides (who were pygmies) on the back of our bikes along a classic Central African 'road' that was narrow, sandy and dotted with so many long and deep potholes filled with rainwater. Although only 30 kilometres, it took about one-and-a-half hours, and once again, I was amazed at Amy's riding ability.

After meeting an English woman who lives in the national park and runs a data-collection project about the gorillas, we started hiking with our pygmy guides and tracker to where the gorillas had last been seen. We trudged through the jungle and were lucky enough to spot some elephants feeding on the salines (jungle openings with streams running through), as well as buffaloes, deer and monkeys.

At times, we found it difficult to keep up with the pygmies as we weaved through the thick jungle. After almost an hour, we met up with two other pygmy trackers who helped us find a group of 13 gorillas, including one massive silverback called Mtombo, as well as six females and young ones ranging from one year old.

We followed this group for over an hour through the jungle, observing a female scratch through the soil for food only metres away, and watching another cross a stream while walking on its hind legs like a human. We were often positioned so close to the silverback that he glanced at — but thankfully ignored — us. It was a truly memorable day.

Then there was the gruelling 30 kilometres back to the Doli Lodge with a pygmy on the back of each bike. That evening, we sat on the boardwalk overlooking the serene Sangha River with jungle foliage lapping at the water's edge and met a German, Philipp, who invited us to his place for dinner. While we enjoyed a great dinner and a few beers, he told us about his work on various conservation projects in the national park and convinced us to stay another day to meet his girlfriend, Michelle, who also worked with the gorillas.

At a nearby village, we made some friends and took plenty of photos. Remarkably short, these pygmies sharpen their teeth into points to help them eat meat, and the women only wear a cloth around their waists. Later that afternoon, our guide took us along the same awful track as the day before to where the elephants grazed at the saline.

We met Andrea, an American conservationist, who took us out to a platform raised among the trees. From a viewing platform we looked over an area of about 400 metres by 200 metres and sat in awe for nearly three hours, watching what seemed like scenes from The Lion King (without the lions). With up to 75 elephants, as well as buffaloes, bongo deer and wild pigs, it was nature at its very best and unlike any other place on earth.

By the time we got up the next day, packed, paid our bills and bid farewell to Philipp and Michelle, it was mid-afternoon. Heading back towards Cameroon, the ride was better because the sun had dried out the road. The first checkpoint didn't cause any problems, and the one with the drunken gun-wielding officer from a few days before was empty. But soon the checkpoints became more frequent, and officers always stopped us and asked for money, thereby delaying our escape from CAR. Each time, I showed them my 'Official Passport' and explained that I was an 'important person'. It always worked.

Waiting for the ferry to cross the Sangha River to Cameroon, I noticed a padlocked door, made of wire and wood, from which three men peered out. I assumed it was a jail — not the sort of place I wanted to end up in. A policeman started asking me for money, but he only spoke French, so Amy and I could pretend we didn't understand (which was true). A man inside the makeshift jail cell started translating for the policeman, who let the man out. The man explained that he'd been locked up over some 'fine' of only 10,000 CFA (US$30). He kindly explained to us about the immigration and customs procedures, and as I turned back to get on my bike, I saw the policeman locking the man back into the 'cage'.

Across the other side of the river, we only rode one kilometre to discover we had to cross another river, or, more likely, the same one that had forked off. There was a barge, but there was no one to operate it — just a few ladies washing clothes in the water. We found out that the man who ran the barge had gone for the day, and that maybe tomorrow we could get across.

As we noticed the clouds growing ominously darker, a man on a *pirogue* canoe agreed to take us and our bikes across the river. I was sceptical, but it was only 200 metres, and there was no other option that day. We unloaded the bikes and sent Amy's across first with all the luggage and her in the *pirogue*. She crossed without any problems. The *pirogue* returned for me and The Mothership — and to my relief we also crossed without plunging into the river.

Then the rain started to belt down, forcing us to wear our waterproof gear (for the first time since Spain) and camp near the village with the Customs office. We were really keen to get out of CAR and return to Cameroon, but a policeman told us the customs officer had gone home. (It was 3.30pm.) The rain fell harder.

Pondering our options, the policeman said he would ring the customs officer if we bought some credit for his mobile phone. We decided against that and chose to wait until the next day. Another man — a kind one, this time — offered a space in his front yard for our tent. Returning to get our bikes, the customs officer appeared from nowhere. He advised us that our *carnet* needed to be stamped by an official inspector. I found someone I'd spoken to earlier in English and asked him to help convince the officer that he could stamp our *carnet*, but the customs officer refused to budge. We tried every angle until I showed him my 'Official Passport', which must've worked because about 20 minutes later he rose from his desk and agreed to give us the stamp.

We were so keen to flee the country that we declined to camp in the front yard of the friendly man and looked for somewhere else further away. Unable to find somewhere suitable, we pulled into a village, which welcomed us; a man called Victor even gave us some bananas. Of course, we were immediately the centre of attention for about 30 kids and a dozen adults all evening while setting up the tent, making dinner, washing up and writing in my diary.

Later, we heard the spine-tingling sounds of kids singing and clapping; we could hear each one taking it in turns to sing a verse, while the others sang the chorus. We got out of our tents and watched them from a distance. It was mesmerising: We were in a jungle village between the CAR and Cameroon borders, where no white people had probably ever stayed listening to these amazing children sing. We sat around a campfire with a few elders before the children joined us. A party soon started with bongo drums, dancing and more singing. It was the perfect antidote to the hassles earlier in the day and such an obvious example of how wonderful ordinary Africans are, but officials from their country are not.

The next day it was 15 March 2007: exactly six months since we'd left London. The final 50 kilometres to the Cameroon border was hassle-free, but everyone — the police, immigration and army wanted money. Again, my trump card, the 'Official Passport', worked like magic.

**CAMEROON — AGAIN**

We punched the air while riding past a sign telling us that we'd reached 'The Republic of Cameroon'. We were really happy to be back, and straight away the Cameroonian border officers did their job quickly, properly and without wanting a single franc in return. We decided to try for a lesser *passavance* (a temporary import permit for our bikes and substitute for a *carnet*) instead of using another page in our *carnet*. (Pages in the *carnet* were running out as quickly as those in Amy's passport.)

To do this, however, we had to go to Yakadouma. Our luck continued when we found the customs officer there, who took us into his office (which looked more like a dungeon) and said we were lucky to find him because he wasn't always available. We explained what we wanted, but he said he didn't have a *passavance*, so we followed him to his home. He did what we asked and not a franc was demanded — such an amazing contrast to the corruptible chaos of the Central African Republic.

We spent our first night back in Cameroon camped on a school yard next to a family of pygmies. We wanted to continue to Mintam along a track that existed according to my GPS, although locals advised that it was now only suitable for walking. We needed fuel, so we found a stall with bottles filled with overpriced petrol that happened to be on the track we wanted. More locals advised us that the track was unsuitable for motorbikes for the same reasons, but others seemed optimistic, which gave us some renewed enthusiasm.

Off we went and, sure enough, it more or less became a walking track full of dirt, which had turned into mud from the rain. At one stage, my bike wouldn't go forward and the back wheel just spun around. On closer inspection, the mud under the mud guard was so thick that the front wheel had stopped completely. The only option was to take off the mud guard, but of course mud then flew *everywhere* while riding.

After about 8 kilometres, we entered a village where the track just disappeared. When asked about the route, the villagers confirmed that it was only a walking trail and was also blocked with many fallen trees. So we gave up, headed back along the same horrendous track, bought more overpriced petrol and looked for an alternate route.

Heading towards Benglos, we came to a fork in the road and asked a man for directions to Sangmelima or Bengbis.

"To the left is good, but longer," he said. "To the right is direct, but rougher."

Of course, we took the latter option, and again the route was little more than a goat path flanked by dense jungle. It was now late afternoon when, just past a village, we saw a massive fallen tree blocking our path. As we got off our bikes and pondered our predicament, about six men raced towards us, picked up the tree trunk and swung it off the path so we could continue.

Almost immediately I had to change another flat tyre. Ignoring a truckload of rude, drunken Cameroonian men, I tried but failed to fix the patches. One of the villagers, who only had one good eye and one leg with a crutch, asked if he could help. I wasn't too proud to say 'yes'. He told a young boy to run off and fetch a tablespoon of white liquid — their homemade glue — and, incredibly, ten minutes later the tyre was fixed! It was too late to look for a camp, so we asked to pitch a tent on the school grounds.

The next morning, we managed to escape before the crowds arrived to gawk at us eating breakfast and packing up. Unfortunately, the track didn't improve. We had to cross a creek by making a 'bridge' out of wooden planks, and then about 10 kilometres past Sangmelima my rear tyre went flat again. There was now no option but for Amy to ride into town with the tube around her neck. She came back with it fixed (for a while). Soon, we were on a decent road — the first stretch of tarmac for the previous 1000 kilometres — and heading towards the appealing beach resort area of Kribi.

I was still angry about my flat tyre when we passed through another checkpoint. I argued with the policeman that we'd been stopped many times before and had shown that all our documents were in order at each checkpoint, so why would our documents not be in order now? Remarkably, he accepted this logic and let us pass. The road soon changed from heavenly tarmac to terrible dirt, and then, yes, my tyre went flat again. With Amy's air filter also clogged with dust, we limped into Kribi. The bikes were getting tired. So were Amy and I. It was time to rest.

We camped along the beach and met Case and Bean, a Dutch couple who, with their three kids, were travelling to Cape Town in an old 4WD fire truck, all nicely kitted out. What should have been a few glorious days of relaxing and swimming at the beach and in nearby waterfalls that plunged into the ocean were soured by the wiring problems on my bike. My frustration peaked when The Mothership wouldn't start and I had to fix it by touch in the pitch dark along a roadside.

Then the rain started; the wet season had finally arrived. *Shit!*

### GABON

We passed through the Cameroonian border with a minimum of fuss and were looking forward to getting into Gabon, another tiny former French colony. Our first impressions, however, were not good: We quickly got into an argument with the extremely rude Gabonese customs officer and rode off to the Immigration post without our correct Customs papers.

Immigration ran smoothly, however, so I thought it would be wise to try again with the customs officer while Amy searched for food. I apologised to the officer and explained what I wanted in a stern voice, and after a moment or two he decided he would cooperate and gave me the required *passavance* for our bikes.

About 20 minutes later, we found a village and asked the chief if we could camp there. Gabon seemed wealthier than other countries in western and central Africa, so the roads were good, and the abundance of signposts was a welcome change. But there didn't seem to be too many reasons to stay long.

The next morning, I was up at dawn again, cleaning the carburettor of The Baja. The bike rode well for 10 minutes before it started chugging again, especially up a hill or when accelerating hard. I tried to fix the problem several times along the road but to no avail. We didn't need to go to the capital, Libreville, for visas this time, but we decided to detour there anyway for the other reason we normally visit a big city: bike repairs.

About 10 kilometres further towards Libreville, we found a campsite by the roadside in a lush jungle choked with singing birds. A sign along the road indicated that we'd crossed the equator, and I realised it had been about three-and-a-half years since I'd been in the Southern Hemisphere.

That night, as Amy cooked and set up the tent, I was determined to fix her bike. Everything seemed okay until I finally tried pulling the high tension lead that delivers power to the spark plug apart. While doing this, the lead simply separated in my hand, which meant it was broken inside and a gap had formed between the wires. I pushed the lead back together and taped it up. I started The Baja and sped down the road with full power. *What a relief!* This had been driving me nuts for days.

With Amy's spark plug fixed, we could avoid Libreville. Instead, we sped across Gabon through endlessly thick jungle, along roads with tall bamboo trees lining both sides almost creating a tunnel, and parallel to the massive River Ogooue. Heading east to Lastoursville on the way to the Congolese border, the roads turned bad — this time, rocky and full of shale. But the scenery remained superb, even if the little flies attracted by our sweat drove us insane.

One night when it rained Amy noticed the tent floor was soaking. I peered out of the tent and noticed that we'd camped in a gully and water was running straight under our tent. I jumped out and quickly made some 'gutters' in the mud to divert the torrent, which worked. Then as the sun rose, we heard a buzzing sound that continued to get louder and louder. Bees had inundated our campsite, including the bikes and helmets, and the swarm seemed to be getting thicker by the minute.

As I jumped out of the tent, the bees were soon in my hair and a few snuck inside the tent, while a pair of dirty socks on the bike seat was a carpet of bees. Amy packed everything up inside the tent and quickly passed it out to me. I raced down the road and placed the gear away from the tent, bikes and bees. The buzzing grew louder, and the bikes were now smothered. With bees now crawling all over me, I cautiously started The Baja and walked it down the road. As I placed my right hand on the throttle, I was stung on the finger. I removed the sting, but it started to hurt really quickly. I returned for The Mothership, but it wouldn't move, as if something was blocking the wheel. I looked down. The back tyre was flat.

I had to pump up the tyre with my head directly in the line with the exhaust pipe to deter more bees from crawling in my hair. When that was done, I pushed my bike about 50 metres away. All that was left was Amy and the tent. As I unzipped the tent, Amy shot out and sprinted to our gear scattered along the road. The tent was now plastered with bees, so I cautiously picked it up by the middle and ran down the road shaking it violently. Sheets and sheets of bees fell off and roared away with an angry buzz. With no time to put on our jackets or helmets, we rode about 500 metres down the hill and packed up our gear properly there. It had been a terrifying ordeal.

The other roads in Gabon were good, but it was raining and misty, and we were soon covered in mud. No fuel was available at Lastoursville, and we needed at least five litres between us to reach the next town, Moanda. While getting my tyre fixed at a repair shop, a Land Cruiser passed with some white guys inside, so we flagged them down, hoping they had petrol or knew how to get some. Three South African chaps, Shaun, Gareth and Jason, said they couldn't help, but magically a local man soon arrived with five litres of fuel for us.

Further along, The Mothership started chugging again, so I reached for the reserve fuel tap and made another daunting discovery: the tap had already been on reserve, so I was now completely out of fuel. I drained a litre from Amy's bike, which lasted about 20 kilometres before I had to drain another. We wanted at least one bike to reach Moanda, where we hoped more fuel could be bought. Again, I ran out, but we did eventually limp into town and rejoiced at the sight of a Shell petrol station.

That night, we found a glorious campsite within earshot of the Poubara Falls. Gabon is simply beautiful, with high plateaus, green hills, lush jungles — and lots and lots of bees. A few buzzed about our campsite again, and hundreds more swarmed all over us the next morning. By now my hand had ballooned from the sting the previous day and was very, very sore, making it really hard to use the throttle. We slowly rode away from the swarm and visited the Poubara Falls. We'd seen a few waterfalls by now and were looking forward to the mightiest of them all: Victoria Falls on the border between Zimbabwe and Zambia.

We reached Franceville for breakfast and rode along a tarmac road to Lekoni. We asked several times for directions to a local attraction, the Lekoni Canyon, and people indicated that we were going in the correct direction. But the track turned into a mini-canyon itself, and at one stage, it wasn't wide enough for my bike with panniers on both sides. We heaved and strained every sinew and muscle we had, and eventually the track petered out completely. Not knowing where the canyon was or the next place we could stock up on fuel, we headed to the Congolese border.

**CONGO**

Along a very sandy track, and with a bald tyre on my bike without even one knob left on it, we reached the Gabonese border — or at least that was what the GPS indicated. There was no Immigration post to check our passports or Customs to stamp our *passavance* for the bikes, so we continued onward, hoping that no one on the Congolese side of the border would care. They didn't.

We reached a village with a banner indicating the Congolese Immigration Office, where a friendly man stamped us into the country. A policeman wearing a Miss Congo T-shirt noted our particulars but advised that the nearest Customs Office was along the road north of the capital, hundreds of kilometres away.

The poverty of Congo was immediately reflected in the atrocious roads and the villagers patting their stomachs and seeking food as we rode past. As it got dark on our first day, we were anxious to find a suitable campsite. We came across a massive pothole full of water stretching from one side of the road to the other. As I tried to ride up on the lip of the pothole used for walking, I plunged into the puddle because my bald rear tyre failed to grip. The puddle was full of mud which felt like glue, so The Mothership was immediately stuck.

After unloading the panniers and everything else from the bike, we tried pushing the bike out, but it wouldn't budge. Then some angels arrived: three women dressed in their finest clothes. They took off their sandals and began pulling and heaving... *Un... Deux...Trois...* and eventually the bike became unstuck. They were such lovely people; we thanked them, gave them some water, and continued our journey. That night, we asked to camp in a village, but the villagers offered us a hut instead. In return, we gave them some pasta and sardines.

The track improved slightly, but it was still very sandy when we reached Okoyo. While filling up with enough fuel from a black marketeer to get to Gamboma, a policeman arrived on a brand new TT-R Yamaha 600 motorbike. My immediate thought was that spare tyres were available. He said that I'd be able to buy a new tyre in the capital, Brazzaville. This was great news.

The roads continued to be good, but the supplies of fuel were not. In Gamboma, we again had to buy petrol at inflated black market prices, and there was nothing in Ngo. We were soon both using our reserve supplies, and it was apparently 60 kilometres to the next petrol station. This had no fuel either, but we asked about at the station and found a nice man who did sell us 25 litres at the normal market rate.

We made it to Brazzaville and met up with Leo and Del again. We spent most of the time in the capital searching for a new rear tyre for The Mothership, but to no avail — despite the policeman saying otherwise. Perhaps, we'd have more luck over the Congo River and in the Democratic Republic of Congo (DRC).

Unfortunately, we were told that the ferry wasn't working because of recent violence in the DRC capital, Kinshasa, which had killed 60 people.

**DEMOCRATIC REPUBLIC OF CONGO (DRC)**
We indulged in a sleep-in before heading to the port in Congo for the crossing to the Democratic Republic of Congo. (Yep, they are two separate countries.) Despite the recent violence, Amy, Del, Leo and I had to cross into the DRC (formerly known as Zaire) to reach Angola on the way to South Africa.

The port in Brazzaville was utter chaos, with people dashing in every direction, carrying all sorts of stuff on their heads. We went to Immigration, which was easy, and then to Customs, which was not — because we hadn't had our *carnet* stamped coming into Congo or at the Customs Office on the way to Brazzaville.

The customs officer said he could give us a *passavance* each on the spot for 20,000 CFA (30€). This wasn't an option, not least because we only had just enough money for the ferry ticket, so the officer took us to see his boss. In the air-conditioned office, I explained that there'd been nowhere in northern Congo to get our *carnet* stamped. Thankfully, he accepted this and stamped the document, using an entire precious page of our *carnet* for the length of our remaining time in Congo (which was only a few minutes).

After buying tickets, we rode up through the gate of the ferry before being stopped by a big, surly policeman who insisted that he needed to put another stamp in our *carnet*. This was clearly not true, but we took deep breaths and reluctantly detoured back to the appropriate building. The head policeman was in a meeting, so we were told to wait. Time for my trump card: I showed my 'Official Passport' and explained how 'important' I was and that I could *not* wait. Again, it worked.

As we returned to the ferry to load up our bikes the process was now even more chaotic. A ferry official told us to follow him down a special ramp while he blew a whistle, shoved people and whipped others with a broken fanbelt from a car to make way for us and our bikes.

We could see Kinshasa in the distance, and the trip only took 20 minutes. As expected, the process of docking, unloading our bikes and proceeding through DRC Immigration and Customs was even more frenzied. One lady even fainted from the heat as she got off the ferry and was crushed under the masses. People were yelling and getting angry, and we were desperate to get off, but we had to wait until all the foot passengers had exited.

After what seemed like a million questions over a few hours, we sorted out all the documentation and were on our way into the Democratic Republic of Congo. The border officials had even wanted to disinfect our bikes, which was ridiculous considering how much disease could've been brought into the DRC by the foot passengers — and they were worried about our motorbikes.

The DRC capital, Kinshasa, was just bearable, but it did have one redeeming feature: a Yamaha dealership that sold new tyres. The tyre on offer was not the knobbly type I needed, a bit thin and cost a whopping US$165, but I bought it so we could escape from Kinshasa as quickly as possible. We camped overnight in a village before suffering what was our most difficult day of the 197 so far.

We just wanted to get in and out of the DRC quickly and rush to the border with Angola only about 100 kilometres away. Immediately past Kinshasa the road deteriorated and turned into a hellhole of mud and ruts caused by trucks. At one stage, my bike was stuck in mud with the texture of glue, and it took six local men as well as Amy, Leo and me to heave it out. The Mothership was now caked in thick mud. Del was also finding it very tough: He fell into a deep puddle and filled his pannier with water, so everything inside was ruined, including his camera.

We strained every muscle just to keep our bikes upright and heading in the right direction. We were all completely covered in mud, and if any local person was kind enough to help push our bikes they'd become plastered in mud as well. Sometimes we had to stop our bikes, get off and walk along or around a puddle to gauge if we could ride through it. Eventually, after an all-day hell-ride that covered only 79 kilometres, we reached Ngindinga. We later met a man who told us that large 4WD trucks take four days to cover this 100 kilometres.

The Cokes we treated ourselves to tasted better than any we'd ever had. Camping outside a police hut in Ngindinga, each of us went to sleep early and completely exhausted.

## ANGOLA

We finally reached the border with Angola. I had to lie under a tree for a while because in recent days I'd been feeling very fatigued and was finding it hard to focus on riding. I put it down to the difficult roads and tough travel we'd had to endure.

The border crossings went reasonably smoothly, although it seemed to take forever at the Angolan side. We only rode for about 20 minutes before camping in the first village we approached, where the people were extremely nice. We'd heard that there were many landmines left over from the civil war in Angola, so we were wary about travelling off the main roads.

But that was the least of my immediate worries.

The next day I knew I was ill, so we rode a short distance to Maquela do Zombo, where we found an Italian doctor, Lara. As I lay under her veranda, away from the hordes, I was getting worse and my body temperature was 40 degrees. The doctor agreed that I probably had malaria, so I quickly took the first dose of Artiquine tablets that we'd bought in Senegal. We couldn't stay at the doctor's house, so once we bought some black market fuel and it was almost dark, the police allowed us to camp in the grounds of the police station.

For the next two days and three nights, I lay on the concrete floor of an Angolan police station suffering from malaria. Not only did I feel terrible but one night the room leaked after a vicious thunderstorm as well. The police were friendly enough towards us, but one morning two local men were brought into the station, and one was whipped once in front of us and again in the next room. Lying in a malarial sweat — one minute shivering with cold, the next sweating uncontrollably — I could hear the man weep and beg for the police to stop the beating.

By the third day I felt good enough to continue. We left Leo and Del behind again because they travelled so slowly. Sometimes the roads improved, but then they quickly turned even worse than before. The continual rain didn't help.

One day while negotiating a washed-out road, I picked the wrong line beside a huge wash-away. My pannier caught the bank on the side of the road, and The Mothership toppled into the crevasse. As my bike fell, I managed to jump clear, land on my side and roll away, but all the mounts holding the dash and mirror were broken. I was okay but more concerned about the bike, which took all of our combined strength to lift up.

Later as I passed a truck parked in the middle of the narrow track, the remaining intact pannier hooked onto the side of the truck's bumper bar and bent completely out of shape. Amy also fell off her bike and bent the sub-frame, so now her back tyre was rubbing on the battery cover under the rear mudguard.

I was still sick while recovering from malaria, and my bike wasn't in much better shape. I felt incredibly disappointed because I'd tried to look after both bikes so well. By now, I had no front brakes left (the pads were down to the metal), and my back brakes were just as bad. Amy's front tyre was almost round (with zero grip), and her chain couldn't be adjusted anymore. I almost felt that the bikes had met their match in Angola.

We often had to ride along roads dotted with white posts bearing the words *Periga! Mina!* (Portuguese for 'Danger! Mines!'). We also stayed clear of a pile of sticks in the middle of the road with a makeshift barrier and a skull-and-cross-bones symbol. It was a live mine that must've washed up from the rains. The roads were littered with abandoned tanks and other military vehicles from the civil war, and old Portuguese buildings marked with holes from bullets and rockets were visible in every town.

Angola was scary, but we made it out. If only just.

**NAMIBIA**

The border formalities on both sides of Namibia were a comparative breeze. At Oshikango, just inside Namibia, we loaded up with fuel and met Derek, a German man who let us stay at his place. It was paradise: There was a washing machine and a place to clean and repair our bikes, and we ate steak for dinner. We also gorged on sausage rolls from a bakery and tried telephoning shops in the capital, Windhoek, in search of spare parts, but were out of luck.

The roads across Namibia were perfect, but not so our tyres. After some more patching and repairs, we stayed at a camping ground with hot showers — our first since Ibadan in Nigeria over two months before. Being in Namibia immediately felt like we were in 'civilisation'.

After a welcome sleep-in and a battle with a dog that chewed one of Amy's thongs, we rode a pleasurable 80 kilometres to Tsumeb, where we found a great shop that sold chain lubes, patches and camping gear. We then went to a supermarket and bought roast chicken and fresh bread. These little things brought us so much pleasure after having gone through so much pain throughout western and central Africa.

We continued searching for a new rear tube without luck, but we were told we would be successful in Grootfontein. Along the way, we stopped for a while at a place where a meteor half the size of a small car had fallen. People had tried to break it up and take bits but had failed because it was so solid. We moved on quickly, however; we were more interested in tubes.

Hoping to fix most of the problems on both bikes the next day we booked into a comfortable camping ground in Grootfontein for the night. Again, we stuffed ourselves with treats like apple juice and chocolate biscuits from a supermarket. Despite not having time to update my blog as much as I'd promised myself (and others), many of the problems on both bikes were fixed. We celebrated with a steak dinner.

Along the road from Grootfontein, we stopped at an animal farm, where we patted a beautiful pet lion through the fence and saw a single wildebeest grazing on the residents' lawn, two cheetahs (that came when called by staff) and a caracal (which looks like a cat). We knew these sorts of animals might be something to worry about when we free-camped in the wilds of southern Africa.

At about this stage it was official: The Mothership was dying. The speedo spline drive had chewed out, so I couldn't use the speedometer, and now there was something wrong with the battery, so I had to push-start the bike. After an early morning walk to see the Giant Baobab Tree — which was disappointingly no bigger than the ones we'd seen in Senegal — we spotted more wildlife along the road, this time a young kudu (like an antelope with long horns). The roads continued to be very good — sometimes long, straight and boring, but we never complained.

At Rundu, we wanted to stay at the Ngepi camping ground which had been recommended to us by Rudy, whom we'd met at the Zebra Bar way back in Senegal, but it was cut off by high waters from the Okavango River. The lodge Ngepi camping ground was still open, however, so leaving our bikes in the car park, we took what we needed and were paddled across the waters in a canoe. Set along the banks of the Okavango (which was choked with crocs, hippos and elephants), the lodge was a perfect place to relax. We could've stayed a lot longer, swinging in a hammock and watching the wildlife, but I was keen to reach Harare in Zimbabwe for ANZAC Day. (I'd always attended ANZAC Day services as a child with my father, a Vietnam veteran.)

For some reason, I started getting a strange and often agonising pain in my right triceps that felt like a hot needle was being pushed into it. A few days later I awoke with a crippling pain in my shoulder. We didn't know what caused it or where to go to get it checked out, so all I could do was take some headache tablets, which seemed to work for a while. I drifted in and out of sleep on the lawn beside the tent with the owner's Labrador, Slim.

The lodge was owned by a South African couple, Marg and Mark. Mark had a licence for helicopters, while Marg had a licence for fixed-wing aircraft, and they also ran a luxury helicopter tour business. Speaking to them inspired me to continue my journey along the east coast of Africa and ride all the way home to Australia. I felt reenergised. Thankfully, my shoulder was getting better, although it was still slightly sore. The suddenness and cause of the pain was puzzling — maybe my body was wearing out from sleeping on a ground mat for the past seven months.

We continued on to the Botswana border through the Mahongo Park, where we saw wildebeest but nothing more, and the Caprivi Strip Game Park, where we spotted loads of elephant dung but no elephants. We did see some hippos later, however, and we heard some more in the water as we pulled up to the Mazambala camping ground. We stocked up on fuel because people kept telling us that there was none in Zimbabwe.

**BOTSWANA**

Travelling through and crossing between Namibia and Botswana was so easy that it felt like a holiday rather than an adventure. But we were only skirting the top northern end of Botswana from the far eastern end of the Caprivi Strip in Namibia to reach the Victoria Falls in Zimbabwe.

Almost immediately after crossing into Botswana, we noticed two elephants alongside the road — the perfect introduction to the Chobe National Park. Riding through the park we saw even more elephants — huge ones — as well as buffaloes and a few massive

Black Mumba snakes basking along the scorching tarmac. We camped at the Chobe Safari Lodge and bought more food from a supermarket. Like Namibia, Botswana is great, with decent roads, reliable fuel supplies and a fantastic range of food. Everything was more expensive, of course, but that was understandable.

**ZIMBABWE**

The ride out of Botswana and into Zimbabwe was like entering another world.

The Zimbabwe dollar was worthless unless you changed the foreign currency on the black market, which was illegal, of course. But everyone did it; they had to. Foreigners can't spend Z$ unless they have a receipt from a bank proving the money had been changed at the laughable rate of US$1 = Z$34,020. We changed a little money at a bank (so we could show a receipt) and then changed the vast majority of our money at the black market rate of about US$1 = Z$1,700,020. (The rate changed daily — even every hour.) We had to pay for some things in US dollars or South African Rand, and petrol was only available through the black market (and even then it was hard to find).

But the reason we were in this crazy country was to see the Victoria Falls, which straddle the border between Zimbabwe and Zambia. We first saw the Falls from afar while walking across a bridge to Zambia and then far closer up from an official viewing platform. It was always such an amazing sight, particularly with the mist giving us the feeling that it was constantly raining. We didn't mind getting soaked. We also booked an ultra-flight to observe the Falls, as well as wild elephants and buffaloes, from above. It was simply stunning.

After finding some black market fuel (bought with Zimbabwe dollars), we continued east. The roads were in reasonable condition but with plenty of corrugations and bumps, and the journey was long, boring and uneventful. The road was bad enough at one stage, however, to snap my bracket (which basically holds down the dash and front fairing up). For two days, I had to ride along holding it up with my left hand until we hit smoother tarmac. At Whange, we sourced another 10 litres of black market fuel from the boot of someone's car. My triceps continued to ache, and at night I couldn't even sleep on my right shoulder because of the crippling pain.

We obviously needed to hole up in Harare for a few days to fix the bikes and do a few other chores, such as answering emails and writing in my blog. Our first impressions of the Zimbabwean capital were positive, but it seems to have a darker side. While looking for the Australian High Commission, we went down one street that was closed from 6pm to 6am. A sign warned us that anyone who disobeyed would get shot. The street was along the front of the palace for President Mugabe.

We found the High Commission and started the process of getting a new passport for Amy. (Getting a four-page emergency passport would allow us to avoid hanging around for two weeks to get a proper passport sent from Australia, but this decision caused us no end of problems later on.)

While looking for a camping ground, we met Ian Jarvis, who allowed us to pitch a tent on his lawn. Rocky, a mate of Ian's, helped me fix my bike. In his mid-60s and an ex-boxer (of course, with a nickname like that), Rocky once had a home with a swimming pool. The whole place was used for functions, but it was closed down by President Mugabe because Rocky is a 'white Rhodesian'. So Rocky turned his house into a 'BYO' brothel, where members of the public were able to bring their mistresses for discreet encounters which — ironically — is frequented by the same government officials who closed it down in the first place. (I even met the Police Commissioner there!)

Rocky invited us to stay at his, um, brothel, and his helpers, Mposie, Select and Akim, made one of the rooms more homely for us. We relaxed and watched Sri Lanka beat New Zealand in a semi-final of the Cricket World Cup on TV. On another day, we went to the Harare Racecourse in Borrowdale for the ANZAC

Day service, wearing our best possible (ripped, but clean) clothes. Arriving about 25 minutes early, we saw what we expected: Everyone else was wearing suits and ties, and we looked like we'd just come from the beach. But our tales of adventure compensated for our informal attire.

The service was good, and I thought of Dad, as always, who'd served in the Vietnam War. Afterwards, the Australian wine and Zimbabwean beer flowed, all courtesy of the Australian High Commission (and, of course, the Australian tax payer). We met plenty of Aussies, such as Dan, Stacey, Ann and Mark (who worked at the High Commission), and swapped stories until the sun went down. We got a lift home with Dan and Stacey, who said we could stay with them in Pretoria (South Africa).

Walking around Harare it was impossible to understand how people could live using the black market. For example, we went to the movies with Dan and Stacey, and tickets cost Z$10,000 each (about AUS$0.30). But we saw a can of WD40 (a lubricant in a pressure can) that cost the Zimbabwean dollar equivalent of US$54! This country has the highest inflation rate in the world — about 3000 per cent per year — and a leader who seems to have lost his marbles.

We spent the rest of our time in Harare hanging out with Rocky and fixing the bikes (of course). Together we fixed the dash, welded up The Mothership, bought a second-hand front tyre, re-bonded the brake pads and made some new chain rubbers for The Baja from a conveyor belt. We also went to a place called Tracks to meet a few local bikers — a strange bunch, but nice enough. On our last night, Ian Jarvis had a *braai* (barbeque) for some South African rugby umpires, which meant more invitations for us to stay across the border.

The road to Bulawayo was good, and the days were sunny, but the scenery offered little. We camped in the bush north of Umuua, and because winter was approaching, it was quite cold at night — something we hadn't experienced since leaving Europe. In Bulawayo, we were approached by a man who worked for a local newspaper, *The Chronicle*. A few minutes later, two female reporters and a male photographer interviewed us about our trip. Sure enough, the next day we were on page three with a colour photo and a headline that read: Two Aussies on African Tour.

In Bulawayo, we stayed with a wonderful couple in their 70s, Henry and Ann (the in-laws of a man we met in Harare). Amy and Ann cooked a delicious meal, and the two of us enjoyed more luxury: a comfortable bed and hot shower.

We rode out to Motopis to see the World's View. This offered the most amazing panoramas and some balancing rocks, as well as the grave of Cecil Rhodes, an English colonialist (after whom Zimbabwe was originally named Rhodesia). We waited for an hour at the entrance of the Matobo National Park, hoping someone would offer us seats in their cars. (For obvious reasons, riding a motorbike through a national park full of lions, rhinos and other dangerous wildlife was not allowed.) But we were out of luck.

Deciding instead to camp nearby, we approached a turn-off that my GPS indicated would be a short cut to the road for Plumtree. After 5 kilometres, the dirt track stopped at a farm house called the Anglesea Stud. A security guard greeted us and told us that the track was a dead-end (similar to the track at the Turriff Farm, where I grew up in Australia).

As we turned around, a 4WD came down the track. It stopped about 200 metres away and waited, which seemed suspicious to us. We soon realised that the car was occupied by two white ladies — the farm owners, Joan and Lara Fodman (mother and daughter, respectively). From a distance, they had thought we were Mugabe's men sent to abscond the last bit of their farm, but we started chatting and they invited us to stay with them in the farm house.

Their dairy farm (with some cows and sheep) was originally 20,000 acres, but it was slashed to 3000 acres after recent legislation allowing Zimbabwean blacks to reclaim 'white farms'. The manager, Marny, invited us to his home, where his wife, Janet, cooked us dinner. Later that evening, there was panic on the farm because a cow was having trouble giving birth. A veterinarian was summoned, but after a huge struggle the calf died. Over several hours, the stillborn calf had to be chopped up while still inside the cow and pulled out piece by piece.

Joan was kind enough to allow us to look after the farm for three weeks while they went on holidays in six weeks' time, but sadly our plans to reach South Africa were not that flexible. As we bid farewell to our lovely hosts, Joan was a little teary-eyed. No doubt she got lonely on the farm.

**BOTSWANA — AGAIN**

Our attempts to cross into Botswana again could not have started any worse.

We quickly made it to the Zimbabwean border town of Plumtree and met a German guy who told us there was a massive queue on the Botswana side of the border. We rode out to see for ourselves, and sure enough, the line of people and cars was over a mile long. We exited Zimbabwe with no problems, but by the time we joined the line on the other side for what looked like a two-hour wait, it was about 3pm. We wanted to reach Francistown (80 kilometres into Botswana) before dark, so trying the 'Official Passport' ruse, we went straight to the front of the line. (I even felt a little guilty about jumping the queue.) But after I got through Immigration, the officer announced that Amy would need a Botswana visa (not normally needed by Australians) because she now had a new Emergency Passport.

This was a problem — and one that could only be sorted out all the way back in Harare. We asked to talk to someone else but had to wait. We were getting really anxious, but the people were snobby and uninterested in our problems. I demanded to see the person in charge.

"She has gone out to lunch," said another immigration officer.

It was now about 4pm. "I don't think so!"

"She has gone home," said the same woman, indifferently.

Now I was *really* angry and called them all incompetent (which, perhaps, wasn't the best way to deal with the situation). Suddenly, the woman in charge appeared, but she just told us what we already knew: that we would have to return to Harare and get a visa for Amy. The woman was very rude, so I told her what I thought about her and her department.

Amy was upset and crying at the thought of returning to Harare about 1000 kilometres away. It was now 5pm, and we had no option but to return to Zimbabwe. To make matters worse, we had no fuel and had spent our last Zimbabwe dollars. I was very angry because I'd thought they were bullshitting us about needing a visa. I had assumed we'd left behind the corruptness of Central Africa and that Botswana was a 'civilised' country. Later, the Australian High Commission confirmed that Amy did not need a Botswana visa for her Emergency Passport. The problem may've been that Botswana Immigration wanted four empty pages after the visa went in but Amy's new passport only consisted of four pages in total, and Immigration needed to use one for their visa.

We stormed out of the building and telephoned Mark, a friend we'd made who worked at the Australian High Commission in Harare. But it was past 5pm on Friday, and of course, there was no answer. With no options left, we decided to return to Zimbabwe, which meant passing the checkpoint along the Botswana border. As we did, we showed the official our *carnet* and other papers for the bikes and told him we needed to go back to Zimbabwe. He waved us through.

For a moment or two, we were both actually *in* Botswana because we had to do a U-turn. We rode about 100 metres to the turn-off for the road back to Zimbabwe and glanced at each other. Immediately, we had the same thought: *We are not going back to Harare.* So we bolted down the road into Botswana, frantically checking our mirrors. Amy's Emergency Passport didn't have a Botswana visa or entry stamp (mine did because I was processed first), but we would worry about that later. We sped down the road as the sun quickly set and arrived at Francistown in the dark.

We tried to think of a few explanations to give to the Botswana immigration officers as to why Amy had no visa or stamp (such as 'they forgot to stamp Amy in'), but the next day, we decided to make up a story about Amy losing her passport and arrange for another Emergency Passport. At a police station, we asked to file a report about Amy's 'lost' passport, but they sent us to the Immigration Office, which was closed on Saturday. Instead, we went back to the police station to complete an affidavit about the passport.

With nothing more we could do, we headed south to the Khama Rhino Sanctuary in Serowe. The 237-kilometre-long road was perfectly tarred, but the countryside was flat and boring. Thankfully, we were allowed to ride our bikes into the camping ground within the sanctuary and set up our tent.

The next morning, as the sun had yet to peek over the horizon and while it was still cold, we joined a safari on an open-top Land Cruiser. After only about 15 minutes, we saw five rhinos up close. They were amazing. In two hours, we spotted a total of 12 rhinos and a few calves as well as giraffes, zebras, wildebeest, springboks, kudus, impalas and warthogs.

We packed up and hit the road for the long haul to Maun, on the edge of the world-famous Okavango Delta. Skirting the edge of the Kalahari Desert the entire way, we completed a boring 537 kilometres in one day — our longest one-day ride yet. At the Audi Camp, I did some more repairs on the bikes. I also telephoned the Immigration Office in Harare to get some ideas about what to do about Amy's 'lost' passport, but they were no help. We tried to relax by the swimming pool but were still concerned about Amy's being in Botswana illegally.

The manager of the Audi Camp, Ron, bought us a beer. He suggested we get to South Africa through Namibia, via a camp called Swamp Stop along the panhandle of the Okavango Delta and the Tsodilo Hills, instead of going through Ghanzi in southern Botswana. While this would involve back-tracking into Namibia, it meant we could stay again at Ngepi, a place we really loved. It also meant we had to quickly come up with a plan for what to tell the immigration officers at the Botswana border about Amy's 'lost' passport. But we did follow his suggestions the next morning.

Pulling into a shop at Supopa for a cold drink and chocolate, we met Alvin, a white farmer from Botswana and the strangest of all the characters we'd met so far. He was probably a little mentally unstable and had trouble talking at times, but he insisted on buying us beers (so he couldn't be too bad). Four beers later, he was still asking us the same questions we'd already answered, such as whether or not Amy had any sisters. It was time to get going again — with a few breaks along the way to relieve ourselves behind the bushes.

As we approached the border to Namibia, Amy became more and more anxious about her passport and visa. We camped at Swamp Stop, which was owned by an Englishman named Phil, and were the only guests. The next day, we rode off to Tsodilo Hills. It looked a little disappointing at first, but we rode 40 kilometres off the main road, set up camp, cooked lunch and had a siesta before exploring the hills on foot. We came across many ancient rock paintings before we found the steep and deep sand track to the start of the trail to the top of the highest peak.

The easy 50-minute climb offered superb views over the Kalahari — very similar to those from atop Ayers Rock (Uluru) in Australia. As Botswana's highest peak at an unimpressive 1395 metres, it shows how flat the countryside is. After dinner, we stumbled across another campfire and chatted to more fascinating and friendly travellers (who also gave us some beer).

## NAMIBIA — AGAIN

Very, very nervously we approached the Immigration post on the Botswana side of the border. The lady official looked at Amy's passport and asked me to find the page with the entry stamp for Botswana. Immediately I explained that there wasn't one because her old passport was stolen and that she'd been issued an Emergency Passport instead. I showed her the affidavit from the police. The officer read the police report I offered as 'proof' and stamped the report and Amy's passport.

*We were out of Botswana!*

It was an enormous relief, but we still had to enter Namibia and could come across the same problem with Amy's four-page passport. But we had even more luck: the female Namibian immigration officer was even nicer than the Botswanian official and joked with us while stamping our passports. Amy would now only need to use her Emergency Passport for one more country, South Africa, before returning to Australia.

It was a quick trip to Ngepi along a road we'd ridden a month before. The flood waters of the Okavango River had now subsided so much that we could ride all the way to the lodge this time instead of taking a canoe. Amy was a little disappointed that Leigh, the owners' niece, had gone and that the puppies she'd grown to love had all found homes, but it was a perfect place to relax. Best of all, we were in the country legally.

I'd been thinking a lot recently about what I — or *we*, if Amy stayed a while — would do in South Africa. It would be the end of her trip and a milestone for both of us to reach Cape Town. But heading on to Russia would mean hanging about somewhere along the way for a few months because the weather in Russia would be too cold and potentially dangerous for travelling until May next year (12 months away). I calculated that it would take about four months to ride from South Africa to northern Iran, which would mean filling in about six months somewhere. And I'd much prefer spending that time in a civilised country like South Africa and possibly getting a job there.

Travelling again along the road to Grootfontein, we noticed two motorbikes approaching us in the opposite direction. Incredibly, it was the boys, Del and Leo. We stood by the roadside and swapped travel stories for a while, but we had to keep going before the sun set. At Grootfontein we caught up with some people we'd previously met there and enjoyed another steak dinner at the same place as before.

The next day, we headed to Waterburg Plateau Park and hiked up onto the plateau, which offered great views but nothing much else. And the 'cheetah park' so was uneventful that I forgot to note the name. We'd seen so much amazing stuff that other places often disappointed us. We thought by now that perhaps we were just riding about and not achieving much while wasting time and money. But we did see some amazing Himba women for the first time. All covered in red ochre, they were posing for tourists, so we carried on without taking photos.

Amy's front tyre was now completely bald and needed replacing and my chain and sprocket were shot, so we headed to the capital for some much-needed repairs. Windhoek (pronounced *vin-dook*) is pleasingly relaxed and not too hectic. We stayed at the Cardboard Box Backpackers because the owner, Chad (who'd we met earlier at the Namibia/Botswana border), said we could stay for free. The bad news was that none of the spare parts we needed were available in Windhoek and had to be sent in from South Africa, which would take a week. But there was no option, and we had free bed and breakfast. Plus, the Windhoek Larger was quite tasty.

I rang the Australian High Commission in Pretoria (South Africa). They advised us that Amy could not get another proper full-paged passport until she returned to Australia unless an 'appropriate person' who'd known her for more than 12 months signed a special form. I couldn't sign it, however, because I was her boyfriend. Finding an 'appropriate person' in Windhoek, Namibia, was impossible, of course. There was nothing to do but wait for our spare parts.

In fact, we had to wait 10 days at the Cardboard Box for the spare parts to arrive. The following day, Amy's birthday (24 May), her new tyres were fitted. Rassie at Suzuki Namibia ordered me a Pirelli MT60 rear tyre which was 150 millimetres wide but could usually only fit a 120–130-millimetre maximum as the swing arm was too narrow, so they had to remove the chain guard to fit the tyre.

We left mid-afternoon for Okahunga, where I tried fitting my new chain and sprocket, which involved using an angle grinder to cut the old chain off. Unfortunately, the front sprocket was wrong; the spline teeth were too small. I rang Rassie, who said he was coming through Okahunga the next day and would drop off the correct sprocket.

We stayed (for what we hoped would be one night) in Okahunga with a man we'd met at Ian's place in Zimbabwe. Then I discovered the chain was too short. Two of the three parts Rassie had supplied me were wrong. I should've checked them before we left Windhoek, but I did order them for an Africa Twin. I rang Rassie *again*, but he couldn't do much on a Sunday.

On Monday, I got up early and rode Amy's bike to Windhoek (75 kilometres away) because The Mothership was still chainless. But not one shop in Windhoek had a 124-link chain, so Rassie ordered the next best thing (a 120-link chain), which would be posted to us direct from Grootfontein.

I rode back to Okahunga on The Baja so angry. It was cold, our visas would run out very soon, and we were stuck at this farm, which we didn't really like. (The owners were nice but just not our kind of people.) Amy was annoyed too; first it was the tyre, then the sprocket, and now the chain.

Early on Tuesday, Amy and I went to the post depot to pick up the chain, which was not only a different size but only 120 links. However, it would have to do. I cut out the required four links and added them via two joining links to the first chain. The chain now had weak spots in the two joining links; not the best while trying to cross the African continent. Again, I rang Rassie and he promised to send a proper-sized chain with 124 links to a future destination, Swakopmund.

We headed north to Etosha National Park, where we booked a safari and saw all sorts of wildlife, such as zebras, springboks, kudus, elephants and even badgers (but no lions or leopards). Relaxing at Etosha allowed me more time to think about my future plans. We were both thinking that while the trip was not over, the adventure seemed to be. I'd felt in the past few weeks that we'd been wasting petrol, time and money. We didn't seem to be making the most of every opportunity and once that started to happen, it might be time to call it quits. The next month would answer a few questions.

I was also now thinking about getting a job as a diver in South Africa and had even applied for a few positions. I still wanted to ride back to Australia, but I needed money to do some other things. To continue up the east coast of Africa, I'd have to spend a lot more money refitting my bike with new panniers among other things. Most of all, I wanted to fly helicopters as a career, but this would require money for training.

A month before at the Ngepi Lodge, we met Paul, a multi-millionaire Belgian who owned the Epatcha Lodge and Spa, a five-star resort near Etosha. He said that if we bought food and drink at his lodge (where rooms cost up to US$300 per person), we could stay there for free. Never before had we stayed anywhere so wonderful. I was having four showers a day and eating meals with five courses. (Paul also owns seven other luxury lodges in Namibia and spends 1.5 million Euros a year on advertising alone.)

Unfortunately, we couldn't stay long at Epatcha, and we set off for Kamanjeb. Along the way, we saw two giraffes (one on the road) and met a Frenchman who'd cycled from France. He'd been travelling for seven months — less time than it took us by motorbike!

At Opawo, we again encountered the amazing Himba people, a tribe where women rub red-coloured ochre all over their bodies and cake their hair with red mud to form huge, long dreadlocks. Also, from the day of their first menstruation Himba females never shower, they only stand over fires to 'bathe' in the thick smoke. At a tourist agency, we found out that most Himba live in the northern areas of Namibia, so we decided to make a 300-kilometre loop north to see and meet them.

Along the way, I spotted a donkey with a Himba lady and child on top and slowed down to tell Amy. But she didn't notice me coming to a stop. *Bang!* She ran right up the back of my bike. I went down, hitting the gravel road hard. I was okay, however, and Amy didn't fall off The Baja. I wanted to be angry, but it wasn't her fault. She was very sorry, so I took a few deep breaths. My right-hand tank saddle bag ripped off but was okay with some tape.

In the Himba region, we stopped a few times and paid about US$1 to take some photos of these tribal people. Along a road that deteriorated into a track of sand and rocks, we pulled over for a break. About five kilometres further on, I realised that my Leatherman (a multi-purpose tool-cum-knife I used every day) was missing. Amy went back to look for it because her bike used less fuel. After 20 minutes she didn't return, so I rode back to look for her. I found her in a Himba village, asking the locals. They helped us search for it on foot, and we eventually spotted it lying on the sandy path.

The track got worse, with more sand and more rocks. Amy fell in a creek-bed, hurting her knee a little. At this stage, I was really starting to get fed up; I wanted to head to Cape Town and finish this part of the trip. I was starting to think about and look forward to the second part, the journey home, and was tired of riding around like we were on holiday.

While continuing the 'Himba Loop', we had one of those typical up-and-down days. The first 'up' was riding through some amazing Himba villages, which consisted of a few mud huts enclosed within a huge *kraal* (wooden fence) about the size of two tennis courts. The *kraal* looked like it would house an entire extended family. The first 'down' was my bike crashing down on huge boulders along the track, which in some parts was a tough as the Amougha Pass in Mauritania.

While fixing my front tyre *again*, a Land Cruiser approached, driven by James and Sherry, two Americans doing an overland trip along a similar route to us. In the scorching sun, we swapped horror stories about African travel, while I swore at the tyre that remained flat. As they gave us some water (which we'd run out of), we warned them about the road they were heading along, the same diabolical track we'd recently tried. We were returning to our camp at Opawo along an improving road when, yep...*another flat tyre*. By now it was late but hot, and we still had no water. James and Sherry arrived on the scene. After listening to our advice, they had decided not to continue down that track. They again gave us more water while I fixed the tyre again. Back in Opawo, while enjoying some chicken and a Coke, we watched the tyre go flat again.

A typical day — up and down!

The road to Palmwag was beautiful and weaved through some mountain ranges. Over one rise, we saw about a dozen elephants. They're called Desert Elephants, although they looked no different to other elephants to us. It was just the name given to them because of their environment — sometimes they even cross the dunes of the Namib Desert.

Near Sesfontein we saw two Himba ladies walking, so we slowed down and offered them a lift. Despite the obvious language barrier, they understood and gratefully accepted. One of them had a baby strapped to her back, but the mother wasn't concerned; we just moved our roll bags back a little and made some room. They climbed on, unsure where to put their feet. It seemed a new experience for them (as it was for us).

It felt quite strange riding with a Himba lady all covered in red mud and paint. Perhaps we should've known that when they got off at their village (15 kilometres later!) our bike seats, the back of our bike jackets and our jeans would be covered in red. They were very grateful and asked to be photographed, but unlike other Himba, they didn't ask for money in return. Our photos perfectly captured their gratitude and sincerity.

For about 30 kilometres before arriving at the Palmwag Lodge, we saw an incredible number and variety of animals, such as zebras, kudus, oryxes (large antelopes with long straight horns) and springboks. That night at the lodge we were woken by zebras and oryxes nibbling on grass outside our tent. And our dinner was delicious — oryxes not only look graceful but they taste superb as well.

We rode down the stunning Namibian coast all the way to Souselvie, home to some of the largest sand dunes in the world. We also visited the old mining town of Kolmanskop, which conjured up images of both meanings of the word 'desert': No-one lives there, and the abandoned town is slowly being completely engulfed by sand. It was such an eerie feeling walking around the derelict houses, and sometimes we had to crouch down to enter a doorway because of the thousands of tons of sand that had drifted inside the houses over time.

I was having more problems trying to rectify my rectifier, which meant the battery was overcharging, causing it to boil and bulge at the seam. I'd been carrying a spare rectifier in my pannier since London, one of several spare parts I'd wondered why I was carrying, but I was glad I had.

From Swakopmund, we rode to Cape Cross along the Skeleton Coast (named after all the shipwrecks) to see the fur seal colony. Thousands of seals were sunning themselves along the beach, barking at each other, splashing about the water, and fighting off occasional jackals that loved feasting on the younger pups. The stench was overwhelming — like nothing else I'd ever smelt before.

We camped at Spitzkoppe, a bizarre rocky outcrop in the midst of the desert. With a highest point of 700 metres above the flat desert floor, the rocks stand out quite dramatically. With all sorts of different shapes, the rocks constantly change colours under the moving sunlight like Ayers Rock (Uluru) and The Olgas in Australia.

Further south towards the South African border, the roads were smooth and empty. On our last night in Namibia, we camped alongside a river and reminisced about our trip, which would end once we reached Cape Town in a few days.

But first we had to get into South Africa, which meant acting 'dumb' (again) at the Customs post. We hadn't got our *carnet* stamped on entering Namibia because we wanted to sell The Baja in South Africa.

I looked surprised at the South African customs officer. "But we've never needed a *carnet* before now." Of course, a quick check of my passport would show the number of countries that we could not have entered without a *carnet*.

But the customs officer just smiled and stamped our documents. We could now sell The Baja.

**TO CAPE TOWN**

A few hundred kilometres down the South African coast — with very little in between — was Cape Town. With the Table Mountain at its heart, Cape Town is the most picturesque city I have ever seen — a far cry from downtown Lagos in Nigeria. For the past nine months, this city had been our destination whenever someone asked where we were going.

And we'd finally arrived. An *enormous* sense of achievement and relief came over us. We had done the trip and finished our adventure together. The bikes had made it, and so had we.

For me, it was almost the end of Part One.

For Amy, it was start of her plans to return home and continue her life in a normal way.

**IN SOUTH AFRICA**

Amy and I stayed in South Africa for about four months. We decided to stay that long for several reasons: to see the country; plan part two of my trip, which meant ensuring the weather would be okay for travelling around Russia; and spend time together before Amy went home. And, of course, to fix my damn bike. (We later sold The Baja to a farmer in Hazeyview, who wanted it for his kids to ride about on his property. This was perfect because the bike couldn't be legally registered for use on the road since it wasn't bought in South Africa.)

We stayed with some old friends and some new ones, which meant hot showers and warm, comfortable beds. In a supermarket near Port Elizabeth, we met Frank, who invited us to stay at his holiday home, which we had to ourselves for three nights. And in Durban we stayed for a few days with John and Arlene, a lovely South African couple we'd met way back in Ouagadougou (Burkina Faso). In Cape Town, I met up with Ricky de Agrela, who I'd met 18 months earlier while travelling in Cuba. He'd completed a Guinness Book of World Records micro-flight trip around the world a few years earlier, so he took us on a joy flight over the city at sunset — an exhilarating experience.

After 248 days, 39,323 kilometres and about 20 tyre punctures, we finally made it to the southernmost tip of the African continent at Cape Agulhas — about the same latitude as Turriff, my home town in northern Victoria. This made me start thinking even more about Part Two, particularly how long I would need (four or six months?) to ride up the east coast of Africa and where I might stay for another two months along the way to Russia. (The idea of working in South Africa didn't eventuate.)

We visited some amazing places across South Africa. We climbed the Table Mountain for one of the most exquisite city skylines I'd ever seen, we visited Kruger National Park for some more amazing wildlife, and we rode along the coast on a Huey, a type of helicopter used in the Vietnam War. (My father, a Vietnam Vet, had told me many stories about the Huey.)

After travelling the entire length of the African continent without being attacked or hurt by a single wild animal, I was badly bitten by a penguin. At Boulders Beach, we walked along a raised boardwalk with wire mesh along each side to (ironically, in my case) protect penguins from humans. We found a penguin stuck on the wrong side of the fence, so Amy said I should pick it up and help. With motorbike gloves on, I grabbed the bird and lifted it over the fence. Swinging its head around 180 degrees, the penguin started pecking at the one inch of bare flesh between my bike jacket and glove. With my wrist bleeding, I quickly put the penguin down on the correct side of the fence while being watched by tourists who thought I was trying to poach it.

Our final trip together was a four-week ride from Cape Town to Johannesburg, from where Amy would return home to Australia. I felt sad; it would be the final time riding together, but we were determined to enjoy ourselves as much as possible. On our repaired and rejuvenated bikes, we saw whales, Amy rode on an ostrich, and we tried surfing in Durban.

We also went bungee-jumping from the highest drop in the world. It took a long time to convince Amy, but she did plunge 216 metre from a bridge to the tiny river below. I'd done one jump before on the Gold Coast in Australia but was still petrified.

It was now winter in South Africa, and we weren't used to (or enjoying) the cold, wet and windy weather — especially in our tents at night. Eventually, Amy received a new, proper passport, but she also had to get an appropriate South African visa inside it from the Home Affairs Office. I also ordered and received a better camera.

Landlocked within South Africa are two strange African kingdoms, Lesotho and Swaziland. We went to Lesotho with Brad and Jolanta, an American couple doubling on their Africa Twin. We entered the 2874-metre-high Sani Pass along a dirt road full of switchbacks that climbed to a plateau. The frozen waterfall proved how cold it really was, and the Africa Twins strained in the thin air.

I now had a major problem — my bike lacked any power. So Amy continued with Brad and Jolanta around Lesotho while I returned to Durban to a Honda dealership (which was closed for the weekend).

That night while travelling along a motorway at 110 kilometres per hour to a friend's place, I suddenly heard a loud screeching of tyres behind me. I gripped my handlebars, hoping like hell the problem wasn't in my lane. But almost immediately I was facing up to the sky as a car slammed into me from behind and shot The Mothership into a wheelie position. I throttled very quickly and pushed the rear brake with my foot, and the bike slammed back down onto the highway at an awkward angle. The handlebars slapped violently from side to side as I gripped as tightly as I could to the tank with my legs and arms to stabilise it. My front wheel hit the tarmac with a wobble, but I managed to keep the bike upright.

I manoeuvred my bike from the centre lane of the motorway to the far left. The car that had hit me pulled up behind. As I switched the bike off, my hands were shaking. I took off my helmet and walked back to the young driver, who was now approaching me. I was too shocked to be angry and simply asked what he was doing.

"I didn't see you," he explained.

"Clearly." I indicated the damage to the rear of my bike and the pannier rails. "You'll have to fix this for me."

Then the excuses started. He said he didn't have a job or any money and had borrowed the car.

"Well," I said, "you need to take responsibility for your actions and ask someone — your parents, wife, girlfriend or boss — for the money. It's your problem. Not mine."

He told me his name (which turned out to be false). Before riding away, I photographed the damage on my bike, his licence plate, and the name of the company (with a telephone number) on the side of his car.

On Monday I got what I needed for The Mothership and rang the company that owned the car. The sympathetic manager agreed to pay for the damage.

I rode back to Lesotho, where Amy, Brad and Jolanta were staying in a village. I arrived at about 10pm after a record 701 kilometres in one day and breaking our Number One Rule: never ride at night. Amy was anxiously waiting for me and gave me a big hug. Again, I realised how much I would miss her.

We arrived in Swaziland during the Reed Festival, when the King selects a new wife (he had 13 already) from a parade of up to 3000 naked dancing virgins. It was an extraordinary sight, with the girls' brightly-coloured beads and jewellery dangling against their dark skin. Apparently the King had already chosen his next bride, so perhaps he just liked to admire the ladies?

Remarkably, it was exactly a year after leaving London that we eventually rode into Johannesburg, Amy's final destination. We were greeted by two friends, Paul and Zoe, who'd also farewelled us a year before from my place in Putney.

What an incredible effort from Amy. From virtually never riding a motorbike before, she had now ridden about 45,000 kilometres — the entire length of the African continent — and done it amazingly well.

For me, it was now Part Two.

*Amy sitting with pygmy tribe people, Cameroon*

*Stuck in a glue pot, DRC Congo*

*Christmas Day, discovering my lost tyre lever in Del's front wheel, Mali*

*The number one highway in Angola*

*Amy, clearing the jungle path in Cameroon*

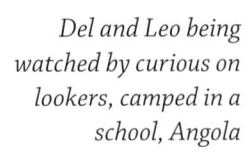

*Del and Leo being watched by curious on lookers, camped in a school, Angola*

*The crash in Angola which caused damaged to the front end*

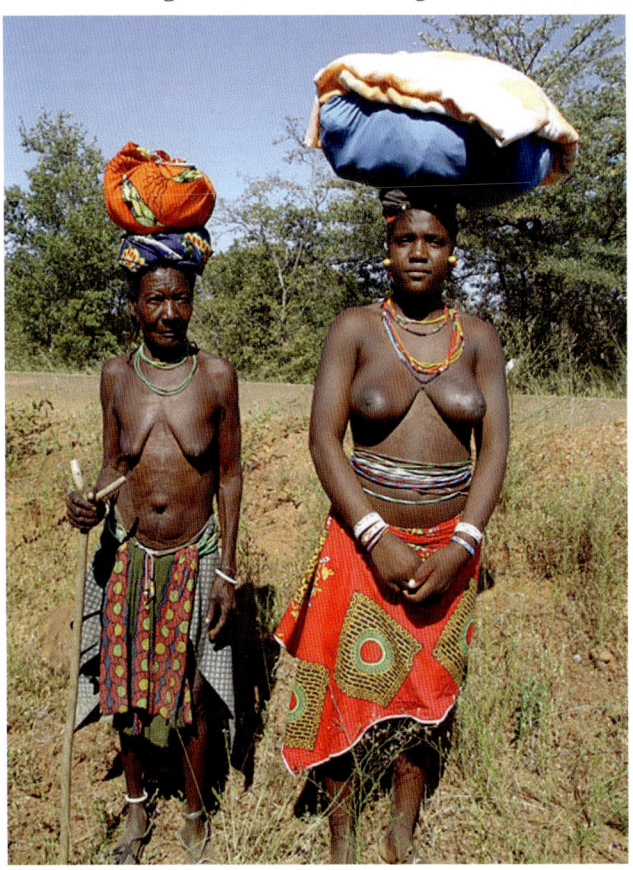

*The young and the old in Angola*

*The single ladies awaiting their turn to parade before the King for bride selection during the Reed Festival, Swaziland*

*Finally made it, Cape of Good Hope, South Africa*

*Frozen waterfall heading up Sani Pass from South Africa into Lesotho*

*Crossing the equator for the second time, now without Amy, Uganda*

*An abandoned hut in the arid region of northern Kenya*

*Young kids protecting their cattle from other tribes, remote north-western corner of Kenya*

*Mursi tribe, unique by putting plates in their lower lip, Omo Valley, Ethiopia*

*A reminder of a war-torn history in north-western Ethiopia*

*The dusty dirty streets of Djibouti City, Djibouti*

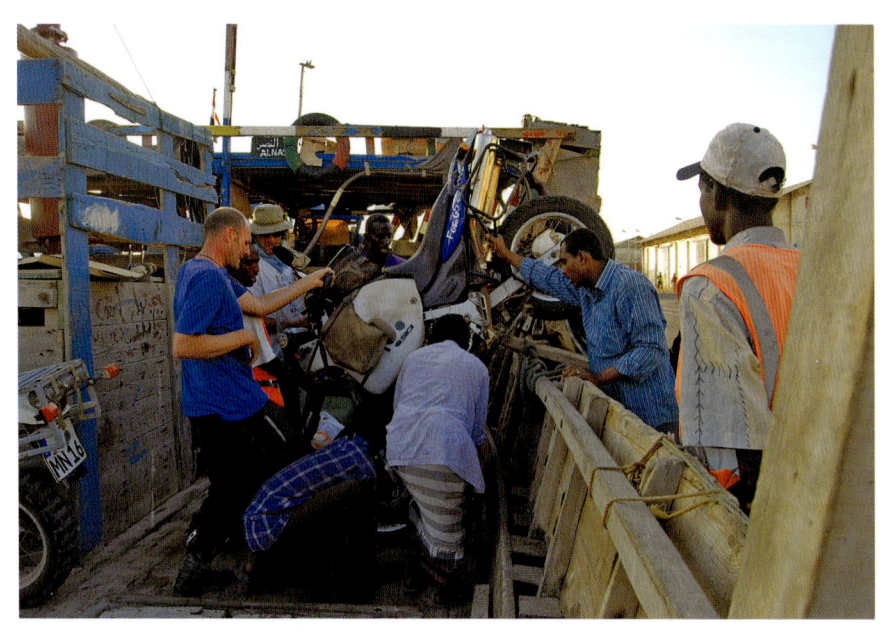

*Rene loading his BMW onto the wooden dhow that would sail us across the Red Sea from Djibouti to Yemen*

*A long journey across the Red Sea aboard the very small wooden dhow*

# PART TWO

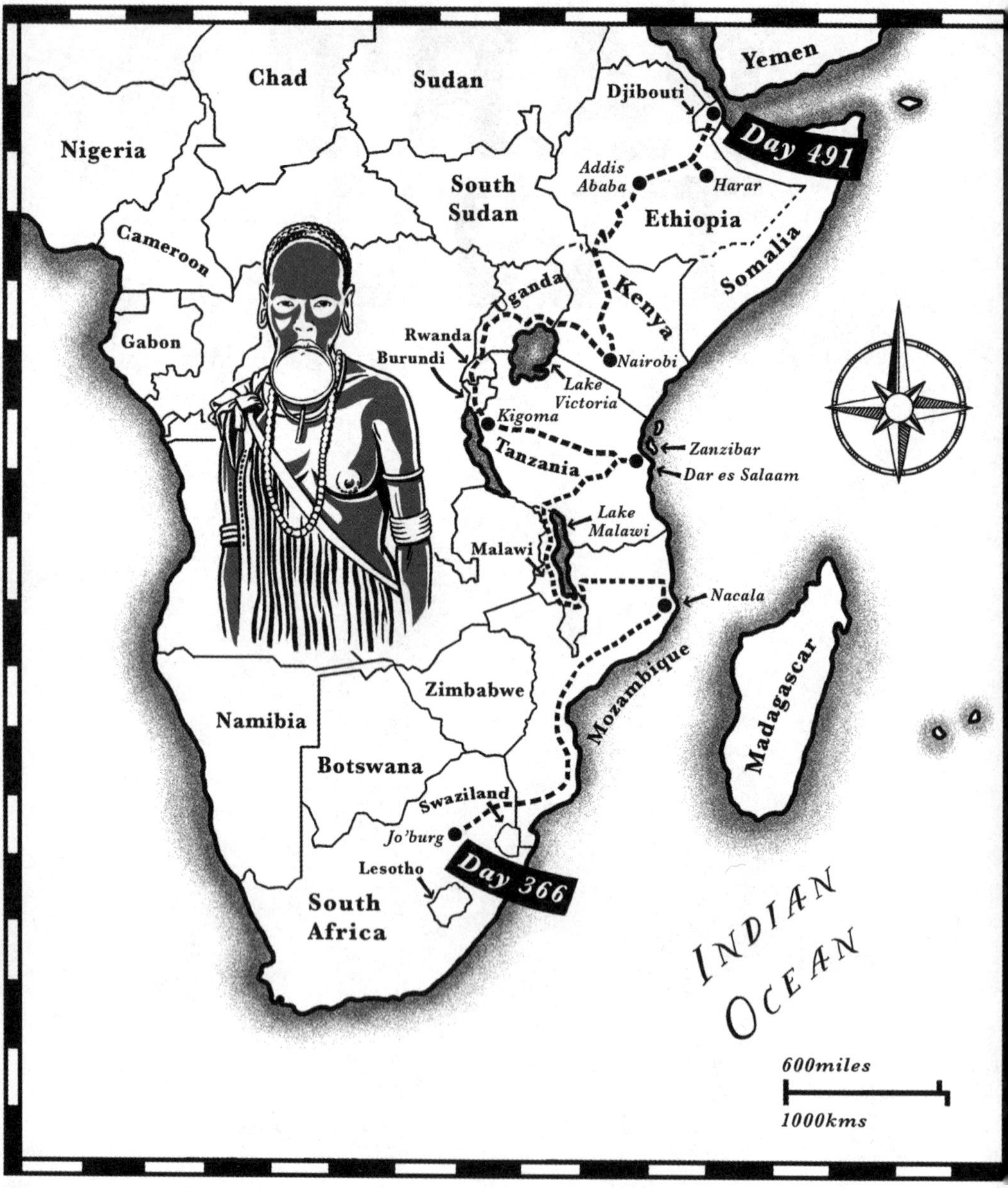

Chad
Sudan
Yemen
Djibouti
Nigeria
Day 491
Addis Ababa
Harar
South Sudan
Ethiopia
Cameroon
Somalia
Kenya
Uganda
Gabon
Rwanda
Burundi
Nairobi
Lake Victoria
Kigoma
Zanzibar
Tanzania
Dar es Salaam
Lake Malawi
Malawi
Nacala
Madagascar
Mozambique
Zimbabwe
Namibia
Botswana
Swaziland
Jo'burg
Lesotho
Day 366
South Africa
INDIAN OCEAN
600miles
1000kms

CHAPTER 4

# Eastern Africa

*Mozambique to Djibouti: 126 Days*

I knew the rest of the trip would be so much harder without Amy. For all intents and purposes, we had broken up but not made it official. (That would happen later.) I started my diary again at Day 1.

Exactly 13 months to the day since we'd left London together, Amy and I said our teary farewells at the Johannesburg airport. While standing in the long check-in line we tried not to mention the inevitable, but the time soon came for her to leave. We hugged and cried. Thirteen months together riding across Africa and now a total separation of around 12,000 kilometres. We were stronger than I'd expected. Amy wished me luck and told me to eat properly, put on mosquito repellent and a few other words of advice I usually heard from my Mum.

Eventually, we stopped hugging. Amy disappeared through to the departure lounge.

I wondered if I'd ever see her again. (I did several months later.)

**OUT OF SOUTH AFRICA**

I now faced what I'd always wanted: riding The Mothership back to Australia, over 50,000 kilometres away — and alone. I needed to prove to myself that I could do it and not quit when it got tough.

With eyes still red, I went to my bike in the airport car park and said, "Just you and me now. Let's look after one another." As I revved up and made the V-Twin rumble, some black maintenance workers resting nearby gave me the thumbs up. I told them I'd come from London and was riding to Australia via Russia.

They stared at me in utter disbelief. "You must be strong," said one of them.

I sure hope so.

The weather on Day One of Part Two quickly turned bad, with enough rain to wet my legs through. I stopped at Nelspruit and wondered if Amy was flying past somewhere above me. I collected two new tyres from Mark at the KTM shop and continued to Hazeyview. I stayed with some friends, Martin and Sasha, in my own cottage while I double-checked the bike, organised some passport-sized photos and bought a new pair of pants from a store called Mr Price.

I was already missing Amy and was still talking to her, both in my mind and sometimes out loud. Very quickly I was realising how hard it was travelling without her, and I hadn't really gone anywhere yet. Already I missed her company so much, especially at night. During the day I was fine because I had something to do, something to focus on: riding my bike. But it hit me so hard whenever I pulled up to a camping ground while the sun was setting. I felt so desperately lonely and began to wonder if I could survive another 10 months feeling like this. I wished so much that The Baja were parked next to The Mothership. Travelling with Amy was so easy most of the time, but my feelings were just one of the things I needed to overcome. I had to cope on my own for once.

## MOZAMBIQUE

I was continually afraid of travelling too fast — not from a safety point of view, but because I didn't want to get to Russia and Mongolia while it was still winter there. But time was money, and I was keen to hit the road, so I quickly headed towards Mozambique. I topped up with fuel because it was cheaper in South Africa, and

I also had to sort out my bike insurance. I even paid a fixer at the Mozambique border to sort out everything.

It was hot — a nice change from the South African winter — as I rode all day to a house owned by Fasie. (Amy and I had met Fasie at his small resort in South Africa, and he had said we could stay at his holiday house.) It was just the sort of place I liked, and with Amy, I could've easily stayed there for several days.

On my first real 'night on the road', I had the usual tuna and pasta for dinner, but I did it all myself; I was going to miss Amy's cooking. She had a real knack. We never went hungry, and the food was always delicious. I knew I had to be strong, but I got so bored in the evenings. *How was I going to cope? Should have I gone home with Amy?*

Whenever I got a rest day, I didn't know how to fill in the time on my own. I was staying at Fasie's place on a lake, and it should've been nice, but it wasn't; I was bored and lonely. I walked to the beach along two kilometres of deep sand. The water was clear and the dunes covered in small trees. To fill in the rest of the day, I went over my maps again and again, trying to calculate how long I'd need to spend in each place so I wouldn't reach Russia too early.

I knew I'd feel better when I meet some other travellers. Staying at proper camping grounds instead of camping in the bush would fix the boredom and loneliness a little but add to the cost of travelling. That night I had dinner with the owner and a worker at a lodge next door, Greg and Curtis. There was also Rod, an eccentric guy who cooked chorizo by burning Johnny Walker in a shallow bowl with a meshed toasting fork on top to sit the meat on.

The next day, the first unexpected adventure of Part Two happened. I loaded up The Mothership and set off down the very sandy track for about eight kilometres to the main road. Once I reached the road, I glanced down to check that my spare tyres (worth US$150 each) were still strapped on — the rear one on the left was, but the front one was not. *Shit!* Along the trail back to Fasie's place, I came across two local men I'd passed earlier walking in my direction.

We talked in very broken simple English (they spoke Portuguese), and they confirmed that when I'd passed earlier I had two tyres strapped to the back, which meant that the tyre was lost between that point and the road. Afraid that someone might've found and stolen it, I asked one of the men to sit on my bike with me and look for the tyre while I rode and checked with everyone as we passed. I was frantic about how and where I was going to buy a new tyre and about the cost. I was kicking myself for not having fitted them earlier and replacing the bald tyres I was still using. Finally, we found the tyre in the bushes.

Of course the spotter wanted money for his efforts, so I struck a deal. I didn't give him money, but I shot back a few kilometres to pick up his mate. Since the people spend their lives walking everywhere and time isn't a worry in Africa, perhaps the spotter would've preferred payment and letting his companion walk. The Mozambiquan people seemed more pleasant and friendly than those in West Africa. For one thing, they don't always have their hands out asking for things.

As I continued, with spare tyres attached more tightly, the weather turned really nasty. While eating lunch in Inambane, I met a Greek couple, Akis and Vula, the first travellers I'd seen since South Africa. They had come down through West Africa in a Land Rover as part of a sponsored 800-day trip around the world. I invited them to come with me to Fasie's other house in Tofo, a nice town with a clear, pleasant beach.

Finally, I got a chance to email Amy. She'd sent me three emails, which I was *so* happy to receive and read. She was finding it difficult to get back into the swing of things. Returning to a normal life was something I was *not* looking forward to.

Sometimes I wished that Amy hadn't gone home, and I was sure she would've stayed with me on the trip if I'd asked her. It had only been five days since she'd left and I felt so lonely at times, but I knew this would happen and I just had to accept it. These feelings wouldn't last forever, of course; maybe in 10–12 months I'd be home.

And once I reached South-East Asia, a region I loved, I'd feel so much closer to home. What lay in between was so daunting — yet exciting — and exactly the sort of thing I wanted to do.

I stayed in Tofo for a few days, more or less killing time and trying not to rush too far too soon. I had free rent, with a hot shower and comfortable bed, but I was also bored and very keen to get going again. I killed some more time by walking along the beach and into town. Also good for filling in the day was visiting the Internet centre, where I received some much-needed emails from Amy. I wished I was back in Australia helping her decide which of the two occupational therapy jobs that she'd been offered on the Gold Coast in Queensland to take.

Akis and Vula certainly helped with my loneliness, but they continued their trip after a few days. (I would later spend Christmas with them in Ethiopia and meet them several more times across South-East Asia. They even visited me at the farm back in Australia.)

I joined a small tour group to go 'snorkelling with the whale sharks' but only saw one shark and some dolphins jumping around. The solitary whale shark was massive, but I only saw it for about 30 seconds. It was something I'd always wanted to do, but I was disappointed. Maybe it was exciting for others, but sometimes I felt spoilt by all the things I'd seen on my travels. Some things just didn't excite me as much these days.

Maybe that's why my dreams had shifted immensely. I still desperately wanted to become a helicopter pilot, but I also had a desire to race motorbikes in the Australian Safari and, ultimately, the Paris to Dakar Rally (which has now moved to South America). But I knew that I wasn't a great rider — certainly not good enough to compete in a rally…yet. I emailed a few newspapers, magazines and Honda dealerships seeking sponsorship for these rallies, but I thought it would probably be a waste of time. (It was. No one bothered even replying.)

When finally leaving Tofo, I encountered my second-hardest day of riding yet. (The hardest was from the Democratic Republic of

Congo to Angola.) The main road was fantastic, but then I made my first mistake of heading to a beach town, Morronguloo, about 13 kilometres off the highway. The road was a little sandy, but despite my very bald tyres I managed to get there okay.

The camping ground was deserted, and it was only 1.30pm. I'd just had four days off and didn't want to hang around there on my own for the rest of the afternoon, so I set off for Pomene, another beachside spot about 50 kilometres further north that I was told was worth visiting. I should've stayed where I was.

The first 30 kilometres wasn't too bad, but I had to ride fast through the sand to keep the front wheel from digging in and throwing me off. The final 20 kilometres, however, were shocking; there was deep, *deep* sand with two deep ruts. I wrestled The Mothership well, but the muscles in my forearms quickly started to ache, and I was sweating hard. I had now committed myself to the track, and it was impossible to turn around; I'd gone beyond the point of no return.

In first gear and with the engine screaming, I bulldozed the bike through the sand. I had to keep a forward momentum to avoid getting bogged. When I did get bogged a few times, I would have to hop off, lay the bike on its side to raise the back wheel out, put sand in the hole, and with all the strength I could muster lift the bike back onto two wheels. I'd traversed these sorts of tracks so many times with Amy. Once again, I realised how much I missed her — and how hard it would be travelling alone.

Utterly exhausted, I rode along some other tracks to the beach, hoping to find harder and fresher sand. But this was another bad decision. I became bogged again within 10 metres. I got off and left the bike planted in the sand. While I stormed away in anger and drank some water under the shade of a tree, I wondered what the hell I was doing here. Stupidly, I still hadn't replaced my bald tyres with the new ones I was carrying, and I couldn't do it in this endless sandpit.

I stopped a local boy on a four-wheeled motorbike, assuming he was from the resort I was headed for (but he wasn't). Although we were unable to verbally communicate with each other beyond saying, "hello," he understood my predicament and pushed the bike while I revved. Then I fell into another massive sandpit, and again the back wheel was spinning into a trench. Once more, the bike tilted to one side forcing me to jump off.

I was so exhausted that I needed to rest again in the shade. A girl about 10 years old and her brother of about six helped me push the bike out of the sand. They heaved and I throttled (the bike, not the kids), and The Mothership eventually escaped from the clutches of the sandpit. By now I was getting so weak, but I had to push the bike for another 50 metres to avoid another sandpit and another spill. I hopped on again, and around a few more bends was my destination. The lodge was mostly empty, but I did meet some kind South Africans. The worse thing was that I'd have to cross the same track again tomorrow.

The next morning, I loaded the bike and pushed it about 10 metres to a harder part of the track. But I got no more than two metres from where I started pushing when the back wheel hit a root. It wouldn't go any further. I had to lay the bike over, fill the trench with sand, lift up the 250-kilogram Mothership again and keep going.

I managed to negotiate the rest of the track and headed north as the rain pelted down. On the way to Vilanculos, the road became good as the potholes disappeared. It was off-season and many camping grounds and backpacker lodges were closed or renovating, so finding a decent place to stay wasn't easy. I chose one camping ground simply because two South Africans and two Brits were there, and I needed a little company. But my sleep that night — the first in a tent during Part Two — was interrupted by dogs constantly barking.

As I continued north, the rain held off except for a little drizzle late in the afternoon. Because the cost of camping grounds in Mozambique was so high, I decided to camp in the wild alongside a river. A fisherman approached and insisted that I pitch my tent next to the mud hut he shared with his wife, two daughters and little boy. They only spoke Portuguese, but it was another great experience.

I'd been travelling now for over a week without Amy and feeling a lot better. Again I checked my maps and realised that I was covering a lot of ground, which was usually good, but not for this leg of the journey. I thought I'd be in Nairobi for Christmas and out of Africa around 1 February as planned. Clocking up 50,000 kilometres since leaving London, I was now about half way home.

After I rode only 200 metres the next morning, the rain started again. I headed inland via a ferry across the Zambezi River which had snaked all the way across the continent from Victoria Falls. There were no petrol stations, so I had to buy fuel from men with drums along the roadside. Once, I nearly ran out, but the seller wanted 40 *metical* (about US$2) per litre, so I only got six litres and hoped to buy more at Caia. But at that town, I had to pay 50 *metical* a litre, which was the going black market rate, even for locals. While filling up with fuel, I met two cyclists (from England and Holland) heading south. They told me what I certainly did *not* want to hear: current track conditions across Malawi, my next destination, were knee-deep in mud.

The roads in Mozambique were fantastic, however, so I could cruise at 90-100 kilometres per hour. There was little traffic, but I did see a bad truck crash. It had happened a week before, but only now was a crane trying to yank the truck from the river it had fallen into. The driver, a South African, was watching. The cut on his leg was nothing compared to the rest of his pain: Five of his mates in the truck were killed.

The landscape was typically African, with scattered vegetation and so many huts made from mud and straw. This often made it very hard to find an isolated place to pitch a tent. I thought I'd succeeded one night by setting up a campsite behind an abandoned house off the road. I cooked dinner and hopped into the tent before realising that someone actually lived in the house — or least under the veranda. I gave him my best friendly 'I'm-an-idiot-please-forgive-me' smile and offered him some chocolate. He let me stay in peace.

In Mozambique the sun rises at about 5am, so I was usually ready to start the day 30 minutes later. One morning, a few locals had already gathered for their morning entertainment, which started the second I got out of the tent. Unfortunately, this always made my regular morning shit problematic. And even when I tried to defecate a little later, someone else saw me, so I had to quickly hike up my pants and try again later.

I found an Internet centre at Nampula and chatted online to Amy. She was still finding it very hard to fit back into a 'normal' life. No one was really that interested in her trip beyond the usual questions, and nobody could relate to what she'd achieved. It wasn't their fault, but she was dejected by their lack of interest.

I headed to the departure point for Ilha de Moçambique (Mozambique Island) and stayed at a camping ground on a dirty beach. I met one couple from Spain, Anna and Antonio, who'd been through West Africa and were now travelling up the east coast, as well as another couple from Perth, Paul and Jacinta, who'd started in Cape Town and were also heading up the east coast. Both couples were travelling by 4WD.

The five of us hired pushbikes and rode together across to the island. The bridge was three kilometres long and narrow, so every time a car approached we had to squeeze past. Ilha de Moçambique was a major centre for slave-trading and formerly owned by Indians from Goa. It was then captured and fortified by the Portuguese before being attacked by the Dutch. Although the history is long and tragic, it's now just a sleepy little island set up for tourists. We walked around the old fort and swam in the ocean pools left behind after high tide.

At Nacala, only 123 kilometres further on, I stayed at Bay Diving, a camping ground recommended by Paul and Zoe (friends from the UK, now in Johannesburg). It was a nice place to relax for a few days while killing time in the Internet centre updating my blog — and fixing my bike. I changed the oil and filter, replaced a broken rear brake pad, put on new tyres and discovered a broken wheel bearing, which was replaced with some Chinese-made parts. I also went snorkelling with a Swedish guy and was stung on the leg by a jellyfish, which was really painful. I'd been stung before, but this felt so much worse. I also bought another tent from a German girl because my tent pole had broken.

The coastal road to the north continued to be reasonably good with just a few potholes here and there. As usual, there were plenty of ups and downs along the way. I got an 'up' when chatting with someone, but the 'down' was riding all day on my own, which made me wonder what I was doing and why.

The police at the checkpoints had been fine, but one day I was stopped three times to show my licence and bike documents. They didn't need to see the *carnet*, but I did have one major problem: My international driving licence had expired. (They are only valid for one year and could only be renewed in the country of issue — in my case, the UK.) I'd tried altering the date on the document from '2006' to '2008', but they noticed the alteration and mentioned the words "pay a fine". So I got out my 'Official Passport' and explained to them about my 'important work' for the Australian Government. I grabbed a pen and paper and asked for the policeman's name. He quickly buckled and let me go.

I headed west towards Malawi, a 500-kilometre trip along the first 'adventure trail' of Part Two. It was really slow going for the first 200 kilometres, with plenty of rocks and maybe 40–50 sandy washouts. (These are deep holes of dust so fine that it feels like riding through water — but worse because the sand engulfs the bike and rider. The depths of these sandy washouts are impossible to gauge, and they are a biker's worst nightmare. They're commonly known as 'bulldust' by Australians and '*fesh fesh*' by Europeans.)

I tried to reach the border town of Lichinga in one day but found a campsite beforehand in an old quarry undiscovered by locals. That night something appeared on one side of the tent — and then something else on the other side. I couldn't tell who or what it was and dared not move. I eventually fell asleep while breathing quietly and never discovered what had caused the sounds.

While riding to Lichinga along glorious rolling hills and past traditional villages, I continued to think about my arrival back home. I imagined riding along Roberts Road, past Torpey's old house, over the hills, through the sandy patch and then over some more hills before the scrub would come into view on my right. Then I would ride one more mile over the channel (which may not exist anymore because it could've been replaced by a pipeline), through the scrub and over one more rise. Appearing through the trees on my left would be where my Mum lives, the house I grew up in. Maybe I would arrive on a Sunday so people could be at the farm to welcome me.

At Lichinga, I found the Mr Chicken shop owned by Tracey and Dwayne (whose parents I'd met in Pomene). Their farm, on which they grew macadamia nuts and bred chickens, was remote, but they did have the Internet. From her emails, I could see Amy was struggling to readjust and desperate to be back in Africa with me. While most of the time I was able to cope travelling on my own, there were many times that I did miss being with her. She is such an amazing person for what she achieved on the trip to Cape Town. But she now needed to face her next challenge: a normal life with a normal job.

But maybe leading a normal life was the true challenge? And riding through Africa on a motorbike was easier?

Tracey and Dwayne were lovely and generous and fed me well — meat, meat and more meat — and I enjoyed the local beer, too. I was especially grateful for being able to sleep in their caravan when it poured. But the skies did clear, and after a huge breakfast of strawberries and cream and scrambled eggs on toast, I rode the final 150 kilometres along a smooth gravel road to the border.

## MALAWI

Both sides of the border went without a hitch. I only had to pay K1200 (about US$10) to temporarily 'import' my bike and K1500 for bike insurance because I no longer had a valid insurance. Even better, people in Malawi (and many other countries heading north) speak English.

I rode to Monkey Bay, perched along the gigantic Lake Malawi, which looks like the ocean when the wind picks up. I found an acceptable camping ground, where I needed to stay a few days because I was travelling far too quickly for the Russian winter. The camping ground seemed empty, so there was no one to share the cost of a snorkelling trip the next day around the lake.

Perhaps this was just as well because I started to feel quite sick. My runny nose and sore back indicated that I may have gotten malaria again. My health and mood didn't improve after I grazed my right knee on a rock while playing volleyball on the beach with some locals. But at least I wasn't the guy who'd died in the village and was the subject of much wailing, screaming and ceremonial singing.

By now I couldn't sleep, and the sore on my knee wouldn't heal properly. I now thought the malaria tablets (Doxycycline) I'd started taking five days before were making me sick, so I stopped taking them. I wasn't really fit to ride, which was okay because I needed to kill some time anyway. And it was so damn hot too.

Still with no real energy, I packed up one morning but had to wait for the kitchen to open so I could pay my bill. While riding along a short track across to the main road, I felt a strange chug and then felt it again. The noise sounded like I'd run out of fuel, which wasn't possible because I'd filled up. I opened the throttle to see if it would clear, but the bike just died.

Immediately looking for shade from the fierce sun, I pushed the bike 20 metres off to the side and under a big tree. I checked the fuel pump while a crowd of onlookers started gathering. The fuel pump was the problem, and I was so incredibly relieved that I'd been carrying a spare one since London. My audience was amazed as I 'magically' pulled a spare pump from my pannier. Five minutes later I hit the starter, and after a few seconds for the bowls of the carbs to fill, the bike roared into life. I was certainly not in the mood or well enough to cope with being stuck out there with no spare fuel pump. (But this raised the next problem: How could I get another spare fuel pump sent out to me?)

Travelling around Malawi was different to the past few months because so many more people walk or get around on bicycles. I guessed due to the increased poverty I'd noticed compared to the last few countries. Once, I passed a truck that had just turned over in the middle of the road, but no one was injured. Then I came across a shallow lake where hundreds of people were fishing with nets.

In Salima I was able to chat online to Amy again. She sounded in good spirits, which helped improve my mood too. Travelling was tough, and I kept wondering what the hell I was doing. Of course, the grass wasn't always greener on the other side, and my 'grass' was green enough to keep me going. I also met Martin and Anna from Holland, who invited me to stay at a village they worked at as part of an NGO education program. I declined because my knee was still hurting and I needed somewhere decent to relax and recuperate.

Instead, I stayed at a camping ground, Cool Runnings, at Senya Bay alongside Lake Malawi. It was quiet and had plenty of grass. A few expats stayed there while working in Malawi, and we all went to a bar. Before going to bed that night, I sat under a tree with a local called 'Porcupine' and watched a fight between two local drunks. (I could've sworn that one of them had been killed, but after getting the beating of his life, he just stood up and walked away.)

By 11 November, Remembrance Day, my health and mood hadn't improved when I stubbed my big toe the previous night adding to my list of problems. Now *that* was sore as hell too. I spent the day swimming in Lake Malawi and checking my bike.

Later, I decided to find Martin and Anna and take them up on their offer of staying in Mkukuhi Village, 30 kilometres away. The villagers danced and sang, which should've been interesting, but I just wasn't in the mood to enjoy it. And sand kept blowing into my pots as I tried cooking a dinner of tuna and pasta (again).

While I was sitting cross-legged on the dirt floor of a mud hut in Mkukuhi to eat dinner with the villagers, the wind picked up again. It was about to rain, so I dashed out of the hut to put the fly on my tent. When I returned, the villagers offered me an entire meal of fish, crushed maize and some green snot-looking stuff. I noticed a mouse scurry across the floor, but I had to be polite and eat what they offered. As a gesture, I placed my now semi-cold plate of untouched tuna and pasta into the middle of the floor for others to share. By the time they all helped themselves to my dish of tasty (but sandy) tuna and pasta, I was left with nothing. The only thing left to eat was something that looked like poo. Thankfully, it didn't taste like it.

I decided that I had the flu, and I just couldn't shake it. I had another restless night as the roosters crowed all night and goats tried to eat my tent. While riding, I felt so tired and just wanted to pull over and sleep, but it was nigh possible with so many people about. I hardly stopped along the 262 kilometres to Kandi Beach, where I planned to drink lots of water and rest. The camping ground was empty, which would normally be a disadvantage, but now I couldn't be bothered meeting anyone. But I did later come across an overland truck (my first) with the usual bunch of Aussies, Kiwis and Brits, including one whose claim to fame was that he cleaned windows on a house in London owned by the Scottish actor Ewan McGregor, who'd completed a similar trip through Africa (but with support vehicles).

As I continued north, my head was feeling a lot better, but my legs still felt like chunks of lead. The decent road veered away from the lake and climbed into the scenic hills before winding through a rubber plantation. I stopped at Nkhata Bay to buy tins of tuna and a plate of fried chips and post a letter to Amy.

While leaving the clean little town of Mzuzu, I noticed a line of stationary cars, so I slowed down. I was then stopped by a policeman. To the right was an oval with two massive dual-motor military helicopters surrounded by Malawians in their finest clothes. As I guessed, it was the President and his entourage. A few minutes later, the engines roared and the helicopters lifted off. I wanted my chopper licence more than ever.

While camped in the Vwaza Marsh Game Reserve, I could make out some hippos in the distance and I found loads of elephant dung, but all the wildlife I really saw were monkeys rummaging for food around the camping ground. Again, I felt depressed because I was missing Amy so much. I also began to realise that my prospects about travelling across China would not be good, but I needed to stay positive and remember that anything was possible.

Along a windy, dirty but pleasant road to the Mushroom Farm camping ground, my speedometer stopped working again. I should've stopped and fixed it then because 70 kilometres later the little white cog inside the speedo drive was stripped, so it was now completely broken. I would have to order these and some other spare parts from somewhere and get them sent out to me from Europe somehow.

Views from the farm high on a ridge spread over Lake Malawi and across to Tanzania. It was there that I met one of the strangest characters yet: an Australian 'half-hippie' called Jo-D, who had busked around Europe. He kept us all entertained by the campfire with his guitar.

**TANZANIA**

My first day in Tanzania was what I called 'TIA!' (This is Africa!). It was the first of many shitty days in this country.

The day started well (in Malawi) as I rode back down to the lake from the mushroom farm where I'd stayed. I passed two people from Ireland, who offered me a Tanzanian guidebook they no longer needed. So far, so good. I then met a French guy on a bicycle with a flat tyre and a broken pump. He was very grateful when I helped him using my pump. He gave me a hearty "God Bless You" as I left, but I don't think the Almighty was listening.

At the Malawi border I filled up my tank, leaving me the *kwacha* equivalent of about US$10. Between the two borders, I wanted to change my remaining *kwacha* for some Tanzanian shillings. As I pulled over, money-changers came running at me from all directions. In the space of a few seconds I was surrounded by dozens of Africans frantically waving money. It was crazy. I told them to slow down and back off, but they wouldn't listen. One man offered me a good rate (too good as it happened), so we swapped notes at the agreed rate.

While that was happening, all sorts of people, mostly other money-changers, started yelling and saying that he'd given me too much money. The original money-changer now wanted to cancel the transaction and get his money back. I agreed as long as he gave me my money back first. He did, so I returned his money. Everyone suddenly walked away and everything went quiet. *What the hell was going on?*

I checked my notes. The bastard had short-changed me by giving me back three banknotes instead of four. The difference was only worth about US$4, but I was so pissed off that I'd let it happen and that he had got away with it. The money-changer was long gone, and the others said they didn't know where he was. Of course, they were in on the scam. (Later, I met two Swedish cyclists who'd fallen for it too.)

Immigration at the Tanzanian border went smoothly, but not so the Customs. The officer was extremely rude and tried her best to process me as slowly as possible by talking to everyone else but me. I was patient, however, and eventually everything was completed.

A salesman wanted US$150 for bike insurance (which would last for the rest of my travels in Africa). I knew the price was too high, so I walked over to another shack that sold insurance. His price was US$100, but he wouldn't negotiate. I returned to the first man and told him about the US$100 policy across the compound. I offered to pay US$70; he said US$80. Because I was so hot and angry, I agreed.

I already hated Tanzania, and I'd only been in the country for two hours. Plus, the chain was crunching from the extra different links I'd put on in Namibia, and my knee had become infected. Both things would need to be looked at soon.

Things did not improve on my second 'TIA!' day in Tanzania. I didn't sleep well because the hotel bed was uncomfortable and the mosquito net kept touching my head. I awoke to some rustling. Somebody was right outside my window. I immediately heard some yelling and then footsteps running from my window only a metre away. I sprang up and noticed that the curtain had been pulled back through the bars and a stick with a hook at the end was being pulled back from outside. (I'd left the window slightly open to catch the breeze.)

I heard screaming and people yelling from everywhere. Pulling on my pants and shirt, I ran outside. In the dark at the far end of the hotel, I could see a man being beaten with some wood. I assumed it was the person who'd just been at my window and was aiming to steal from my room.

The man groaned more from the beating while guests and staff yelled at him in Swahili. Suddenly, he got free and started running towards me. Before he reached me, he turned, jumped onto a roof and escaped. I hurried back to my room to see if anything was missing. I couldn't see that anything had been taken.

I tried going back to sleep, but couldn't. I wasn't so much worried about the robber, but I was kept awake by the *muezzin* loudspeakers calling followers to the mosques. I was now back in an Islamic country.

Outside my room the next morning, I noticed a small bag with some tools that the robber had obviously dropped while trying to rob me. Then I realised my mobile phone was missing. He must've been able to reach the phone through the window. I didn't use the phone for calls (because I had no SIM card), but it was a handy alarm and calendar and included a list of telephone numbers of friends and contacts.

There were more problems later that morning with my chain. I had a new set waiting for me in Nairobi, but that was still 5,000 kilometres away. Now the speedo, choke and chain were no good. The Mothership seemed to be falling apart around me. After trying to order some spare parts and contacting Amy at an Internet centre with an incredibly slow connection, my dejection worsened with the discovery of another flat tyre. I'd now lost interest in my trip — well, maybe just the African section. I knew my misery was probably due to what had happened in the previous 24 hours and was sure things would get better. At least they couldn't get much worse.

Things did improve while I was riding through Mikumi National Park. I saw giraffes, zebras (dead and alive), elephants and springboks — the first wild animals I'd seen since South Africa. The roads were sometimes scenic and other times dead boring, but I eventually made it to Dar es Salaam. The Tanzanian capital was surprisingly calm on a Sunday, which suited me fine.

I found the ferry for Mikadi Beach, where I stayed at a camping ground. There were five overland trucks with tourists also heading to my next destination: Zanzibar, the infamous Arab slave-trading island. The ferry ticket was really expensive (US$70 return), and it seemed like hard work getting there (because I couldn't take The Mothership). But I'd never been to Zanzibar before — and certainly would never be coming back to Tanzania ever again.

The main village, Stone Town, reminded me of Morocco with its Arab influence and narrow streets. On the second day, I was going to hire a motorbike (a Baja) and look around, but I became ill. It felt like malaria (again), so I went for a test (again), and the result was negative (again).

I needed to rest, so I went back to the camping ground on the mainland. Soon, my burps stank of rotten eggs and I had an attack of the runs that was green. A nurse staying at the camping ground diagnosed me as having giardia. (This is a severe type of dysentery commonly contracted by eating something contaminated with faeces.) *Great, I'd eaten shit.* The manager of the camping ground arranged to get me tablets and rehydration satchels. I felt worse before I actually got any better, and the pus from the cut on my knee was still a problem.

After three full days of rest and medication, I was almost back to normal — knee and all. While recovering, I calculated that it was about 40,000 kilometres to get home, which at an average of 200 kilometres a day was about seven months. I wasn't enjoying hanging around and waiting for the Russian winter to pass, but I researched and found out that even in March (the start of spring) the *maximum* temperature could still be only 2 degrees Celsius. I decided that as long as I was in Almaty (Kazakhstan) no sooner than 1 April, I should be okay.

I decided to head to Burundi, another country that had been gripped by civil war for decades. I always took notice when people warned me about places, but with Amy I seemed to only take on half the risk. If we both agreed to go somewhere potentially dangerous, we went. Now there was no one else to ask and discuss things with.

Sunday was the best time to travel out of Dar es Salaam, and I headed west for the very last time. From Burundi, I would head in a gradual easterly direction all the way back home to the farm in Turriff. Along the road, there were a few buses and trucks (which sometimes forced me off the road) and huge speed-humps at the start and finish of every village and bridge.

At an Internet centre in Morogoro, I found out Amy's latest news: She hated being back in Australia and had had a small car crash (but was okay). She was quickly learning that the Big Bad World wasn't so easy and that friends were not always forever — some, maybe, but not all. I had been in her shoes. She was starting out afresh and finding it hard, but I knew she would come through. It was the same for me and this trip. We both needed to get on with life and enjoy it. And I had to take each day, kilometre and puncture at a time and remember what an amazing thing I was doing. I vowed to enjoy every day — good or bad.

Camping in the bush in Tanzania was problematic. One night, I was going to camp under the stars but heard loud noises that repeated over and over again. It wasn't a cat, but I didn't know what it was. I did see a jackal when I pulled up, but these noises seemed like something else. It was just one more time that I'd wished there were two of us. Amy would've been really worried, and I would've laughed. But here and now, I had no choice but to pitch my tent.

During that night, whatever it was got closer and louder. I did see something large — maybe a hyena — run along a ridge near my tent, but nothing else. The jungle was strange, with so many noises and shadows. I imagined what it was like for my father in the jungles of Vietnam with people trying to kill him. He was incredibly brave.

At Tabora, I met a Chinese guy who could tell me about a road to Kigoma. (No road was listed on my map, GPS or guide book — only a railway line. The alternative was a very long detour.) In broken English, he said the road was bad but then said it was okay — except for one impassable bit where the water might clear in a day. To avoid the lengthy alternative, I decided to give it a go; I could ride along the train track for that impassable section.

At the beginning, the road was great (for Africa, anyway), but I got my first rear puncture since leaving South Africa. What a disaster that was. Back in Durban I'd put a liquid in my rear tube to prevent flats, but after so many kilometres it was now like black liquid shit that made fixing the hole impossible. In despair, I threw the tube high into a tree and fitted my only spare tube. Later, just as I was tapping the final tent peg into the soft ground, it pelted with rain.

The road to Kigoma was still acceptable until Malagarasi, where it headed into a swamp. I looked around, found a harder surface and negotiated the rest of the way to Kigoma without any drama. The road actually improved as I passed some refugee camps full of Congolese. Kigoma was unexciting, and I was glad to bump into two Swedes on pushbikes, who suggested I stay at their hotel. It was the cheapest place in town and, perhaps not surprisingly, also a brothel.

## BURUNDI

The day I crossed into Burundi was amazing — the sort of day I would never have expected.

As Burundi and Rwanda don't apparently have ATM machines, I stocked up on Tanzanian shillings and fuel in Kigoma. But I was nervous. I'd done some research and asked plenty of people, and it seemed that Burundi was safe enough. Yet, for some reason, I was worried. *If so, why go? Why put myself in danger?* These thoughts were probably a result of being alone. With Amy, we could've shared our concerns, but by myself I questioned things more. Perhaps that was a good thing.

The mountainous road to the border was beautiful, and I was *so* glad to be leaving Tanzania. Despite all the hassles — being scammed and robbed and contracting giardia — the Tanzanian border procedures were straightforward. At a checkpoint on the Burundian border, I was asked for my passport, but the official had no idea what he was looking at or searching for, so he eventually waved me through. The Immigration post was further up the road in the first town, Madimba.

As I approached Madimba, I noticed hundreds of people walking and riding bicycles in the opposite direction. My immediate thought was that they were all fleeing the country because something terrible was happening. But it wasn't anything like that — just a coincidence. I was given a transit visa, so I only had 72 hours in Burundi.

As the tarmac road twisted down the magnificent mountains to Lake Tanganyika, I spotted hippos in the water. As I stopped to take some photos, the usual crowd gathered, but they were very friendly. On the way to the capital, Bujumbura, I passed so many soldiers with AK-47s and other ancient weapons lounging about. (Apparently one rebel group still remained in Burundi, but it was small and not very active — or at least I hoped that was true.)

While flicking through my out-dated guidebook for somewhere to stay, I noticed a few people with white faces. I hoped somebody would offer me a place to stay. Sure enough, a car pulled up and

David, an American, gave me a bed for the night. A lovely guy in his mid-60s, he is married to a Burundian woman, Gloria, and has two children. Like other expats in the region, David is very religious, but only once did he suggest that I also help spread the 'word of peace'. I was eaten alive my mosquitoes while staying there but was assured that malaria rarely existed at this altitude.

My leg had also become painful. A sore had formed like a huge boil on the back of my thigh. It was difficult to reach and in a painful position for a bike rider. Over several days, I tried squeezing it like a pimple, but it just got bigger and bigger. Some days, it actually felt like something was moving inside. By the time I'd reached David's house, I had squeezed it so many times that I had a bruise around the area. With a mirror, I could now get a better look. I heated up my Leatherman knife with the aim of lancing the sore and gave it one more squeeze. I squeezed it so hard that my eyes started to water.

Then something white shot out onto my leg. Feeling immediate relief from the pain, I wiped my finger across the white stuff on my leg and held it up. It was moving. I felt sick. On the end of my finger was a wriggling maggot. (Later, I found out that a certain species of fly lays eggs on clothes while they dry. When you put the clothes on later, the eggs hatch and burrow into your skin. That maggot had been growing inside of my body for over a week.)

## RWANDA

While leaving Burundi was easy, getting into Rwanda was not. First of all, the three-day visa cost a whopping US$60, and then Customs would not allow my bike into Rwanda without a valid *carnet* (which I no longer had). After some discussion, they allowed me and my bike into the country with an import permit (in lieu of a *carnet*) for 15,000 Francs (US$30).

Rwanda seemed more developed than Burundi, but I kept thinking about the horrors of the genocide in 1994. At Butare, it started raining again, but I couldn't find a hotel (and camping in the wild wasn't an option). Sunset was approaching when I came across the entrance to the Nyungwe Forest National Park, which I wanted to ride through. The guards told me there was a camping ground 36 kilometres inside the park for only 3000 Francs (US$6). I rushed along the mountainous road (about 2500 metres high) and through the clouds with one headlight. Not only was travelling at night dangerous but I was missing the amazing jungle scenery.

At the camping ground, I was told it would cost me US$20 to camp. (US$6 was what locals paid.) On top of that, I would have to pay a US$20 park entry fee — a total of US$40 for one night's camping. I refused these 'foreigner-only' prices, and again breaking my own rule about riding at night, I kept going. Using all my concentration, I avoided hitting any animals or falling into any potholes. Eventually, cold, tired and wet from ploughing through one too many puddles too quickly, I found a very basic guesthouse (at which I was the only guest). But this also cost me US$20 and didn't have hot water, despite promises.

My impressions of Rwanda were not good, but I couldn't stay more than three days anyway. I hoped things would improve once I'd left Africa, and I was keen to reach another continent. The problem was that I was still far ahead of my scheduled departure date from Africa, which was not before 1 February. That was still two months away — longer than the time it had taken me to ride from Cape Town but with less distance to cover.

Maybe I could travel around Ethiopia with Antonio and Anna — who would arrive at roughly the same time I would — or with Lisa, an acquaintance from London heading out to Africa for a vacation. Or I could stay in Dubai with Kathy and Craig (friends of Amy's I'd met in London) for a few weeks before hitting Iran. The good news was that the Russian winter had finally started, so I planned to be in Almaty (Kazakhstan) in three months.

Heading north, the road was good for a while, and then it turned into gravel hell as my kidneys shook, but the views along Lake Kiva were magnificent. Unlike in other countries, the kids in Rwanda ran away from me petrified, and the adults weren't very pleasant either. Or perhaps my patience had completely disappeared. While I was considering my route at Giysen, a crowd of Rwandans gathered and started touching me, poking everything I had and asking for money.

I asked them to stop. Some listened — most did not. "Fuck off!" I said.

"Fuck! Fuck! Fuck!" they repeated back.

I gestured for them to move away because I was leaving, but they didn't. When I started my bike, a few scattered because of the air and noise from the exhaust. I tried riding away, but one of them held on to the back of my bike and stopped me from leaving. I got off the bike while they continued to laugh like hyenas. I opened the blade of my knife to scare them. This worked. They all scattered. I shouldn't have done it, but they were crazy — literally. I explained their behaviour to a policeman who'd arrived, and he told them to keep moving away from me.

I needed to get out of Africa — and quickly. I wanted to be in Thailand, far away from this maniacal and chaotic environment.

There was no chance of a sleep-in on my last day in Rwanda as the gardeners started working about two metres from my tent at 6am. My impressions about the Rwandan people were countered by the kind offer of tea and toast by the receptionist at the camping ground.

As I headed to the Ugandan border, the morning air was clear and the scenery simply stunning, with three volcanoes visible from the road and one peak ringed by cloud. The mountains are home to the famed gorillas, but I wasn't going to pay US$500 to see them.

## UGANDA

Leaving any country rarely presents problems, but entering the next one often does.

At the quiet little border post, I left Rwanda easily, but my concerns about crossing into Uganda without a *carnet* were justified. The Ugandan official said I couldn't enter the country at this border but would have to cross at a different border and leave a deposit upon entry (and then collect it when leaving). This wasn't an option, so I explained my lack of fuel and cash, and the crazy cost of going back into Rwanda. He didn't know what to do with me, so he agreed that I would pay 35,000 shillings (US$20) to complete the paperwork he should've done in the first place.

In Kisoro, I was thankful to find an ATM machine, glad to be riding on the left-hand side of the road, and happy that Ugandans speak English. I stocked up on supplies and checked the Internet, hoping to read a few emails from Amy.

I was in for a shock.

Plenty of her emails were waiting for me, but the most recent one made me want to immediately get out of Uganda and head home. Amy didn't exactly say so, but it seemed that she wanted a break from me — or even to break up. She said there were 'many things she had never told me'. I could only wonder what that meant — and that it was so tough being back home. (It wasn't that great for me alone in a shitty little Ugandan town, either.) I now felt a million miles away from home. (Not that I really had a home. There's the farm, where Mum lives, but nothing else.)

I stared at the ceiling of my room with a knot in my stomach. Of course, I could pull out of the trip at any time, but why? And what did I expect, making her wait 10 months for me anyway?

Then something happened that would have a profound effect on my relationship with Amy.

I met an American doctor called Arti (of Indian origin) who was working in Kisoro. She offered me a spare room. While drinking Nile Beer and watching DVDs, we got along really well — and with a combination of my wanting a morale boost and her needing reassurance about her work in Africa, we laughed and flirted. There was a real chemistry between us, but I didn't intend to take it any further. She did make me feel good, and it had been a long time since I had had these sorts of feelings. I realised she felt the same way — and, well, what happened that night should be obvious…

It was something we both needed, but the implications later for Amy and I were enormous.

I hit the road the next day minus my neck scarf (or 'buff'), which I'd somehow lost. I rode through the thick rainforest of the beautiful Dwindi National Park. My bike started playing up, suffering a lack of power in the thin air as it did in Lesotho. It couldn't have been the spark plugs, which were only a couple of months old, so I kept going, trying to be positive about my bike and about Amy.

With the bike steadily improving in the lower altitude, I weaved through the amazing Queen Elizabeth National Park along potholes that I sometimes hit hard enough that the bike shuddered beneath me. I spotted loads of deer, elephants and buffaloes, as well as a lion perched in a tree. As I pulled over to take some photos, I noticed another lion nearby, about 40 metres away and watching me intently. I was even more concerned about dangerous wildlife nearby when I had to pull up along the roadside in the jungle to tighten my chain. I also discovered that another wheel bearing had gone. I hoped The Mothership wouldn't need fixing until Fort Portal, thankfully only another 100 kilometres along a tarmac road.

On the way, I passed the equator and took some more photos. In a camping ground on the rim of a volcano with a lake in its cone, I hoped to find some company, but it was empty. While trying to change the wheel bearing, I had to sit down again and take some deep breaths. Amy's email had hit me *really* hard. I couldn't handle it, and I cried. I had never missed her so much as I did at that moment. But there was no option: I had to pull myself together and fix the wheel bearing.

I spent hours trying to fix the bike, but it defeated me — and I accidentally smashed my thumb with a makeshift hammer. I gave up and lay in my tent. I was alone, dirty and hungry but too tired to cook. I started talking out loud as if Amy were there. I wanted to find the courage to stay positive, but I couldn't. I stopped writing in my diary that night because I was too upset.

The next day, the drama with my bike continued. I tried getting the bearing out, but it wouldn't budge, and I had the wrong tools. So I carried the giant rear wheel down the hill and waited for a car to take me into town. George, the camp owner, was also waiting by the side of the road. A car took us half way, and then I continued the bumpy ride on the back of a 90cc motorbike.

Thankfully, the mechanic got it fixed quickly with a proper hammer and levers. Having no energy or interest in eating since yesterday, I wanted to buy some food, but the 10,000 shilling note (US$6) I'd been given somewhere as change was a fake. Then, as I was repairing the bike at the camping ground, I damaged the other side bearing and had to go through the whole process of going into town again for more repairs.

I was hesitant about entering the Internet centre and reading another sad email from Amy. There were more from her, but I was too depressed to reply.

The really rough road towards Masindi stopped at a bridge or causeway that had been washed away. Following a local as he walked, I rode through the water with two guys at each side in case I toppled over. The water was flowing fast, but I managed to get through.

At the dusty, decrepit town of Masindi, the gateway to the Murchison Falls, I wrote a long email to Amy — a final, last-ditch effort to fight for our relationship. I decided it would be my last email; if nothing came from it, I would never ask or try again. If she wanted it, I would have to let go of her and respect her wishes. The only good news was that Lisa, an acquaintance from London, would bring some spare parts for the bike with her to Ethiopia.

Along the road north to Murchison Falls National Park, the bike and I were soon plastered in dust. Again, there was a dual-pricing system, with foreigners charged far more than locals to enter the park: US$20 for me and even more for The Mothership. But I'd come all this way, and I'd probably never come again — and money didn't seem to matter after the recent news from Amy.

While trekking in the park, the chimps put on a kind of 'sex fest'. The solitary female of the group had it off with all the males about a dozen times in the hour I was there, with each little session lasting about three seconds. With my fill of monkey porn, I headed to the falls, which were quite spectacular. (The water eventually runs into the Mediterranean via the Nile.)

While the park wasn't too touristy, no one else was about, so I rode on to the Red Chilli Camp Site on the Victoria Nile (as it's called there). I rested up and planned the rest of my trip in sections: Stage 1 was getting to Nairobi, Stage 2 was getting out of Africa, Stage 3 was getting to the United Arab Emirates (UAE) via Yemen, Stage 4 was going on to Mongolia, Stage 5 was continuing to Laos via China, Stage 6 was going from there to Australia, and the final leg would be from Darwin to the family farm at Turriff.

Although the road was good and I was making steady progress towards Kampala, the drivers were maniacs. Again, I cracked. I'd been forced off the road about a dozen times by various vehicles overtaking on the wrong side of the road coming towards me. As some idiot in a Toyota 2.8 litre diesel did the same, I furiously gave him a middle-finger salute while pointlessly shaking my head and fist at him. Then came the final straw. Another car sped towards me on my lane while overtaking and flashing its lights to force me to move over. Again, I had to plough into a ditch and stop along the gravel roadside.

I was indescribably angry. Looking down at the gravel, I saw a rock the size of a golf ball. I picked it up, placed it on my lap, and pulled back on to the road in anticipation of the next idiot to run me off the road. I didn't have to wait long — about two minutes. This time it was a taxi-driver. I waited until the vehicle was just ahead of me, forcing me to swerve from my lane, and I threw the rock at the taxi's windscreen. I just didn't care about the damage or consequences; I'd been playing chicken with these idiots for far too long.

It was another incident that made me wonder if I had what it took to finish my trip. I was so tired of all the shit. It was becoming really tough, and I was questioning if I had the energy for what lay ahead. I knew what I did was wrong, but they had brought it upon themselves. The impact and noise of the rock hitting the windscreen was huge, but I kept going. I never found out what happened to the car or its passengers.

The Ugandan capital, Kampala, was hectic, and the traffic just as maniacal. As a truck turned at one intersection, its rear wheels were cutting a shorter turning circle than the front, so its trailer hit my pannier. I had to make way by barging into two more motorbikes. Not needing to stay in Kampala, I happily headed out to Jinja, about 80 kilometres further on.

At the Nile Explorers Backpackers, I met up again with Jim and Sherry, the two Americans driving a Land Cruiser whom I'd met in Namibia. I enjoyed catching up with them over a cold beer or three, but the backpackers staying there were crazy, so I found a quieter spot to camp. That evening I thought someone was trying to break into my pannier as I heard the lid clanging. I bolted upright in my tent and felt for the zip in the dark, but something hard was blocking the tent door. I quickly jumped out of the other door to confront whoever was messing with The Mothership. I then noticed that my bike had fallen over onto the tent. The bike had been on its centre stand, but one side had slowly sunk into the ground because of the rain. I heaved it up and went back to sleep.

An engine mounting bolt nut had come off and my chain problem had returned, so I had to stay there another day to work on my bike. I was keen to get to Nairobi but worried about entering Kenya without a *carnet*. I was even warned by one guy in a 4WD that it wasn't possible. I stocked up on supplies in Jinja but couldn't find anyone to share the cost of a rafting trip down the Nile.

Instead, I managed to organise a tandem kayak (which I'd never done before) with a guide called Henry. The rapids were huge, and not being in a large raft was really scary. The first rapid was massive — Class V — and we capsized. I got stuck on some rocks, and as the water pushed me over the edge, my feet and knee hit the rocks hard and dislodged some skin.

Eventually I clutched the safety kayak (operated by another experienced guide) and broke free, wondering if I'd actually fractured my foot. Feeling a little better, I climbed into the safety kayak. I wasn't so keen to hop back into my two-person kayak with Henry, but I had no option. From then on, we worked well and only capsized once more.

That evening, I relaxed with a few beers and tried to enjoy myself at a barbecue. Watching the antics of the crazy backpackers in the bar, I wondered if maybe I had finally grown up. Mum would be pleased.

### KENYA

I awoke feeling sore: in the head from last night's beers and in the knees from kayaking.

I agreed to give a lift as far as Nairobi to Chris, a sort of hippy who did a weird 'food prayer' before eating her vegetarian food. As usual, getting out of Uganda was easy. But, as expected, Kenyan Immigration wanted to question me about where I'd been because of an Ebola outbreak. (I lied.) For the bike, I just filled out a Customs form and got it stamped. No money. No hassles. Then Chris announced that she'd left her bracelet at a restaurant on the Ugandan side of the border. Thankfully, the police on both sides understood and let us through and the bracelet was still there.

Not long into Kenya the weather turned really nasty, with the wind sweeping white waves of rain and hail across the road. It was the worst weather I'd ever ridden through. I turned on the headlight but still couldn't see, so I frantically looked for somewhere to pull over and shelter. The storm only lasted 20 minutes, but we were absolutely soaked.

It was still freezing by the time we reached Eldoret, where we stayed in a cheap (but quite nice) hotel. I was asleep by 7.30pm and slept almost 12 hours. In fact, I slept so well that I didn't hear Chris, whom I'd heard earlier drop a fart loud enough to wake the dead from across the room.

It was now only about 300 kilometres to Nairobi, the end of Stage 1, Part 2. A petrol station attendant persuaded us to take an alternate route, which was good for most of the way. It even turned cold as we climbed to 2700 metres and crossed back over the equator and into the Southern Hemisphere. Soon we were in the Kenyan capital, Nairobi — also known as 'Nai-robbery' because of its extreme crime rate.

At the Jungle Junction camping ground, the guests were quiet, the grass was green and the food was tasty. Checking my emails, I found out that Antonio and Anna were in Nairobi, but they were ready to leave very soon because they'd obtained their Ethiopian visas. I wanted — in fact, I *needed* — to travel with them to Lake Turkana (Northern Kenya), one of the most amazing and primitive places on earth. To do this, extra fuel for my bike needed to be carried in another vehicle. I also wanted some sense of security because of the lake's remoteness and armed bandits.

Staying only five kilometres away, Antonio and Anna agreed to wait for a few days. This gave me time to change the oil, replace the spark plugs, upload some photos, and obtain the all-important Ethiopian visa. I also needed a rest. They noticed that I'd lost weight, so I suppose I hadn't been looking after myself too well.

The day I started preparing for the trip to Lake Turkana was a public holiday, so nothing much was open, which included the Ethiopian Embassy. I rode to the Karen Camp ground, where some spare parts (rear tyre, chain and sprockets, plus two oil filters) had been transported in an overland truck from South Africa. I'd arranged this in Cape Town, thereby saving myself from having to carry them.

(Amazingly, the German man that ran Jungle Junction had a brand new Africa Twin fuel pump, which I bought from him at a premium price. I felt at ease having a spare because fuel pumps are a constant source of problems with Africa Twins, as well as rectifiers blowing and batteries overcharging, which I'd already experienced in Namibia.)

All was going reasonably well, although I was missing Amy, of course. I wished I could be back home to give her a big hug and tell her that everything would be okay for her. I just wanted her to find happiness within. Then maybe we could have a chance to be together.

After I eventually got my Ethiopian visa, I had to get an exit stamp from Kenya because there was no Kenyan Immigration post along the route we would be taking. I also got another email from Amy, who'd sent me a letter to Karen Camp, so I took another trip out there. Luckily, the letter arrived the day before I was leaving. It was lovely to read her words as I slowly devoured the Cherry Ripe chocolate bar she'd sent me.

Just before we left for Lake Turkana I fell extremely ill, with a horrible burning in my stomach. I thought I'd have to go to hospital, but a Dutch couple, Ilvy and Ilja, gave me some powerful tablets (painkillers) that worked a treat. The pain disappeared the next morning. So, while Antonio and Anna left for Lake Turkana, I stayed one more day to make sure I didn't have a reoccurrence of the sickness. (I didn't.)

On the way out of Nairobi, I saw a dead man. He'd just been hit by a car a few seconds before. He was lying on the roadside, wide-eyed and with his body twisted and blood streaming from his head. There was no point in stopping. I was also keen to get out of Kenya quickly to avoid the chaotic post-election rioting (that would soon lead to many deaths).

Accompanying me as I rode out of Nairobi was a 4WD driven by an Australian couple, Jacinta and Paul — whom I'd met in Mozambique, and another belonging to the Dutch couple, Ilvy and Ilja. We only travelled a short way to Nyahruru to meet up with Antonio and Anna. The bike was running smoothly, and it was newly cleaned (as were my clothes), so I was primed for a new adventure. And I had some company for a few weeks, which would be a nice change.

As we headed into the unknown and skirted around Mount Kenya, the countryside became more barren, with little more than thorny acacia trees. The first 30 kilometres were tarred, but beyond Rumuriti the road turned ugly. 'Civilisation' now ceased to exist. Although only 250 kilometres from Nairobi, a vibrant city of flat screen TVs and huge supermarkets, the local people here in the north western region of Kenya wore the most amazing beads around their necks and piercings in their ears. It was hard to take photos, however, because the people always demanded money.

It was only after lunch on day two of our travels through the Rift Valley that I had my first flat tyre since Tanzania. I fixed it quickly, but the hole was on the wall of the tube where it flexed most, so sure enough, 10 kilometres further on the tyre went flat again. I decided to put in my new tube instead.

It was enjoyable with six extra people to chat with, but I wished Amy was with me too. As I started heading closer to the Middle East (only three to four weeks away) and Asia, I wondered how much time I would be travelling on my own. I was sure I would survive, but it was daunting. I was still loving the trip but also looking forward to riding home to the farm.

The north-west corner of Kenya is one of the most amazing places in Africa. The landscape is harsh, full of sharp rocks and thorn trees, so I was constantly wondering when my next puncture would come. The Samburu people are so beautiful. Women wear 10 to maybe 100 rings of beads around their necks, while the men and women paste ochre in their hair and around their necks. We gave a Samburu man a lift and got some great photos of him.

After loading up with extra fuel (at US$3 per litre) for the rest of the trip into Ethiopia, I went over a hill and saw a group of six to eight men with machine guns. I stopped, a little concerned, but quickly realised they were really just boys — one was as young as 12 years old. They had an assortment of machine guns, except one who just stood staring at me. A man armed only with a spear approached and tapped my helmet. I slowly removed it and gestured for him to wear it, slipping it over his head. This broke the ice and everyone smiled. The boys said they were 'warriors' fighting cattle rustlers from other tribes, but they were friendly enough to us. We took some more great photos of them with their 'toys'.

Not long after, I understood the remoteness of where we were going and felt completely in the wild. Paul and Jacinta had to turn back to Nairobi because they were headed in another direction, so with my Dutch and Spanish friends, I delved deeper into this remote corner of Kenya. Heading towards Lake Turkana, the scenery was extraordinary — like it would be on Mars. The roads were tough and made of volcanic rock, often forcing me to skate on my bike from one side of the track to the other. When I stopped once for a photo, the wind blew my bike over, snapping my front brake lever in half.

During the intense heat one afternoon, I was negotiating a sandy track and moving a lot quicker than the 4WDs. I would often pull up and sometimes wait 20 minutes for them to come into view before I'd set off again. At one stage, I saw a dry riverbed of white sand in front of me and to my left a two-wheeled track diverting off. I then noticed that the track I was using had no signs of use, so I needed to get off quickly. I slammed on both brakes, and The Mothership started sliding. Then I saw it: the riverbank had washed away, with a one-metre drop into the sand. I knew I wasn't going to stop in time, so I stood on the foot pegs and steadied myself for the impact. A dirt bike would be fine, but the full-loaded 250 kilogram Mothership was like an anvil on wheels.

I managed to reduce some speed, but the bike went over the edge. The suspension fully compressed with a huge jarring bang, and I came to a complete stop. The bike was planted in the sand but still upright as the dust washed over me. For a while, I just sat there alone on the bike. Peering down the riverbed, I noticed a lady with a leather-hide skirt and beads around her neck standing by a huge hole. A small child appeared and poured water into a container. The lady had seen my near-crash and came towards me. Without saying a word, she offered me a drink. After flicking pieces of wood and other debris from the surface, I drank the muddy water. Although we are worlds apart, human nature is constant.

Life around Lake Turkana was obviously extremely tough. Somehow, people and animals had evolved so they could survive by drinking small amounts of water from the salt lake. Men constantly move their camel and goat herds looking for something to eat, while kids run around wearing no clothes at all. We came across some tribal people who were desperate for water, so we traded what little we could spare for some photos. Their world is so far removed from ours.

During our entire trip to this region we did not see any other travellers.

**ETHIOPIA**

As we knew, there was no Kenyan border post, but we'd already had our passports stamped out in Nairobi. On the Ethiopian side, there was a little tin shed where some bored officials wanted to see our passports for the hell of it. We all knew we'd have to get our entry stamp for Ethiopia in Omarate, about 60 kilometres further up the track.

Our main reason for visiting this part of the country was to find some amazing tribes, such as the Hammer people with their bizarre ceremonies. We saw a young boy jumping about four times over about six cows lined up side by side as part of ritual to reach 'manhood'. Just before that, women in the boy's extended family (such as sisters and cousins) worked themselves into a trance by blowing whistles and horns and then 'begged' to be whipped by other men. This obviously caused the women's backs to bleed and huge gashes to appear, but the wounds were quickly soothed with a white milky solution.

At the market towns of Turmi, Dimeka and Sinka, we tried a local dish called *engira* — spicy meat or vegetables on top of huge pancake-like bread. It was tasty but resulted in almost earth-shattering flatulence from all who consumed it. At Turmi, we celebrated Christmas. Ilvy and Ilja took some Polaroid photos of the group, which they gave me along with a bottle of Coke. Exactly one year before, I'd celebrated Christmas in Mali with Amy.

Besides company, there was another good reason for travelling in groups around this part of the world. The 4WD belonging to the Dutch couple broke down at the bottom of a dry creek. We towed it out using a winch from Antonio's vehicle, but it still wouldn't start. Working for hours, we tried everything (I even successfully removed the complete immobiliser system), but still nothing. Then I had a brainwave: Give it a push-start. The 4WD fired up, but we had to repeat this several more times over the next few days. (I found the problem later. The earth lead from the battery had corroded.) Then Antonio's spring hanger (a bracket that holds one end of the suspension to the chassis) on the rear broke, but between us we were able to fix that too.

Normally, visiting villages in which the Mursi tribe lived meant paying a hefty entrance fee (about US$25), so we made up a story about visiting to research and give aid and I showed my 'Official Passport'. Again, it worked. The Mursi were the most amazing tribe we visited. The women wear huge plates in their lips and ears, and the men wear nothing — except for AK-47s slung across their backs.

After leaving the Omo Valley, we entered the very scenic Ethiopian Highlands, where I completely ran out of fuel for the first time ever (after about 60,000 kilometres). This happened because I had to travel an extra 60 kilometres or so, using precious fuel to back-track. Somehow I'd missed the others in their 4WDs come past me in a busy town. I still thought they were behind me, when in fact they were actually in front. I got within 15 kilometres of Shashamene but ran out, even after pouring fuel from my stove into the tank. I had to push The Mothership for an hour (over 4 kilometres) in the blistering heat before the others finally came back. Thankfully, they were carrying extra fuel for me.

While I was riding one day, a girl herding cattle threw a huge stick at me. I had to duck as it whizzed past my head, but I kept going. A little further along, a boy threw some kind of fruit and hit me in the chest with a thud. I casually stopped, got off my bike and pretended not to notice him standing only 30 metres away. He just stood by the roadside, wondering what this alien from The Mothership was doing. I then sprinted towards him. Screaming, he fled and quickly veered off the road into a thick bush. He was stuck there like a terrified fly in a spider's web.

I pulled him out and marched him down the road, holding his arm while a man, who I assumed was the boy's father, came towards us. Using hand-signals and a rock, I explained what the boy had done. The old man was suitably furious. As I handed the boy over I gave him a boot up the bum, which was nothing compared to the belting the old man started giving him. I felt like a bully as I left the boy in tears, but I hoped he'd learnt his lesson. Of course, there were thousands more like him across the region.

After two weeks in the bush, we finally arrived in Addis Ababa, where we celebrated the New Year and the completion of an amazing adventure along the Lake Turkana route. Of course, being in a capital city meant getting another visa — this time for Yemen. But the Yemeni Embassy told me I would need a 'Letter of Introduction' from the Canadian Embassy (which served as a de facto Australian Embassy) and that the Yemeni visa would cost 600 *birr* (US$32). The Canadian Embassy wanted 450 *birr* for this letter, and it was closing down for the Ethiopian Christmas long weekend. Instead, I decided to apply for the Yemeni visa in the next country, Djibouti. (In hindsight, this was *not* a brilliant idea.)

My fellow travellers departed in different directions. I started feeling a bit strange — lost again. From her emails, Amy was still having a tough time back home but trying her best. Sometimes I felt I needed to tell her to be free and not consider me anymore. Maybe I should let her go so she could make the right decisions and follow her dreams, although I'd love to encourage, support and help her with those dreams. I wasn't feeling in the right frame of mind; I still loved the adventure and riding, but I didn't want outside factors playing on my mind. Maybe I needed to free myself of her hassles and focus on the rest of the trip, which would be an enormous challenge and huge test of my character.

I soon met up with Rene, a Canadian guy on a BMW 650 Dakar bike, and Hugh, whom I'd first met in Abuja (Nigeria) a year before outside the Angolan Embassy. Rene was also heading to Yemen, so we decided to team up, even though I would've preferred to travel there on my own. Even better, I wished I could be travelling there with Amy. But my immediate plans were thwarted by more illness.

We were due to leave for Djibouti on (Ethiopian) Christmas Day, but the night before I awoke freezing, forcing me to get into my sleeping bag under the blankets. I assumed it was the altitude because Addis can get cold. The next morning, after trying to send an email to Amy (but the Internet was down) and getting some more money, we departed. But I felt exhausted immediately.

Along the way to Awasa, the road and traffic were good because of the public holiday. Despite my ill health, we pushed on and rode into the mountains (which were around 2300 metres high). It was cold, and finding somewhere to pitch a tent was difficult. As usual, I cooked pasta for dinner and then just collapsed into my sleeping bag, clothes and all. Although the overnight temperature was quite mild, I awoke in a pool of sweat and my pillow was soaked.

The next day, we went to Dire Dawa so Rene could apply for a visa to Djibouti (which I'd already got in Addis Ababa). Waiting in the hot sun, I felt freezing cold. I knew I was getting worse. At the next town, Harar, we stopped at a crappy hotel where I lay in bed with a headache and pain all over my body. I felt like I was about to catch fire. Using a thermometer from my first aid kit, I checked my temperature: 39.6°C. Dripping with sweat, I took a three-wheeled taxi to a hospital. After maybe 45 minutes, a pleasant English-speaking doctor took some blood and tested me for a few things, including typhoid. But the result was obvious: I had malaria again.

I immediately started a course of tablets and was soon feeling good enough to see a tourist show called The Hyena Man. We walked to the edge of the walled city, where amongst the rubbish and sewerage drains a man started yelling in the local language, Amharic. Slowly, hyenas appeared from the bush, gingerly approaching him as he held out raw meat from the end of a short stick. The climax of the show was when the hyenas snatched meat from the man's own mouth.

After a sleepless, malaria-induced night, I felt a little better, so we rode 50 kilometres back to Dire Dawa for Rene's passport and Djibouti visa. But I was in bed at 10am and slept through the entire day — this time, thankfully, in a nicer hotel. With a day's rest and spaghetti for dinner, I felt good enough to tackle the ride to Djibouti the next day. The landscape was arid but beautiful. Tanks from a previous civil war were still scattered along the road as we came close to the border with war-ravaged Somalia. The wind picked up, forcing me to use my limited energy to steady The Mothership. I watched the kilometres count down on my GPS as I approached my final country in Africa.

## DJIBOUTI

I had no *carnet*, so I told the Ethiopian customs officer a story about me crossing into the country at Omarate, where I was told I could use my Kenyan Temporary Import Permit (TIP). They accepted my story. The Djibouti immigration officers seemed high on *qat* (pronounced 'chat'), an addictive leaf that gets them stoned, and they stamped me through without any problems.

At the Customs shed, one man — his teeth riddled with decay from chewing *qat* — wanted to see my vaccination book. I handed it over, which made him quite confused, then happy. The officers asked to see my *carnet*. I explained that I didn't have one, which also made them quite confused, then happy. It was surreal. Everything I said, they did. I felt like a Jedi Knight controlling their minds. Obviously stoned, the officers stamped whatever they had to stamp and let us go. We continued into a strong headwind along a road lined with plastic bags, goat herds and trucks waiting to take fuel into Ethiopia.

My first impressions of the capital, Djibouti City, were not good. In fact, it's a shit hole. But Rene and I only needed to stay for as long as it took us to get a visa for Yemen. A helpful official at the Yemeni Embassy, Riad, explained that we had to return the next day because it was Friday, the day of prayer in this Islamic country, and that Rene would need a 'Letter of Introduction' from his own embassy (which I didn't need because there is no Australian representation in Djibouti). Riad also added that a boat for Mocha in Yemen would be leaving at 2pm in two days' time. Another guy also seeking a visa suggested it might be possible to pitch our tent at the British Consulate.

Armed with all this information, we rushed to the Canadian Embassy for Rene's 'Letter of Introduction', but it was closed, of course. In fact, it was only open between 9 and 10am. *Shit!* We wanted to get on that boat to Yemen, and we dreaded paying for a hotel because a large French military presence and wealthy shipping crews had made Djibouti City a very expensive place to stay.

I contacted a pastor mentioned to me by someone in Nairobi, but he said there was no room at the mission, so we tried the British Consulate. Eventually, we found it, but a man at the gate said it was closed and the Consul was asleep. The guard suggested we come back 30 minutes later. After eating a disgusting baguette with meat and chips, we went back and met Alain, a man who was about 65 years old and wearing a lengthy sarong. Alain was a French lawyer who also acted as the British Consul. He lived in a magnificent home with a swimming pool and a garden with outdoor showers and toilets. He said we could camp there. It was perfect.

While unpacking our gear and trying to contain our excitement about such a lovely, free place to pitch our tent, the Consul came back out to the garden. He opened up the doors of the guesthouse and said that we could stay there instead. It had two bedrooms, TV, air-conditioning and — wait for it — a maid who washed our clothes. *Heaven!* Somehow, we — an Australian and Canadian — had scored five-star luxury at the British Consulate in Djibouti run by a Frenchman while seeking a visa to Yemen before sailing on a boat owned by an Indian. And it got better...

Alain rang the Canadian Consul (who was Greek!) and asked him to ring the Yemeni Embassy at 8.30am on Saturday so that Rene would not need a 'Letter of Introduction'. The Internet there also had the fastest connection I'd seen since leaving South Africa, so I could upload photos onto my blog.

We went to the Yemeni Embassy at 7am sharp on Saturday. This was a waste of time because it didn't open until 8.30am (although Riad said to be there at 7am). We waited and waited — and waited some more — until about 1pm, only to be told that the embassy had just run out of visa stickers. We would have to come back on Monday. This caused two immediate headaches: we would miss the next boat to Yemen, and could we stay longer at the 'Hotel British Consulate'?

We rode out to the port and asked around for info on the next boat. It seemed there would be no problems getting a boat to Yemen, but the process was unclear and the departure would be chaotic. Alain and his wife let us stay with them longer and regaled us with their travel stories, which included being kidnapped by Somalis.

While we did enjoy the amazing luxury and hospitality at the Consulate, we hated hanging around Djibouti. I just wanted to get out of Africa. To fill in time, we rode to Lake Assal, a salt bowl and the lowest point in Africa (156 metres below sea level). While taking some great photos and enjoying our lunch, we could see where the earth is actually splitting apart — so much so that one day this tiny portion of Africa will actual break off and become an island.

We went to the port again the next day. As we knew, there was no regular schedule: One boat had left the previous evening, and the next could be in two or three days. We went back to the Yemeni

Embassy and waited another three hours before being told that stickers for our visas had still not arrived from the Yemeni capital. The Ambassador personally apologised and promised that our visas would be ready at 10am tomorrow.

We returned to the embassy the next day, but, of course, there were still no visa stickers. Who knew when — or *if* — we'd ever get out of this hell hole? To make matters worse, we had to move out of the 'Hotel British Consulate' because Alain and his wife were going away. We asked the Greek Consul working for the Canadian Embassy about a bed but were spectacularly unsuccessful. (If you don't ask, you don't get.) We hoped that during lunch with a German priest from the Eglise Protestante Evangelique church we'd be offered somewhere to stay, but instead a couple, George (from Greece) and Alina (from Romania), offered us a spot to pitch our tents in the backyard of the Coldspot Internet café they owned.

The latest news was that we would receive our visas on Saturday morning, more than a week after we'd first applied, and that a boat for Yemen would be departing later that day. Hanging around in Djibouti was so depressing, and the more I researched the '-stans' (such as Tajikistan and Kyrgyzstan) online, the more I got dejected. The problem was all the 'Letters of Introduction' required for each visa. I wanted to ride through this beautiful part of the world and not detour an extra 5000 kilometres around the '-stans'.

If that wasn't discouraging enough, a contact in China emailed to say that it would not be possible to travel alone around China on a motorbike. Driving a car, truck or van was possible for a price, but not on The Mothership unless it was in a group of other vehicles. (Officially, a guide needed to accompany tourists, but this wasn't possible on motorbikes.) The only other option was to cross into China illegally by the 'Truck Method'. (That is, I would load the bike onto a Mongolian truck heading into China and then unload it after crossing the Chinese border. But I knew I'd panic every time I'd see a cop.) Only time would tell, I suppose, but I was determined not to give up.

Rene and I met another biker on an Africa Twin, an American guy who lives in Germany called Michael. Aged about 40, he was a ladies' man who tried his moves and chat-up lines at every opportunity and was successful more often than not. On Saturday, the three of us packed up our gear and again headed to the Yemeni Embassy. We waited for one-and-a-half hours, but still nothing. Then Riad, the official who'd been helpful before, said the Consul wasn't coming in that day. We screamed at Riad, so he suggested we go to the Consul's home instead.

With Riad on the back of my bike, we rode back into the city centre, where the Yemeni Consul lived in a horrible little unit (as far removed from the British Consul's home as possible). After being led through some empty rooms, we met the Consul, a little man almost lying on the floor, wearing nothing but a towel. A piece of tissue was stuck to the side of his face where he'd cut himself shaving. Facing the TV (which was showing a dubbed episode of Gilligan's Island); I sat cross-legged on the floor next to the Consul while Riad explained in Arabic about our urgent need for visas.

As I suspected, the Consul suggested we bring our passports to him, so we went back through the traffic to the Yemeni Embassy. And this was when the situation got even *weirder*.

Michael's passport was being held by two embassy helpers we dubbed 'Tom' and 'Jerry'. When Michael asked for his passport and visa application form, 'Jerry' wouldn't hand it over. Michael asked again, so 'Jerry' passed the passport back to Michael but tore up Michael's visa application form while ranting in Arabic. Back at the Consul's home, the Consul was now dressed in a long Muslim-style cloak, but the tissue on his face remained. Our visa applications were slowly being processed, but the Consul wanted 'Tom' to help, so Riad, Rene and I went back to the embassy *again* to collect 'Tom'. We all had to fill out the visa application forms again. 'Jerry' was now in trouble with the Consul for ripping up Michael's application, so the Consul had to ring the actual Foreign Minister in Yemen, who insisted we write a letter of complaint about 'Jerry'. Michael also had to explain what happened to the Foreign Minister on the phone.

But we didn't care about *any* of this. We just wanted a visa so we could catch the bloody boat!

Another man arrived and announced that he was captain of a boat that would leave tomorrow *'inshallah'* ('God willing'). This, of course, could mean anything — or nothing. Eventually, 10 days after first applying, the Consul placed working visa stickers into our passports — as the tourists' stickers still had not arrived, of course — and we were ready to go.

But the Consul insisted we stay for lunch. We didn't have much choice and nowhere else to go anyway until the next day. We feasted like kings as more and more Yemeni dishes of meat, soup, noodles and stew were brought out. The Consul also gave us his brother's telephone number in Yemen, which could prove useful because his brother was the Head of Police.

Later, we heard that two days before, a couple of Belgian tourists were gunned down in cold blood by Al-Qaida at a roadblock in an area of Yemen we had to pass.

**SAILING TO YEMEN**

It was a full moon as the lights of Djibouti City faded along the horizon. I sat on my pannier, leaning back against the engine room wall, with The Mothership tied down beside me and goats and sheep as fellow passengers. The bikes constantly rocked while the boat battled the swell. After waiting for hours at the port, paying US$130 for each bike and rider, and dealing with Djibouti Immigration and Customs, we were shocked at the condition of the boat. It was old and wooden, and we thought that if we didn't get kidnapped by Somali pirates we'd probably sink and drown.

Having no choice, of course, we departed at 8pm for the 16-hour journey to Yemen. According to my GPS, we only travelled at about 13 kilometres per hour. I wore my motorbike jacket and fleece, and as I lay on the floor under the moon, seawater would occasionally splash over the edge and hit my face. I grabbed a tarpaulin next to me and covered myself a little, but it stank of rats. Not surprisingly, I hardly slept as we motored towards Mocha.

After 16 months and five days travelling through 32 countries, I was finally leaving Africa. Already feeling like a distant land, The Dark Continent was now just a memory — no longer a reality.

Tomorrow: another country and another world.

Russia
Day 6
Kazakhstan
Almaty
Uzbekistan
Tashkent
Kyrgyzstan
Turkmenistan
Tajikistan
China
Mashhad
Tehran
Afghanistan
Iraq
Iran
Pakistan
Nepal
Bandar-e Abbas
Dubai
Saudi Arabia
UAE
Muscat
Oman
India
Yemen
Sana'a
Salalah
Arabian Sea
Djibouti
Day 492
600miles
1000kms

CHAPTER 5

# Middle East & the '–Stans'

*Yemen to Russia: 206 Days*

**YEMEN**

The port at Mocha was a graveyard of old sunken ships of all sizes rusting away to nothing. Our wooden dhow docked near a massive red super-tanker from Norway, while about 40 camels surveyed the scene. Fixers and various other men flocked when they saw us and our bikes. They wanted to charge a ridiculous amount just to move the bikes all of two metres from the boat to the wharf. Instead, I found some planks of wood — not to hit the men hassling us, but to make a ramp. Of course, one false move and the bikes would have plunged into the sea, but we made it.

After someone checked all our belongings, we packed everything back into the panniers and went to find Immigration and Customs. Sitting on the steps of a run-down building, I looked around at the mess: plastic bags and dust were everywhere, as well as hundreds of goats and cows being herded on or off the boats while camels were being airlifted by crane and rope. The few cars travelling by boat were complete rust-buckets with bald tyres. The customs officer who could stamp the documents for our bikes was, of course, at home, so we had to wait. Once again, I handed the officer my (now useless) Temporary Import Permit from Kenya, and again it worked.

Welcome to the Middle East.

Mocha was a dump, full of more plastic bags and dust than the port was. Every man seemed to be chewing *qat*. (I don't think I saw one woman in the whole town.) Our nerves about being in Yemen were heightened further when a white van pulled up abruptly and a young man jumped out and looked at us. He went back to the van and gestured to his companions, who passed him an AK-47 rifle. But he just walked past, bought something from a shop and hopped back into the van, and the driver sped away with wheels spinning. Yemeni men carry AK-47s like we carry mobile phones. Apparently there are three guns for every man, woman and child in Yemen.

As we headed out of Mocha, thick dust blew across the road. Our first checkpoint was only 15 kilometres before the major town of Ta'izz. The soldiers carried guns and demanded to see our passports but were extremely friendly; one even gave us bottles of cold water while another rang people in high places (such as the police) and hotels for us in Ta'izz. They also gave us a kind of energy drink, like Red Bull. They didn't seem to want to let us go — but for the right reasons.

When we stopped at another checkpoint, the police already knew about us, so they escorted us with lights flashing and sirens wailing through the dense traffic to Hotel Rooma in Ta'izz. The police yelled through their loud-speaker for traffic and pedestrians to disperse while running through red lights and along roundabouts the wrong way. (They even paid our hotel bill!) After we checked in and rested up, three men were waiting for us at the reception. They explained that they were police and wanted to arrange a meeting the next day with the local Governor of Security.

As requested, we entered a building full of soldiers with machine-guns and climbed stairs to a room with five men and another man behind a huge desk. While one policeman, Jeemal, translated, we asked the Governor about the security situation in Yemen, especially after the murder of the Belgian tourists. They assured us that it was safe to travel, but we weren't so certain. Some reporters — one of whom was a woman covered from head to toe in a black *burqa* — took notes and photos. We were given some water and soft drinks and asked to come back for lunch at 2pm. After another round of handshakes and smiles, we left.

To fill in time before lunch, Jeemal took us to a castle and mosque and a museum dedicated to an old Imam. During lunch, the Governor insisted we move to another hotel (which cost US$200 a night) at their expense, but we politely declined, preferring to stay where we were. The Governor then had to leave, leaving us three with a few of his aides to finish off the massive feast.

After all that eating, we rested again before visiting an evening market with our 'babysitter'. We certainly did not like being escorted around by a policeman, but we couldn't refuse — and it was probably for our own safety anyway. The Yemeni people seemed very welcoming, and the hospitality so far was second to none, but I still felt a little nervous. The thought that anything could happen to us still lingered in the back of my mind.

Rene, Michael and I did manage to escape Ta'izz. Winding high through the mountains, we quickly learnt how to cope with Yemen's maniacal car drivers. We had to ride at the same pace as them, or else they'd stop to see if we were okay because they assumed that our 'huge' bikes could travel fast up through the mountains when the opposite was actually true.

By the time we reached the capital, Sana'a, we were exhausted. Again, my bike struggled in the thin air at the high altitude (above 2000 metres), but we made it. We stayed at a hotel in the old part of the city, one of the oldest in the world, and some would claim one of the most beautiful. But I was ready to leave as soon as I got there.

At the Ministry of Tourism, we had to wake up an official to give us the permit we needed to travel across Yemen and on to Oman. We got the permit but were told we couldn't use the inland route we wanted and had to travel along the coast instead — and we had to use an escort. We ambled around the market for a while, but that was enough. I was tired (or perhaps sick) of Muslim countries and big cities. I was ready to head south to the coast and get out of Yemen.

The next day was one of extremes. Not far from Sana'a, we came across our first checkpoint of the day. The police said we couldn't continue without an escort and had to return to Sana'a. We explained our plan and eventually convinced them to provide an escort. After waiting a few hours in the blistering heat, a car arrived from Sana'a and escorted us to Dhamar. At Dhamar, we decided to skip the second-largest city, Aden, and head east further inland towards to Shuqrah. On the way, Michael's fuel pump blew, but luckily I had the spare I'd picked up in Nairobi and it was fixed in 10 minutes.

With our new escort vehicle, we passed through a landscape of rocks, rocks and more rocks. At the edge of a plateau, the views were truly amazing, with the road below resembling a tangle of string. Weaving our way through a few tight bends, we came across a mangled car lying in the middle of the road. It was a complete mess — and so was the driver, with his body ripped in half, stomach all over the road, and head missing.

We quickly realised what must've happened. Only seconds before, the car had careered off the road from above like it had fallen from the sky. Without using brakes or high on *qat* (or probably both), the driver had simply driven over the edge from at least 100 metres above us. If we hadn't stopped for some photos a minute before, the car might've fallen on to us.

We were now even more anxious to get of Yemen.

Along the way to Shuqrah, one of the escort policemen allowed us to fill up our tanks for free. But we had to camp outside of town at the back of a police hut (and near the squalid toilets and on top of rocks) because some particularly nasty men were roaming around Shuqrah with AK-47 rifles. Still about 1000 kilometres and four days from Oman, I was so glad to be travelling with Rene and Michael. I would've hated Yemen even more if I'd been riding alone.

The next day, we headed along the coast, but after about 80 kilometres we stopped at another checkpoint and got a new escort vehicle. We saw a cyclist who I soon realised was Lars. (Amy and I had met him in Namibia many months before.)

I walked up to him with my helmet on. "G'day, Lars."

He looked surprised. "How do you know my name?"

When I removed my helmet, he instantly recognised me. He explained that he'd been cycling around parts of South America but had become ill and returned to his home country, Sweden. Now fully recovered, he flew to the Arabian Peninsula with the idea of cycling home from there. We were complaining about *our* escort, but Lars wasn't even allowed to ride and had to travel across Yemen sitting in the back of a police truck with his bicycle. Clearly, he wasn't achieving what he'd set out to do. Lars joined our convoy, which now also consisted of a Yemeni soldier wearing fingerless bicycle gloves in control of a rotating anti-aircraft gun mounted in the back of a Land Cruiser.

Every day, the scenery was stunning like the moon, with so many old volcanoes and lava fields. The road was good, so we travelled quickly, and the weather was hot, so we enjoyed dipping into the ocean from our beachside camp sites. We continued along the coastal road to Al Mukalla, where we again had to check in with the Tourist Police. We were now in the Hadromat Region, the birthplace of Osama Bin Laden. I thought that if Bin Laden were hiding out there in the countryside, no one would ever find him. (Of course, he wasn't. And later they did.)

From Al Mukalla, we were allowed to continue to Oman without an escort. Lars joined our own personal 'convoy' as we put Lars' gear on Rene's bike, the bicycle on Michael's motorbike, and Lars himself sat on the back of The Mothership. Not surprisingly, Lars had had enough of Yemen and was grateful for our help: It would've taken him seven days to cover the rest of the trip, while we hurried the final 585 kilometres to the Oman border in two days. We all felt freer without escorts and were able to camp in the sand dunes.

As we stopped at Saybut to collect some water, the usual crowds gathered to watch us. The people and culture seemed to be changing as we headed east, with less *qat* being chewed and fewer people wearing *jambiya* (Yemeni knives) in their belts or carrying AK-47s across their shoulders. The coastline was flat with some sand dunes and then turned rugged as we veered through mountain passes and even through a few tunnels. The Mothership was performing well, even with a passenger.

For Lars, disaster struck while we looked for a campsite about 4 kilometres from the Oman border. His bicycle was strapped to the back of Michael's motorbike, and as he negotiated a rocky track the back wheel of the pushbike hit a rock, buckling the wheel beyond repair. There was no choice but to take Lars and his broken bike all the way to Salalah in Oman, where he hoped to get a new wheel or rim.

Yemen had certainly been up and down: great scenery but escorts we didn't want, and cheap fuel (about US$0.30 a litre) but restrictions wherever we wanted to go. Yet, despite everything we had a good laugh. I enjoyed everyone's company, and Michael and I got along particularly well. Rene decided that he might change his plans and travel the same route as me instead of going through India, but I wasn't sure about travelling all that way with anyone. I'd rather travel most of the way home on my own. And if I were to ride with somebody the whole way, it would only be with Amy.

## OMAN

Eventually we were stamped out of Yemen and rode into Oman. The change was incredible and immediate: The border officers were neatly dressed, polite and spoke good English. The functional buildings had computer terminals and the surrounding areas were clean. Again, the Omani customs officer was happy to stamp my (useless) TIP bike permit from Kenya. I just hoped it would work for me when entering Iran. (It certainly did not.)

At Salalah, we checked into a hotel and rested. We lazed about, checked emails, watched TV, drank beer (for 5€ each) at a luxury resort, and pigged out at Pizza Hut — none of which would've been possible anywhere in Yemen. The only similarity between Oman and Yemen is the spectacular scenery.

Lars couldn't get his bike fixed at Salalah, so he caught an immediate bus (with the damaged bike) to the Omani capital,

Muscat, to buy a wheel or rim there. Rene decided to stay a while longer in Salalah, so Michael and I headed towards Muscat through more than 1000 kilometres of flat, empty nothingness. Along the way, we met two Australians, Billy and Trish, on a BMW R100 and Kawasaki Sherpa 250 (respectively). They were travelling in the other direction, so it was great to gather current information about Iran and the '-stans'. What they said made me feel far more confident and excited about travelling there.

The next day we hoped for an early start, but were covered in fog and everything was wet — despite being in the middle of the desert. As the weather improved at about 9am, we hit the road with a slight tail wind. There was nothing to see along the desert highway — no trees or hills, just a black strip of tar dissecting the landscape forever.

But I did see something ahead that looked like a wall. A thick blanket of sand with gale-force winds suddenly approached us with a ferocity I'd never experienced in the Sahara. For 400 kilometres we rode at an angle as the wind blew sideways into us, and the road beneath our bikes was barely visible. It was so windy that sand got caught in my eyes and mouth even though the helmet visor was down and clipped shut.

If that wasn't bad enough, Michael got a flat tyre. Fixing it by the roadside, we felt like we were sitting in a sand blaster. There was nowhere to shelter, so we continued to a town called Adam, where the wind still blew but the sand had gone. We camped in the backyard of a two-storey house under construction, with a fence acting as a windbreak.

By the next morning, the wind had dissipated but dust still hung in the air all day long. We detoured to Sur along the north-eastern tip, but there was nothing special to see or do there, so we continued along a three-lane highway to Muscat.

Spread out around rocky outcrops, the capital offers luxuries like proper service stations and McDonalds as well as expats, such as Bob, an American geologist working in the oil industry who invited us to stay at his place. With hot showers, cold beers and the chance to clean our clothes, it was the perfect place to relax. From her emails, it was clear that Amy was still having a rough time. She was not coping being back to 'normal' life and wanted to quit her job as an occupational therapist. I needed to speak with her as soon as possible.

In a few days, Michael planned to continue to Dubai and then head in a different direction (because he travelled on a US passport and couldn't get a visa to Iran), so we decided to hang about Muscat for a few more days and camp at the beach.

Amy sent me another email asking if she could come over and see me. I told her exactly how I felt in a long email and said she could come to Dubai and continue the trip with me.

But in my own mind, I still wasn't sure. Did I want to travel on my own, or not? I only had six or seven months to go — not long, really. I just wanted to be me and for her to be her and for us to enjoy each other.

I had to wait until the next day for Amy's reply because the Internet centre (like everything else in this part of the world) was closed between 1 and 4pm.

Camping out on the beach, all I could do was think about Amy. I just hoped she was okay and all that I said in my email made sense. I wanted it to work out for us, but I also wanted her to be 100 per cent sure she really *did* want to be with me. I hoped to talk to her by phone — and maybe even meet her — in Dubai.

But something else happened that took over my life.

## UNITED ARAB EMIRATES (UAE)

Michael and I easily crossed into the UAE, where I stayed with Kathy and Craig, friends of Amy's. Two days later, after having dinner with Michael (who was staying elsewhere), we walked outside the restaurant. I almost buckled to my knees.

My trip was finished.

The Mothership was gone.

Not only had the bike disappeared but all the attachments had disappeared as well: my GPS (with every single kilometre of the 65,032 I'd travelled since London recorded), tools, and spare parts.

I registered the theft with the police, who drove me around Dubai for several hours early in the morning looking for the bike, but to no avail, of course. All I could do was cross my fingers and hope that someone had just taken it for a joy ride and not dumped it into a river or the ocean. People told me that Dubai was the safest city in the world, but now my bike had been stolen.

I rang Amy the next day. She was an angel and wanted to help. She asked people to donate some money for a new bike so I could continue my trip. A friend of the people I was staying with, Abbas Al Lawati, was a reporter at *The Gulf News*, one of the largest regional newspapers. He ran a story about the theft, which made the front page.

This prompted more offers of help, including free use of quality second-hand motorbikes from England (and one from the UAE) as well as more offers of money from people. I was overwhelmed. I set up a 'donate' button for three to four weeks on my blog, and people I didn't know from across the world sent me money. Soon, I'd received US$3000 in donations.

And, just as importantly, so many people — often strangers — sent me encouraging comments urging me to carry on:

"Rob, my heart goes out to you. I've just read about your problem."

"You made it over the Congo and the tough bits. This should be a minor setback."

"If anyone can come out of this situation it is you. Don't give up."

"You have been following your dream, and it ain't over yet. Keep your head up."

About one week later, Amy decided to come out to Dubai. She wanted to help me with my bike and join me for the rest of the trip. She felt so unsettled back home and wanted to give our relationship another chance. It was so great to see her again, of course, but things had changed. According to the email I'd received back in Uganda we had broken up. And I hadn't told her what had happened with the American lady on that lonely night.

I also met a lot of people in Dubai who offered me places to stay, including Colin Mercer, a Scot who managed a business which painted super-yachts for the Sheiks. He was into his dirt bikes, and his hospitality was legendary. Another was Sean Linton, who ran a bike shop called Gecko's.

Sean suggested I approach the Al Futtaim Honda dealership in Dubai. They agreed to give me a brand new Honda CRF 450 on the proviso that during the rest of my trip I would raise awareness for their chosen charity: The Dubai Centre for Special Needs. I was happy to help in that way, of course, but the CRF 450 was an endurance racing bike and I much preferred my Africa Twin off/on road bike. As it happened, I found another Africa Twin for sale in Abu Dhabi (not far away in UAE) of the same year and model — just a different colour. Al Futtaim Honda paid for it (US$4000), but the deal would take three weeks to complete.

And there was another problem. I wasn't a resident of the UAE, so I couldn't register any bike in my name. I could take it out of the UAE and travel anywhere, but I couldn't bring it into Australia unless it was registered to me. I rang the Customs Department in Australia — and even took up the matter with my Member of Parliament back home — but nobody could do anything. Customs advised that because I could sell the bike in Australia, they could not bend the rules. I explained that I planned to ride it thousands of kilometres and it would be worthless by the time I arrived home, but the answer was always, "no".

In the meantime, the Honda PR machine was rolling along. To help promote the charity, I appeared on local TV once and on radio twice and was interviewed several more times by local newspapers. I even featured in two editions of *Wheels* magazine. I was a guest speaker at a lunch for heads of Australian businesses in Dubai and wheeled my bike into the Dubai Centre for Special Needs to show the kids what I'd been doing for the previous 19 months.

I even made the Australian newsstands, with stories about me in *The Age*, *Sydney Morning Herald* and *Herald Sun*. But it was draining doing the interviews and solving problems with the new bike's registration while still hoping that The Mothership would be found. Plus, it seemed that Amy couldn't join me on the trip anytime soon because of the additional logistical headache of her, too, buying a motorbike in UAE and taking it back to Australia. I wished I'd let my sister lend me the US$4000 for the second-hand Africa Twin when she offered. If so, I wouldn't have all these extra commitments and problems and Amy and I might've been closer to riding back home.

My life was now a whirlwind. The only positive about my extended layover was that the winter in Iran and Russia would be well finished by the time I got going. As a distraction, I spent a lot of time riding in the desert with Col on his dirt bikes. Sean also let me use his workshop to prepare my replacement Africa Twin. His shop specialised in rally-racing, particularly for the Abu Dhabi Desert Challenge. (This is similar to the Paris to Dakar Rally but involved racing 'only' 3000 kilometres over five days in the desert.)

Gecko's had a Honda CRF 450 rally bike for sale, which would be ideal for the Desert Challenge rally. I started dreaming about entering this event in November and maybe, later, the Paris to Dakar Rally (which is a *very* expensive option). I bought the bike on my credit card and left it at Gecko's with the idea of returning to Dubai (most probably from Bangkok) for the rally. (I spent the US$3000 of donations on a new GPS, tools and other equipment for The Mothership as well as on living expenses for the time I was stuck in Dubai, an expensive city.)

Thanks to Hein (a South African), I was able to race in the last round of the Dubai Baja season on one of his bikes. Racing is always something I'd wanted to do, but I'd never done it before and had no idea what to expect. This was a desert track through the dunes with 85 riders given two-and-a-half hours to complete as many laps as possible.

The race was fast, and the track was rough. By the first lap I could hardly hang on to the bike that bucked and kicked beneath me. I wasn't the only one tiring quickly and getting bogged as the top guys in the professional class whizzed past. I crossed the finish line with every muscle in my body aching, but I was glad that I'd finished. I was happier still when I was presented with the third-place trophy for the class I'd entered. But I could hardly move the next day, and the blisters on both thumbs were so bad that Amy had to open bottles of water for me.

Sorting out the registration of the new Africa Twin continued to be very frustrating, and I felt that I'd lost momentum. Previously, I'd been worrying about reaching Russia too soon; now, the problem was the opposite. I had to leave the UAE by 1 June and ride north to Russia, across Mongolia and south through China before the bad weather started again.

And because we couldn't restart the trip anytime soon, Amy and I started to drift apart. The final straw was when she read an email from the American lady in Uganda and found out about my fling. Amy was crushed. She'd quit her job and come all the way to Dubai (a city she hated) to give our relationship one last shot. But I had ripped her heart in two. I knew right then we could never be together again.

Then my luck turned around.

"Mister Roberts?"

I glanced at the phone but didn't recognise the number. "Yes."

"We have found your bike."

"*What?* Really? You found it!?"

"Yes, Mr Roberts, we have it. You can come tomorrow morning and pick it up. But it does have a broken rear tyre."

I thanked him profusely. I could not believe it. The Mothership had been found — and with only a flat tyre!

After a sleepless night, I rushed to the police station, brimming with anticipation about recommencing my trip. I wouldn't have to worry about registering the other bike, and I could be in Iran in a week or so.

But I was wrong.

The Mothership had been virtually destroyed. It looked like it had been hit by a truck or dropped from a 20-storey building. The instrument panel was smashed, the tank crushed in, the ignition had been skewered by something like a screw driver, the blinkers were ripped off and broken wires were everywhere, the pannier racks were gone, the exhaust pipe was bent, and so on and so on. Almost every single part of the bike was broken or missing. It was a write-off.

I was shattered. At that moment, I actually wished I'd never seen the bike again. I had hoped it had been ridden around by somebody and not destroyed. But...

I started thinking. If the frame was still okay, I could transfer parts of the new African Twin onto the old frame, paint it black and do an engine number change on the paperwork. I wouldn't have to worry about any registration because essentially the frame or chassis of a vehicle *is* the vehicle — that's what is registered.

At Gecko's, I stripped The Mothership of all the remaining broken parts and welded the original frame where it was cracked. With the help of a Filipino guy, Aris, and Chris Cargill, I transferred all the parts from the second-hand bike bought in Dubai to the naked frame of The Mothership. After about 12 hours, The Mothership was reborn. Within the following 10 days, I'd had the new registration papers couriered to me from the UK reflecting the 'new' engine number.

After four months and 19 days in Dubai I was now ready to continue.

**IRAN**

The day I finally left UAE, Amy left my life.

I was exhausted and anxious about what lay ahead; being in Dubai for so long, I knew that I'd lost momentum. And I was distraught about Amy going back home. Together, we loaded up the rebuilt Mothership, and with Amy and her gear on the back, we took the short ride to the airport. We had said goodbye before in South Africa, but this time we both knew that it was over. Amy tried to be strong, though a few tears rolled down her cheek — and there were a few down mine, too. I knew I was letting go of a great girl, but I was stubborn and had been for a long time: I had to finish this trip. We hugged and wished each other the best. She was strong for me. That was typical of Amy.

I rode straight to Port Khailid in Sharjah. From one queue, I received a boarding pass; from another, I got an exit stamp in my passport. I then rode 500 metres to the ferry, which was a Catamaran. I couldn't see how the bike could get on, but some crew lashed ropes around the engine bars and pannier rails and hoisted it up from the dock and into the hull of the boat. After making sure it was secured tightly, I sat down and contemplated that I was actually leaving the UAE with my bike — well, some of it at least.

I tried sleeping on the six-hour journey, but it was just too uncomfortable. Two hours before arriving in Iran, a strange combination of feelings overcame me. I felt scared, thinking my bad luck would continue from the UAE; I felt rushed, with pressure to make up time wasted in the UAE; and I felt so anxious about the visa nightmares across the '-stans'.

I'd read that a 'Letter of Introduction' for some countries could take two weeks to organise, and I now did not have the luxury of waiting around for paperwork. I tried to remain positive, remembering that I was undertaking a once-in-a-lifetime experience. By the time the ferry arrived in Iran, the pressure had built within me to the point that I felt defeated. I was ready to cry.

The ferry docked at 10.30pm in the port of Bandar-e Abbas, where I breezed through Immigration. Customs was closed, however. I asked around, and the consensus was that I'd have to leave the bike at the port until tomorrow, but I had no local money and nowhere to change foreign currency to pay for a taxi into town. One guy lent me about US$10 worth of *rials* and provided the name of a hotel to stay at.

The receptionist at the Homa Hotel wanted to charge me US$87. Of course, I wasn't going to pay that, so they asked me how much I would spend. I said US$10. He did some calculations and offered me a room for US$67. I glared. He suggested another place, the Atlas Hotel.

Wasting more precious *rials* on a taxi, I was told that the hotel was full. I then took another taxi to another hotel, where I got a decent room for US$16. I was now broke. I still had to find a way to get The Mothership into Iran without a *carnet*. And I was utterly dejected because Amy was not with me but probably in Bangkok instead. I was also very anxious about how the next day would unfold. Sitting in the bare room with only a bed, my tank bag, little money and some dry chicken to eat, I suddenly could not control my emotions. I started to cry.

The new day brought nothing but misery. I dragged myself out of bed and went back to the port. I got within 50 metres of my bike when a guard asked to see my passport. He spoke no English and I spoke no Farsi (the language in Iran), but I understood that I needed a permit to enter the port. I got the permit, found my bike, and waited for someone at Customs who could speak English. Mohammed eventually came and explained that I had to go to the Shipping Office in town to get a stamp.

Staff at this office wanted to charge me US$50 for 'port fees'. I refused, but they wouldn't budge, so I had to go back to the port to get some money stored on the bike. Back at the Shipping Office, I got my stamp, but Customs at the port insisted on placing the stamp on my *carnet* (which I hadn't had since leaving South Africa). *Shit!*

I tried every argument and every angle, but they would not compromise. There were now two options — both terrible. I could return to Dubai, or I could freight the bike across Iran to the next country. But I wanted to ride through Iran, and freighting the bike would cost a fortune.

Still hanging around the port at 6pm, Mohammed offered to put me up at his place. That evening, I also managed to get an email from Amy. She was in Bangkok and doing well. I wished so much that I were there with her and not in Bandar Bloody Abbas without a *carnet* or motorbike. I also saw an article online from *The Gulf*

*News* announcing my successful departure to Iran, so going back to Dubai wasn't really an option either.

I was fortunate to be staying with Mohammed and his wife, who prepared a dinner of chicken, rice and chips, all eaten with special yoghurt. He set up two mattresses on the floor of the lounge room — one for me and the other for him. He explained that he didn't sleep with his wife, but I didn't ask any more questions. (Presumably this was for religious reasons.)

I awoke the next day, accepting that freighting my bike across Iran was the only alternative. I needed to transport The Mothership to Mashhad, about 1500 kilometres away and near the border with Turkmenistan. But would I still have the same problems for that and every other country without a *carnet*? I emailed Paul in London and asked him to arrange a new one for me urgently. (Paul was a contact at the Automobile Association in England who organised my original *carnet*.)

With great trepidation, I went back to the port with Mohammed. At Customs, I told them a small lie: When I received my Iranian visa in Dubai, the immigration officers had said I could take my bike with me into Iran without any problems. I also showed them a world map with the route I'd taken through all the countries that had allowed me in so far. I added that I hoped Iran would not be the only country that would stop my journey. This seemed to swing things a little in my favour.

Then one of the Customs Officers made a sudden announcement. "You will ride your bike across Iran."

And so began the longest and most brutal paper-trail I'd ever experienced in my entire life. (But it sure beat the alternative of going back to Dubai and waiting for a *carnet* from London or freighting my bike across Iran to Turkmenistan.) With Mohammed's invaluable help, I went backwards and forwards to over 20 different people, offices and departments to get countless signatures, stamps and photocopies and to make payments for insurance, storage and whatever else they needed.

*Spectacular scenery of Yemen*

*A familiar sight all across Yemen*

*Camping in the desert with Michael, Oman*

*The last photo of the Mothership in Oman before being stolen only days later in Dubai*

*The sight of the original Mothership after police told me they had found it*

*Building the new bike with the old motor, Dubai*

*Dirk and 'The Old Lady', Tajikistan*

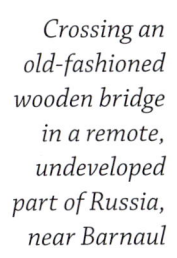

*Crossing an old-fashioned wooden bridge in a remote, undeveloped part of Russia, near Barnaul*

*The entrance to the Tunnel of Doom and the Lada we followed*

*We made it, on the other side of the Tunnel of Doom*

*Horsemen at full gallop fighting for the headless goat, Kyrgyzstan*

*Dirk and his ride for Kok Buro, Kyrgyzstan*

*The pre-match 'ball' for Kok Buro*

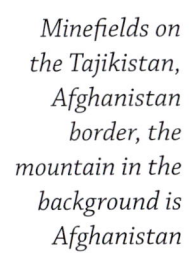

*Minefields on the Tajikistan, Afghanistan border, the mountain in the background is Afghanistan*

*Plenty of reminders of the old mother Russia across the ex-Soviet States, this one in Tajikistan*

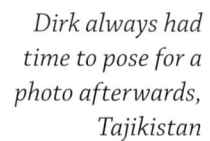

*Dirk always had time to pose for a photo afterwards, Tajikistan*

*The Mothership always attracted some attention from all ages, Kyrgyzstan*

*Dirk amusing soldiers on Tajikistan/ Afghanistan border*

*Waiting at a checkpoint in Tajikistan*

*Happy kids, Tajikistan*

*Dirk being watched by a young Mongol girl*

*Golden teeth were very popular in Turkmenistan*

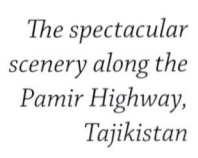

*The spectacular scenery along the Pamir Highway, Tajikistan*

It went on and on and on…and on. Then, just as the whole process had nearly finished, a customs officer said the Shipping Office had given me the wrong document (or maybe somebody else's instead of mine), so on to that office one last time and then back to the port again.

Without Mohammed's assistance, I would've been screwed. I bid him a grateful farewell and nervously rode towards the gate for one more stamp. And that was it. I couldn't believe it. I had achieved the near impossible: entering Iran without a *carnet*.

Before leaving Bandar-e Abbas, I was able to talk to Amy. She sounded happy and was meeting people. I was so glad she was doing okay. I also felt in good spirits — until my bike died 20 kilometres from the port. (It was the fuel pump again, but I quickly changed it with another pump Michael had replaced for me in Dubai after lending him mine in Yemen.)

I decided to make up time and head straight to Mashhad near the Turkmenistan border and then continue on to Uzbekistan as soon as possible. It was now the middle of summer, and the temperature didn't drop even when I rode into mountains over 2000 metres high. Once, I passed a pipe with gushing water, so I stopped to dunk my head into the cool water. It was so refreshing (and I hadn't had a shower for a few days).

The roads were always choked with trucks, buses and cars, but I was 'only' forced off the road twice in the first day. (It was amazing how relaxed I had become when this happened.) There were a few checkpoints, but the police created no problems. As I got stuck behind traffic in one tunnel, the fumes burned my eyes and throat, and the air temperature inside must've reached 50 degrees Celsius. I emerged at the other end gasping for breath.

My plan to camp one night near Sirjin was thwarted when a car coming in the opposite direction moved into my lane while flashing his lights. He pulled up and waved for me to stop, which I did. He ran back to me, pulled out his wallet and produced an ID card. It showed a photo of him in a military uniform. After a quick discussion, it was apparent that he was there to escort me to Sirjin. (I assumed the town was unsafe and therefore wasn't a great place to camp.)

I followed him, and we stopped just outside of Sirjin to wait for his colleagues from the secret police. The sun was sinking, and I was almost out of fuel. His colleagues eventually arrived and noted my details. I followed them to the petrol station, where 40 cars were lined up (but with a police escort I went to the front of the queue).

I told them I wanted to camp, so unfortunately they took me to a public park full of people with techno-music blasting. The police told me to pitch my tent at a spot next to the military guards, some with machine guns and others with batons. Later, I was approached by two soldiers. Using hand gestures, the skinnier one asked me if I 'needed company', while his fatter friend added that he was a 'good friend'. I didn't. In fact, all I wanted to do was swap my tent for a locked cage.

After a sleepless night made worse by a 4.30am sunrise, I packed up and waited for my escort. I hoped Iran wouldn't be a repeat of Yemen, with police restricting my travels so much, but the escort let me continue alone after another 50 kilometres. I crossed nothing but desert, with probably the hottest weather I'd encountered on all my travels so far. There were laybys every 50 kilometres with water taps where I would soak myself. This cooled my body down until I was completely dry again 10 kilometres further on.

The first thing I had to do in Mashhad was find the Turkmenistan Consulate. On the way, I came across the only other tourist I'd seen in Iran: a guy who looked like he was from Pakistan riding a pushbike with lots of luggage. In a thick English accent, he said he knew of a good place to stay: a guest house run by Vali (who speaks good English). At the guesthouse, I met two Swiss cyclists, Luc Henry and Mark, who were waiting for their Turkmenistan visa. The information they shared was not good: I needed a visa for Uzbekistan before I could get one for Turkmenistan. Even worse, the Uzbekistan Embassy was in Tehran. If all that wasn't bad enough, the border I wanted to cross was closed.

With all fingers crossed, I went to the Turkmen Consulate and applied for a transit visa. Talking through a hole in the wall the size of an A4 piece of paper, the consular official asked if I had a 'Letter of Introduction', which I didn't. He stared at me silently and then waved me away. But I didn't move. Eventually, he asked for my passport.

"Do you have photocopy of passport?" he asked.

"Yes."

"Do you have onward visa?"

"Yes, for Kazakhstan." That was a lie.

He took the photocopies. "Come back next week."

"What day?" I asked.

He said to come back in 10 days. There was no other option.

In the meantime, I needed to go to Tehran and spend a few days there getting my Uzbekistan visa. I hoped the Iranian capital would be more interesting than Mashhad, which is a particularly holy city.

Leaving The Mothership at the guesthouse, I took a 16-hour bus ride to Tehran on Saturday night with Luc Henry and Mark, the two Swiss cyclists. It was hell, and I couldn't sleep. We went straight to the Uzbekistan Embassy, where the official said I needed to apply through a travel agency that deals with 'Letters of Introduction' because Uzbekistan and Australia have no formal ties.

Knowing this already, I had made some arrangements with a travel agency online. While waiting around for the Uzbekistan visa, I thought I'd try my luck with a visa to China. This meant first going to the Australian Embassy to get a two-lined 'Letter of Recommendation', which cost a hefty US$30. But when I returned to the Chinese Embassy and saw the queues of people — some of whom had been there all night — I gave up. (The embassy only processes 50 visa applications a day, and only three times a week. And I was given the queue number 99.)

I got an email from the Swiss cyclists (who had returned to Mashhad) to say that the Turkmenistan Consulate in Mashhad was now closed and would remain shut for 10 days. (So sick of waiting, they decided to detour through Afghanistan instead!) My only option was to apply at the Turkmenistan Embassy in Tehran, and amazingly, I received a five-day transit visa the next day. Still in Tehran, I went back to the Uzbekistan Embassy, but it was closed because of an Uzbekistan public holiday. I did get the visa the next day for a whopping US$105. By now I was seriously running out of US dollars.

After being propositioned for sex about six times — by men! — and waiting around drinking tea for days on end in cafés, I was keen to get out of Tehran. To avoid the overnight bus back to Mashhad I caught the overnight train, but I still didn't sleep, especially with men snoring and kids jumping around.

I missed Amy so much at times like these.

**TURKMENISTAN**

I woke up at 6am, ate breakfast, borrowed some US dollars from Vali (the guesthouse owner) and escaped from Mashhad. With the air cool and the traffic bearable so early, I covered the 185 kilometres to the border in no time. The lack of *carnet* confused the Iranian officials for a while, but everything was explained in all the papers I'd obtained at the port in Bandar-e Abbas. The procedure to get out of Iran took less than 30 minutes, while getting in lasted three days.

Riding over a bridge to the Turkmenistan border, I noticed an instant difference in the people: They looked more Asian, with rounder heads, and were wearing shorts and driving Russian-made cars. At the border, a doctor noted details from my passport (for which he charged US$13). I then waited a while before being taken to Customs, where I was given a map with all the roads I could use to reach Uzbekistan. I got my bike insurance easily and my pretend *carnet* stamped, but the whole crossing cost me US$60. One official asked for an extra US$10, but I just laughed and rode off.

The countryside across the Garragum desert was as flat and boring as Iran. One problem now was that I was almost out of US dollars, and I didn't want to change too much (or preferably anything) into the local currency because I'd be crossing into Uzbekistan the next day. I was forced to camp in the dunes and eat canned baked beans and bananas all day. I had some issues with my bloody fuel pump too, so I put a new one on.

The searing heat and the sore back I'd developed woke me just after dawn. While I was filling up with fuel near the Uzbekistan border at Farab, a kid offered me a rock melon and others wanted me to take their photos. Most men and women had gold teeth (sometimes both rows were all gold) like their late and slightly demented leader, President Turkmenbashi, who erected a huge statue of himself in the capital.

**UZBEKISTAN**

Exiting Turkmenistan was easy, and amazingly, so was crossing into Uzbekistan, although Customs Officers were still confused that I had no *carnet*. It was always a good feeling entering a new country — and crossing two within a couple of days was doing wonders for my spirits. I was making good time, and there were fewer hassles than I'd expected.

My first stop was the holy of city of Bukarra, an ancient place with many buildings over one thousand years old. I found a cheap and comfortable room where I could flick through endless TV channels of junk and revel in the air-conditioning. I also enjoyed a traditional meal of *palau*, which is rice, beans, vegetables and something that tasted like (but wasn't) mashed potatoes. I washed it down with a *Sarbast* beer, my first for a long time.

It was still incredibly hot as I continued to Samarkand the next day. The tarmac on the road was bumpy, and drivers of the little Russian-made cars that resembled a square box always wanted to overtake me but would then slow down when in front. Travelling was tough enough on a motorbike, so I wondered how the cyclist (from Taiwan) I met was coping. I saw a few more cyclists in Samarkand, including a Brit I'd met in Mashhad and Luc Henry and Mark, who had some hair-raising stories about their travels by bicycle through Afghanistan. Most travellers I met were coming from the east, and not one had a positive thing to say about getting into China. They added that there would be real headaches getting a visa for Russia (which might cost me US$300!) and China (because of the Olympics and protests in Tibet).

These negative reports started to seriously affect my attitude, and I looked into flights from Ulan Bator in Mongolia to Bangkok, but the cost for me alone (let alone the bike) would be US$1200. Once again, I was sick of the trip and the hassles. Plus, it was Friday and I still had not received my 'Letter of Introduction' for Tajikistan.

Samarkand is full of mosques and minarets, but nothing much else, and once the sun rose it became unbearably hot. I was keen to continue to Tashkent, the capital, where I got a room by the train station. Once again, I bumped into the two Swiss cyclists who'd travelled there by train to get their visas to Tajikistan. Trying my luck again at the Chinese Embassy, I waited two-and-a-half hours to be told that I had to get my visa for China in Mongolia.

Then I tried for a visa at the Russian Embassy. About 100 people were trying to squeeze into the building through a little door. I pushed and shoved for an hour or so before I was finally allowed in. But the officials told me that to get a transit visa for Russia I would need a visa for Mongolia — all of which I had to sort out in Almaty (Kazakhstan).

A few days later, I finally received a 'Letter of Introduction' and stood in the sun for a few hours applying for a Tajikistan visa, which cost US$100.

**TAJIKISTAN**

The day I crossed into Tajikistan was one of those hopelessly frustrating stuff-ups.

I had to leave Uzbekistan quickly as my visa to Kyrgyzstan (which I'd got in Dubai) would run out soon, and I would need time in Kazakhstan to apply for my visa to Russia. I rushed 180 kilometres to the border but was told that it was closed to westerners. The immigration officer rang someone who explained in English that I'd have to cross at Kakobad, 30 kilometres to the east. This didn't seem too bad.

But it was. When I approached the border at Kakobad, a sign indicated that it was closed to *everyone*. Some officials told me to head north for 50 kilometres and try there. Checking my map, I didn't know whether to trust their advice or try at a border 200 kilometres further west that I knew would be open and accessible to foreigners. I took the safer option and arrived at the western border about five hours after I reached the first one. Other than forgetting to get my pen back from the border official who borrowed it, the crossing for me and the bike was painless.

Thankfully, the scenery improved, with large distant mountains, some permanently capped with ice. The road turned to dirt as kids started waving and yelling, "hello, hello." I eventually reached a bridge with a line of cars about 200 metres long. I asked a man, who offered the familiar gesture of crossing one wrist over the other to indicate that the bridge was closed. But he added that it would reopen in 40 minutes so, for once, the timing was good. There were only two hours of daylight left, and I wanted to find a campsite soon.

While waiting and eating, I met someone who would become a long-time travelling companion and firm friend.

Dirk was also riding an Africa Twin (which he called The Old Lady) from his homeland in Belgium to Australia via India. We chatted and drank Coke and then hopped onto our bikes as soon as the bridge opened to avoid the scramble of cars lined up to cross it along a single lane. The scenery became even more spectacular, with sheer ravines, steep mountains and raging rivers weaving through the valleys below. We eventually found a spot to camp in the backyard of a house just off the main road, but I didn't sleep more than one hour as trucks and cars whizzed past us all night.

The 130-kilometre-long road to Dushanbe, the capital, was dirty and dusty, with a few rocky bumps. The scenery was a nice change as we veered around several massive peaks, but along the way we came across The Tunnel. In an email, Rene had warned me to 'avoid the fucking tunnel at all costs'. Dark, full of water and 5 kilometres long, The Tunnel was a shocking place to ride a motorbike, but we'd missed the turn-off for an alternate route across the mountain. There was now no other option.

The entrance to The Tunnel looked like something from a horror movie. We could see massive puddles across the road and water gushing out of the tunnel but nothing else because there were no lights inside. A small 4WD Lada stopped in front of us so the driver could put a rag over the air intake pipe to stop splashing water from being sucked into the engine. He kindly suggested that we follow him so we could gauge the depth of the water by watching his car dip into the puddles and potholes.

Very quickly, the water was about half a metre deep, so our boots were instantly full — and the water was cold. As the 4WD Lada in front of us crawled along the gravel, potholed surface that we could not see, I was getting really worried. This was insanely dangerous. At times our bikes would sink into water-filled potholes one metre deep, and the 4WD was creating huge waves in front of us as water sprayed everywhere. More disconcerting was all the water dripping from the cracks in the roof. Other trucks and cars were coming the other way, also spraying water in all directions. Some vehicles had even parked, perhaps defeated, while others had broken down and were pushed up against the wall. We had to focus intently. Our adrenalin was pumping as the fumes stung our eyes and burnt our lungs.

Eventually, after about four kilometres, the depth of the water in The Tunnel reduced to about 10 centimetres and I could see light at the end. While most people back home would be in bed or sitting down to breakfast, I was riding out of 'The Tunnel of Doom', soaking wet, muddy and freezing in the 2500 metre-high mountains of Tajikistan. Dirk and I were ecstatic about what we'd just accomplished.

Thankfully, the road to Dushanbe improved and the final 40 kilometres were billiard-table smooth. But we dropped altitude quickly, so the temperature started to soar as we hit the plains. The first two hotels we tried were full, but we were allowed to camp in the garden of the second.

Our first chore was to find a man called Dishlod Curaiwo for a permit to enter the Pamir mountain region and to formally register in Tajikistan. I insisted that we get these permits by the next day because I did *not* want to hang around all weekend and I was *sick* of waiting. (I'd only ridden 10 out of 28 possible days since leaving Dubai.) Plus, my Kyrgyzstan visa could run out before I'd even used it. To make matters worse, I had the runs.

At 11am the next day, I got a call saying that our permit for the Pamir Mountains — one of the main reasons I was visiting this part of the world — would be ready by 4pm. This would allow us to leave the next morning and not have to worry about any other paperwork until I reached Almaty (Kazakhstan), where I prayed that I could get visas for Russia and China.

The road out of Dushanbe was straight and flat but with a strong headwind and some rain. Soon enough, the road deteriorated and turned into a rocky track of patchy tarmac as we wound through the valley and into the Pamirs. With the temperature dipping as we reached 3252 metres, the road hugged the border with Afghanistan, which was just across a flowing grey river. We waved to some residents of that troubled country. At one stage, as we reached 4200 metres, the altitude gave me crippling headaches, but my body soon adjusted. The Mothership wasn't in much better health, but it kept chugging away.

As we continued weaving towards Khorog, my speedometer stopped working and we pulled up to fix it on a volleyball court in a village. We also stopped to wash ourselves at a hot spring. We had to be naked in the single-sex baths, but I could only manage about two seconds up to my neck before I screamed and jumped out. A huge man, whom we called 'The Big Bear' because he was covered from head to toe in hair, said something to us in Russian. From his gestures, we assumed he was saying something like, "Come, hop in, it's not hot." Slipping into the water without testing it first, he immediately jumped straight out again with a scream.

Dirk smiled. "Well, it's even too hot for The Big Bear."

We camped outside of Ishkashim in another beautiful area of snow-capped mountains, but we were being spoilt with these amazing landscapes every day. Across the river only 20 to 50 metres away was Afghanistan, but the Wakhan Valley is a world away from the war, although we did see plenty of warning signs about land mines on our side of the river-cum-border. We tried crossing a bridge over the river and asking a guard if we could walk into Afghanistan for a quick look. He made his answer quite clear by forming a 'gun' with his fingers and placing it under his chin.

It was good to have company, and Dirk and I got along well. With his blond hair and wiry face, my first impressions of this crazy 36-year-old were not good; I thought I'd never be able to get rid of him. But I soon changed my mind, and we became best mates. Starting his adventure in Belgium a few months earlier and travelling via Turkey and Iran, he was now heading in the same direction as I was for a while on the way to Australia. He was relaxed and easy-going, and we worked perfectly as a team. And he could fart like no one else on earth.

Dirk and I decided to slow down a bit — because of paperwork, not the bikes. Dirk was thinking that if he couldn't get a visa to China in Bishkek (Kyrgyzstan), he would come to Mongolia with me and try to get a Chinese visa there. But according to his Kyrgyzstan visa, he couldn't enter that country for another 10 days, while I had to enter in about four days. We whiled away time by taking photos, wallowing in hot springs, drinking from fresh streams and stopping at roadside tea shops.

A few people liked throwing rocks at us, and one day we'd had enough. We caught one of the kids and kicked him up the backside. This prompted two men to run down the road toward us, carrying shovels.

"Do you think they want trouble with us?" I asked Dirk.

"I'm not hanging around to find out!"

So we scarpered off quick smart. We also met two cyclists, European guys in their late 50s. How they managed to ride across these mountains on bicycles at this altitude was beyond me.

About 10 kilometres before the turn-off to the Pamir Highway, we passed an old Russian *Uaz* van parked along the road. I thought nothing more of it until we reached an intersection, where three westerners — part of a group of seven Polish alpinists (mountain climbers) — were standing. They explained that their van had run out of fuel, so they needed to reach the next town, which was 20 kilometres away. Dirk took one of them into town to buy some petrol. After they refuelled, the van needed to be push-started, and although the local driver had no idea what to do, it did start. At an altitude of about 4000 metres, we were all exhausted, so the Poles bought us dinner that night.

The Pamir 'Highway' (which is just a road, really) stretches along the Pamir Mountains from Khorog in Tajikistan to Osh in Kyrgyzstan. The scenery is extraordinary, a real change from the Wakhan Valley we'd been following for the previous four days. The people had round, weather-beaten faces like I'd imagined the Mongolians would have. The locals lived in *gers*, which are large round tents with chimneys in the middle spewing out smoke. We saw long animals like moles, or perhaps marmots, running to their holes as well as plenty of yaks — but almost no trees anywhere.

After negotiating another 4000 metres-high pass, we finally reached Murgab. We caught up again with the Poles who shared their watermelon and vodka.

The next day, Dirk and I intended to cross into Kyrgyzstan, but his visa wasn't actually valid for another week. Dirk's bike was also causing problems, so we stopped — at 4000 metres and close to the Chinese border — to change his spark plugs. The scenery around the remote town of Karakul was quite something, with snow-capped peaks around a huge salt lake. I never understood why — or even *how* — anyone would live in places like this.

## KYRGYZSTAN

To avoid hanging about waiting for Dirk's visa to become valid, we decided to tell the Tajikistan border officials that Dirk was suffering from 'altitude sickness', so he needed to cross into Kyrgyzstan and get to lower altitudes quickly. Inside the little hut that served as the Tajikistan Immigration post, Dirk lay on a bunk bed, 'suffering' from his 'sickness', while a policeman noted our details.

Things didn't start well when another official took my glove, unclipped his pistol from its holster and waved the pistol in my face, saying we could swap my gloves for his pistol. But it was a joke, so I laughed appropriately. Our ruse had worked better than expected, and we were soon both stamped out (despite the 'gravely ill' Dirk running after a roll of toilet paper careering down the hill).

As we rode past the final barrier and around a corner, just out of sight from the Tajikistan border control, Dirk's bike stopped again. At 4500 metres and in no-man's land between Tajikistan and Kyrgyzstan, we did some makeshift repairs to his fuel pump.

Over another pass, we headed down to the Kyrgyzstan border, where Dirk's acting skills would need to be superb once more. Sitting in a little room, the Kyrgyzstan border official checked my visa and made some notes. He then opened Dirk's passport. Dirk was about to say something regarding his 'altitude sickness', but the official picked up a date-stamp and stamped both our passports.

"Okay, you go," he said.

And we did. We hopped onto our bikes, rode to the Customs post and were waved through. Roaring along a tarred but bumpy road across a flat plain, we tooted our horns and waved with delight at some soldiers.

The first stop, only 20 kilometres from the border, was Sary Tash, a cold, remote place with stunning views of the snow-covered Pamir Mountains back over in Tajikistan. We stayed in a house owned by some locals (for a small fee), where we enjoyed a tasty traditional dinner of bread, potato and cabbage. The Pamir 'Highway' that finishes at Osh was good but dusty in places because of road works. With no cheap accommodation available, we decided to camp 30 kilometres out of Osh in an old building that looked like a village hospital.

That night, I desperately needed to talk with Amy. I wanted for her to be with me or at least to see her. I was always thinking about her — no more than at that time. I knew there seemed to be only two options: letting Amy go, or trying my hardest to make things right. But the latter was impossible, stuck in a mountain village thousands of kilometres away.

The next day, my spirits lifted. Along the excellent road towards Bishkek, the capital, we met two more cyclists (from Spain). Later, we swam in Lake Toktogal because the weather was so damn hot, but it soon started to rain. By that afternoon, we felt like we were freezing to death while travelling over a mountain pass at 3184 metres. In a gully below, we saw loads of people and horses, so we decided to check out what was happening.

Someone explained that they were about to start *kok boru*, a traditional game where men on horses fight over a headless goat and drop it in an area marked by rocks. Banned during Soviet rule, there seemed to be no teams or even rules — just every man and horse for themselves — in one of the world's most incredible 'stadiums': a grassy valley surrounded by towering peaks.

First, someone cut the throat of a live goat and chopped off its head and hoofs. One horseman took the heavily-bleeding goat about 300 metres away and dropped it on the ground. At a signal, about 15 horsemen galloped towards the lifeless goat while whipping and yelling at their horses. Still riding at full speed, the first man there leaned to the ground, picked up the goat and tried to drop it at the marked spot in order to score. But, of course, all the others wanted the goat just as much, so they pulled and jostled at the carcass while the horses crashed into each other. The horsemen often galloped with no hands on the reins while tugging at the carcass held by someone else. Often, they charged into the crowd, which had to scatter.

As we were the only westerners, they asked if we could ride a horse. Stupidly, I said, "yes". Some of the delighted spectators quickly found me a horse and threw me the 'ball' — the headless goat. Suddenly, I was the target as the more experienced players tried ripping the carcass away from me. They were so strong and fit, and after about two minutes I was absolutely stuffed. But they were kind and let me 'score' by placing the goat at the scoring spot (even though I missed it).

Not to be outdone, Dirk (who couldn't ride a horse) was given the carcass and put on a donkey, which pranced around while a local whipped it. The crowd erupted when Dirk dismounted (which wasn't hard because his feet almost touched the ground).

Totally exhausted, we pitched our tents behind a nearby farmer's shed in a spectacularly lush area with masses of horses and *yurts* (also called *gers*), the large round tents they live in and use as shops for selling fermented mares' milk. It was a gorgeous scene that I desperately wanted to share with Amy.

In contrast, Bishkek was unexciting. And the bad news was that Dirk would have to wait around for two weeks to get a visa for Kazakhstan. This was not part of my plan, especially as I wanted to get home by around 1 February next year (about seven months away) and return from Bangkok to Dubai for the motorbike rally. Having to wait for someone is a good reason why travelling alone is often preferable.

On the other hand, we did enjoy travelling together, and the arrival date back home was just a focus point; I wasn't bound to it. So I decided to hang around Bishkek and try some traditional cuisine, such as fermented mares' milk (which tastes as horrible as it sounds). To fill in the time, we rode to Ata Arch, a gorge about 30 kilometres from Bishkek, where we hiked up a mountain to an unimpressive waterfall and I got sunburnt.

I also spent time updating my blog and organising my entry to the Desert Challenge rally in Dubai. Amy hadn't emailed for a long time. I had mixed feelings: I hoped she was okay, but I knew she was keeping her distance. Again, I felt that I was over this trip and its hassles (like waiting days for visas), but I did have a lot to look forward to in the next few months. This included riding around South-East Asia, a region I loved; loading The Mothership on to the boat to Darwin for the final leg; and setting foot onto Australian soil for the first time in over five years.

On the day that Dirk obtained his Kazakhstan visa, I got the runs. I spent an entire day lying on my back with stomach cramps and running to the toilet.

## KAZAKHSTAN

Dehydrated and drained from the diarrhoea, I slowly packed up before riding 20 kilometres to the border. Getting out of Kyrgyzstan was a breeze — both of us were processed in three minutes — and it only took a few minutes longer to get into Kazakhstan. The first thing I did in Kazakhstan was shit myself — quite literally (but I won't go into details).

I survived the 200 kilometres to Almaty, the capital, where we stayed with Max, a real character whom Rene had also met and stayed with. Max is a 'genuine' biker, with tattoos, chains and belts (whereas I am someone who just rides motorbikes). This was a chance to fix my bike, relax, recuperate (and clean my underwear) — and, of course, get visas for Mongolia and hopefully Russia. It was hot, but I gradually recovered from what seemed like a recurrence of the giardia I caught in Tanzania.

After waiting a day for it to open, we arrived at the Mongolian Embassy at 8.45am with great anxiety. A sign informed us that the embassy opened at 9.30, so we sat on the road in the shade. An official came out of the embassy at 9.05 and asked if we wanted a visa. We said, "yes", so he told us to come inside. We filled in the application forms and paid our fees (US$58 each). He told us to collect our visas the next day. So far, so good.

We went to the Russian Embassy to ask about visas even though we didn't have our passports with us. After waiting only 10 minutes, we filled in a form and approached the window to enquire about transit visas. The official said that if we returned the next day with our passports and bike papers, we could get the visa almost on the spot. *Amazing!* This meant we could leave for Russia very soon, with no more crap about visas until we reached Ulaan Baator, the capital of Mongolia, and had to apply for visas to China.

Still with my recurring stomach problems, we returned to the Mongolian Embassy the next day to collect our lovely 30-day visas, which were valid for three months. After some photocopying, we collected our Russian transit visas almost immediately. Getting two visas in one day was almost unheard of. For other countries, I sometimes had to wait a week or more just to get *one* visa.

It was time to head to Russia. Max insisted that he and his biker mate on a 'chopper' (cruiser-style motorbike) escort us out of town as a farewell. We left late but were determined to get some distance under our belts before sundown. We camped that night on grass in an old creek bed between fenceless paddocks. We still had about 900 kilometres to the Russian border.

With the sun up so early and no need to hang around Kazakhstan, we travelled 873 kilometres the next day. A lot of the time, it felt like a rollercoaster, with huge bumps always keeping me alert — and awake, because the scenery was dead boring. The wind also blew hard, and the Kazaks drove like lunatics. Twice, Dirk was nearly driven off the road, each time with potentially fatal consequences. When we entered a pine forest, he also got bogged in sand, so I had to go back and help him lift up The Old Lady.

The Russian border would mark a significant turning point. I'd been travelling north since Cape Agulhas (the most southerly tip of South Africa) for about 12 months, but I would soon be heading south all the way home to Turriff.

The farm was still 20,000 kilometres away, but it did feel like the 'home stretch'. There was still a long, *long* way to go, of course, and I needed to take one day at a time. All the unknowns were always racing around in my brain — especially about China. Would I get a visa? Would my bike be allowed in?

*Would I get caught if I took my bike in illegally?*

**RUSSIA**

Kazakhstan was disappointing. The men were often drunk on vodka, the land was so barren and the roads were always terrible. I wasn't sorry to leave, and thankfully, it didn't take long to get out. We didn't have a Customs Declaration for the bikes, which wasn't our fault because we were never given one when we entered Kazakhstan. The customs officer didn't bother arguing or investigating. He took the easy option and waved us through.

Russian Immigration went without a hitch, but we also need papers for the bikes, so we waited in line at a Customs room for about 40 minutes.

A big Russian man standing in line looked at me and said *"Atkuta?"* ('Where are you from?')

"Australia," I said.

"Ah, kangaroo!"

The others waiting in the room laughed. The big Russian felt proud about his comment.

I smiled and asked him the same question. *"Atkuta?"*

"Russia!" he announced with great pride.

I paused for a moment and said, "Ah, Kalashnikov!"

During the immediate silence, Dirk and I glanced at each other with unease before the Russian burst out laughing. My joke went better than expected as the room full of Russians joined in with the mirth. After about three hours, we were eventually cleared.

The road was flat, straight and boring, but the big difference between Russia and some of the '-stans' was the greenery. There were fields and fields of wheat and numerous farm sheds, but no one seemed to have any fences. At our first stop in Rubscouk, we loaded up on burgers (which were horrible) and *rubles*, the local currency. We also noticed (especially after being in Iran) that the further we travelled across

Russia, the shorter the skirts seemed to be. All the Russian women (in summer) like to wear tight shorts or mini-skirts and low tops. They all looked like the blonde tennis player Anna Kournikova.

But we didn't stop anywhere for long because we were keen to push through to the Mongolian border by the next day, before it would close for the weekend. Near Ajisk, we took what seemed like a shortcut on our map to save time. But it didn't — in fact, far from it. To start with, the road was good, like Switzerland with rolling hills. We ticked off a lot of kilometres, but then my bike started chugging. The battery was flat.

I switched off my headlights (according to Russian law all vehicles must use headlights at all times) and checked the horn. The horn was okay, so the rectifier was still charging the battery, but the battery was dead. I'd only bought it a short while before in Dubai, but it was a cheap Chinese variety. We rode on using the GPS because the network of roads was only slightly less incompressible than all the Russian signs in the Cyrillic alphabet.

We turned left (the first of many mistakes), which led us along an 80-kilometre loop that finished along the main road we'd previously used but only 10 kilometres further on. Then the road we chose turned to gravel. It was late, and we needed to camp, especially because my left boot was completely covered in cow shit after driving through the world's largest pile of dung.

We started early again the next day, knowing there were still 100 kilometres to the main road and 300 kilometres more to the Mongolian border (that we needed to cross that afternoon). We soon reached a typical Russian hillside village where all the homes were log cabins, but we needed to reach Ust Kan, 60 kilometres further on. Our map indicated a road alongside a river, but the track petered out at a camping ground. While asking directions there, we ended up eating breakfast with a Russian man who spoke German (which Dirk could understand) and 20 kids who were on a camp, it seemed, to teach them some discipline.

The Russian got his map out and announced that the road which continued for another 18 kilometres to a town was no good for a car, but okay for motorbikes. I should've heard the alarm bells, but I accepted his word. Sure enough, the road turned to complete crap, barely more than a series of rocky creek beds.

We hit our first major obstacle after only two kilometres: a collapsed, incomplete bridge. We laid down some planks and walked the bikes over one at a time, waiting for the rotten wood to collapse beneath us. The rest of the road was a combination of rocks, slush and mud before we reached a huge boulder that signalled the end of the track. Using small rocks, we created a path over the bigger boulder and pushed the bikes over, but the bash plates (that protect the exhaust pipes and sump) slammed into the rocks. With more banging and crashing of the bash plates, we immediately came across the next obstacle.

A huge tree had fallen across the track. Our first thought was to burn through it, but after a while we managed to lever it away. Further on, we bulldozed our way through the thick forest and pushed our bikes around more fallen trees and through huge potholes. It was crazy and exhausting; in two hours we'd only covered 400 metres. The track was barely 15 centimetres wide in places, and Dirk fell into the bushes a few times.

Soon enough, we reached a point that seemed even *worse*. We walked further on to investigate and agreed that the track was utterly impassable on any form of vehicle — even walking would be tough. Of course, this meant enduring everything again on the way back. And we were wasting so much precious time; we'd only travelled six of the 18 kilometres to the town since leaving the Russian and the 20 ill-disciplined kids that morning. There was no way we were going to make the Mongolian border (which closed on weekends), meaning we would waste two more days as well.

We slogged our way back along the track and did well until we reached the 'bridge', which was now more dangerous because of the drop-off on the part of the bridge we had to pass first. Totally exhausted, we laid more planks across the 'bridge' and lifted, pushed and grunted hard enough to get The Old Lady up across the main plank and onto the other planks we'd laid down a few hours earlier.

While helping to push my bike across, a plank broke beneath Dirk. He fell, pulling my bike towards him. I couldn't hold my 250 kilogram bike alone any longer, so it fell on top of him. He screamed for me to pull The Mothership off him, so I ran around and somehow heaved it off his leg. I really thought his leg was in a bad way until he said, "I was always a bit of a screamer."

We wanted to laugh but didn't have the energy. We made it across the bridge and struggled along the rest of the track. I reached another camping ground with some other Russians, who asked if I wanted some *chai* (tea). I managed to nod and smile. With whatever energy I had remaining, I took off my jacket. I was covered in sweat.

I soon heard Dirk approaching the camping ground, and I turned as I heard an almighty crash. I ran to where Dirk lay with his bike on its side among the rocks. He was *totally* exhausted, with no energy left to even ride his bike any more. The sympathetic campers gave us tea (with plenty of energy-boosting sugar) as well as fruit strips and a Twix chocolate bar. We decided we'd had enough for that day and camped there. This gave us a chance to recuperate and to wash our smelly clothes and our smellier selves in the river. Later that evening, more Russians arrived at the camping ground carrying AK-47s.

That was the hardest road I'd ever attempted on this trip — or at any other time in my life — and the beer offered by the Russians never tasted so good. They also cooked us a meal with cabbage and shared their bottles of Vodka and Cognac.

Now that the border to Mongolia was closed for the weekend, we had more time. We went fishing with the Russians who gave an AK-47 to Dirk and a semi-automatic 12-gauge shotgun to me. I wondered how we were going to shoot fish, but the Russian signalled to us that the weapons were for protection against bears. But we saw no bears (or fish).

The next morning, we packed up and exchanged email addresses with the Russians. One of them said the group were in the 'mafia' and that I should call him if I ever got into trouble. As a farewell, they fired some AK-47s into the air. I tried shooting the rifle too. The noise and recoil were unbelievable.

We made our way back to Ust Kan along the comparatively wonderful road, but it felt boring and unchallenging. My dash mount snapped (which happened on my first bike in Zimbabwe) with one of the two supports broken, which would have to be welded as soon as possible. We still had to travel to the border with Mongolia quickly because we only had two days left on our transit visa for Russia. As we continued, the road was great and the scenery absolutely stunning, with alpine forests and snow-capped mountains. The countryside later changed to the treeless plains we expected in Mongolia.

At Kosh Agac, while we were eating *largmun* (a tasty broth of noodles and meat), two Russians pulled up to look at our bikes. I asked them about a welder. They drove away and returned 15 minutes later to take me to a mechanic with a welder. I took my dash apart and welded up the support. We spent our last few *rubles* on fuel and headed to Tshanta. Very near the border, we saw some wild, double-humped Bactrian camels and did some maintenance on our bikes, but we were told to move on by trigger-happy soldiers.

We were invited to stay for our last night in Russia at a riverside campsite with some French and English people riding motorbikes and cars in the charity Mongol Rally (in which vehicles cannot cost more than £500). There was also a load of very drunk Russian border guards who were pissed off with these foreigners. I tired of them quickly too and went to bed.

Staring at the amazing stars and listening to the horrible Russian house music in the distance, I wondered about the Next Big Question.

China.

Day 698
Ulaanbaatar
Mongolia
Erenhot
Ger
Xi'an
China
Three Gorges Dam
East China Sea
Kunming
India
Myanmar
Laos
South China Sea
Thailand
Bangkok
Malaysia
Banda Aceh
Sumatra
Indonesia
Java
Bali
East Timor
Dili
Yogyakarta
Day 868
600miles
1000kms
Timor Sea

CHAPTER 6

# Asia

*Mongolia to Indonesia: 171 Days*

**MONGOLIA**

Of course, a little country called Mongolia stood in the way between me and China.

To get out of Russia, Dirk and I waited a few hours until 12pm, at which time, of course, the border closed for two hours for lunch. So after cooking another meal of tuna and pasta, we did a few chores such as washing our clothes under a tap and hanging them over our bikes. Finally, after another two hours — seven hours after we'd started — we were let through.

The road immediately turned into gravel for five kilometres to a surprisingly new building at the Mongolian border. Most of the 20 cars and four bikes waiting there were part of the Mongol Rally, which started at London and ended in the Mongolian capital, Ulaanbaatar, where participants donated the vehicles to local people.

The Mongolian side was another nightmare as we shifted from one person to another and back again for an hour. After changing some money, we were stopped at another little wooden shed. We knew we didn't have bike insurance and they would want to sell us some.

"We have insurance," I lied.

"Let me see."

I showed the man what I said was my *insurance* — that is, the worthless Temporary Import Permit I got way back in Kenya. He studied it hard.

"International," I lied again.

Dirk presented his Belgium registration papers as *insurance*.

He waved us through.

We continued down the crappy gravel road into Mongolia, a country that had lingered in my mind since leaving South Africa. But I felt a little sad as I thought about Amy and how much she would've loved to be here. Instantly, I missed her even more than usual.

The landscape was barren, with long flat plains with mountains along both sides and not a tree in sight. Across the immense grassy spaces, horses and yaks were grazing in areas with no fences. We headed straight to Olgii to buy fuel and food and were surprised at the selection on offer at the small store. That night, we found a pleasant place to camp on grass and alongside a stream. Mongolia seemed to be one massive, perfect campsite.

I soon regarded Mongolia as the last wild frontier, especially considering the way people rode into town on horseback and tied up their transport in front of a shop. And the roads were a joke — like one giant paddock with trails heading in every direction. According to the GPS, I was closer to London (7000 kilometres away) than home (10,600 kilometres) in a straight line, although it had now been two years since I'd left England. But I still felt close to home, with maybe only seven countries to go — if I could get through China. Before that, however, was the small matter of riding about 2000 kilometres along dirt tracks just to reach the Mongolian capital, Ulaanbaatar.

The country and people of Mongolia are quite unique. The endless green grass is dotted with round, white tents called *gers* (or *yurts*). The people are mostly nomadic and raise horses, camels, goats, sheep and yaks, and the shepherds' faces are weathered by the extreme climate. Mongolians really live like they would've done

300 years ago. They ride horses along the streets of sleepy villages and use camels and yaks to transport their worldly possessions in wagons made of wood.

The skies were clear and blue but often windy and dusty. The sunsets were truly beautiful, and we often camped at places offering spectacular views, with yaks wandering about nearby. Overnight it was freezing, but the days warmed up when the sun shone.

I should've been exhilarated by the countryside and excited about my travels, but I felt empty and lost. I checked my email, and there was nothing from Amy. I had to face reality. It was completely over. I had to let her — and us — go from my mind.

As the days went by, we had the usual dramas with the bikes, of course. Dirk got a puncture, and so did I after hitting a sharp rock that also bent my rim a little. After pumping up my spare tube, I was ready to go, but then that went flat. The spare had three holes in it, so I threw it away and patched up the tube with the original hole.

By the time we reached Clavadon, my dash mount had snapped in half completely and I needed a welder. We were directed to a Mongolian Army base, a ramshackle place with gates hanging off the hinges, cows wandering about, and a few army trucks that looked like they hadn't moved for a decade.

The base was manned by a few Mongolian soldiers doing almost nothing, so they were glad to have something to do. They supplied the welding equipment and a massive diesel motor which powered the generator while Dirk welded as best as he could. The soldiers asked for 1000 *tugriks* (US$8), but the highest ranking officer firmly said Dirk should pay no money.

Along the sandy tracks, Dirk had another spill, which battered his confidence. He is a good rider, but when he falls it plays on his mind. Amazingly, we also passed some cyclists, one of whom gave us some bad news: getting a visa to China in Mongolia was not possible.

On the second-to-last day before reaching Ulaanbaatar my rectifier failed, which meant it supplied too much charge to the battery, but I hadn't notice until the battery blew up. I was now screwed. The bike couldn't go anywhere. (I could monitor problems with the rectifier, but this time I needed a new battery.)

There was no choice but to find a *ger* and ask a local to take The Mothership in a truck to Tsertgergul, which was 45 kilometres away. It was disappointing because it was the first time in the 75,000 kilometres I'd ridden so far that my bike had moved without me on it. Incredibly, we found a new battery that would do the job. It was made in China, but there was no alternative. I disconnected one of the three phases supplied to the rectifier to reduce its output so it wouldn't blow up the new battery.

Most of the final 300 kilometres to Ulaanbaatar was tarmac, a wonderful change after 1500 kilometres of dirt tracks. We stopped at a monastery called Harkorin, where Dirk's goggles were stolen, which was annoying. When the road temporarily turned bad, my dash mount snapped again, so I had to hold it up with my hand for the last 150 kilometres.

The first thing we did when we reached Ulaanbaatar (commonly shortened to UB) was look for the Chinese Embassy. This would be my third attempt at getting a Chinese visa — and also my last chance. On Monday, we came prepared with a fake airline 'ticket' and an 'itinerary' (created through a travel agency). We also offered proof of a 10% deposit for two weeks' accommodation (which we had no intention of using, so we would lose the deposit). We were unsuccessful, however, because we needed photocopies of everything and proof of how much money we had.

On Tuesday, the embassy was closed. On Wednesday, the official accepted our applications after we got there one-and-a-half hours before opening and then lined up in the rain for another hour. And on Friday, we picked up the visa. (Usually, tourists are issued a standard 30-day visa, but because of security around the Olympics we were given what we'd requested with our fake 'itinerary': a visa for 16 days. We weren't sure this would be long enough to cross China. And we didn't know yet that we'd be riding through China on different motorbikes.)

We filled in the rest of our days in UB washing and fixing the bikes and frequenting an Irish bar, which seemed as far removed as possible from Mongolia. We stumbled across Mike, the German guy I'd travelled with across the Arabian Peninsula. The three of us spent several riotous evenings sharing new stories and laughing about old ones.

Despite all the warnings, getting a Chinese visa was surprisingly easy. Far more difficult was getting the bike over the border and riding it across China. After some more enquiries, it seemed impossible because the Chinese authorities did not want motorcyclists travelling alone. This meant reverting to Plan B: riding 700 kilometres to the border, transporting our bikes into China in the back of a truck, and off-loading the bikes further into the country.

Of course, this would be highly illegal, but we had no choice. Dirk and I were now joined by Izabella, a girl from Poland whom we met at the Chinese Embassy. It was Artic conditions as we rode about 500 kilometres towards the Chinese border, and I cursed myself for sending home my winter riding gear. Along the way, we spotted a fence in the distance and entered a compound with two *gers*. We asked if we could pitch our tents nearby. A man invited us inside the *ger* to drink tea (really just salty balls made from camel or goat milk) and thaw out next to the stove. He later took pity on us and allowed us to sleep on the floor of the comparatively cosy *ger*.

All the time we were travelling to the border, we were still unsure whether or not we'd be allowed into China. If not, we would have to ride all the way back to UB and come up with another plan. At the border town of Zam uud, Izabella found a truck driver, a half Kazak/Mongolian called Narrka, who'd given her a lift a few weeks before. Being Polish, Izabella spoke to him in Russian and explained our problem about crossing the border with our bikes.

He said we could load our bikes onto his truck. We managed to do this with a makeshift ramp that broke, resulting in The Mothership nearly crushing me. After much yelling and pulling on our part, the bikes were in the back of the truck and strapped down securely.

Then it hit me again. We were now illegally transporting our bikes into China.

Crossing out of Mongolia on foot was easy. With the bikes still in the truck, we hitched a ride to the Chinese side in an old Russian UAZ jeep (which was also smuggling a man hidden under a tarpaulin in the back). Crossing the next border went reasonably smoothly, and before we knew it we were in China. But our bikes were *not*. They were still in the truck at the Mongolian border.

We waited and waited in the fierce sun. I soon became petrified. *Would our bikes get in? And what would happen if they didn't?* We saw a truck belonging to Narrka's mate, who indicated that the truck with our bikes was coming soon. We got excited. It was happening. We started planning our next route.

But more time passed. We were still waiting. We noticed Narrka's mate on the phone. He approached us and said we needed to go to the truck.

This was *not* good.

I slowly walked 500 metres back to the Chinese Customs terminal and entered the building wearing my friendliest smile. One man, who spoke a little English, immediately explained that our bikes could not come in to China. I tried everything. I made up stories about how one bike was broken, how we couldn't fly our bikes from Mongolia because the plane wasn't large enough, and how we planned to transport the bikes to Xi'an before freighting them to Bangkok. They understood what I was saying, but their answers were the same.

Reality was quickly setting in. The bikes — and, therefore, we — could go no further. Perhaps I'd always expected it, but to get so close…

I tried gesturing a bribe, but again the officials gave a firm, "no". Feeling that I'd tried everything, I walked back to tell Dirk and Izabella. I then realised there might be another problem. A young

Chinese policeman at a gate wanted to see my passport. I explained that the Customs Officers wanted to see Dirk and Izabella, but he shook his head and made it plain that the three of us would not be allowed back into the Customs building, although he didn't know why. We argued with the policeman for 30 minutes while Narrka was very anxious to offload our bikes and get into China.

Eventually the policeman saw the light and allowed us back into the Customs building. Dirk and Izabella tried their negotiation skills, but to no avail. There was now only one alternative: riding our bikes back into Mongolia. But that created another problem: we'd been stamped out of Mongolia, and we were now stuck in no-man's land.

Narrka was now getting calls from his boss asking him why he was still at the border. The Chinese Customs Officers said we could not ride back into Mongolia; instead, we would have to leave our bikes at the border and collect them in a day or two. I made it clear that this was *not* an option, so they relented and allowed us to take the bikes immediately back into Mongolia.

We had to return to the Chinese Immigration Office in a car to collect our passports. Izabella jumped out at the border as we said our quick farewells. She certainly did not want or need to go back to UB. The Immigration officials cancelled our entry stamps, which meant our precious Chinese visas were still valid. The officials escorted us out of the door and pointed us to the direction of Mongolia. Meanwhile, Narrka was not happy about being forced to drive back into Mongolia.

Dirk and I clambered into a jeep full of Mongolians for the short trip back to the Mongolian border. With no ramp or other way to unload our bikes, we commandeered two men standing about interested in the commotion. As they hauled our bikes straight out from the back of the truck, our 250-kilogram machines hit the ground with a thud. Narrka bid us farewell but not before we slipped him a considerable payment for all the trouble we'd caused.

At the Mongolian Immigration post, we simply said, "No China." The officer laughed as if to say, "You two ain't the first." We were taken to the main office, where the boss quickly took out a stamp and gave us visas for Mongolia.

As we rode back into Mongolia without our helmets on, I glanced at Dirk and we burst out laughing. It was all we could do because the situation was so surreal. But, of course, we were now further away from getting into China than we were that morning. People had warned me that crossing the border into China with my bike would be impossible, and perhaps I should've listened, but at least I tried my best.

As I went to sleep that night, little did I know that things would get even more absurd the next day — beyond anything that I'd experienced during almost two years of travel.

During the night, I awoke thinking a car with its headlights was approaching. I soon realised it was a thunderstorm, but I felt safe from the rain in my tent. The first 30 kilometres of the 668 kilometres back to Ulaanbaatar were easy enough along the dusty Gobi Desert tracks. It started raining, which made the sand firmer and the dust settle, but the rain got heavier. The Mothership skated across the surface of the slippery plains, but we managed to keep the bikes upright before taking shelter at Saynshand.

I often travelled faster than Dirk, who was less confident on dirt tracks at times. He always told me to carry on and said that he would catch up with me later.

So I did. And, one day, he did not.

I thought it would be the last time I'd ever see Dirk again.

From Saynshand, we decided to follow the train line to the north. After five kilometres, conditions became even worse and the ground was as slippery as ice. I turned back and decided to take another track that we'd used a few days earlier. I thought I saw Dirk following me in the distance through the pelting rain. Finding a higher and firmer track, I was soon travelling some 70 to 80 kilometres per hour. I had to keep going. I was soaked and freezing. This was not place to stop and wait for Dirk to catch up.

About 90 minutes later and 100 kilometres further on, I arrived at the next town. I walked into a small wooden shack, where a man in the shack could see I was frozen to the bone. Without saying a word, a lady also in there started a fire in the stove and placed a chair in front of it for me. I decided I would wait there for Dirk.

An hour passed and the fire had almost died out. I was warmer but more worried. I waited another hour, but there was still no sign of Dirk. My fears grew. I knew riding was tough in the Gobi, especially in that sort of weather, but I was only 100 kilometres from where we last saw each other. I knew he should've arrived a long time ago. It was dark and still raining, but I had to make a decision: I could either continue on and catch up with Dirk later or look for him.

But I had no idea where he would be. Dozens of tracks lead in all directions. He could've been anywhere. I rode out of town and tried to look for him, but it was hopeless and pointless. So many tracks spread across a 3- or 4-kilometre width, and I could only see a few hundred metres ahead of me in the rain and dark.

I decided to continue north to Ulaanbaatar. By now, the Gobi had turned into an ocean. I had to ride with my helmet visor up because I couldn't see anything with the tinted lens. The rain whipped my cheeks and stung my face like needles. The wind grew stronger. I could no longer feel my hands; they hardly functioned on the throttle. I kept telling myself that I had to carry on. There was nowhere to camp anyway.

I then saw a light from a *ger* in the distance. Smoke was pouring from the chimney. My survival instincts told me that I had to stop. I needed shelter. I rode over to the *ger* and prized my fingers from the handlebars. The occupants must've heard my bike, and I saw the door open.

Standing at the entrance was a dwarf. The absurdity of the situation made me smile for the first time all day. I entered the *ger*, dripping wet and frozen to the core, and smiled at the old lady and young boy also there. They stoked the fire, which helped dry out my boots, gloves, jacket and every layer of clothes I had on. They cooked me a dinner of rice and mutton, served up with lots of hot salty and milky tea. After dinner, they placed a thin mattress on the floor of the *ger* and gave me a blanket. I lay down, completely exhausted, with the wind howling and the rain pelting outside.

But I couldn't sleep. I'd left Dirk out there, and I don't know where he was. I should've looked for him. *But how?* That night, it was impossible to write in my diary the mix and depth of my feelings. I was scared, worried and sad. I missed Amy so much I wanted to cry. But was it Amy I missed? I wasn't sure. Did I do the right thing by Dirk? What could I have done anyway? Had he ran out of fuel? Fallen off his bike? Broken his leg or knocked himself out? I knew I should've turned back and looked for him, but I might've put myself in danger too.

And what could I do the next day? The only option was to continue to UB and wait there for Dirk. He could've taken any of the 20 or more roads to the capital that snake through the Gobi Desert. But I had done wrong by Dirk — broken some unwritten rule about bikers looking after each other. Yet there was nothing I could do. The wind was still howling outside, everything on me and with me was soaked, and I had a crippling headache.

I had had some low points on my trip, but this was the lowest. I desperately wanted to wake up the next day and find that Dirk was okay. In fact, I wanted the next month to pass so I could be in Thailand. Better still, I needed the next four months to go by so I could see Amy.

But would I ever see her again? I wanted to cry. I wanted to scream. But I needed to sleep even more badly. *Where the hell was my mate?*

I awoke as soon as the sun was up. The dwarf heated up leftovers from last night's dinner. The ground outside was drying quickly, but my boots were still wet. I must've rested them on the pot-belly stove the previous night because the zip was melted and the top of my boot was burnt.

I continued to UB. Along the way, I bought some fuel with what little money I had left. While warming my hands on a stove, I switched on my mobile phone (which normally didn't work way out in the desert) and waited for Dirk. About 30 minutes later, I received a text from a number I didn't know. I read it eagerly.

It was from Dirk.

*Jesus, what a relief!* He'd fallen off his bike in the mud and rain the day before, but he was okay. I waited until 11am for him to catch up before deciding to wait again at another town 100 kilometres further on. I made it there with half a litre of fuel remaining in my tank.

As I approached some tourists to change money, I saw Dirk riding over the hill. I was so incredibly relieved to see him. When he pulled up, we hugged each other tightly and laughed. We celebrated with a Snickers chocolate bar each before loading up with fuel and riding the final 80 kilometres to UB.

He explained what had unfolded in the 'Gobi Ocean'. He had seen me switch sides at the train line in search of a better track but didn't immediately follow. Not long after, he came to grief and slid in the mud, falling about 20 metres from his bike. Even further back was his pannier, which had ripped off during the crash. In the freezing, wet weather and in the middle of nowhere, he tried fixing The Old Lady, but it took some time to beat the panels into a usable state. While doing this, a mangy dog appeared, shaking from the cold. It sat beside him and looked at Dirk as if to say, "Get me out of here!" Glancing at the dog, Dirk had said, "And I thought I had problems."

It felt so strange being back in UB. We spent several days in the capital doing what we should've thought about and done in the first place: shipping our bikes to Bangkok and riding across China on other motorbikes bought inside the country. It was a simple plan and we would've saved ourselves a lot of drama and time. But we did have a great adventure.

We found a German company that would freight our bikes to Bangkok via Seoul. We had to strip them down first — for example, take off the handlebars and disconnect the battery — to make the bikes as small as possible to meet the dimensions required by the air freight company. Then we bought tickets for the afternoon train to the Chinese border.

## CHINA

This was 15 hours of hell.

The train authorities sell eight tickets to a compartment that only has six beds. The Mongolians have local knowledge, of course, so they arrived early at the station to claim their beds. After an old man tried to kiss me, I found refuge in an overhead luggage rack where I managed to get an hour's sleep. Well, maybe.

We arrived at Zam uud, where we'd tried to cross into China one week earlier. Again, we exited Mongolia easily, but our cancelled entry stamp did confuse the Chinese immigration officer for a while. This was the first time on this trip that I'd crossed a border without having to deal with Customs.

Our plan was to buy two motorbikes in Erenhot, the border town on the Chinese side. Of course, this was far easier said than done, but we did find two at US$563 each. Mine was okay, but Dirk's wouldn't start, so we ordered another, which Dirk and I fixed up.

The gears on our bikes were so different to those of the Africa Twin. Instead of one down and four up on the gear shift, all the gears on the Chinese bikes were down to six and back up to neutral. It was also possible from top gear to click the lever down once more. This would hit neutral, and one more down would see you back into first gear. While test-driving and building up speed, Dirk accidently went from top gear to first, so the engine let out a huge screaming whine. The bike then 'popped'. That was that. We quickly wheeled the bike back into the shop and asked for another one.

We eventually rode out of Erenhot flat out — which meant about 75 kilometres per hour. Almost immediately, Dirk's bike started leaking fuel, so we returned to Erenhot and changed the carburettor. While that was happening someone stole a bungee cord from my bike.

We rode out of Erenhot again. Within seconds, all I could think about was how the hell I was going to ride all the way across China on this heap of shit. It was a Chinese-made 150cc Sunik and gutless as hell. What could make matters far worse was that we had no licence, registration papers or even number plates between us. All we had was a scrap of paper with Chinese characters that acted as a 'receipt' (but could've really said anything).

We rode about one kilometre further away from Erenhot than we did the last time before Dirk's bike was again leaking fuel, so we limped back to Erenhot. Eventually, the problems with Dirk's bike were fixed and we made some distance, but problems with the bikes continued throughout Inner Mongolia. Dirk lost his speedo, rear brake light and fuel gauge and had to kick-start his bike every time because the electrics didn't work. His bike was falling apart around him as he rode. We really thought that all we'd have left to sell at the end was the frame and motor.

My immediate impressions of China were not good. The next town, Datong, was a mess. So many houses, offices, roads and bridges were under construction, and the air was choked with so much dust and pollution that it was hard to breathe. Passing through the industrial and mining heartland of China was depressing. It was easily the dirtiest region I'd ever visited in my life. The world was witnessing China on centre stage with the Olympics, but I was sure few knew what was happening in the rest of the country. I had really negative feelings and just wanted to get out.

Motorbikes are not allowed on expressways in China, so we had to use alternative roads, which are terrible. More bolts fell off our bikes. According to our map, we should've passed the Great Wall of China. As the age-old myth says, the Wall can be seen from outer space, but somehow we'd missed it. But we weren't keen to stop for long anywhere. We had to keep going for as long as the bikes held together — which probably wouldn't be long. The other major problem was that our visas only lasted 16 days, which we thought would be long enough with our normal bikes, but not these.

Western China was one of those really tough sections of my trip where again I questioned what I was doing. I needed a *long* rest. Or maybe I just wanted to finish the trip, and get something new in my life. I had to get my life in order, and I was not appreciating what I was doing. We laughed as more and more of our bikes fell off or stopped working, but at other times I got so tired of all the travel and hassles.

While some Chinese people were nice, many were strange and most had disgusting habits. One night, we found a crappy hotel with decent beds in a town I never found out the name of. The owners of a nearby restaurant (choked with cigarette smoke) liked us and took photos of us with each member of their family. When we asked for the bill, the owner said we didn't have to pay.

But later I went to a communal bath area in our hotel (because the shower in our room didn't work), where three Chinese men stood and watched me. One even took a photo of me in my 'birthday suit'.

Within 50 kilometres of Tiayuan, the road was so bad that we decided to (illegally) use the expressway. As we sped through the toll gate, the lady in the booth stared at us in shock. Before she could say or do anything, we were hurtling down the motorway. While clocking up a glorious 90 kilometres per hour, car drivers and passengers gawked at us. *Jesus, what were we doing?*

We had to crouch really low when we saw police in the distance and spotted some more at the next exit. Again, we zipped down the side of the toll booth and weaved past unnoticed. But we decided not to risk that again (for a while, at least).

At a petrol station, Dirk's bike wouldn't start again, and I realised I had only one bolt left (from four) on the front faring that surrounds my headlight. My backside was getting really sore because the padding on my seat had compressed so much that I felt like I was sitting on the frame. Every bump reverberated through my whole body, and my headlight popped out and couldn't really be fixed. I was certain it would pop out completely at any moment and bounce down the road.

All road signs are in the Chinese script, so to avoid going the wrong direction (again) we had the bright idea of asking a man at a hotel reception to write all the big towns we'd need to pass in Chinese characters. The language barrier was really tough. We never knew how to pronounce words correctly — despite maybe 10 attempts — and everything took so much time. Checking into a hotel was never easy, and even ordering a beer was a headache sometimes.

We did get caught by a traffic cop once. I thought it would be the end of our trip across China. As we stopped at some traffic lights, the officer approached us, waving his baton and blowing his whistle. He stood in front of us and directed us to pull over. Realising there was no alternative, we reluctantly did what he demanded. Almost immediately, a massive crowd gathered. Fortunately, one of the onlookers spoke some broken English and translated. Apparently, we couldn't ride our bikes without registration. The cop also wanted to see our (non-existent) licences.

We quickly made up some stories about being told that we didn't have to register our bikes for 30 days after purchase and were going to Beijing to get this done. I also showed him my out-dated International Driving Licence, which meant nothing to the Chinese policeman. It was all too hard for him, so he let us go on our unregistered and uninsured bikes, without number plates (and for me, a valid licence). I gambled that because China is so bloody big authorities wouldn't know the rules from one province to the next.

Riding in China was exhausting. We constantly dodged trucks, cars, bicycles and even people. The Chinese drive, ride and walk with tunnel vision, turning whenever they want. It reminding me of riding through Africa, where I just hoped I'd survive each day.

We were riding one day along a road under construction, so there were even fewer rules than normal about which part of the road vehicles should use. Dirk was following a Honda Civic, which suddenly slowed down for a speed hump. Dirk had no time to react and slammed into the back of the car. He went down. I thought it was serious, but he got up, unharmed, with his bike lying in the middle of the road.

The Honda Civic just kept going, probably thinking the noise and bump to his car had been caused by the speed hump and not the bike. Dirk's bike was okay. There wasn't much that hadn't fallen off to damage anyway. We later caught up to and passed the car, which now had a dented rear bumper with a vertical black line from Dirk's tyre.

Our first major stop was Xi'an, home to the famous Terracotta Warriors. The 8000 or more figures of soldiers, horses and chariots that dated back to 200BC were amazing, but I found it hard to get too excited about an attraction so full of tourists. Plus, Dirk had been there before. At the train station, we arranged to meet up with Izabella, who'd caught a train from the Chinese border about two weeks earlier. But we couldn't stay long in Xi'an because we only had 12 days left on our Chinese visa and 3663 kilometres to reach Laos.

It was at this time that home seemed closer than it had been for a long time — certainly the closest geographically for about five years. I kept thinking about what it would be like on my last day of the trip riding into the farm back home… But what would I do the day after I arrived? Or the following week? Move somewhere else? Get a job? But where? I did not have a clue.

The next morning, I awoke with sore and blocked eyes from all the pollution. Worse, I had put my smelly boots outside the hotel window, but it had rained, so they now stunk *and* were soaked. Izabella wanted to join us as far as the Three Gorges Dam despite our warnings about the bumpy roads and crappy bikes.

As we eventually found our way out of Xi'an, I nearly hit three pedestrians who simply did not look where they were walking. I also smashed into the back of Dirk's bike as he slammed on his brakes to avoid a truck swerving in front of him. None of us were injured, but my left-hand indicator was shattered. Another time, a car overtook a truck as Dirk was passing them and ran him right off the road into a forest thick with trees.

We continued south towards Laos on the 'Vibrating Toothpicks', which is what we called our bikes because they felt so skinny beneath us and vibrated like nothing else. The scenery was increasingly spectacular, and the pollution and dirt seemed to be long gone. But we still had six days to travel about 1800 kilometres to Kunming (where we needed to apply for a visa to Laos) and another two days to reach the border.

We only had time to stop at the Three Gorges Dam. Riding across a bridge high above the water, we spotted a bungee-jumping station. Dirk and I had to do it. While I was lining up, someone wrapped towels around my ankles before securing a rope, which was all taped together with duct tape, to them. Suddenly this seemed like a *very* bad idea, but I had to go through with it because Dirk had already jumped. I'd done it before, including with Amy in Africa, but I still felt that my heart had stopped until the bungee cord yanked me up from certain death below.

At about this time, our bikes were literally falling apart. Dirk's 'Toothpick' vibrated so much that one of his rear shockers failed and lost all its fluid. This meant that every time he throttled on what power the bike had, the rear wheel would twist, causing the chain to jump off the sprocket. Until it got fixed about 50 kilometres later, he had to stop at least every kilometre to put the chain back onto the sprocket.

The scenery in the middle and southern parts of China was stunningly beautiful, with tiered rice-fields sloping down the mountains and ancient clay-tiled buildings. We constantly saw ducks waddling across the roads, bullocks carting hay, and Chinese ladies ambling along and carrying all sorts of things in baskets across their shoulders. Most days it rained and we never travelled without wet boots, but with the appalling pollution of the Northern provinces gone, I felt that China had redeemed itself.

After all these months together, it was still great travelling with Dirk. He always made me laugh and was more patient than I was. Izabella was good company, too. On 14 September, we celebrated

Dirk's birthday — and the two-year anniversary of the start of my trip — by walking into the kitchen at a restaurant and picking the largest chicken from a cage. About 45 minutes later, we scoffed it down with a few beers.

*Two years!* Sometimes, I couldn't believe it. There have been so many memories — but that is all they were now. And the memories were slowly slipping away from my mind.

Our last day riding into Kunming was eventful. We had spent all morning on a terrible, windy road, so we tried our luck on the expressway again. Everything was fine until we were spotted at a toll booth by a policeman. We dodged the barrier and sped through. Sure enough, 15 minutes later, I saw flashing lights in my mirror. The cops sped past with sirens blaring. They screamed at us in Chinese over the loudspeaker on top of the car.

This was it. We'd pushed our luck too far this time.

As we pulled up, one of the policemen hopped out of the car. He looked serious but seemed okay. His colleague, however, was *mightily* pissed off with us, waving his baton and yelling frantically at Dirk. But after we removed our helmets and they realised we weren't Chinese, their mood changed. The Angrier One put away his baton and rang somebody, while the other took photos of us using his mobile phone.

The Angrier One explained to us in broken English what we already knew, but we played dumb. We expressed 'surprise' that we couldn't ride along the expressway (and didn't have to pay a toll), so they escorted us for 10 kilometres to the next exit. Once we were off the motorway, we all swapped photos of each other and shook hands. Away they went.

And we went straight back onto the expressway as soon as we could. It would've simply taken far too long to travel across China otherwise. But — perhaps for our sins — we got punctures three times and had to mend each without tools. (We'd sent our tools with our other bikes to Bangkok.) With great relief, we limped into Kunming.

We rose early the next day and rushed to the Laotian Embassy. We were told that a visa for Laos would take one week to process. We explained that our Chinese visa would run out in three days, so for one-and-a-half times the normal charge we collected our visas that morning. To celebrate, we found a small bar with a jazz band from Argentina and polished off a couple of bottles of wine.

Despite my hangover the next morning, we needed to keep going. We tried the expressway again but were turned back. We tried again later by zipping through a toll gate, but then I immediately got a flat tyre. Riding back up the ramp the wrong way and passing the toll booths with looks of astonishment from staff, I waved as I wobbled past on a flat tyre. I replaced the tube with one that was smaller, but that only lasted 25 kilometres before it was flat again. I fixed that, and then 20 kilometres later, the same. We only covered 100 kilometres that day, which meant riding 750 kilometres in two days before our visas would run out — and hoping like hell there were no more problems with the bikes.

The next day, we managed to sneak onto the expressway through a toll gate. (It was always exciting to zip through, but I did smash a mirror a few times while dodging the toll gates because the gap wasn't wide enough.) Thankfully, there was little traffic, so we made 200 kilometres before being stopped at the next toll booth. Again, we pulled off our helmets to show that we weren't Chinese and acted dumb. Again, the police didn't have a clue what to do with us, so they waved us on.

The final part of the expressway served us well for another 500 kilometres. As we passed over a mountain, I noticed the sort of jungles I'd seen and the humidity I'd felt before in Southeast Asia. That night, I slept within 50 kilometres of a region I really loved, with familiar countries, people and food.

I almost felt home.

## LAOS

Somehow we got out of China and into Laos while still aboard the 'Vibrating Toothpicks'.

At the Chinese side, we cleared Immigration easily, and there wasn't even a Customs post, so they let us ride our bikes out of China. But we wondered if we'd have the same trouble bringing our bikes into Laos. We showed our bike 'papers', which consisted of a receipt written in Chinese and a small manual which included pointless information like the number of gears, to the Laotian immigration officer.

The immigration officer took one look and said, "I can't read this." I shrugged. "Neither can we."

It was all too hard for him, so he waved us through. I now felt my goal of riding all the way home was so much closer. All we had to do was survive on the 'Vibrating Toothpicks' across Laos and get into Thailand, where we would pick up The Old Lady and The Mothership in Bangkok in about 10 days. I also had to prepare for the Desert Challenge rally in Dubai.

After coping with China, Laos was so relaxed and slow-paced, with minimal traffic and no horns tooting or people yelling. At our first overnight stop at Oudomxai, we ate at an amazing restaurant and found a very dark and loud discothèque, but we headed back to the guesthouse for a few beers on the balcony instead. All I wanted to do in Laos was relax. The people are so gentle and kind, and I quickly fell in love with the country once again. With only 500 kilometres to the Thai border, we had plenty of time to collect our bikes in Bangkok, so we lazed about in Luang Prabang and indulged in tasty food and beer.

But we couldn't help ourselves. To reach the border, we decided on a route through the jungle that was more challenging than the main sealed road. And it was challenging — especially through the mud and rain that swelled the rivers. At times, we had to wait for a river to subside a little before asking locals to help push the 'Vibrating Toothpicks' across a bridge or carry them across on bamboo rafts that battled the strong currents. We stopped off at the renowned Plain of Jars, which is, well, an assembly of huge rocks carved like jars across a plain.

One day it was pouring so hard that it was impossible to see, but we 'tooth-picked' our way through the muddy trail until we came across a huge river where about six people were sitting under a little hut, waiting for the deep, wide river to subside. We waited with them for an hour until people arrived at the opposite bank. They started carrying their scooters across the river by hand, so we decided to do the same with their help.

Then we came across the muddiest road I'd ever been on in my entire life. Initially, we thought it completely impassable, but we poked along, mud-hole by mud-hole, and eventually came out the other end. Reaching the Thai border along this route was quite an achievement, and we were surprised the bikes had made it.

But we were *really* looking forward to being reunited with the Africa Twins in three days.

**THAILAND**

We bid farewell to Izabella, packed our bikes and proceeded easily through the Laotian Immigration and Customs posts.

We then crossed the mighty Mekong River on a long, narrow boat which docked at the Thai Immigration Office. The office was at the top of about 30 very steep steps, but with the aid of some local men we carried the bikes up with us. We hoped like hell our luck would last and we'd get the bikes into Thailand. The paperwork took two hours, but we made it in with assistance from the helpful officers at Thai Customs.

As we pulled away from the border, Dirk and I punched the air. I was so excited that I forgot which side of the road I was meant to be on (the left, not the right as in Laos). Finding myself staring at the face of a petrified girl on a scooter coming towards me, I quickly swerved and missed her by millimetres. I could hear Dirk laughing under his helmet.

We had planned to reach Bangkok, which was over 700 kilometres away, the next day, but we quickly decided to make it in one. Again, we broke Rule Number One: Never ride at night. But we really wanted to reach the Thai capital and celebrate crossing China, getting our old bikes back, and being so much closer to home. As the sun set, the rain started getting heavier, and despite being in the tropics we felt chilled to the bone. I couldn't see through my tinted visor and had to ride with it up. The rain stung like bees against my cheeks.

Dirk's headlight had long ago fallen off, so he followed close behind me with his left blinker flashing to help him at least see the edge of the road. We both knew it was insane riding on these sorts of bikes in the rain with hardly a light to guide us through the darkness. When we stopped for fuel at about 11pm, we were so cold that we couldn't even turn our heads to talk to each other; we had to twist our whole bodies instead. As we stood there shaking, we knew the idea of staying somewhere overnight, removing all our gear and saddling up the following morning in our soaked jackets and boots was not an option.

I turned my body to Dirk. "I need a piss badly."

He just smiled. "I am pissing now."

We didn't want to stop or get back on our bikes — or even piss in our pants — but we had no choice. We had no feeling in our hands to undo our fly. The warmth of the urine was also a short relief.

By about 1am, the rain had stopped as we rode into Bangkok. Although we were still freezing, our joy about arriving in the Thai capital outweighed everything else. We rode side by side down Sukhumvit Road, and under the Sky Train we revved the 'Vibrating Toothpicks' as much as we could to celebrate our arrival. And at that exact moment, Dirk's exhaust pipe fell off. His bike now bellowed like a Harley-Davidson whenever he screwed the throttle. (He did it for the noise, not the power. The bike had none.)

We rode straight to Soi Cowboy (a strip full of bars), parked the bikes and ordered beers. We heartily celebrated our safe arrival after riding 720 kilometres in the dark and rain from Laos. More so, we commended ourselves for surviving on the crappy motorbikes from one side of China to the other and all the way down through Laos to Bangkok. We were frozen to death and had pissed our pants and were now absolutely shattered with exhaustion.

The next day, we got word that The Old Lady and The Mothership had arrived early, so we went to the airport to be reunited. It took us all day to clear the paperwork and a few more hours to put them back together. The first time I hit the starter button and heard the rumble of the faithful V-Twin engine I got goose-bumps. It was a wonderful sound.

Strangely, it took a while to get used to the heaviness of the bike again, but once I screwed the throttle I felt like I was going to launch into outer space. From the airport terminal, we turned onto the highway, where I screwed the throttle even harder and, to the delight of a row of taxi-drivers, rode up onto the back wheel. We weren't sorry to say goodbye to the 'Vibrating Toothpicks', which we gave to a Thai family who'd lived and worked with a friend of Dirk's.

After a few days of well-earned R&R, I bid farewell to Dirk, who decided to stay longer in Bangkok. With time to kill before the Desert Challenge rally in Dubai, I headed to Cambodia and caught up with Akis and Vula, who were in Siem Reap near Angkor Wat. I had last seen them in Ethiopia, and, like me, they were still on their around-the-world journey.

**CAMBODIA**

It was such a joy travelling on The Mothership again. It didn't vibrate, and parts didn't fall off. The seat felt like a sofa in comparison to the seat on the 'Vibrating Toothpick'.

I arrived at the border late and was quickly stamped out of Thailand. At the Cambodian side one kilometre further on, I was told the customs officer had gone home for the night, so I would have to return to Thailand. I insisted nicely that this was not an option, so after much discussion the Cambodian immigration officers said I could sleep the night in a hammock inside the hut.

After two years and about 40 crossings, I was stuck for the first time at a border. That night, the mosquitoes nearly carried me away while the heavens opened up and rain hammered on the tin roof. The next morning, the customs officer arrived and cleared me fairly easily.

About half way to the capital, Phnom Penh, I attempted a slight detour. (Yes, you'd think I would've learnt by now.) About half-way, as the sun was setting while it still rained, my front tyre became so caked with mud that the wheel stopped turning and I fell off. (This also happened in Cameroon when Amy and I tried a similar track.) I wasn't hurt but was temporarily defeated, so I turned back to the last town.

I checked out a few guesthouses, but they all smelled like rats, before a Cambodian girl invited me to stay with her family. They cooked me rice and fish, let me use their (cold) shower, and offered me a private room with a welcome bed.

In Phnom Penh, I had the pleasure of catching up with Jarrod, a mate I hadn't seen for about 12 years, who was teaching there. The beers flowed while the old stories got better and longer.

But I didn't have much time before the rally started in Dubai, so I continued to Siem Reap, where I caught up with Akis and Vula, the Greek couple I'd first met in Mozambique almost a year before to the day.

As a motorsport enthusiast, Akis was able to provide some useful advice about the Desert Challenge rally. I'd been to Angkor Wat five years earlier (while my arm was still in plaster from the accident in Thailand), but I was still astounded by the amazing architecture and serene location. I was also pleased that the area had changed little since then.

I needed to hit the road early the next day to reach Bangkok by 4.30pm for a flight to Dubai four hours later. The road was crap, and within 10 kilometres of the border with Thailand the bike's engine just died. Initially, I thought it was the fuel pump, but when I smelled the sulphur I knew the problem. *Shit!* My battery had exploded again, as it did in Mongolia. This was confirmed when The Mothership failed to start when I pushed it.

As I wondered what the hell I was going to do, a guy on a chopper bike pulled up. (It was another one of those strange things that sometimes happened to me on the trip.) He was dressed in leather, chains and rings, boasted some mean tattoos, and looked Cambodian, but he spoke with an American accent. And by his speech and breath, I could tell he was really wasted.

I explained that my battery was beyond repair, so I needed to reach the next town, Poipet. While offering me some grass to smoke, he said he'd tow my bike all the way to the border. I declined both offers, explaining that I needed to keep my mind clear (and being towed by him would've been disastrous). Instead, I flagged down a utility truck and loaded the bike on the back for a negotiated fare.

Looking back, I could see the wasted biker having the same problems. His bike wouldn't start either, but I couldn't stop to help him. Bangkok was still 300 kilometres away, and I had a plane to catch. Luckily, I quickly found a mechanic in Poipet, but the only option was transferring a second-hand battery from an old chopper bike I found leaning against the wall. As I rode away, I realised that the battery had blown because the rectifier was overcharging, and my indicator blinked furiously, which also told me it was getting too much energy.

## THAILAND — AGAIN

I rushed to the border and was quickly stamped out by Cambodian Immigration, but with no time to waste I avoided Customs completely. On the Thai side, I got my passport stamped but was told I couldn't enter Thailand without bike insurance. The officer told me to buy insurance at the next town, but I had no time for that either. I extracted an unrelated piece of paper with all the writing washed away by the rain. I apologised about the state of my 'insurance document', which he studied. I could almost see the little cogs in his brain turning. He soon realised he had no idea what the document said, but incredibly, it worked. He filled out some forms which I signed and let me go.

I cleared the Thai border by about 1pm and rode frantically towards the airport in Bangkok. Desperately worried about my battery blowing up again, I pulled over and disconnected one wire from the alternator to reduce the amount of power coming in. I wasn't sure it would work, but the bike lasted until I reached Bangkok.

I collected some gear from where I'd been staying the first time with Dirk, scoffed a quick lunch of noodles, and headed to the airport. I left The Mothership with Ross (a friend of a friend) from the local Harley-Davidson dealership and continued by taxi. I made it on the flight to Dubai with a few minutes to spare.

I was now on my way to meet possibly the toughest challenge I had ever faced.

**THE ABU DHABI DESERT CHALLENGE, DUBAI**

As I flew into Dubai, I couldn't stop thinking about the rally. I'd invested a lot of money in it and needed to do well. A Top 20 finish would be nice, but I was an inexperienced rally rider and would probably be happy with just finishing.

After two days in Dubai, however, I was an emotional wreck. I quickly realised how much needed to be done before the rally. I found out that the bike I'd previously bought in Dubai wasn't prepared yet and my rally jacket hadn't arrived from the UK. Everyone else seemed so professional, but I was disorganised.

The 'Prologue' consisted of a quick lap around the Dubai motocross track to determine the starting order for the following day. With about 60 motorbikes and 20 quad bikes entering the race, I went around the track slowly but confidently, wondering if the solitary hour I'd spent in the desert two days earlier had been enough training. I found myself in the starting position of 57th out of 80. I was happy with that.

On Day 1, I got up at 4am and with Shaun Mayer (a South African I'd met last time I was in Dubai) loaded the bike onto a trailer and set off for Abu Dhabi, which was 150 kilometres from Dubai. We got no further than 10 kilometres before I noticed that a bag with Sean's boots and clothing had fallen off. We turned around and found the boots but not the clothes. What a great start.

After greeting Sheik Mohammed ben Sulayem, official sponsor of the event and a champion rally driver, I rode 50 kilometres with the other contestants to the starting line. As I saw the professionals scream off into the desert on their factory KTM bikes, I wondered what I would do: Would I scream off into the desert too? Or fall off? I was so nervous as the clock ticked away.

Soon, my countdown started: 20 seconds…10…5, 4, 3, 2, 1. Go!

It was a long race — 2500 kilometres over five days — and people had warned me that riders burn themselves out on Day 1, so I went at about three-quarter pace for a long time. I quickly got the hang of the track, which was mostly flat without too much deep sand, and started passing a few other bikes. As the day wore on, I grew in confidence.

I passed four quad bikes scattered along the route. The riders were okay but telling someone (most probably their mechanics) by mobile phone that their machines were broken. For the final 40 kilometres, I felt confident enough to plough through the dunes, which tossed the bike like an ocean swell.

Inevitably, I was caught out. The bike fell, and my head slammed into the side of a dune. A little rattled, I picked up my Honda CRF450 Rally bike and made a quick inspection. Except for a mouthful of sand, the bike and I were fine. I reached the finish line in one piece in 17th place overall. I was ecstatic.

On Day 2, I managed to stay on my bike all day, but during the 300 kilometres I wasn't able to overtake anyone, although no one caught me either. I was reminded to be careful when I came over one rise and saw a bike on its side and the rider about 30 metres away, lying on the ground. Another rider had stopped, so I continued on when they gave me the thumbs up. Again, at the end of the day I felt good and had finished 13th fastest for the day. I was up against some amazing riders and couldn't believe I'd done so well. Plus, I was on a 450cc, and half the field were using stronger 690cc bikes.

When starting on Day 3, I was surrounded by well-known, professional riders, and we all rode together in a group for about 300 kilometres. Their intense speed forced me to go faster to keep up with them. The pace was blistering. Sometimes, we'd hurtle more than 120 kilometres per hour across the desert, while at other times we'd slide down the slopes of massive sand dunes. On my first spill, with only about 40 kilometres to go, they careered ahead. I tried catching up but failed. I was exhausted as I approached the finishing line and fell over one more time. But I was now in 11th place overall.

Still exhausted when I started Day 4, I soon dropped to about 20th, but after the half-way point I made up some places. I finished 15th overall and 4th among riders in my 450cc class. The top Portuguese 450cc rider, Ruben Faria, had broken his back that day, which, of course, was terrible for him, but it moved me into 3rd position in my class.

On the fifth and final day, I was really nervous because I knew I only had a 30-minute lead on the next 450cc rider, Helder Rodrigues. I really wanted to maintain a 3rd position for my class. There was less sand as we headed back along the flat terrain towards Dubai. During the compulsory 15-minute break half-way, I was told that Rodrigues had only made up 30 seconds on me. Later, I saw the leading 450cc rider on the side of the track. He was out of the race, so I was now in 2nd place. Although I made a navigation error, I still had time up my sleeve.

I kept telling myself to calm down and ride carefully — but, of course, I wasn't listening. As I reached 90 kilometres per hour, I hit a sand dune and flew through the air end over end into a huge mound of dirt on the other side. I landed on my head and rolled on my back, with my feet landing last.

I waited for the pain to set in, but it didn't. I sat upright and paused. Still, there was no pain. I stood up, not believing that I felt fine.

I sprinted back to my bike (which looked okay), picked up a few things that had fallen off, and started it. I thought nothing was going to stop me finishing, but I had ripped the power cable from the GPS, so navigation was now quite hard. My only option was to slow down so another rider would overtake me and I could follow that bike.

Then I saw the finishing line. I had travelled 2200 kilometres over five days and not only finished but also received 2$^{nd}$ prize for my class. And I was an amazing 11$^{th}$ overall. Not bad for a rider without any sponsorship and only one hour's worth of training!

I received my trophy from the Sheikh himself live on local TV. After a welcome shower, I changed into some clean clothes and attended a gala dinner as a trophy winner. It was an experience I would never forget. It also showed me that I could do anything I set my mind to. I had made my dream come true in every way.

**THAILAND — AGAIN**

When I returned to Bangkok, I discovered that the documents and paperwork I needed to continue were not there. Somehow, I'd lost my registration papers. I had to have proof that I legally owned The Mothership in order to cross borders.

I thought I could just ring the relevant department in the UK and sort it out, but I was wrong. They advised me that because my bike had been out of the UK for longer than 12 months it was officially listed as 'exported'. Therefore, they could not issue new papers without some sort of 'investigation', which could take at least six weeks.

But I was ready to leave for Malaysia *now*. After some more running around, I managed to find a copy of my registration papers on an email and print them out. It was only a copy, but I didn't want to wait around for six weeks to get an answer from the UK, which could be bad anyway.

The roads heading south from Bangkok are excellent, and I made up some distance quickly. I stopped at Ao Nang, a popular beach area, where I saw more tourists than I'd ever seen before. I'd been there five years before with Clint and was amazed how much the town had changed, most probably because of the tsunami in 2004.

The noise, people and shops made me miss the wonders of Mongolia, the unknown of Africa, and the wild scenery of Central Asia. The trip now felt more like a holiday and less of an adventure, but I did love travelling on The Mothership along the same roads that I'd travelled before in crammed buses.

**MALAYSIA**

Crossing out of Thailand and into Malaysia was a breeze. In fact, Malaysian Customs never even asked to see my registration papers — or anything else for that matter. It was one of the easiest border crossings possible. I only wished they were all like that. But then again, where would the fun be if they were?

I only needed to go as far as the island of Penang, where I stayed for a week, sorting out things like updating blogs and finding tyres. I also sent an application to the Department of Infrastructure & Transport back home so I could import my bike into Australia. This felt like another step closer to home, with only Indonesia and East Timor remaining before I was on the final leg to the family farm. I also had to find out about a ferry to Indonesia. Or I should say *ferries* because my bike was due to leave the day before me on a separate boat.

This would probably cause problems collecting the bike at the other end, especially as the port in Belawan (Indonesia) is closed on weekends. The other problem was that the freight company warned me that the last guy who'd tried to bring his motorbike into Indonesia without a *carnet* was fined US$600. But I'd heard horror stories like that for Iran and Kenya and got through.

Staying at the same guesthouse was the Greek couple, Akis and Vula, whom I'd recently met again in Cambodia (as well as Mozambique and Ethiopia before that). They planned to catch the same boat to Belawan, so we considered travelling across Sumatra together. At least I would have some company over Christmas and the New Year. (I'd planned to celebrate the latter in Bali, but waiting around for the ferry forced me to change plans.) From Sumatra, I wanted to take four to six weeks to travel 6000 kilometres across several islands as far as East Timor. I still planned to be on home soil by early February and back at the family farm two or three weeks later.

The only problem was that I would be travelling along busy, windy and undeveloped roads and taking ferries between each island, right smack in the middle of the tropical wet season.

**INDONESIA**

Finally, my bike — as well as the 4WD belonging to Akis and Vula — was loaded from the port of Butterworth (on the Malaysian mainland near Penang) onto the ferry bound for Belawan on Sumatra. The boat was old and wooden but seemed like the QE2 compared with the dhow that took The Mothership and me from Djibouti to Yemen. This boat would take 16 hours to reach the port, while we would take the faster ferry the next day.

Immigration into Indonesia seemed to take forever, and I was tired and hungry from not eating all day. We immediately searched for — and found a few hours later — the boat with the 4WD and motorbike. I could see The Mothership parked on its centre stand in a warehouse. In contrast, the 4WD was still aboard and didn't look like it was going to move for a while.

At Customs, I received the bad news I'd been dreading: no *carnet*, no entry. But the helpful officials said that if I waited two days until Monday I could pick up the bike if I paid a deposit (which I could later collect when I left Indonesia). I told them I was in a hurry and needed the bike the next day. They agreed that was possible. To make sure, the Customs guys allowed me to sleep there overnight.

This was a mistake. The Customs building is open 24 hours, and some of the officials on duty at 11pm decided to crank up the Indonesian-language karaoke (and porn) with speakers blaring about one metre from my head. Earplugs offset the horrible singing to some degree, but the bass still pounded through my body. And I got eaten alive by mosquitoes.

The next morning, I tried again to get my bike into Indonesia without a *carnet*. One helpful official started the paperwork by asking how much my bike was worth. I lied and said US$1000. Sick of waiting, I went back to the dock and managed to push my bike as far as the gate, but, of course, the policeman needed to see my 'letter of release'. This action of pushing the bike to the gate seriously angered the Customs Officer, who thought I was trying to get away without completing the paperwork or paying the deposit.

The officer told me to go back to Customs, and his mood did not improve when I went to the wrong Customs building. Finally, we began discussing the situation. The only option was for me to pay a cash deposit of US$1000 (the value of the bike.) I lied again and told him that I didn't have that sort of money.

I knew I needed to leave a deposit so that I wouldn't sell the bike in Indonesia, but I was concerned about my chances of getting the deposit back while crossing at the small, distant border with East Timor. I asked the officials to lower the value of the bike — and, therefore, the amount of the deposit — but they wouldn't do that. The paperwork trail had started. (I should've said the bike was worth US$500.) I again explained that I did not have US$1000 in cash, but they still would not budge.

They suggested I visit the Australian Consulate in Medan, the capital of Sumatra, and talk to the Consul. This seemed a stupid and impractical idea because the Consulate wouldn't be open for two days, Medan was a four-hour return trip, and I wasn't sure the Consul could help anyway. In the end, I had no choice. I agreed to pay the US$1000 deposit. They assured me I would get my money back when I left Indonesia, but I wasn't so optimistic. I signed the form.

This started an even longer bureaucratic nightmare of more documents, photocopies and signatures that took so long that Akis and Vula left, with plans to hopefully meet up later. When it was time to pay the 'port fees', there were more disagreements. The official wanted US$80, while I offered US$25. But he knew I was serious and really pissed off, so we agreed at US$35. He also wanted another fee for helping me (which was his job anyway), but I only gave him US$5. This prompted more arguments between us.

By then, I'd had enough of Indonesia and wanted to escape. But I hadn't even left the dock, and I still planned to travel another 6000 kilometres across the country…

Eventually, after about 24 hours, I went back to the dock, packed up my stuff, changed into my riding gear and sped away, wondering if I'd get my US$1000 deposit back when I crossed over to East Timor in about six weeks.

Along the way to Medan, I tried to get on the motorway, but the man at the toll booth gestured for me to turn around. (Like China, motorbikes are not allowed on motorways.) But I 'waved' back and rode on it anyway. I nearly got all the way to Medan, but I was stopped by a police car with a blaring siren and loud-speaker about 200 metres from the exit I needed. I thought about doing a runner because they could never keep up with me, but I imagined that an Indonesian jail would be no fun. I pulled over and played 'dumb'. The police escorted me to the next exit 200 metres away. I'd managed a good distance already

I rode into Medan hungry, tired and upset with everything. I felt like I'd had enough. My mood didn't improve when a guy wanted to charge me 5000 *rupiah* (AUS$0.50) rather than the normal 1000rp at the McDonald's car park.

I headed towards Lake Toba but couldn't find a decent hotel in my price range. By now, my energy and spirit had gone completely. I asked a few passing motorcyclists about a *losmen* (cheap hotel) but still had no luck. A friendly man called Agus, who spoke a little English, gave me directions to a *losmen* and then insisted I go to his place. I resisted because I was so tired and just wanted to sleep, but Agus was persistent.

I sat in his house for two hours, finding it hard to keep up a conversation in pidgin English and eating the food offered after stuffing myself at McDonald's. After the rain stopped, I followed him back to a hotel with a shitty room, which was at least was quiet and cheap. I felt like I was in Iran. I didn't want to cross Indonesia, but I knew I would. I simply had to.

I'd also been thinking a lot about Amy and how much I still missed her, especially at times like these. I wished so much I could make it up to her, but it was too late; the damage had been done. And Amy had met somebody else and was happy, which I was glad about. But I realised that I still loved her and wished that I'd never hurt her. I wanted so much for her to be with me or to be going home in a month or so to see her. But it would not happen.

I was unsure whether to head north to Bukit Lawang or south to Lake Toba, but the Greek couple persuaded me to meet them at the former. The next day, I set my alarm for 5.30am, but I needn't have bothered. The mosque next door woke me an hour beforehand. I also wanted to start early to avoid the crazy but slow traffic, with its millions of motorbikes.

My only reason to visit Bukit Lawang was to see orang-utans in the wild. I'd seen the gorillas in central Africa and other orang-utans in Malaysian Borneo, and I wasn't so sure I wanted to see any more, but I was glad I did. We got right up close to the beautiful orange creatures with their crazy hair as they loped down from the jungle canopy to feed on fruits handed out by the park rangers.

We then travelled further north through Aceh province, which was in the opposite direction to where I wanted to go, but I enjoyed travelling with Akis and Vula. It was still really hot when we camped at a restaurant by the side of the road. This was the first time I'd used my tent since Mongolia.

The next day, I heard a grinding noise from the back wheel. I pulled over but couldn't see anything obviously wrong. I started the bike again, revved it up and heard the same noise as the rear wheel turned on the centre stand. I took the rear wheel off and, sure enough, the bearing in the sprocket hub was stuffed. While we were wondering what to do, a local man who was watching us sped off on his motorbike. He quickly came back with a spare, and we fixed the bike in a few minutes.

Later, while riding in front, I stopped for some water and waited for the Greek couple to catch up. But they didn't show. Worried, I went slowly back along the road. I then checked my mobile phone. There were five missed calls and a text message that explained the bad news.

*Robbo. Engine is completely off. Leak oil. Disaster!*

I found them an hour later. The engine had seized up or something, but they had no idea why and couldn't do anything about it. We eventually found a truck to tow them to the next town, Sigli, about 30 kilometres away. We parked my bike and their broken-down 4WD in the car park of a bank and searched for a hotel. Of the three available, two were full and the other was way too expensive and dirty. We returned to the bank and asked the guard if we could camp in the car park. He checked with the bank manager, who agreed. But being only two metres from the road we didn't expect — or get — much sleep.

The next morning, Akis found a truck driver who agreed to tow their vehicle to Banda Aceh, at the very northern tip of Sumatra. I really needed to go in the opposite direction but decided to head north with them because it was close. In Banda Aceh, I bid farewell to Akis and Vula, who planned to return to Malaysia.

While riding around the city, I tried to imagine the huge tsunami crashing its way through the crowded streets, where so many people had no hope. In the middle of all the tin shacks in which people now lived was a huge flat-bottom barge about the size of two tennis courts and five or six storeys high. The 2600-tonne vessel had been swept three kilometres inland by the waves.

I didn't stay long because I had to head south. The coastal road started off okay but soon got worse. The scenery and coastline were beautiful, but travelling was so slow because of the potholes and windy roads. In two hours I was only covering about 60 kilometres as the crow flies. The coast was also scattered with more reminders of the tsunami, such as the bare trunks of tall palm trees with all their leaves ripped off. As on most days at this time of year, clouds circled during late afternoon and by 5.30pm rain was bucketing down.

I continued to enjoy the scenery through western Sumatra, but the trip soon became boring. I was also emotionally drained and lonely. The fun had gone, and I was looking forward to the end of the trip. I had wanted to see a few things across Indonesia but now just really wanted to ride home. But I knew these thoughts were not constructive. I was still about 12,000 kilometres from home, half of which would be spent battling crazy traffic across the islands of Java, Bali, Lombok, Sumbawa, Flores and Timor.

On Christmas Eve, I took a dip in the volcanic Lake Toba in a region where most people are Christian. There was a festival atmosphere around the place, but I felt more alone than ever as I lay in my cheap, musty room during another storm. That evening, I met a Swedish couple who'd been on the road for five months. They also felt they were not getting all they could or should from their travels. This made me feel a little better. I'd been traveling for over two years, yet they were tired after only five months.

I enjoyed sleeping in on Christmas Day, the first one alone on this trip. I spent the morning fitting the new back tyre I'd picked up in Georgetown (Malaysia), but my air compressor wasn't powerful enough to force the tyre to pop onto the rim, so I found a mechanic who had one that could. While eating an unappetizing Christmas lunch of a hamburger and chips, I thought about where I'd spent each Christmas Day since leaving home. Five years ago, I was with Clint in Chang Mai (Thailand), then with Amy in Sweden, and then in Morocco with Amy (on a previous holiday). Along this trip, I was in Mali with Amy and then in Ethiopia among ancient tribes. Next year, I hoped I would spend Christmas with my family.

The next morning, I caught the ferry back across Lake Toba to Parapat, from where I would join the Trans-Sumatran highway. With all the crazy traffic and even crazier drivers I felt like I was back in Uganda. All I could do was hope that I'd make it out alive. But, of course, I had to stop for flat tyres along the way, which always drew large crowds of locals. One of the locals spoke good English and asked about my religion, a conversation I'd had many times before. He just could *not* believe that I had no religion, but he was pleasant and funny — if perhaps a little too honest when he said I smelt and asked why I didn't wash myself.

After crossing the equator again — for the 5th and final time — I was now back in the Southern Hemisphere. The scenery through the mountains and jungle of southern Sumatra continued to be stunning, but the roads were always so busy. One lapse in concentration and it could be all over for me and the bike.

The Indonesians were very nice — sometimes *too* nice when all I wanted was some peace and quiet. Finding an 'undiscovered' campsite was often difficult, and once two wild pigs came running from the grass as I pitched my tent. Some nights, I'd cook noodles for dinner with the stove I hadn't used since Mongolia. And soon enough, I was starting to enjoy the travel again because I was camping and the trip felt more like an adventure than a holiday. I was also clocking up more and more kilometres and had a mission: to finish and get home.

After covering 2572 kilometres across Sumatra, I caught the ferry to Java, easily the most populated island in Indonesia. Crossing the strait was like entering a new country, but I was sure I'd get sick of ferries soon enough. As the boat docked at Merak, the weather was appalling and the traffic twice as bad as Sumatra's. I was soon averaging less than 40 kilometres an hour and constantly breathing in car fumes. I dreamt of the long roads and emptiness of Australia, where I'd be able to use the full range of my gearbox and not have to change gears every two seconds.

I reached Bogor, an hour south of Jakarta by expressway, which was now virtually a suburb. I checked into a smelly, stale room with a bucket shower, but I got what I paid for. That night, I opened the door to a well-dressed man who looked (and was) gay. He offered me some 'ladies for the night', which I declined. While shaking my hand, he rubbed my palm with his finger. I shuddered and slammed the door. With all sorts of strange activities in and outside the building, I was obviously staying at a brothel — again.

The traffic seemed to get more and more insane the further I went across Java. At a petrol station, my battery died, but The Mothership fired up again after a push start. The cause bothered me, and I prayed it wasn't the rectifier causing problems. About two kilometres later, the bike died again. The battery either wasn't getting charged or wasn't holding the charge. As the rain got heavier, I heaved the bike under the veranda of what happened to be a Youth Hostel. Soon, I could see the problem — the battery wasn't getting charged because one of the wires had broken — and I was able to fix it quickly. I was lucky because I met two Spanish backpackers at the hostel, who gave me all the information I needed about travelling around Java, including to Mount Bromo and Mount Merapi.

Further east, as my blood continued to boil because of the insane traffic, a truck drove into my pannier, nearly making me crash into a family on a scooter to my left. Furious, I grabbed the truck's mirror to twist it around, but the mirror disintegrated in my hand. That night, at an Internet centre, I found out that Dirk was now in Darwin. A part of me wished I was there too.

I spent New Year's Eve in Yogyakarta after covering a comparatively long 300 kilometres in one day via a beach with black volcanic sand like in Cameroon. Finding a room in one of Indonesia's most popular cities on New Year's Eve was a real problem. All the hotels I tried were either full — with Indonesian tourists, not foreigners — or charged too much over the holiday period. I spent two hours visiting 15 different hotels until I relented and paid US$28 for a room. This blew my daily budget, but the room did have a swimming pool, air-conditioning and a hot shower (which I desperately needed). It was also a chance to get some laundry done.

After a few celebratory beers on New Year's Eve with Jeremy, an English guy I'd met in Lake Toba, I awoke with a headache and stayed in bed all day. (My tolerance to alcohol had been greatly reduced.) But it did feel good to relax, enjoy a few more (much-needed) hot showers and reflect on the upcoming year. *What would 2009 bring?* A lot of new things, I supposed — finishing the trip and getting a job, obviously. But *what*, *where* and *when* were The Big Questions. It was exciting but daunting. And would I get to race motorbikes again? To do that I needed to earn some money.

From Selo, on the slopes of Mount Merapi, I planned to climb one of Java's most active volcanoes. I met a really nice Indonesian guy who took me to his house, where his family fed me and offered a bed. He also gave me lots of information about the climb. I had planned to do it alone, which meant starting at 1am in time to reach the peak for the sunrise. But when I got up, it was still raining hard, so I went back to bed. When I got up later, I'd lost interest and decided to move on. I couldn't wait around for days for the weather to clear.

I camped the next night on the slopes of another active volcano, Mount Bromo, at about 2100 metres. My tent was covered with white ash the next morning. I was able to ride my bike all the way to the base, climb for only two minutes to the cone, and then clamber down inside the volcano where the sulphur gas spewed out (and made me feel a little ill).

The next morning, I rode to a viewpoint for the sunrise over the volcano, but the entire view was obscured by clouds. It then started to rain, so I went back down the winding road to the lava field but took a few wrong turns and ended up along some rocky tracks. These mountain trails were hellishly rough, and I worried about my bike with its ongoing problems, especially the faulty rectifier. The Mothership felt tired, and perhaps she too wanted to go home in one piece.

The ferry trip across to the third Indonesian island, Bali, was only five kilometres. This was where I had had my first overseas holiday with two mates from the football club when I was 20. About 11 years later, I was back there after having visited about 100 other countries since. It seemed a lifetime ago.

The main tourist hub, Kuta, was only 100 kilometres away. It had changed a lot, especially the prices, and I wasn't used to being surrounded by so many foreigners, especially young Australians. I had nothing in common with these people anymore: I was a traveller, and they were tourists. They were in Bali for the same reason I went all those years ago — clubbing, drinking and shopping — but I was now different.

However, I did decide to stay in Kuta rather than the remote port of Ende, from where the ferry would leave for Timor in a couple of weeks. From Kuta, I contacted the Australian import company to find out about my application for bringing the bike back home. I got some great news: Everything had been approved, and Mum had even received all the paperwork.

Now I could transport The Mothership on the boat to Darwin and start the final leg. I also received a message from Penelope Perkins. (She was Amy's best friend, whose mother owned Perkins Shipping, which had services from Dili to Darwin.) Penelope advised me that I should be able to get my bike onto a Perkins ship to Darwin for free. She was also trying to arrange a berth for me on the same boat. Alternatively, I'd have to book a flight from Dili (East Timor) to Darwin for myself.

I was watching the Paris to Dakar rally (now in South America) on the Internet. This again 'fuelled' my desire to race. I was confident that I had what was needed to do well. I also wanted to participate in the Aussie Safari and Finke Desert Race, but the problem was money. I didn't have much left, and by the time I got home I'd have nothing. (And I still owed Dirk over US$2000 for shipping my bike from Mongolia to Bangkok.)

I eventually left Bali for Lombok, the next island to the east. I allowed myself eight days to reach Ende for the infrequent ferry to Kupang on Timor. Although it was raining again, I reached the port of Padangbai quickly. I tried to convince the ticket-seller that my bike was only 150cc (to pay half the fare), but he knew I was fibbing when I showed him the bike's papers (which I had photo-shopped to make '742cc' look like '142cc'.) He frantically tried to find the number indicating the engine capacity on the bike but eventually gave me the cheaper fare. I paid my dues, however, by missing the ferry. Waiting an hour for the next one gave me time to plaster some duct tape over the stamp on the engine indicating the bike was 750cc.

By the time the next ferry had docked at Padangbai, loaded up and set off, it was past 4pm. The strait between Bali and Lombok is only 65 kilometres wide, but the trip took four-and-a-half hours. The sunset was beautiful, but I arrived in the dark and had to stay in a shitty little *losmen* near the port. It was bucketing with rain as I walked down the street to eat some more *nasi goreng* (fried rice). I checked my tank bag, and yep, it was soaked. Everything inside — including my customs papers — was drenched.

I wasn't in a hurry to reach Ende on Sumbawa Island and wait there for days for the ferry across to Timor, but Lombok is only about 60 kilometres wide, so it took me no time to reach the next ferry to the next island. This time, I payed the full fare for the bike because I couldn't be bothered arguing. It even felt good being honest.

Two hours later, I was riding across what seemed like another new country — Sumbawa. There was so little traffic in comparison to the other islands, but the roads were worse than on Java or Bali. The locals weren't used to tourists, either. The first night, about 15 people watched me set up camp. I felt like I was back in Africa. Although the scenery was beautiful, there wasn't much to see. The highlight of this region would be the Komodo Dragons, the giant lizards that live on Rinca Island further east.

My sister Belinda sent me an email with loads of great ideas about my arrival day, which made me realise, perhaps for the first time, that I really would be finishing soon. I hoped a few people would be at the farm to greet me — including Amy, but I knew that would be impossible. Maybe she should have been riding with me on that final day. Of course, that's history, but I still thought about her a lot.

I'd been traveling for so long that chores such as pitching my tent, wondering about fuel and writing my diary were normal. The trip was now my life and had been for so long. And I was almost finished. I also received discouraging emails about work prospects. It seemed to be the wrong time to be looking for the sort of jobs I wanted.

On my last day on Sumbawa Island, I rode past a group of five kids. One threw a piece of hard fruit at me, which smashed into my windscreen. I slammed on my brakes and turned around, but they'd all run off — except for one who I knew had not thrown the fruit. When I caught this boy, he quickly explained that it was his mate — now hidden in the jungle — who had thrown the fruit. I led him down the road to some elders. The boy explained to them what his friend, Erfan, had just done.

A huge crowd quickly formed. One man spoke some English, so I told him I wanted to see Erfan's parents. Another man said that Erfan's parents were dead. I assumed this was a lie and angrily insisted that I talk to the people who looked after the boy. This stumped them. They didn't respond, so I threatened to call the police. They panicked and talked more amongst themselves. The police soon arrived and took me to see the boy's parents.

Erfan's mother and father were very old, so I explained the situation nicely (with the aid of the man who spoke English). I said that I was a tourist who wanted to enjoy their very beautiful country and bring money to spend, but I did not get a very good impression when kids threw stuff at me. Plus, it was dangerous and could easily cause an accident. It all ended well as I shook hands with the parents and the police apologised to me.

Arriving at Sape, on the far eastern end of Sumbawa, at about 2pm, I went straight to the port. I confirmed that there would be a ferry that evening to Flores Island. To kill a few hours, I went to a restaurant that Dirk had mentioned to me. Amazingly, the staff was even expecting me (because Dirk has passed through and told them

*Cold beer, machine guns and Russian Mafia at the end of a hard day's riding, Russia*

*Working on the bikes on on the border of Russia and Mongolia before being found and moved on by the Russian Army*

*A very friendly young Mongolian girl*

*Double humped 'Bactrian' camel, Mongolia*

*The long green plains of Mongolia*

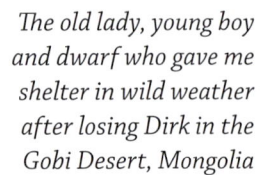

*The old lady, young boy and dwarf who gave me shelter in wild weather after losing Dirk in the Gobi Desert, Mongolia*

*Dirk inspecting our new 150cc Suniks that we would ride 8000 kilometres from Eronhot to Bangkok*

*Hotel parking for the Toothpicks in China*

*Roadside cafe in China, dumplings were always a sure thing*

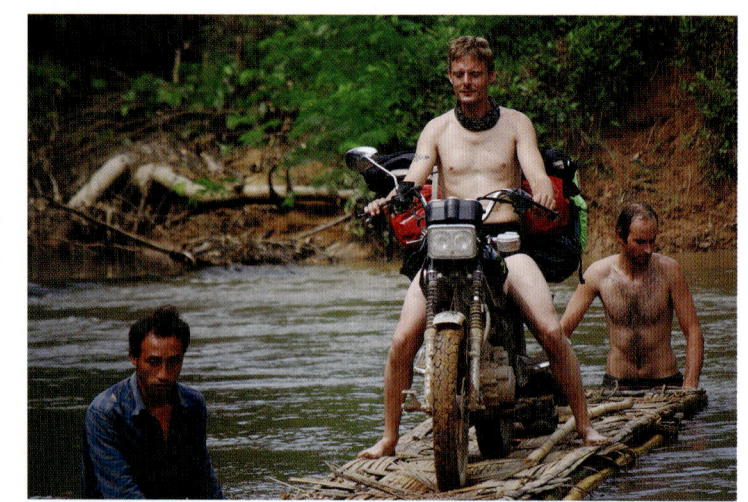

*Negotiating rivers in Laos on the toothpicks*

*Beautiful Laos*

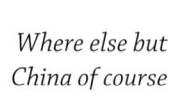

*Where else but China of course*

*At the start of the desert race — in the background, the World Number 1, Marc Coma, Dubai*

*Receiving my medal on live TV from Sheik Mohammed ben Sulayem in Dubai after the UAE Desert Challenge*

*The end of the Rally — if this is what racing is all about count me in*

*Camping at the foot of Mt Bromo, an active volcano in the background, Java, Indonesia*

*Captain Pedro from the Philippines, in the bridge of the Kathryn Bay, bound for Darwin*

*The red centre, Finke Track, Northern Territory*

*Just in case I forgot, Northern Territory, Australia*

*Rounding the final bend on the family farm, 899 days after leaving London*

*One very happy lady, my mum, and I at the farm on my final day*

*The end of a journey*

about me). I went back to the port, and guess what? The ferry was going to leave tomorrow because the seas were too rough. The five other western tourists waiting at the port were also disappointed with the news, but I had plenty of time before I needed to reach Ende.

At 8pm, I was told the ferry would leave at 4am the next day. I was sick of travelling by — and waiting for — ferries, and the journeys seemed to get longer. From Sumbawa to Flores was officially eight hours, and from Ende (on Flores) to Kupang (on Timor), it would be 18 hours. And the boat from Dili to Darwin would take two days.

Despite all the noise, I managed to fall asleep on my mat along the floor of the port. At about 1am, somebody woke me to say that I could buy a ticket and get on board, which I did although I was still half-asleep. After loading my bike, I found a spot to lay down my mat and make myself comfortable — well, as comfortable as possible with adults talking so loudly and every baby screaming and crying.

After nine hours, we docked at Labuan Bajo, the small laidback port on the far western tip of Flores. I stayed at another hotel recommended by Dirk. At lunch, I met two Italian guys also planning to see the Komodo Dragons on Rinca Island the next day, so we decided to travel there together.

Early next morning, the three of us caught the slow, noisy wooden boat to Rinca. We were surprised we had to pay 205,000rp (US$20) to enter the National Park but were soon rewarded by seeing two of the mighty lizards (the world's largest species) hanging about for food scraps at the park headquarters. The largest was fat, lazy and about 2.2 metres long. After paying the entry fee, which included a guide for a one-hour hike, we were told that it was the wrong season to spot the Komodo Dragons. Sure enough, we didn't see any more and had to make do with some monkeys.

Rinca's other attraction is snorkelling, but this was unappealing because of the rain. Reluctantly, I did jump in and have a quick look, but I saw nothing exciting underwater and got out. I was bloody freezing, and it rained most of the way back to the port. Overall, the trip was disappointing and expensive, but perhaps it's easy to expect too much. It's hard to experience in a few hours what we see on amazing TV documentaries. But I was glad I went, and the people were nice; all the kids wanted to say, "hello."

I still had plenty of time to reach Ende, and I planned to stay somewhere half-way. The road was windy and the scenery beautiful, but it would not stop raining. I didn't fancy pitching a tent on the soggy ground, so I continued going to Ende. On the way, I passed the ferry terminal, which was about 15 kilometres from town, and asked about the schedule. The place was empty except for one man washing his clothes. He pointed to the 'Monday' on the calendar of my mobile phone. That was good. The ferry for Kupang was leaving on time. Then, he explained the bad news: the ferry wasn't leaving until the *following* Monday, which was 10 days away.

*Shit!* I did not want to spend a week or more waiting for a stupid boat — and certainly not in Ende. This would also seriously delay my arrival date at the farm. I asked some people at my hotel, but they could only say that the ferry was often cancelled at this time of year.

*Shit again!* If the weather was still crap, the ferry may not leave for another week after the following Monday. There wasn't much to do but pray for blue skies so the ferry would leave in three days and not 10. With motorbikes screaming past all night and cars tooting their horns, Hotel Flores was not a good place to hang around. I checked out and set up camp at the port.

Because no ferries were running during the bad weather, the ferry terminal was deserted except for the one man who lived there. Later, he told me even *worse* news: There was no ferry at all this time of year because of the rough seas. I decided that my only other options were (a) convince the other ferry service, Pelni, which is for only passengers, to also take my bike, or (b) charter a boat — but Kupang was 269 kilometres away, and no one at the port was interested because of the bad weather.

With time to kill I rode to Kelimutu, a remarkable series of coloured lakes set among volcanoes. Each lake is a separate colour because of the different dissolving minerals. One advantage of travelling in the rainy season was that I virtually had the lakes to myself. I planned to stay there and see the lakes again at sunrise, but it was raining (like every day). Instead, I returned to Ende and checked into the quieter Mentari Hotel. They had Wi-Fi, so I was able to get some information online about boat schedules. The remaining option seemed useless because the next Pelni ferry from Ende to Kupang wasn't due to leave for another 10 days.

The situation was so frustrating. I was quickly losing any patience I still had left, especially because the weather had been perfect (with rain, but no wind) for the previous few days. I'd been in worse situations and wasn't worried, but I felt so close to home. I was going nowhere fast. It was now almost a year to the day that I'd been waiting in Djibouti for a boat (and visa) for Yemen.

On the first Monday that the ferry was originally due to leave, I got up at 6am and went to the terminal just to make sure the ferry wasn't there. Of course, it wasn't, but I had to be 100% certain. Finding information about the current schedule was so bloody hard too, not only because of language barriers but also because of the different ways that the Indonesians deal with things.

All day on that Monday, I asked around about the ferry, but all anyone knew was that it was cancelled. I was aware of this. *But for how long?* One week, or two? Or even longer? If someone could tell me, I could make a decision. But they couldn't, so I didn't.

Another option was to get all the telephone numbers of all relevant people, including the ferry company in Kupang where I assumed the ferry would leave from, and ring them while waiting in Bali. Although I vowed to never return to Bali, its surf, decent rooms and good Wi-Fi was 10 times more appealing than staying any longer in Ende.

While Flores Island was beautiful, I'd soon run out of things to see and do. Flying back to anywhere else but Bali was risky because of irregular flights in case I needed to quickly get back to Ende for the ferry. Plus, some of the locals had become very annoying. Some even yelled, "Fuck you!" when I rode past. I was sure they didn't know the meaning, but it made them laugh.

My other concerns were that the weather would get worse — and the ferries even less reliable — next month, and soon I might have to go on a 'visa run'. (This would involve flying to Singapore and returning to Bali on the same day to get another 30-day visa on arrival back to Indonesia.) I decided to go to Bali and wait there.

On the day of departure, I parked my bike inside Hotel Flores and walked back to the other place I was staying. It was now 10am. I had to leave for the airport in 30 minutes. I thought I'd give Anton from the ASDP ferry company one final call. I asked the same question, and he gave me the same answer: Yes, the ferry would leave Ende for Kupang this Monday (in five more days). Although I had heard this before, it gave me some hope. Still dubious, however, I asked the hotel owner to ring Anton and ask the same question in Bahasa Indonesia. She got the same answer too.

Should I now go to Bali, or wait in Ende until Monday? What if I went to Bali, but there were no empty seats on the return flight to Ende? To make sure, I booked a return Bali-Ende flight for Sunday, the day before the ferry was due to leave. This allowed me at least four days to surf, eat and relax on the holiday island.

Strangely, I felt happier in Bali than I had a couple of weeks earlier. I tried to surf but got tired quickly. I spent the rest of the time eating, relaxing and, of course, ringing the ferry company offices.

Dirk rang me to say he would be at the farm when I arrived. So if I could get the ferry on Monday, I could be home on 28 February or, more likely, a week later, but that also depended on the boat schedule from Darwin.

I then got some encouraging news: Anton confirmed that the ferry from Ende would definitely leave for Kupang at 8am on Monday. If all went well, I would then need to travel from Kupang (West Timor) to Dili (East Timor) in one day to catch the weekly

Perkins cargo boat leaving for Darwin on 28 January. I certainly did not want to miss that boat and have to wait around somewhere else for another week, especially Dili, which is an expensive town to stay. At the border, I'd also needed time to get my US$1000 customs deposit back.

My bike was still at Hotel Flores when I flew back to Ende. After yet another plate of *nasi goreng*, I rode to the ferry terminal. Encouragingly, the port was a little livelier. There was also a notice — in Indonesian, of course — with Monday's date and the word 'Kupang'. It looked promising.

To fill in a long afternoon, I washed some clothes in a bucket with fresh water from a well and cooled off in the sea. Later that afternoon, I panicked when I found out that taking my bike on the ferry would cost 230,000rp (US$25), a little more than I had. I rode back into town in the dark to use the ATM machine. After a terrible night's sleep at my campsite near the terminal with trucks arriving all night, I got up at 5am to check for the ferry.

The ferry was there.

After I waited for 10 days, it had finally arrived — although I knew that in 24 hours I would be aching to get off it.

Travelling on ferries was always an experience. Inside this one, there were two giant speakers playing nothing but loud Indonesian pop music which almost hurt my ears, but the Indonesian passengers loved it. I couldn't sleep, of course, and there was nothing to do but read my book and watch movies on my laptop. Thankfully, the ferry was relatively empty: perhaps about 30 people, five cars and a dozen bikes. I was so glad that the ocean was actually as smooth as silk.

Watching a truly magnificent sunset, I couldn't help but think the trip was almost over. My ultimate freedom was coming to an end. Perhaps in less than one week I would be in Darwin — certainly in no more than two. Fast approaching was a 'normal' life with a job, which would mean staying put and sleeping in the same bed every night. I would miss the adventure and the people I'd often meet, but I would no longer need to check maps all the time and worry about a *carnet*. It was fitting to complete the final leg from Darwin to the farm on my own.

The ferry arrived in Kupang at the ungodly hour of 1am, so I found a bit of ground in the shadows along a seawall to pitch my tent among the grazing pigs and goats.

"Hey, Mister!"

I had managed to drift off for a couple of hours until a man approached me at 5.30am. I looked up at him, and he walked away. What was he doing? Trying to see if I was alive?

Although the sun wasn't yet over the horizon, I could feel the day's warmth starting to creep in. I packed up and rode into Kupang to find the Customs Office and get my US$1000 deposit back. After I eventually found the office and waited for it to open, a Customs official rang their office in Belawan (the port where I'd entered Indonesia). The upshot was that I had to get my deposit refunded at Atapupu, on the border with East Timor. I did not like the sound of that at all. They assured me that there was a bank at Atapupu and I would get my money back.

But time was not on my side. I needed to reach Dili by that night to get on Thursday's boat. This would leave me one day in Dili, the capital, to organise my trip to Darwin and clean the bike thoroughly before it would be allowed into Australia. I had no choice but to ride on to the East Timor border.

## EAST TIMOR

The road through West Timor (still part of Indonesia) wasn't too bad and there wasn't much traffic, but the scenery was quite dull. I arrived at Atapupu at midday and tried to explain about my deposit. Again, they rang the Belawan Customs office to confirm. The problem now was that there was no bank at the border, but there was in the last town, which was 30 kilometres further back. Riding there and dealing with the bank would take time, and in four hours the border would close for the day.

The Customs guys understood my plight and gave me two options. If I wanted my deposit back in US dollars, I would have to return to the bank — but there was no guarantee that the transfer of money from Belawan would be processed that afternoon. Or they could give me the deposit in Indonesian *rupiah*, and I could cross the border immediately. This meant having literally millions of *rupiah* notes which I couldn't spend in East Timor, but I agreed because I did not want to spend a week in Dili waiting for next week's boat to Darwin.

Of course, we argued about the official rate of exchange, but I managed to get US$993 worth of *rupiah*. They also wanted US$50 for processing the paperwork quickly, but we agreed at US$18. With all the signatures in the right boxes and a very thick wad of *rupiah*, I rode the last 12 kilometres to the border. In no time I cleared Customs and Immigration on both sides.

Then it hit me. I was in East Timor, the last foreign country on my trip. The more I thought about it, the more excited I became. I grinned, punched my fist into the air and patted the tank of The Mothership.

"Well done, girl," I said. "You got me here."

As I rode on to Dili, it was clear that East Timor had had an unsettled past (or beginning). There were so many gutted, abandoned buildings and people living in shacks with straw roofs, and the roads were in a bad way. But I was content, happily waving to as many locals as possible. Of course, they didn't have a clue that I'd just ridden from the UK, but their smiles and waves did give me a sense of victory.

Dili seemed so different to the countryside. The streets were filled with UN vehicles and soldiers with rifles. It was a strange place — and extremely expensive because so much of the economy uses the US dollar (which was a bugger because I had wads of *rupiah*). I emailed my contact at Perkins Shipping in Singapore and got the reply I needed: The bike could be shipped to Darwin with me on board.

The main thing left to do was wash my bike. I met two German guys also shipping their bikes to Darwin, who'd been cleaning their bikes all day and still had not finished. But I only had half a day available to clean The Mothership in order to satisfy the very strict Australian quarantine conditions (about importing anything with mud and possible insects and diseases).

My very last day overseas was one of extreme lows followed by extreme highs. Perhaps this was fitting. I needed to start at the SDV office, the local representative of Perkins Shipping, to fill out forms for the bike and find out what time the boat would leave. One of the German guys asked to come to the office with me on the bike.

We were soon stopped by a policeman.

"Shit, I need a helmet," said the German guy.

I stared at him. "You could've told me!"

The German guy just got off the bike and walked away. The policeman spoke no English, so I had to follow him to the station. (As the rider, I was responsible and would be fined. But the German would repay all my costs.)

I was now wasting precious time. Someone at the police station who could speak English explained what I now knew. I would have to pay a fine. The policeman also wanted to see my bike registration papers for East Timor. I explained that I was a tourist passing through and showed him where Customs had stamped the bike in. He couldn't understand any of this and wanted to fine me for not having registration papers as well. I quickly produced my import approval papers for Australia and explained that I needed to get the bike on the ship that day. Eventually, he started to see the light and agreed to only fine me for the helmet.

But the paperwork was building and time was passing, especially when I had to follow the cop to the Transport Department to pay the fine. It was then that I realised that East Timor was one hour ahead of Indonesia and that I'd lost another hour of valuable time. I went from window to window pleading to pay the fine so I could get out of there.

One sweet lady took pity on me and began the process. She returned to explain that there was a problem with the 'system' and that I would need to come back later to pay the fine. With time running out, this was not an option, so the lady disappeared again and then led me into another office where there were more discussions (in the local language). By now, the lady was really concerned about my situation — even more than I was. With the 'system' still down, they decided that the only option was to let me go and not pay the fine at all.

I had to explain this to the policeman, who insisted that I fill out one more declaration form before I went. I asked the cop who'd pulled me over to lead me to the Perkins Office, but we seemed to be heading out of town. Sure enough, he led me to the Perkins Container Yard and not the office.

It was past 9.30am by the time I arrived at the correct office, and I hadn't achieved *anything*. I got things sorted in that office at last, but the cop was waiting for me outside. He explained that I needed to pay US$20 for the declaration form and go back to the Transport Department again. I didn't know if this was true or not, but I was not going back there again so I paid the cop US$20. He smiled and left. (The German later reimbursed me for this too.)

It was already 10.30am by the time I started the massive job of cleaning my bike all over at the Tiger Garage. I started scrubbing the seat and rear wheel and did not stop for four hours. I didn't have any more time anyway. I had to get Customs and Immigration stamps and put the bike in the container. Riding from one place to the other, I tried dodging the dirt and dust along the roads. I got through the Customs inspection of my bike with a minimum of fuss.

At Immigration, I met an Australian, Captain Paul Doney, who delivers yachts. He said he would've given a lift that night for me and The Mothership to Cairns. He then offered me a job as a deckhand along the east coast of Australia.

From the SDV office, I followed two guys in a utility truck to a shipyard, where they put The Mothership into a container. It needed to be tied down, and some guys at the shipyard wanted US$10 for four metres of rope. I said no, and they didn't bother arguing. Meanwhile, my lift to the shipyard had disappeared, so I waited and waited for them to come back. By 4.30pm, I gave up and hitched a ride to the port on a truck.

Sweaty, hungry and exhausted, I found the *Kathryn Bay*, the Perkins ship that would take me to Darwin. It was huge — such a far cry from the wooden dhow I took across the Red Sea to Yemen with some sheep and goats and a squat loo that went into the ocean. The *Kathryn Bay* is a container ship, so only stockman bringing cattle or Special Forces soldiers are normally allowed on board, but I was promised someplace to bunk down.

I approached and shook hands with someone wearing Perkins overalls.

"Allan Roberts?" he said.

"Yes." What great service, I thought. He knew my name and was expecting me.

"Welcome aboard," he said. "We have been expecting you. Please follow me."

I followed him on board, where I met Pedro, the captain. The whole Filipino crew were polite, and the boat was spotless. I was shown to my room. It was amazing, with an en suite, sitting area, double bed and air conditioning. And the shower was so hot.

There was a knock on the door and a voice outside. "Dinner time, sir."

I sat at the captain's table, devouring steak, salad, soup and dessert. I could not believe the five-star service. It was the most incredible way to end this part of my journey and the best possible way to travel to Darwin. It was 'first world' luxury and an ideal preparation for the 'normality' of Australia.

As I watched my final sunset in a foreign country, I saw a Blackhawk helicopter circle the skies above Dili and dreamt of the perfect sleep.

But it didn't happen. I was sick with a headache, annoying coughs and fever. Perhaps I had malaria again, or was exhausted after all the dramas of the previous day? I rested and thought about what was going to happen very soon. I would see the coastline of Australia within a few hours.

As we approached, however, Captain Pedro advised that the port in Darwin was busy. We would have to anchor for a day and wait. It didn't bother me.

One more day didn't seem too long after everything I'd waited for.

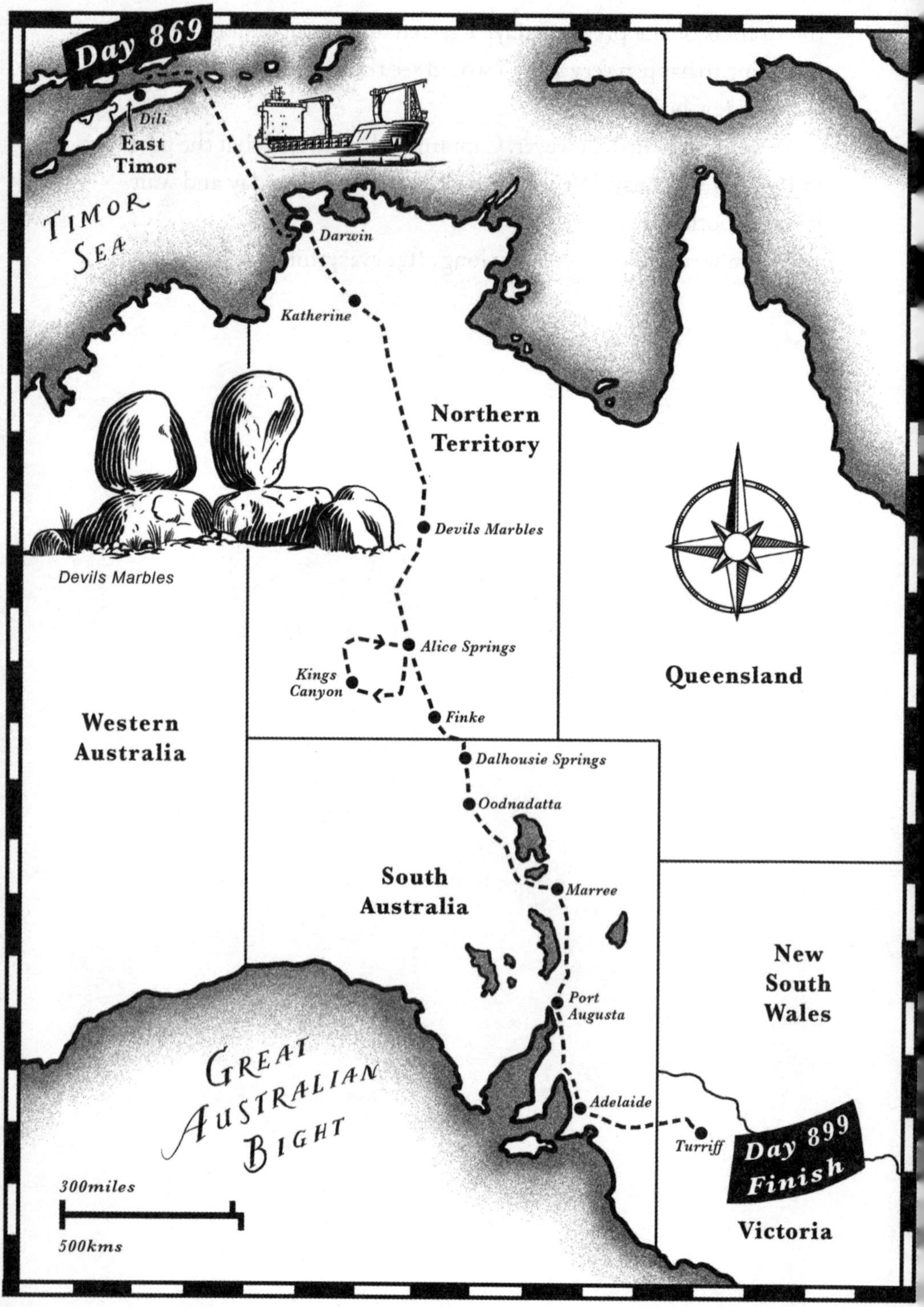
Day 869
Dili
East Timor
TIMOR SEA
Darwin
Katherine
Northern Territory
Devils Marbles
Devils Marbles
Alice Springs
Kings Canyon
Finke
Queensland
Western Australia
Dalhousie Springs
Oodnadatta
South Australia
Marree
New South Wales
Port Augusta
GREAT AUSTRALIAN BIGHT
Adelaide
Turriff
Day 899 Finish
300miles
500kms
Victoria

CHAPTER 7

# **Home**

*Darwin to Turriff: 31 Days*

**DILI TO DARWIN**

My aim was to ride the bike the whole way from London and never fly. I succeeded, but ironically, it was The Mothership that took a plane ride (from Ulaanbaatar to Bangkok) while I crossed China and Laos on the 150cc Sunik. Fittingly, I would arrive in Darwin on the *Kathryn Bay*, with my trusty steed stowed underneath.

But I was still anchored about one kilometre off-shore. I could see Darwin but couldn't touch home soil for another 24 hours. The trip from Dili was quite rough, so I didn't sleep well as the huge ship rocked in the waves. But now in Darwin Harbour, the seas were calm, although there was still plenty of rain.

After waiting a while, I could not wait to get off the boat and start my ride back home. I knew it would be so enjoyable, with no more ferries, borders and bullshit. It had been about five years and 40 days since I'd left Australia and had never been back since. An impulsive decision to join a mate for a while in Thailand turned into a life and job in the UK for two-and-a-half years and then riding across Europe, Asia, the Middle East and Asia. And soon I'd be home after 100,000 kilometres, three continents and 59 countries — and another 24 hours on the boat stranded in Darwin harbour.

But the delay did give me time to reflect. I wondered if I'd changed. I didn't feel that I had, but people do grow and things do alter.

## AUSTRALIA

Finally, the *Kathryn Bay* docked.

It only took about 30 minutes to complete all the paperwork for me to enter Australia, but I still had to deal with Customs and Quarantine about The Mothership. In the meantime, I visited some mates and did things I hadn't done for over five years. These included getting Aussie dollars from an ATM machine, going to a drive-thru bottle shop, and spreading Vegemite on my toast. Darwin was quiet, almost empty, with virtually no traffic. It was just a welcome relief.

I confirmed my arrival date back at the farm for 28 February, in four weeks. But I was soon already four days behind schedule and about AUS$1200 lighter in the pocket. Getting my bike into Australia was a lot harder and more expensive than I thought. First of all, I had to pay AUS$96 for someone from Quarantine to inspect my bike, which took 10 minutes, but it got through, which was a huge relief. Second, I had to fork out a whopping AUS$435 for GST (Goods & Services Tax) to import my bike, which I had already bought and owned. Third, there was the AUS$550 I had to pay for shipping the bike from Dili. (Penelope from Perkins Shipping said the company would pay, but I decided not to ring and ask. I was simply very grateful for even being allowed on the ship.) And finally, there was the cost of AUS$55 to get 'import approval' for The Mothership. Adding insult to injury were the wasted days.

I'd now spent the equivalent of one-and-a-half month's budget just getting my bike from Dili to Darwin. I felt so disappointed, and many of the positive vibes about being back in Australia disappeared. I also felt insignificant. I certainly was not expecting a hero's welcome in Darwin, but on the road in Africa and Asia I met so many interesting travellers whom I swapped stories with. Suddenly, I was just another Aussie.

I also felt sort of lonely in a strange way. I watched people drive to work or walk along the footpath. Nobody was smiling. They all looked like robots, towing the line. Very soon, I was missing the craziness of Africa and the people of Asia, who laughed and didn't take life as seriously as my fellow Australians. But I probably wouldn't miss setting up the tent, checking oil levels, crossing borders and dodging crazy drivers on shocking roads.

My mood was not improved by the horrific cough I now had — or by the thoughts of ending up in a dead-end job — and certainly not by the high cost of living in Australia. Often in Africa and Asia, fuel, food and accommodation combined would cost about AUS$20 a day, yet I spent that amount on a SIM card for my mobile phone, which was soon eaten up after a few calls and text messages.

Before leaving Darwin, I did two more things. I spent another AUS$250 to get a commercial dive medical, the first step towards obtaining a diving job, and I was interviewed for an hour on the local ABC Radio about my travels (which I always enjoyed talking about).

After a week in the Northern Territory capital, my first day riding into the Australian countryside was a long 880 kilometres straight down the Stuart Highway. It rained on and off but enough to soak me through. The rain also meant that several parts of the road were underwater and some cars were even stranded. It felt good riding through 30 centimetre-deep water knowing there was a safe tarmac surface beneath. I pitched my tent at the Banka Banka camping ground but couldn't sleep much because of the millions of mozzies, the heat and my cough.

The next morning, I'd had enough and set out off at 5am. As I stopped at the amazing rock formations at the Devils Marbles, I immediately discovered something else I'd forgotten about Australia: the swarms of flies in the outback. Reaching Alice Springs by lunchtime, my first stop was a chemist. I needed tablets to kill this cough before it killed me.

I rode down to Erldunda, the turn off to Ayers Rock, where I met another mate, Al, whom I'd worked with in the UK. He'd driven up from Adelaide in his 4WD. After resting for a while in an air-conditioned roadhouse, we camped at a place where the flies were just as bad as every other time I stopped. Thankfully, they disappeared after sunset as we enjoyed a barbecue dinner. For the next few days, Al and I looped around the McDonnell Ranges (skipping Uluru/Ayers Rock, which I'd visited before) and headed back to the Alice via the Kings Canyon and some remote waterholes. I'd travelled around this area as a 16-year-old with my dad. Of the few places I still remembered, nothing much had changed. Somewhere along the way, I created another milestone: I hit the 100,000-kilometre mark.

I bought some knobbly tyres for our next leg across the dirt roads down to Finke and beyond, along the Oodnadatta Track. Travelling along the Finke Track also gave me a chance to check out the conditions because I hoped to participate in a race there, hopefully with some sponsorship. At Finke, we gave out lollies to some Aboriginal kids, which reminded me of being back in Africa. We continued along more great roads through some more amazing Australian countryside.

I'd often dreamt of the peaceful Australian desert and its straight roads while riding through places like Indonesia, with its insane traffic and tooting horns. In no time, we made it to Dalhousie Springs, an amazing oasis. We had a refreshing swim, but again, our enjoyment was spoilt by the swarms of bloody flies. Our next stop was Oodnadatta, with lunch at the Pink Roadhouse, and then on to William Creek, where we camped.

In some ways, I now felt I was just going through the motions. But I was really happy to ride through this part of Australia, along dirt tracks in the desert rather than using the boring highway, and it was great catching up with Al.

As we rode further into South Australia to Port Augusta, it felt strange seeing familiar sights. I wasn't sure what to think or how to feel. I felt sort of removed from 'normal' society. All I could talk about now was my travels. I didn't know about anything else. Perhaps I would feel somehow distant when talking with old friends. Before the trip, I used to be the life of the party, but I knew it would take time to adjust and find my feet again — return to a 'normal' life.

Al and I continued south to Adelaide, where I had a few days to kill before arriving at the farm on Sunday, 28 February, when a barbeque and party with family and friends had been organised by my sister. With only 400 kilometres to go, it seemed such an anti-climax to wait around at Adelaide, a city I'd lived in before (and would live in again).

In Adelaide, it was great catching up again with Clint. Over five years ago, he'd urged me to meet him in Thailand, which led to an amazing chain of events: breaking my elbow, meeting Amy, moving to London, and completing this incredible journey.

As much as I wanted to finish this trip and get back home, I wondered… If I had another AUS$10,000 in my bank account, would I just turn around, head north and catch the next boat to South America? I could then continue riding and doing what I knew and loved: being free without the confines of a calendar. My trip was the ultimate example of freedom. I had no one to answer to, and every day I decided where I would go, eat and sleep, and what I would do.

The day finally arrived.

It was time to head east and go home. With clear blue skies and a cool breeze, I donned my jacket and loaded up The Mothership with all my gear for the last time. I pulled on my helmet for the final 400 kilometres to the farm at Turriff in northern Victoria. I left Adelaide early to give myself plenty of time to arrive at the pre-arranged time of 1.30pm.

I left South Australia and crossed into Victoria, the last change in time-zone. Within a few hours, I reached the country town of Speed, where I attended primary school. With a population of about 30, it seemed even more of a ghost town on Sunday morning.

I saw a huge sign with balloons: "Welcome home, Robbo. Only 8 kilometres to go."

Suddenly, I was overcome with emotion. I now realised it was only a few kilometres until the last turn before heading down the dirt road to the farmhouse. Although it had been over five years, the bumps along the road were all so familiar.

As I slowed down for the final turn, I noticed another sign: "The dirt road you've travelled from London to find, 4 kilometres to go".

As I had done thousands of times before, I stopped my bike to take one final photo. I glanced at the familiar sign which indicated Roberts Road. This was my track, the last one I would travel after 899 days.

I wondered who would be at the welcome party my sister had organised. What would I say to them? Perhaps Amy would be there? She was such a huge part of the journey so long ago. Although I travelled with her, and later with so many others through so many countries, in the end it was my journey. I was so glad to be arriving alone.

Around the final bend, I waved as I passed another banner: "FINISH LINE". Waiting for me was a crowd of about 90 family and friends, all cheering, waving and clapping. But Amy wasn't there.

I pulled up, switched off The Mothership for the final time and stepped off. I saw my mother, as well as my sister and her husband and their three children, who'd been born after I left Australia five years ago.

My mother rushed to me and hugged me tightly as tears of joy rolled down her cheeks. My sister cried too. They were just so happy to finally have me home and not need to worry anymore about where the hell I was. My nieces also hugged me but were shy and unsure about the strange Uncle Al they'd never seen before.

Among the hugs, kisses, handshakes and back-slaps from family and friends, from behind I heard a familiar voice. "Welcome home, Robbo." Immediately, I recognised the accent. It was Dirk, with beer in hand.

I'd finally achieved my dream. I had come the hard way home.

But what would I do tomorrow? I had nowhere to go and nothing to do.

Perhaps an even harder journey was about to begin…

The End

*So, what happened to all those amazing characters who shared my trip?*

**AMY**

When Amy returned from Dubai, she attended a wedding, where she met the man she is still with. She changed careers and became a sonographer (dealing with ultrasounds for pregnant women). Sadly, we have barely spoken since. I think she now lives in Perth.

**DIRK**

Dirk and I are still best mates. He never returned to his factory job in Belgium, but he now works on a dredging barge that travels all over the world. With plenty of time off, he manages to catch up with me two or three times a year. He came to Dubai to act as my mechanic during the Abu Dhabi Desert Challenge in 2011. We had planned to work together at the 2014 Dakar Rally but late in 2013 whilst Dirk was on break in Thailand from work in Columbia he had a serious motorcycle accident, suffering three compound fractures to the right forearm, two compound fractures to lower right leg, a broken right knee and the doctors were unable to save what was left of his right foot, amputating and leaving only the heel. I left my work to be by his side in Bangkok after the accident and helped him get through the worst days of his life. He is busy on his road to recovery. Dirk may have lost half of his foot but he hasn't lost his sense of humor.

**AKIS & VULA**

Continuing their around-the-world journey in a 4WD, the Greek couple came to Australia and drove all the way from Sydney just to see me at the farm two months after I returned. They eventually returned to Greece but didn't stay long, instead taking a job managing a game park in Tanzania. After a year, they moved to Italy when Vula became pregnant. I visited them in 2012, just before she gave birth to a beautiful little girl, Anastasia.

### LEO

Leo worked as a tour guide in Namibia for a few months before returning to Spain on Christmas Day (to surprise his parents). He went back to Vietnam and toured there on his motorbike for a while, but he didn't stay long. Since then, he has been doing freelance work and is now based in Berlin, where he's learning German. With no wife or kids, Leo plans to spend the European winters continuing his travels by motorbike.

### DEL

After four and a half years of travelling, Del returned home to the UK and opened a coffee bar with his brother, which they sold a year later. Currently, he works as a taxi driver in southern England, which allows him time to visit Leo occasionally. Del bought a CCM 644, which he is doing up and plans to ride for short trips around the UK and Europe.

### OLLY

Olly's love affair with motorbikes continues. He became friends with Charley Boorman, who rode with Ewan McGregor on the famed 'Long Way…' series of books and TV shows about their travels by motorbike. Olly also recently travelled on a Harley-Davidson with his wife from Las Vegas to San Francisco via the Grand Canyon and Monument Valley.

### MIKE

After leaving Dubai, Mike went to Thailand and then shipped his bike to Japan, a country he loved. He continued on to Vladivostok (Russia) and Mongolia, where Dirk and I met him again. Back in Germany, Mike started a new job in a new city. We occasionally email and reminisce about those 'great' days in the Middle East and the parties in Ulaanbaatar (Mongolia).

**RENE**

A year after finishing his trip, Rene returned to South Africa to visit Colette, a girl from Cape Town he'd met while he was there. They soon got married and had a baby boy. Rene now runs guided motorbike tours across Africa for six months a year, while the rest of the time he's in North America, explaining the joys of adventure travel at speaking events and promoting his book *The University of Gravel Roads*.

**AND ME, ALLAN...**

I worked with my brother-in-law on the family farm for six months and then found a job in the oil and gas industry. But I still found it hard to accept the 'Australian' way, so I moved to Bangkok for two-and-a-half years while working offshore back home. I also completed all of the seven commercial helicopter exams but haven't yet done the flying hours.

In 2011, I again entered the Abu Dhabi Desert Challenge but crashed out on Day 4. But this hasn't stopped my dream of entering the world's toughest off-road rally in 2014 — the Dakar Rally (these days based in South America) — Unfortunatley without my great mate and reliable mechanic, Dirk. I am now based in Adelaide, but The Mothership has retired to the family farm. It has not moved since my return.

# THANKS

*Amy for sharing an amazing part of the adventure*
*Dirk for the endless laughs, adventures and great memoires mate*
*Paul and Zoe Gherkin for the many camping trips to Salisbury Plains*
*Del and Leo for all those laughs and stories*
*Michael for the journey across the Arabian Peninsular*
*Rene for those long days in Djibouti*
*Colin Mercer for your amazing hospitality in Dubai*
*Paul Greenway for taking on the project*
*Bill Wood for your patience*
*Vanessa Fisher for typing all my diaries into word*
*My mum and my sister for everything*
*Neil Roberts for giving me the skills*
*And the following, Akis and Vula, Ilvy, Anna and Antonio, Paul and Jacinta, Ilja, Olly Vine, Ricky De Agrela, Al Margitich, Andy and Axel, Gecko Motorcycles, Al Futtaim Honda, Shaun Mayer, Chris Cargil, Tim Ansell, Jocelyn Perkins, Allen Erskine, Speed Lions Club, Jim Gordon, Jean Menzies, all those who gave support when my bike was stolen*